"IT WAS FUN WHILE IT LASTED," SHE SAID LIGHTLY.

"And it could be that way again," he whispered.

"Oh, you have time for me now? Is that it? Or is it that you think you might be bored here and I'm convenient? Well, sorry, but you can forget it," Amy replied sarcastically. "I'm not the least bit interested."

"Are you sure of that?" Jordon persisted, his thumb lifting her chin as he bent down to brush his lips along the delicate line of her jaw. His arm went swiftly around her. "Remember the nights we had," he murmured, trailing warm kisses over the curve of her neck. "I remember all the pleasures we shared, and so do you."

And Amy did. Only too well. The tender taking power of Jordon's hard body was engraved in her memory along with every moment of ecstasy and her own answering ardor. . . .

A CANDLELIGHT ECSTASY SUPREME

BREAKING
THE RULES

Donna Kimel Vitek

A CANDLELIGHT ECSTASY SUPREME ™

Published by
Dell Publishing Co., Inc.
1 Dag Hammarskjold Plaza
New York, New York 10017

Dell ® TM 681510, Dell Publishing Co., Inc.

Candlelight Ecstasy Supreme is a trademark of Dell
Publishing Co., Inc.

Candlelight Ecstasy Romance®, 1,203,540, is a registered
trademark of Dell Publishing Co., Inc.

ISBN: 0-440-10834-9

Printed in the United States of America

First printing—April 1984

To Our Readers:

Candlelight Ecstasy is delighted to announce the start of a brand-new series—Ecstasy Supremes! Now you can enjoy a romance series unlike all the others—longer and more exciting, filled with more passion, adventure, and intrigue—the stories you've been waiting for.

In months to come we look forward to presenting books by many of your favorite authors and the very finest work from new authors of romantic fiction as well. As always, we are striving to present the unique, absorbing love stories that you enjoy most—the very best love has to offer.

Breathtaking and unforgettable, Ecstasy Supremes will follow in the great romantic tradition you've come to expect *only* from Candlelight Ecstasy.

Your suggestions and comments are always welcome. Please let us hear from you.

Sincerely,

The Editors
Candlelight Romances
1 Dag Hammarskjold Plaza
New York, New York 10017

CHAPTER ONE

Amy Sinclair stood watching and waiting at her office window. Some distance to her left, sea oats scattered in the sand swayed lazily in a gentle late summer breeze while beyond, the sun-silvered ocean tumbled rhythmically into a creamy surf along the Virginia coast. For once Amy had no time to take pleasure in her surroundings. Her attention was riveted on the white car just entering the grounds. Slightly nearsighted, she had to squint as the Ford sedan pulled into a parking space but at last she was able to read the insignia painted on the front door. She turned back toward her desk with a heartfelt sigh of relief. Someone from Security Unlimited had finally arrived and she already felt more confident that the rash of burglaries that had been plaguing the exclusive community of St. Tropez Run would soon be brought to a halt. The departing security chief and his men hadn't been able to put a stop to the break-ins. Desperately as they had tried, they hadn't unearthed one clue that might have led them to the person or persons responsible for the robberies, and in the security business, ineffectiveness is not tolerated. So it was out with the old and in with the new; Security Unlimited would now be responsible for stopping this unexpected miniwave of crime. Amy herself had recommended the agency to her superiors in the real estate and development corporations that provided services and privacy to the wealthy residents of the country-club–like community. From experience she knew that Unlimited was one of the topnotch security consultant agencies in the country but that had not been her only reason for her recommendation. Perhaps, as importantly, she had been determined to prove to herself that her memories of three years ago no longer hurt her. What had happened might not be forgotten but at least she had forgiven. In a way she had done what she had done to set herself free from the past.

Satisfied now that she had acted in the best interest of her employer and herself, Amy smoothed back a wavy honey-gold tendril of hair from her temple before checking with light slender fingers the neatness of the loose chignon on her nape. She settled back in the swivel chair behind her desk just as the expected knock on the door came.

Instead of merely sticking her head in as usual, however, Trudy Smith, the receptionist, entered the office with a conspiratorial smile and closed the door behind her. "Well, our new chief of security is here," she announced, her gamine face alight with good humor and some excitement. "And I must say he looks better in his uniform than old Henry does."

"Henry's not that old and it doesn't really matter how his uniform looks on him. He's a nice person and I'm going to miss him," Amy replied but had to smile teasingly at Trudy's unabashed exuberance. "Besides, don't you ever think of anything except good-looking men?"

"Oh, sure I do." The receptionist's grin became impish as she qualified, "But not very often."

"I can believe it." Laughing softly, Amy tidied a stack of papers on her desk. "But even if you do tend to have a one-track mind, I'm sure you can concentrate on business at least long enough to show the new security chief in. He might not appreciate having to cool his heels out there while we're gossiping about him."

"Now that you mention it, he doesn't impress me as the overly patient type." With a comical arching of her eyebrows Trudy swung around toward the door, opened it, and beckoned the visitor in. "Miss Sinclair will see you now. Amy, this is—"

8

"We've met," a deep rumbling male voice interrupted. And, ignoring Trudy's look of great surprise, Jordon Kent stepped into the office, meeting Amy's widening blue eyes as they darted up from the desktop to stare directly into the amber depths of his. The expression on his darkly tanned face was an enigma, revealing nothing of what he was feeling, if indeed he was feeling anything. His mouth neither moved in a semblance of a smile nor tightened with displeasure. He simply stood inside the doorway, holding Amy's gaze as he added almost as an afterthought, "In fact, Miss Smith, Amy and I have known each other for quite a while, although it's been a long time since we've seen each other. Hasn't it, Amy? Exactly how long has it been?"

"Three . . . four years; I'm not sure which," Amy lied, miraculously regaining her breath enough to steady her voice, although for one terrifying instant she had felt she might never breathe again. She could have told Jordon the precise date she had last seen him over three years and two months ago if she had been willing to be truthful with him. Intense pride prohibited honesty in this instance and she determinedly arranged her own features into bland, composed lines. Through sheer willpower she tried to slow the trip-hammering beats of her heart until at last the blood rushing in her ears ceased pounding so loudly and the tight, painful knots in her stomach began to ease to some extent. She managed a half smile that she prayed conveyed a cool carelessness, then turned her attention from Jordon to her obviously puzzled and frankly curious receptionist. Amy nodded briefly. "Thank you, Trudy. That'll be all for now."

After Trudy made a quiet but none-too-hurried exit, Amy had no choice except to look at Jordon again and she was not so nearsighted that she couldn't see him clearly, although he remained standing some distance from her desk. Deliberately, she flicked a glance over him, but even that swift, supposedly indifferent appraisal created an all too familiar and well-hated catch in her chest as she recognized how little he had actually changed since she had last seen him. And Trudy was right. He was

9

impressive, rather dashing, in fact, in the neat, perfectly fitting khaki uniform of a chief security guard which accentuated sun-streaked brown hair and eyes the odd compelling color of burnt amber. His facial features were strongly hewn, his once perfectly straight patrician nose a bit crooked since being improperly set when he had broken it as a teen-ager. It was a very minor flaw that in no way detracted from his unadulterated male attractiveness. Actually, the slightly crooked nose enhanced his appeal as a man, lending an endearing touch of individuality. And his mouth, so firmly molded, the lower lip fuller and shaped sensuously . . .

After several milliseconds of allowing herself to look at Jordon, Amy motioned him toward the chair across from her while requesting, "Please sit down." Yet when he strode forward, her eyes were once again riveted on him. Tall, subtly muscled, he was slim to the point that when he stood still he gave the impression he might be somewhat gangling, even awkward; but when he moved, that first erroneous impression was instantly forgotten. He carried himself with powerful ease and flowing grace. Watching him simply walk had always fascinated Amy, and now as he moved toward her, she forcibly averted her gaze, mentally shaking her head to reassemble her thoughts. This wasn't the time to indulge in such nonsense. That time had come and had long since gone away. Only after Jordon had settled himself in the opposite chair did she look up at him again. Then the fragile mantle of protective composure she had woven round herself threatened to disintegrate when Jordon spoke before she could, thus breaking the silence between them.

"Amy," he began, regarding her intently. "It *has* been a long time."

"Yes." A growing insidious tightness squeezed at her throat but didn't noticeably alter her voice. "As I said, it's been three or four years."

"Closer to three, and I want to explain again why you didn't hear from me for—"

"No need to explain to me, Jordon," she calmly interrupted, shrugging and lifting a silencing hand. It was far too late for further explanation, even too late for apologies should he attempt to offer any. She simply wasn't willing to listen. Yet she smiled as brightly as she possibly could across the desk. "I understand everything. After your father died, you threw yourself into running the agency and you had to do so much traveling. Then you got involved in expanding operations into other cities—a perfectly natural ambition—so I really do understand. How could I not? After all, you told me in no uncertain terms that you had no time for anything except the agency."

A tiny frown nicked Jordon's brow and his chin rested on long steepled fingers while he continued closely observing her face. "I did get completely wrapped up in the business for a while. There was a great deal that had to be done and you're right—I wanted to expand. But I think I could probably have explained that to you a little less harshly."

"Oh, were you harsh? I don't remember. Looking back, it seems to me you were just perfectly honest. I asked you why we were hardly ever seeing each other and you told me why. That was that."

"Still, I could have been less abrupt about it."

Despite the catch that recurred in Amy's chest, she blithely tossed up her hands. "Ah, well, people come; people go. Relationships begin and end. We just drifted away from each other. What else can we say? Sometimes things like that just happen." And, of course she knew that from bitter experience. Glancing down briefly at the desktop, the thick fringe of her lashes veiling her eyes, she recalled the twenty-two-year-old she had been, falling in love with Jordon, becoming intimately involved, then having to wait helplessly as a closeness she had believed they shared dissolved into nothingness as if it had never existed. She had not been the first relatively naive young woman to face such an experience and knew for a certainty she wouldn't be the last. But three years ago that realization hadn't eased her pain in the

11

slightest. Now she could find some comfort in it, mainly because she knew she was wiser than she had been then. Never again could she be twenty-two and so foolishly vulnerable and dreamily unrealistic. The lesson Jordon had taught her was etched indelibly in her heart and mind. Now, wondering ironically if she should be somewhat grateful to him for teaching her that cautious is better, she raised her eyes; but when they met his once more, gratitude was the last thing in the world she felt. She had thought she had forgiven him, but now that he was here in the flesh, sitting a mere three feet away, she was no longer so sure of that. Still, pride enabled her to act as if she had. "Whether you were harsh or not doesn't really matter now, does it, Jordon? I mean, all that's water under the bridge."

Surveying her expressionlessly, Jordon slowly tapped his index fingers against his chin. "About two months after we had that talk, I did have a chance to get in touch with you," he told her, his words more a statement of fact than an apology. "I tried to call you."

"Oh, you did call eventually, then?" she asked, remembering long nights of praying for her phone to ring but trying to sound neither disbelieving nor sarcastic nor bitter. "I didn't know that."

"Your phone had been disconnected; you'd already left Alexandria. I was a little surprised. I didn't expect you to just go."

"Oh?" The curve of her brows rose. *He hadn't expected her to just go?* How dare he say that when he had practically issued her an engraved invitation to forget about him and she had decided the best way to try to do that was to get out of the town where he made his home. Now he was acting as if he couldn't imagine having anything to do with her decision. Old resentments bubbled hotly up but she suppressed them and even managed to maintain a somewhat fixed smile. "Well, I guess I did leave sort of suddenly, but when Coastal Realty and Development in Virginia Beach offered me a position, it was such a golden opportunity I couldn't pass it up."

"I see. And are you satisfied with the way your career is going?"

"I'm not disappointed. I started as assistant to the assistant manager at one of Coastal's resort properties, then became assistant manager at another. And now I'm the coordinator here at St. Tropez Run."

"Coordinator meaning what exactly?"

"Assistant manager," Amy said drily, wry humor surfacing despite her tension. "Coordinator is just a fancier title. I still take care of all the mundane details while Evan Price, my boss, stays in his Virginia Beach office, wheeling and dealing and planning other profitable developments like this one." Her smile faded and obvious concern caused the edge of her teeth to sink into the soft fullness of her lower lip. "Actually, St. Tropez Run is Evan's pet project and he's terribly upset that four houses here have been broken into in the past three weeks. But I imagine you've already spoken to him and he told you that."

Nodding, Jordon continued lightly tapping his chin as his narrowing eyes traveled over her face questioningly. "Price also told me *you* suggested bringing in Security Unlimited to help stop the burglaries. I couldn't help wondering why you recommended my agency?"

"Why shouldn't I? Your agency has an excellent reputation for solving problems like this," she answered flatly, failing to mention another, perhaps more important, reason. By recommending his agency, she had believed she was proving to herself that she was truly over him while at the same time magnanimously directing some new business his way. Never for a second had she imagined her generosity would bring him personally back into her life again, but he was here and maybe next time she'd think twice before trying to be noble. An old adage popped into her mind: No good deed ever goes unpunished. And tempted at that moment to believe it, she leaned back in her chair, a rather cynical quirk of a smile touching her lips before quickly vanishing. "Now, I want to ask you a question, too. Why are you

13

here yourself and why undercover as a security guard chief? I'm sure you have many highly competent investigators you could have sent instead. And besides, since you've branched out of the Washington, D.C., area and now have offices in several states, you must be very busy with executive duties. So I don't understand why you felt this matter needed your personal attention."

"I could say I simply got tired of all those 'executive duties.' Or I could say that Coastal Realty is such a potentially lucrative client that I want to personally make sure these burglaries are stopped so my agency can begin to serve all their security needs." He moved forward in his chair, elbows on armrests and the message in his eyes seemed deliberately indecipherable as his deep voice lowered. "Or I could say I came personally because I knew you were here and I wanted to see you again."

"You could say that but I wouldn't believe it for a minute," Amy said icily, masking the old hurt that tried to resurrect itself inside her. She forced it aside, denied it new life, and regarded Jordon mockingly. "Your second possible reason makes much more sense. You want to stop these break-ins so Coastal Realty will hire Unlimited to provide for all the company's security needs. You came here personally to be certain everything works out just the way you want it to. Believe me, Jordon, I know all about you and how ambitious you are."

"Correction—you knew about me three years ago and about how ambitious I was then," he countered, a bland expression lying over his sun-bronzed rugged features. "But that doesn't necessarily mean you know about me now. Maybe I've changed."

Amy's hands, clasped in her lap, involuntarily clenched. Her softly shaped lips thinned and twisted derisively. "You? Change? I sincerely doubt that. A leopard doesn't change his spots."

"Leopard?" Jordon's slow smile was disturbingly provocative. "I distinctly remember some of our . . . um . . . more intimate moments when you told me my eyes reminded you of a tiger's."

And they still did. Even as she glared angrily into those amber

14

depths, Amy recognized the tawny gold glint that beckoned, half-hypnotizing her, and threatening to free disruptive memories best left locked away in the darkest farthermost corner of her mind. Her heart felt as if it leaped up into her throat and she looked away quickly, sitting up straighter, shoulders squaring, chin lifting. "Enough of this nonsense," she commanded. "You didn't come here for us to discuss old times so if you want to talk about anything at all, it has to be the burglaries and what we can do to put a stop to them."

"If you insist," he drawled, something too reminiscent of amusement edging his voice. "If you don't want to talk about our past history, we won't . . . at least for now. I have quite a few questions to ask you about the situation here anyhow."

"Would you care for coffee before we begin?" she hastily asked, but not because she felt any desire to be gracious. She simply had to escape him, if only for a few precious minutes. When he accepted her offer with a brief nod, she rose from her chair, moved around the desk, and walked past him at a natural unhurried pace, resisting the growing urge to race out of the office and not return until she was certain he had left it. She mustered the willpower to at least appear composed, and after opening the door, she paused to look back. Jordon swept a lazy gaze over her from the tips of her toes to the top of her head. He had turned slightly in his seat to watch her move across the room, and she cursed silently at the realization that he had made her feel as self-conscious as any adolescent. Nevertheless she met his gaze without flinching. "You still like your coffee without cream and sugar?"

"Ah, you remember. Yes, I still take it black, thanks."

Amy neither smiled nor replied. When she turned to step out of the office, leaving the door ajar, Jordon watched her walk across the reception area toward the table bearing the coffee maker. His narrowing eyes drifted slowly over her once again, following her long shapely legs upward, defining the gentle swell of her hips, and lingering on the enticing indenting of her narrow waist, then the straight implacable line of her back. Her navy skirt and pristine white blouse covered but couldn't conceal her slender yet amply curved form. She was a lovely woman and Jordon felt a stirring of desire, remembering three years ago when she had lain so often in his arms, her warm, lithe body attuned to his every touch. Despite an initial and quite natural uncertainty, she had soon responded to him with a passion that had further inflamed his own. In the rare idle moments he had spent since last seeing her, he had often recalled the pleasure they had given each other, and although she obviously didn't believe him, she *was* one of the reasons he had decided personally to investigate the burglaries at St. Tropez Run. When he'd learned that she had recommended his security agency to her superiors, he had wanted to see her again, if only to discover whether or not she was still the same young woman he remembered.

She wasn't. Not precisely. There were some subtle differences in her. Lovely and intelligent and delightful as she had been three years ago, she now possessed qualities that made her even more intriguing. Of course she was older, more sophisticated . . . but perhaps *sophisticated* wasn't the right word for it. Self-assured better described her and she also seemed much more self-contained. Before, she had been totally open, all her feelings easily readable, while now she was more mysterious, more adept at concealing what she was really thinking. Were there some highly volatile emotions hidden beneath the cool, calm professional exterior? Very probably, unless she had completely changed her personality. She had never been cold. On the contrary, she had been naturally warm and passionate and it was unlikely that even the passing of three years had changed her as drastically as she seemed to want to make it appear. Yet there was always the slim possibility she *had* changed that much. Was this new somewhat glacial demeanor of hers coming from an inner frigidity or was it simply an icy veneer that could perhaps be thawed? Watching as she poured coffee into two mugs, Jordon wondered what he might be able to do to go about trying to melt it. . . .

A few moments later when Amy walked back into her office, she was all too well aware of how closely she was being watched. The flesh of her nape beneath her collar grew hotter and hotter, yet she managed a polite smile when she handed Jordon his coffee. Then, to deny him the opportunity to say anything at all remotely personal, she plunged right in to the business at hand while sitting down again behind her desk. "Okay," she began, smoothing her skirt with her free hand. "What questions did you want to ask me about the burglaries?"

Jordon looked at her over the rim of the coffee mug raised to his lips. He took a slow sip. Relaxing comfortably in his chair, he stretched his long khaki-clad legs out before him, as if he were settling in to ask her a great many questions. When he noticed Amy glance at her wristwatch, a smile etched attractive indentations into his cheeks beside his mouth. "This won't take too long, I promise," he told her. "First, I'll tell you what I already know about St. Tropez Run and then you can fill me in on any details I leave out. All right?"

"Fine," Amy murmured, trying to forget that he had once been her lover and to think of him only as an investigator with whom she wanted to cooperate to stop the string of burglaries. After all, that was why he was here anyhow. His reason for seeing her was in no way personal. By repeating that in her mind several times, she was able to relax to some extent. Laying her arms on the desktop, cupping the mug of steaming coffee in both hands, she gave him her undivided attention. "Of course, I want to help in any way I can."

Jordon nodded. "I understand St. Tropez Run isn't a really typical exclusive community. Ads are describing it as 'a new concept in luxurious living' because Coastal Development provides many extra services to the residents. Besides maintaining the streets, golf course, and other recreational facilities, Coastal also supervises the domestic help, the housekeepers, maids, and gardeners."

"Even the part-time baby-sitters who might only come in for

a few hours in the evening," Amy added. "Everyone who works in St. Tropez Run is really an employee of Coastal. The residents they work for pay the salaries plus a fee to the realty company because we guarantee that anyone who works here has first been thoroughly investigated and found reliable."

"We?"

"Well, I meant Coastal. I'm not personally involved in investigating prospective employees."

"Who is, then? Who investigated the people who work here now?"

"Latham Security Service, the agency you're replacing. They've been in charge of security since the first residents moved into St. Tropez Run two years ago. And, according to some of the employees I've talked to, they did some very thorough checking."

"Maybe not quite thorough enough," Jordon mused after another sip of coffee. Looking at Amy, he thoughtfully tugged at the lobe of his right ear. "But Latham doesn't actually do any hiring because that's one of your responsibilities, isn't it?"

"I've done all the hiring for the past year. That's how long I've been here."

"Tell me exactly how you go about it."

"Frankly, there isn't much to tell. It's a very simple procedure, Jordon," she said blandly. "One of the residents might decide she wants a live-in housekeeper and calls me. I check the files to see if anyone Latham has already investigated is available. If no one is, I interview new people until I find one who fits the requirement. Latham checks references and does its investigation. If they find nothing wrong, I hire the person, pending final approval of the resident, of course. Sometimes there are personality conflicts and things just don't work out. When that happens, I start all over again. It's as simple as that."

"It would be simpler if the residents did their own hiring," Jordon remarked reasonably. "But I suppose they feel that references could be forged and aren't nearly as reliable as thorough investigations. How do the employees feel about that, though? Some of them must resent having their lives examined in such detail?"

"Times are hard. Most of the people here are just relieved to get a chance to work," Amy reminded him softly. "But, yes, many of them do resent the fact that their references are practically ignored and they have to be investigated and I can't say I blame them. Still, I guess they're lucky they aren't required to take lie detector tests, too."

"I take it for granted then that the people who live in St. Tropez Run are very security minded."

"I think you could safely say that," she answered, a trace of a rueful smile touching her lips. "A twelve-foot chain link fence surrounds three sides of the development and the Atlantic Ocean borders the other. There's only one road leading in and there are always two guards posted at the gate. If you're not recognized as a resident, you don't get through unless you have a bright red entrance pass from this office in plain view through the windshield on your dash. But that's why these people wanted to live here. They were promised security, which is why they're terribly upset about the break-ins. They didn't expect these things to happen at St. Tropez Run."

Again Jordon nodded, thoughtfully tapping one lean finger against his cheek. "Evan Price mentioned that some of the homeowners don't live here year round and often rent their houses to people who have been investigated and approved. You handle all the rental arrangements, don't you?"

"Yes, and I know what you're thinking. It's crossed my mind, too, that one of the temporary residents might be responsible for the burglaries. But as you said, they're all thoroughly investigated. You'd think no one would want to come here badly enough to go through all that. There are certainly other beach houses and expensive resorts they could go to but, amazingly, most of the people who rent one of these homes act as if it's some sort of status symbol to be screened and approved for a brief stay in St. Tropez Run."

Offering no comment on her observation of the sometimes strange quirks of human nature, Jordon placed his empty coffee mug on Amy's desk, then laced his fingers together across his flat midriff. "Tell me about the permanent residents. In general."

"In general they're all wealthy," she replied, far more relaxed now than she had been. He was making this easier for her than she had imagined it would be. But then, this was business, which meant he would naturally be businesslike. For once that was a quality she could appreciate in him, although it was the very same quality that had caused her so much pain in the past. But that was over and done. For now, she had to be more concerned about getting through this meeting with him as easily and smoothly as possible, for her own sake. And to answer his question more completely, she became more specific. "Many of the residents are executives or lawyers, doctors, or dentists. Many are retirees, one of them a former Army general."

"I have the names of the one's whose houses were burglarized, but which was first?"

"Mrs. Church, a widow. A priceless carved jade chess set was taken along with a very valuable painting and all her jewelry, including the diamond solitaire her husband gave her when they became engaged," Amy said, eyes darkening compassionately. "If only they had left that. . . . She was heartbroken when she found it was gone, too."

"It usually does hurt more to lose something of sentimental value than anything else," Jordon said quietly, then reached into his hip pocket for a worn black leather notebook. After flipping through a few pages, he had obviously refreshed his memory. "Oh, yes, and Price mentioned a boys' home located about two miles from here. Do you—"

"I know some people would like to lay the blame for these break-ins there, but they really have no reason to," Amy interrupted tersely. "Those boys aren't delinquents. They're just orphans and it's not fair to try to blame them for everything simply because they're parentless."

"I'm not blaming them for anything, Amy. I'm only trying to be thorough."

"Well, you're on the wrong track there."

A smile tugged at the corners of his mouth. "Still leaping to the defense of all the less fortunate, aren't you?"

"Somebody has to."

"I couldn't agree more," he murmured, his amber eyes seeming to plumb the depths of hers. "Your need to defend the helpless always was an endearing quality and an admirable one, too."

Amy stared at him, searching his face for some sign of duplicity, and when she found only a seemingly candid expression, she dragged her gaze from his in some confusion. He had actually meant that, which surprised her immensely. In the past three years she had come to think of him as a dispassionate, emotionless, coldhearted man, one who considered her compassion for life's unfortunates very foolish. But obviously he didn't and she wasn't sure what to make of his unexpected reaction.

"If it makes you feel any better, I doubt very much if any of the young men at the boys' home were involved in the burglaries," Jordon added when her baffled silence continued. "Considering all the security measures here, I doubt they could have gotten in, which makes me think these robberies have been inside jobs. Tell me what you know about the security guards my men will be replacing tomorrow."

"Henry Owens and his men?" she exclaimed softly, shaking her head. "Oh, Jordon, you're on the wrong track again. I know all these men and they couldn't be involved. So you're wasting your time if you suspect—"

"Amy," he cut in, his voice low but commanding. "At this point in my investigation, I have to suspect everybody closely associated with this community."

"Everybody?" she questioned, tensing, her tone sharpening. "Even *me*?"

"I can't afford to assume you couldn't possibly be involved in the burglaries" was Jordon's astounding answer. "It's my responsibility to check everyone out. You understand that."

"No, I don't understand that. I don't understand you. I never have," she uttered, rising up from her chair, her anger and bitter resentment so intense that she was very nearly trembling. Rose color mantled her cheeks as defiance flashed like blue fire in her eyes. "Are you out of your mind? How can you even think of including me on your list of suspects? For God's sake, Jordon, you know me!"

"I *knew* you, but that was three years ago," he reminded her, his inscrutable eyes capturing and holding hers. "And even then we only knew each other something less than three months, not a very long time, you have to admit."

"Long enough for you to—" Amy snapped, then broke off abruptly before accusing him of seducing her and leading her to believe they could have a future together when he'd known damn well there was no chance of that. She refused to give him the satisfaction of realizing how emotionally involved she had been and how lost she had felt when everything ended. Nor would she give him any further indication that his present suspicions about her infuriated her and even hurt a little. After all, she had only known him as long as he had known her yet she would never even entertain the possibility that he might be involved in some criminal activity. On a personal level, she knew she couldn't trust him as far as she could throw him but she still believed him to be a professionally ethical, honest man. Obviously he was too cynical and jaded to be able to have the same faith in her, but that was his problem. She couldn't allow it to be hers, and staring coldly at him, she tossed up one hand in a dismissive gesture. "If nearly three months of working at the same hotel where I worked didn't teach you I'm trustworthy, then I don't know what would. And I really don't care."

22

"I'm not saying I don't think you're trustworthy and you're certainly nowhere near the top of my suspects' list," Jordon said quietly. "But in order to make this a completely thorough investigation, I'll still have to do a check on you."

His logical tone merely fueled her anger and, scarcely able to control her temper, she turned her back on him to look blindly out the window. "Do whatever you please. It makes no difference to me if you check up on every minute of my life from the day I was born," she muttered, clenching her hands tightly together in front of her. "Just be sure you do what you came here to do—stop these break-ins before I . . ."

"Before you what?" Jordon prompted when she stopped mid-sentence. "Amy, are you getting a lot of heat from Coastal Realty because of the situation here?"

"Oh, well, you know how it is," she murmured, rather surprised at his perception but tensing all over when she heard him get up and approach her. Imagining she could feel the very warmth of his body as he stepped up behind her, she wouldn't turn around and pointedly gazed out the window as she shrugged. "These burglaries have upset everyone, residents and executives at Coastal alike. And, since I'm the company's representative here . . . well, you understand. If the problem isn't solved soon, they might start thinking about looking for a scapegoat. And my career won't be worth much if that happens."

"So you had another reason for recommending Unlimited," Jordon said very softly, putting a hand on her shoulder to turn her around. "You personally need my help."

Her spine stiff, Amy flexed her shoulder, and could not breathe deeply again until he had dropped his hand away. She shook her head. "I recommended your agency because it's one of the best, but I had no idea you'd conduct this investigation yourself. But of course if you help save my job by ending these robberies, I'll be very glad."

"I'll certainly do my best."

"Fine. That's all I ask," she said briskly, moving as if to step past him. "Now, if you have no more questions, I am busy."

"You've changed, Amy," Jordon said, ignoring her hint and blocking her way around the desk. His deep voice lowered. "Lovely as you were three years ago, you're even lovelier now."

"How kind of you to say so. But if you'll excuse me . . ."

Shaking his head, he stepped nearer and reached out once more to cup the back of her slender neck in one large hand, as he whispered, "We had something very wonderful together then. Remember?"

"I remember," she muttered, swallowing hard, pulses pounding. He was too close. She could detect the faint scent of spicy aftershave and clearly see the taut smoothness of his lean, tanned face. Tall and straight and strong in the khaki uniform, he was too disturbingly masculine and she felt her heart would explode if she didn't put more distance between herself and him. She took a step back. "It was fun while it lasted."

He moved after her, the pressure of his hand on her nape increasing. "And it could be that way again."

"Oh, you have time for me now? Is that it? Or is it that you think you might be bored here and since I'm convenient, you can use me to while away the time? Well, sorry, but you can forget it," she replied sarcastically. "I'm not the least bit interested."

"Are you sure of that?" he persisted, his thumb lifting her chin while he bent down. When his lips brushed along the delicate line of her jaw and she tried to twist free to escape him, his arm went swiftly around her and he drew her close against him. "I didn't have time then because the agency almost went under when my father died. I had to save it. But everything's different now."

"You're damn right it's different. I—" she began, but the attempted protest was silenced as her mouth was swiftly, softly possessed by his. Her breath caught in her throat. Her eyes closed of their own volition as his firm masterful lips feathered over the soft shape of hers until she had the presence of mind to turn her head to escape them. "*Stop*. I don't want—"

24

"Remember the nights we had," he cut in, trailing warm kisses over the curve of her neck, his low voice muffled against it, his breath caressing her sensitive skin. "I remember all the pleasures we shared, and so do you."

And she did, all too well. The tender taking-power of Jordon's hard body was engraved in her memory along with every moment of ecstasy and her own ardent responsiveness. And when the tip of his tongue sought the hollow at the base of her throat, drawing erotic patterns there, and a forbidden rush of warmth spread like wildfire over and through her, she clung to reality with a vengeance. Loathing herself for even that instant of weakness, she resisted, pushing violently at his chest.

"Take your hands off me right now," she demanded through clenched teeth, cursing when his arm remained around her waist and he refused to release her completely. All the resentment she had tried to conceal burst out as if a dam had suddenly broken, and her hands balled into tight fists. "What kind of idiot do you think I am? I'm not a half-wit. I'd have to be an absolute fool even to consider getting involved with you after what happened. I was twenty-two and in love, or at least I thought I was, which is just as bad. And you used me, Jordon, then told me you didn't have time for me anymore and walked away. You shouldn't have done what you did."

His eyes darkened with regret and he immediately released her. "Amy," he began softly, "I was twenty-nine years old and the future of the entire agency was suddenly in my hands. And you . . . wanted more from me than I was ready or able to give. The thought of any kind of commitment scared me like hell. I didn't have time to—"

"So you said, very bluntly," she snapped. "And I got the message loud and clear."

"I was too blunt. I admit that. But I never meant to hurt you and I'm sorry I did."

"Oh, I got over it fast enough," she lied straight to his face. "So don't worry about it. Besides, you taught me an invaluable

25

lesson. Now I know the last kind of man I'd ever get involved with is one like you."

Looking down at her face and into her lovely sapphire eyes, flashing with anger, Jordon glimpsed the emotionally volatile inner woman he had suspected she tried to hide. He nearly succumbed to a rising desire to touch her again, but thought better of it. *Later.* It would be unwise to try to rush her, but he did feel it was only fair to warn her he was not one to give up easily. "I'm a very determined man, Amy," he advised, half-smiling. "No matter how often you say you won't get involved with me again, I probably won't accept that as your final decision."

Refusing to honor that remark with an answer, her right palm itching to make contact with his cheek, she turned quickly on one heel and started to walk around the other side of the desk. "I don't have time to walk down memory lane any longer, Jordon," she announced haughtily. "I have a great deal to do, so I'll have Trudy show you to your quarters now."

"Later, if you don't mind," he replied nonchalantly. "At the moment I'd rather drive through the development and have a look around."

Amy halted midstride. "We prefer to call St. Tropez Run a community."

"I beg your pardon. Then I want to drive through the community."

"You'll have to have a pass to get through the gate." Going back behind her desk, she opened the middle drawer, brought out a brightly colored pass, then had to refrain from slapping it down hard into the palm of the hand he held out. "Please try to get back here before five thirty, since Trudy goes home then."

Jordon walked to the door. "I'll see you later?"

"Not today. I have so much to do that I'm sure I won't have time to talk to you again after you come back."

That knowing smile still lingered on Jordon's mouth but, mercifully, he said nothing more before leaving Amy's office.

When he had gone out and closed the door quietly behind him, she released a long, tremulous breath. She hadn't needed this to happen. She already had enough to worry about: the burglaries and the effect they might have on her position in the realty company. Pressing her fingertips against her forehead, she sighed, wondering how easily sleep would come tonight after he had managed to arouse all the old memories. She shook her head. She was over him. Memories couldn't hurt her now; even Jordon himself couldn't hurt her. It had taken almost three long years for her to find contentment without him; she refused to let his sudden reappearance in her life upset her equilibrium.

CHAPTER TWO

Amy strummed her fingers on the desktop, her patience growing thin. For the fifth time in as many minutes she looked at her wristwatch. It was ten until six and still Jordon hadn't returned to the office. "Just like him to be so inconsiderate," she muttered aloud as her strumming increased in tempo. When he hadn't come back by five thirty, she had told Trudy she needn't stay late simply to show Jordon to his quarters. It would have been ridiculous, not to mention cowardly, to detain the receptionist just for that, despite Amy's intense reluctance to perform the task herself. She wasn't eager to see Jordon again, especially today. His unexpected appearance this afternoon had unnerved her considerably and she was planning to spend this evening alone, regaining the composure she was certain to need during the remainder of his stay at St. Tropez Run. But then, it probably wasn't going

27

to be that easy anyway. One brief evening of trying to shore up her defenses against him might not be nearly enough to shield herself from the still disruptive effect he had on her senses, an effect she had been momentarily powerless to fight today when he had kissed her.

Of course, Jordon had always been a sexually attractive man, adept at arousing her passion sometimes merely with words, expert with his caresses and kisses. Despite his very winning way with women, however, there was no excuse for the way she had responded, even briefly, this afternoon. His treatment of her three years ago should have made her totally immune to his brand of sensuality. She had assumed she was, but was now no longer as sure of it.

"Damn," she whispered, uncertainty shadowing her features until she resolutely tightened her jaw. She would simply have to take herself in hand and also prevent Jordon from catching her off guard. Once his rare combination of magnetic virility, intelligence, and sense of humor had been irresistible, but she was older, wiser, and far less susceptible now. She would resist him!

Busying herself with paperwork to avoid fuming impotently about how late Jordon was, Amy passed the next several minutes without looking at her watch again. It was only when she heard the outer office door open, then the footsteps in the reception area, that she checked the time. Three after six. Removing her purse from one desk drawer and the keys to Jordon's quarters from another, she didn't look up when he opened her door and came in.

"I was gone longer than I expected to be," he announced, approaching Amy. "Sorry if I kept you and Trudy waiting."

"I let Trudy leave at her regular time. I'll show you where you'll be staying myself."

"Then I'm sorry for keeping you waiting."

"No problem" was her offhanded reply as she tucked the straw clutch purse under one arm and stood. At last she looked

28

at him without smiling. "We can go now, unless you want to ask me more questions about the burglaries."

"No questions. I will be needing your personnel files, though, including present employees and any former ones who left their jobs less than a year ago."

Amy's chin came up a fraction of an inch. She pressed her lips firmly together and started to lay her purse down. "I suppose you want those now?"

"Tomorrow sometime will be soon enough."

"Then I'll pull all the files for you early in the morning," she said rather stiffly. "Including mine."

The hint of sarcasm in her voice didn't alter his expression one whit. He simply nodded. "I'll pick them up sometime before lunch."

"And is there anything else you'd like me to do for you?"

"That's all I ask . . . at the moment," Jordon said, straight faced despite the somewhat amused and provocative note in his low-timbred voice. "But I'll certainly let you know when I want something more."

In no mood to respond to his teasing tone, Amy marched past him toward the door. "If you're ready now . . ."

After following her through the reception area into the saffron glow of early-evening sunshine, Jordon watched as she locked the door to the offices. A soft salt-scented breeze stirred wisps of her honey gold hair that had escaped confinement, but when he lifted a hand to brush a tendril lightly back from her right temple, she stiffened, then hurriedly preceded him along a winding flagstone path.

"Your quarters are at the other end of the clubhouse, near the beach. We'll cut through the gardens," she informed him after a couple of his long easy strides had enabled him to catch up. "We could go through the building but I usually go this way just to get a breath of fresh air."

"This certainly isn't your run-of-the-mill clubhouse," he commented, slipping his hands into the pockets of his pants. "And my guess is that it was built approximately thirty-five to forty years ago."

"Great guess. To be exact, this place is forty-two years old. You see, before this property became St. Tropez Run, it was a private estate. This was the main house," Amy explained, relieved to discuss the impersonal topic. She glanced up at the vast gray-stone mansion with its decorative turrets at each end. "When the community was still only an idea, I understand there was some talk of tearing this house down and building a modern clubhouse. Fortunately, wiser heads prevailed and it wasn't destroyed after all. It would have been such a shame if it had been. You really should try to walk through it sometime while you're here to see how soundly built and elegant it is."

Jordon smiled down at her. "Sounds like a fine idea, especially if you're volunteering to give me the tour. How about tomorrow?"

"Impossible," she said flatly. Her pace brisk, she took a short-cut through the formal gardens, bypassing banks of vibrant red shasta daisies and beds of more exotic flowers to reach the far end of the mansion. "I'll be far too busy all week to give any guided tours. But you can wander through the house on your own or Trudy can show you around, whichever you prefer."

"I prefer to wait until you have time to show me around yourself."

Then you'll be waiting until hell freezes over was the cutting response that came to mind, but she didn't voice it, pretending instead that she hadn't even heard his last remark. She turned off the walkway, stopping before a massive mahogany door which she unlocked with one of the keys she carried. Opening it, she stepped across the threshold, switching on the lights in a small foyer with double doors to the left and right.

"These were once the quarters for the housekeeper and chauffeur," she said, unlocking and opening the right-hand doors, then preceding Jordon into a small sitting room containing a fading damask sofa and chair and a few plain functional pieces

30

of antique mahogany furniture. "The chauffeur lived here, I was told. It isn't elegant but it's nice enough. It's really like an efficiency apartment with this room, one bedroom and bath, and a tiny kitchenette. I hope you can make yourself comfortable."

Moving into the room toward her, Jordon nodded. "Looks fine to me. And who lives across the hall?"

"Oh, those are the coordinator's quarters," Amy replied, then added rather smugly when he speculatively cocked one eyebrow, "I don't live there, though. Since I work here all day, I want to get away evenings so I kept my apartment just south of Virginia Beach. That's only about three miles away, so I can get here quickly when I'm needed."

"Pity," he murmured, tawny eyes narrowing. "I suppose that means I live in the house alone?"

"Oh, don't worry about that. There's plenty of activity in the clubhouse upstairs until at least twelve every night. It does get very quiet after everyone is gone, but try not to let the silence bother you. I know there are some people who claim this place is haunted, but *I* certainly haven't seen any ghosts."

A low chuckle rumbled up from deep in Jordon's throat. "Surely you didn't say that hoping I'd lie awake all tonight, listening for strange noises?"

"Heaven forbid. I was only trying to reassure you," she answered, her wide, innocent gaze at variance with the slight tugging of the corners of her mouth. "Really, I'm sure you'll be very comfortable staying here. Henry Owens was. In fact, he was a little sad when he had to move out this morning. Oh, and speaking of Henry, his men will be replaced by yours tomorrow morning, right?"

"Two at the gate and another patrolling in a car during the day. Two cars at night."

"Hopefully they have better luck controlling the situation than Henry's guards have had," Amy said pensively, nibbling her lower lip. Then, remembering Jordon's suspicions, she felt compelled to defend the outgoing security team. "Of course, it

31

isn't as if Henry and his men haven't tried. But even the sheriff's deputies couldn't come up with any clues after the burglaries. Whoever is breaking into the houses certainly seems to know exactly what he's doing."

"All criminals make mistakes eventually. This one will, too," Jordon said confidently. "If he doesn't stop operating in St. Tropez Run, we'll catch him."

"I just hope it's very soon." Amy started back toward the door. "Well, I'll let you get settled in now. You'll find a few items in the kitchen: bread, milk, eggs, and whatever other essentials Trudy bought when I sent her to the store today. But if you don't find anything you want, or don't want to bother making your own dinner, you can have something brought down from the clubhouse dining room."

"I have a better idea," Jordon murmured, catching her by one hand, stopping her in midstep, and turning her around toward him. His darkening gaze held hers. "The two of us can have dinner together somewhere."

Amy's expression grew frosty. "Thank you, but no. I make it a rule not to accept dinner invitations from men who suspect me of being a jewel thief."

"That's not a very good excuse, Amy, since I explained to you why I have to check you out," Jordon softly said, the ball of his thumb drifting slowly back and forth over the back of her hand. "You really don't like me very much anymore, do you?"

She was trying her best not to, but he was such a damnably likable man, even more now than he had been three years ago. It was as if time had mellowed and gentled him, enhancing his appeal; but then again, this was probably no more than an act he was putting on for her benefit. Cursing herself for being gullible even if for only a moment, she pulled her hand from his and made her way to the door, where she stopped short to take another key from her purse. She tossed it toward Jordon.

"For the offices," she explained tautly as he caught it easily in his left hand. "In case you want to start work before I come in tomorrow morning. Your office is the one next to mine."

He slipped the key into his pocket. "Sure you won't change your mind and have dinner with me after all?"

Turning her back to him, she moved out into the foyer. "Sorry, but I have to go home and feed my cat."

"I certainly wouldn't want your cat to go hungry, but, Amy, remember what I told you this afternoon," he called after her, his deep voice melodiously enticing. "I'm not going to take no as your final answer."

Amy left without so much as a backward glance. She stepped outside, but even the early evening air did little to cool her overheated skin. Scowling, she hurried around the gray-stone house, the low heels of her navy leather pumps tapping out a staccato beat on the flagstones as she walked toward the shaded space where she always parked her green Chevette. Her chest felt tight; every muscle in her was tensed until, little by little, she willed herself to relax. Yet her lips remained pressed firmly together. Jordon thought he could play a game with her again, but she would soon show him that this time he would have to play the game by himself. She had played it with him once and lost badly; she wouldn't risk losing again.

The black cat with white paws wound around Amy's ankles. When that ploy achieved no results, she turned onto her back, exposing her furry white underbelly and plaintively meowing.

"I'll scratch your back later," Amy informed her, glancing down with a smile. "Right now I have to finish making this salad. I'm hungry." When the cat, never one to give up easily, meowed again, she shook her head. "Come on, use your nose, Skeeter. You must smell that fish broiling. Don't you want some of it?"

When Skeeter's answering meow was punctuated by the ringing of the front doorbell, Amy abandoned the salad, brushed her hands over her apron, and padded barefoot from the kitchen through the living room, trying not to tread on the cat, who managed to be underfoot every third or fourth step. Although she was virtually certain her visitor was her downstairs neighbor, Erica, who came at least twice a week to complain about her husband of eight months spending too much time with the "boys," habit prompted Amy to stretch up on tiptoe to look out the peephole in the door. Her heart gave a little lurch; she sank back down on her heels. It wasn't Erica outside after all. It was Jordon, and being caught off guard for the second time in one day was almost more than she could handle. For a split second confusion reigned. She couldn't think straight. Then, for a brief moment, she considered not opening the door to him; but at last an inherent unwillingness to give in to cowardice made her reach out and turn the knob. She opened the door less than halfway, a tactic usually reserved only for door-to-door salesmen.

Still in the crisp khaki uniform, his thick brown hair slightly windswept, Jordon met her somewhat hostile questioning gaze and smiled. Shifting his weight from one foot to the other, he surveyed her jeans, yellow tank top, and the pristine white apron tied around her narrow waist.

"How did you find me?" Amy asked coolly before he could speak, her grip on the door so tight that the edge dug painfully into her palm. "I didn't tell you exactly where my apartment was."

"That's why I had to go to the office and check your file for the address. I neglected to tell you something this afternoon that I wanted you to know before you go into work tomorrow morning."

"Oh? What is it?"

Jordon glanced around. "I'd rather not discuss it out here. I'd like to come inside."

Amy hesitated a long moment. Then, with extreme reluctance, she opened the door wider and stepped aside. When Jordon moved past her into the living room, she gestured toward the sofa. "Won't you sit down?"

He complied, grinning when the cat made a mad dash by him

34

to bound beneath the coffee table where she lurked and eyed him suspiciously, her long tail switching slowly back and forth. "Pretty cat," he commented while Amy settled herself on the edge of the chair opposite him. "Had her long?"

"Since she was a kitten, about ten months."

"Animals do make a home seem a little less lonely when you live by yourself, don't they? I've been thinking seriously about getting a dog."

Amy merely nodded, unwilling to discuss either pets or loneliness, especially the latter, with this particular man. "Now, what is it you forgot to mention to me this afternoon, Jordon?"

"It's a small detail but important," he said, relaxing on the sofa, one arm extended across the back. "I think it would be best if you don't tell anyone at St. Tropez Run that I own Security Unlimited. Just introduce me as the new chief of security and maybe if someone on the inside is pulling off these burglaries, he won't feel the need to be extra cautious."

"That makes sense. And will you be using a false name?"

"I don't think it'll be necessary to go that far."

"Fine. So I'll tell everyone you're the new security chief and that's all," Amy agreed, although her expression was vaguely puzzled. "But you didn't have to drive here just to tell me that, Jordon. You could have phoned."

Smiling, he shrugged. "To tell the truth, I had another reason for coming. After you left, I decided it would be too boring to have dinner alone, and since you're the only person I know here, here I am."

"I thought I made it pretty clear that I wouldn't go out to dinner with you," Amy said, her words crisp and precise. "But if I didn't, let me tell you again: thank you but no, I don't want to go out to dinner. And even if you don't know anyone in the immediate area, you don't have to dine alone. You have an agency in Norfolk, so you obviously know people there. Drive up and have dinner with some of them."

"Why should I drive all the way up there when you're right here and I know you?"

"Because I said no, that's why. I'm not available, Jordon, so you'll have to find someone else. I'm busy."

"Oh, you have plans for tonight? Are you going out with someone?"

Amy heaved a disgruntled sigh. "That's really none of your business."

"I take that to mean no. If you were going out with someone, you would have just said so," Jordon stated flatly. "So if you don't have a date, what's going to be keeping you so busy?"

"Something important. I plan to wash my hair," she retorted irritably. And when she actually detected a glint of amusement in his amber eyes, resentment erupted anew in her. She stood up quickly, hands clenched into fists at her sides. "I don't know what you're trying to prove, Jordon, but it's really rotten of you to try to have fun at my expense and I don't appreciate it one bit."

"I'm not having fun, Amy, I assure you," he said softly, the amused glint vanishing, his expression growing somber. "If anything, I'm making a serious effort at charming you into a truce. Obviously I'm having very little luck, but I have to give it one more try. I'd still like to have dinner with you."

"No," she repeated, although slightly mollified. "Even if I wanted to, I've already started dinner here."

"I realized you might have but I came anyway. I thought you might invite me to have dinner here with you."

"But . . ."

"Come on, Amy, you're from Georgia originally. Where's that famous southern hospitality?" he persisted. "I'm a stranger in a strange place and it wouldn't be very gracious of you to allow me to have dinner by myself my first night here."

"Jordon, you're—"

"Besides, I didn't come empty-handed. I brought wine." Lithely rising up from the sofa, he looked into her surprised eyes.

"I bought red and white since I didn't know what you'd be having. It's in the car. I'll go get it. It's a gift from me to you even if I'm not invited to share it."

She raised her eyes heavenward. "You're breaking my heart."

"Yes, I can see I am," he murmured, smiling ruefully. "Well, I'll get the wine, then leave, since I'm obviously upsetting you."

"Don't be silly," she retorted, pride forcing her to appear far cooler and more composed than she felt. "You're not upsetting me in the least."

He gave her an expectant look. "Well, then?"

She hesitated only an instant. "Oh, all right, Jordon," she finally acquiesced, feeling he was issuing a challenge her self-respect wouldn't allow her to refuse. "Would you like to stay for dinner?"

"I'd be delighted. How nice of you to ask and what a surprise," he said, a small smile touching his mouth. "I'll bring in the wine."

"Fine. I'll check the fish; it should be nearly done. If I remember correctly, you enjoy fish, don't you?" she asked, although the question was totally unnecessary. She remembered correctly, all right, everything she had ever known about him, all his likes and dislikes. There was probably nothing she had forgotten, much to her regret. But as long as he didn't realize that . . . "Or am I wrong? Do you hate it?"

"Not at all. It's one of my favorites. And I have a very good white wine to go with it."

"Sounds delicious." She gave a polite smile. "Now, if you'll excuse—"

"Amy." Catching her lightly by the arm, he stopped her as she started to turn away. "I'm glad you asked me to stay because I *was* beginning to think you were afraid to be alone with me."

"Afraid? No, I'm not afraid of you," Amy said, and it wasn't a lie. She wasn't afraid of him, but he did make her uneasy, and the uneasiness was growing now with the warming tingling effect his lean fingers were having on her bare arm. She pretended his

37

touch was having no effect at all. "And it certainly doesn't bother me to be alone with you."

"Truce, then?"

"We'll see, Jordon. I'm not promising anything."

"At least for tonight," he insisted quietly, his steady gaze holding hers. "You can't go on forever without forgiving me, Amy."

"Oh, I forgave you a long time ago," she replied, although she was even less sure of that now than she had been this afternoon. "It's just that I've never forgotten what you did."

"Then, I'll have to see what I can do to change that, won't I?"

"I wouldn't waste my time if I were you. There's nothing you can do to change it."

"Never underestimate me, Amy. I've already warned you: I can be a very determined man," he told her, his voice low and appealingly husky. Then, leaving her with those words to mull over, he started out to his car.

In the kitchen a moment later a tiny frown marred her smooth brow. With Jordon's words echoing in her head, she couldn't really concentrate on what she was doing and basically operated instead on automatic pilot, checking the fish, then getting back to the salad. Standing at the counter, tearing tender lettuce leaves into a wooden bowl, she once again almost wished she had never recommended Jordon's agency to Evan Price at Coastal, although Jordon was a highly effective, thorough investigator and probably had a better chance of stopping the break-ins and thereby saving her job than almost anyone else. Maybe her job wasn't that important. Oh, she enjoyed it and didn't want her career to suffer for any reason, yet something akin to apprehension crawled along her spine. What exactly did Jordon have on his mind? Why was he here tonight and being so charming? Why, at the start of an important investigation, did he want to waste time on her when he had had no time for her at all three years ago? What did he want? Was his conscience finally beginning to bother him? Was he trying to appease it by trying to gain her full and unconditional pardon? Or was this what she had feared—simply a game he was playing to while away time?

These endless questions bombarded Amy's brain but she could find no answer to any of them and she became increasingly tense. When Jordon appeared in the doorway of the kitchen carrying one bottle of red and one of white wine, she gave him a cursory glance, then continued slicing oval-shaped Italian tomatoes into the salad.

"Hello, cat," she heard him say. Out of the corner of her eyes she looked in his direction as he bent over, his hand outstretched to stroke Skeeter.

"You might want to think twice before you do that," Amy cautioned, looking away to pick up a cucumber. "She'll probably stratch you. She doesn't like strange men."

"Oh?" Jordon murmured. "Then I must be an exception."

Amy turned, the curve of her brows lifting as she watched Skeeter rub against his ankles, content beneath his hand on her narrow back, her purring audible even at a few feet distance. "Well, I guess I kept her waiting for a back-scratching too long, so she went elsewhere for it," Amy muttered, ridiculously feeling as if she had been betrayed. It seemed for an instant that even her pet wasn't worthy of trust, but she soon dismissed that thought as silly. She smiled ruefully to herself. Skeeter, after all, was only a cat; she wasn't expected to have good taste. But what about instinct, the inborn ability to size up people? Mere myth, Amy decided. Animals were probably capable of being as gullible as humans on occasion.

"I'll put the wine in here until we're ready for it," Jordon announced, leaving the cat and approaching the refrigerator. "I had it sent down from the club house restaurant so it was chilled, but it's been in the car for a while."

"It should be fine, then," she muttered, wondering if only one bottle of white wine would be nearly enough to get her through this meal.

As it turned out, dinner was quite enjoyable, relaxing and at the same time stimulating. Naturally, Amy had never forgotten what an interesting man Jordon was, but tonight was like living over the first dinner they had ever had, as if she were rediscovering him. Knowledgeable in a vast variety of subjects, he was a wonderful conversationalist and as one topic led into another and another, Amy became too involved in their discussion to remain tense. Still, in the back of her mind, she realized Jordon was the reason all the men she had met since knowing him had seemed dull. Before tonight she had convinced herself she felt that way only because of a somewhat adolescent memory of him as being exceptional. Now she knew different. He *was* special. His intelligence was keen, his wit quick. He made her laugh and he laughed because she was able to amuse him. Sometimes they agreed; sometimes they expressed opposing ideas; but, together, they made each other think. It was exciting, and she had to make an effort to remember that Jordon had hurt her so badly that she had never been able to trust any man since him, at least not nearly enough to become seriously involved with anyone else.

After dinner Jordon insisted on helping with the dishes. He washed; Amy dried and put away. When they had finished, they carried their coffee into the living room, where he settled himself comfortably on the sofa once again. She had thought he might leave soon after the meal, but he seemed in no hurry to go, and she wondered fleetingly if he had come to see her tonight simply because he had felt lonely in his quarters. Perhaps even loners like him experienced moments when they needed to be with somebody. Unwilling to dwell on the possibility that he could ever be even temporarily vulnerable, she banished that thought to a far corner of her mind. Placing her cup and saucer on the coffee table, she sat poised on the edge of the cushion at her end of the sofa. She glanced at Skeeter, who, replete after her portion of fish, had commandeered the chair and was now snoozing peacefully. A faint smile lingered on her lips when she turned toward Jordon.

"I can offer you ice cream if you'd like some. I didn't make a dessert. Too many calories."

"I can't imagine why you have to worry about that. You're thinner now than you were when we met."

"You say that as if you think I'm skinny," she said wryly. "I'm certainly not that."

"And that's not what I meant. You're not at all skinny; in fact, you're . . . er . . . very nicely rounded. But you are more slender than you were. You've lost some weight."

"A couple of pounds, not enough to be noticeable. Maybe you just can't remember how I was such a long time ago."

"Don't kid yourself, Amy," Jordon advised, his deep voice lowering. "I memorized every inch of you while we were together and I haven't forgotten exactly how you looked and how you felt in my arms."

His very tone and the almost searchingly intent way he was looking at her made her heart do a crazy little somersault, then settle into a too rapid beat. Danger signals were set off in her head and an overwhelming need to protect herself caused her doubtfully to shake her head. "I find that impossible to believe," she said. "How could you have had to time to remember what I was like when you've totally wrapped yourself up in your business for the past three years?"

"I suppose I deserve that," he conceded, his lean dark face expressionless. "And I guess it made you feel better to say it."

Trouble was, saying that hadn't made her feel better at all. In actuality she now felt worse. The conversation was becoming too personal and she was getting tense again, feeling as if her nerves were being stretched tauter and tauter. Inwardly she sighed, averting her gaze from him to stare for a second at the floor. When the silence between them became prolonged, she gestured weakly.

"How's your mother?" she inquired, grasping the first safe subject she could think of. "Well, I hope."

"Very well, actually. She remarried last year. He's a retired doctor and they seem quite happy."

"I'm glad," Amy said sincerely. "Your mother is such a nice warm person. I always was fond of her."

"And she was fond of you. She was terribly disappointed when she learned you had left Alexandria."

"Oh?" Amy's brows lifted mockingly. "And did you tell her you weren't?"

"No, because I was disappointed when I found out you were gone," Jordon claimed, leaning forward to put his own empty cup and saucer on the coffee table. "And to set the record straight, I didn't tell you I had no more time for you. I simply told you I wouldn't have nearly as much time to spend with you."

"Right. And then you didn't call or see me for the entire six weeks before I left Alexandria. A rather cowardly way to give someone the brush-off."

A muscle ticked with fascinating regularity in Jordon's tightening jaw. "We declared a truce. Remember?"

She shrugged. "I told you I couldn't promise it would last long."

"We'll just have to give it another chance, then," he demanded rather than suggested. "How's your family?"

He certainly didn't give up easily and she was tired. Sometimes it's far less exhausting simply to go with the tide rather than try to fight against it and, to her, it seemed this was one of those times. Slipping back on the sofa, she made herself more comfortable. "My family's fine," she finally answered. "My father hasn't retired yet and Mother's still busy gardening plus making a fuss over my brother's three kids. She's the typical grandmother, getting a kick out of spoiling all her grandchildren."

Jordon smiled. "And does she ever ask you when you're going to provide her with some more to spoil?"

"Heavens yes, every time I see her and at least every other

time I speak to her on the phone," Amy said, chuckling indulgently. "Why do you ask? Do you get that same question from your mother?"

"Whenever she gets half a chance to ask it." Loosening his uniform tie and undoing his collar button, he grinned. "And do you ever get this line: 'If you don't get married and have children soon, I'm going to be too old to enjoy them'?"

"Mothers must belong to some secret society. They all ask the exact same questions," Amy said, her laughter light but genuine and infectious. "But I suppose that's their prerogative."

"I guess," he agreed.

But his smile softened, became more sensuous as his gaze wandered over her finely molded features. Her amused blue eyes met his and the quick flaring of light in the amber depths told her at once that his mood had suddenly changed. For a moment that seemed an eternity, she couldn't look away. She caught her breath. Then, willing herself to move, she started to stand.

"I . . ." she began, her voice strained. "W-would you like more coffee?"

"No, Amy," he murmured, moving with awesome quickness and purpose toward her, his hands coming out to span her waist and draw her toward him. "Right now I only want—"

His words halted as he immediately proved to her precisely what he wanted. His finger lifted her chin and he swiftly lowered his dark head, and before she could react, his lips were on hers, softly stroking yet taking. For a few confusing seconds she was too stunned to resist him, but when his tautly muscular arms slipped round her waist, she was abruptly jolted into awareness by what was happening. Her entire body went tense. She threw her hands against his broad chest and tried to push him back while dragging her mouth from his.

"No! Stop!" she gasped. "*Now.*"

He paid no attention. His touch remained gentle, but he easily overcame her attempts at resistance, rendering them useless. Catching both her hands in one of his, he pressed them back against her, and when his knuckles sank warmly into the cushioned softness of her breasts, a riotously erotic thrill shot through her so savage in intensity that she nearly panicked and tried all the harder to break free of his embrace.

"Jordon, let me go," she muttered, holding herself stiffly. "I don't want—"

"Be still, Amy. You want the same thing I do. This and this," he whispered, kissing each corner of her mouth again and again. "And this."

Then his warm firm lips were on hers once more, brushing, caressing, and evoking tremors that ran all over her. As his teeth closed tenderly on the full curve of her lower lip, nibbling, nipping, tasting, an insidious invasive warmth spread through her legs, and her heart hammered wildly in her breast.

"No," she breathed, both her voice and her will weakening, and when the tip of his tongue sought the moist sweetness of her mouth, she could no longer deny herself the dizzying delight of his kiss. Her lips clung to his, taking and giving. Beyond rational thought, capable only of feeling, she softly sighed and kissed him back, a fever rising deep within her. When Jordon slowly released her hands they went back against his chest, but this time to graze over the broad expanse up to the strong column of his neck and across his shoulders. Her slender fingers feathered down his arms then back up again along the lean, powerful line of his upper body. And as she cupped his face in her hands while her lips parted wider beneath the sweet compelling pressure of his, he sat back, gathering her hard against him.

Half reclining across his thighs, she pressed nearer, the enticing curves of her slim body yielding to his firmer flesh. As he cradled her closer, his kisses deepened and she returned them with a fervor that soon equaled his. His large hands ranged over her, exploring the line of her slender thigh, the swell of her buttocks and hips, and her trim waist. His fingers slipped beneath her top, grazing her bare flat midriff then probing the rising lower slope of one breast, searing her skin through the gossamer sheer fabric of her brief lace bra. Amy moaned softly. One of her hands covered his, pressing his palm into her warmly resiliant flesh.

"Amy," he groaned, cupping the weight of both her breasts in his hands. "You feel so good, smell so good, *taste* so good."

"*Jordon,*" she breathed, then was lost in the fierce commanding power of his kiss as his mouth descended upon hers once again. Swept away in the remembrance of the nights of ecstasy they had shared together, of the gentle yet insistent thrusts of him deep within her, she melted against him, all feminine and acquiescent. For three long years she hadn't felt so vital and alive and exquisitely responsive. Since Jordon, no other man had ever made her feel more than a faint flicker of physical desire and she had never even been tempted to share an intimate moment with any of them, although some had been more handsome than Jordon, perhaps as successful, and certainly more considerate. Still, she had never been able to respond to any of them with even a fraction of the passion he always seemed able to evoke in her, the fiery passion he was evoking now. It seemed an eternity since she had wanted anything as much as she wanted him at that moment and she ran eager fingers through his thick, vibrant hair.

"Amy, honey, it's been too long," he whispered roughly, as if reading her thoughts. "And I want you so much."

Her head fell back against his supportive arm, exposing the creamy curve of her neck to his burning kisses. He drew back slightly, leaning over her, his broad shoulders blocking the golden glow of the lamp behind him. She gazed up at him, her blue eyes drowsy and glimmering with desire. Lifting a hand, she drew one fingertip down the bridge of his nose, feeling the slight bump that was his memento of the improper mending of that break years ago. And it was that one small gesture that tugged at her heart more than any other. How many times, before and during and after lovemaking, had she run a fingertip along his nose? So many that she couldn't begin to count them; but those times had been long ago when she had been young and foolish and, ultimately, she had dearly paid for that foolishness. How odd that such a simple caress, the mere touching of his nose, could trigger all the memories of their affair, from beginning to bitter end. And in that deluge of memories, desire waned. Passion had clouded her mind, but now it was clearing and she realized that for the last few minutes she had been playing the fool for him once again. As his hand skimmed across her flat abdomen and he lowered his head as if to kiss her once more, she shook hers.

"No," she said firmly, her newfound resolve strengthening, enabling her to sit up and move away from him. "Jordon, I want you to leave now."

"Amy, I—"

"Just go."

His hands gripped her shoulders; he turned her around to face him. "Is this your little revenge, Amy? Playing the tease and then saying no? If so and you think that's going to discourage me, you're badly mistaken. I've tried to tell you I won't give up so easily."

"Well, you might as well give up!" she exclaimed heatedly, reproach-darkened eyes boring into the tawny depths of his. "What happened tonight will never be repeated, I can promise you."

"Never say never, love," he cautioned softly, a semblance of a smile drifting across his lips. "It's useless to make promises you can't keep and there's no sense in your trying to fight this. We still want each other as much as we ever did."

Shrugging his hands off her shoulders, she rose to her feet and haughtily swept a hand toward the door. "Leave now, Jordon."

"If you insist." He got up and walked across the room before pausing to look back at her with a faint, too-knowing smile. "Tonight was just a new beginning, Amy. All the old feelings are still there for both of us."

"That's where you're wrong," she shot back, but before the last word had left her lips, he had closed the door behind him, leaving her alone in a sudden heavy silence. Outside his footfalls receded on the stairs, and with an impotent curse she spun around on one heel, raking her hand through her hair. He was wrong; he was. All the old feelings weren't still there. Once she had believed she loved him and what she felt for him right now was far from love. Instead, she felt . . . well, she didn't know exactly what she did feel, but it most certainly wasn't love.

Unable to stand still a moment longer, needing to do something, anything, to take her mind off Jordon, she started clearing the coffee table. When she rattled a cup against its saucer, Skeeter stirred on the chair cushion, lazily lifting her head up.

"Some help you were. You could at least have arched your back at him instead of being so friendly," Amy muttered, sighing when the cat showed her total lack of concern by yawning wide and gazing up through narrow, slitted eyes until she nodded off again.

Walking into the kitchen, Amy couldn't blame the cat for what had happened. She could only blame herself. And perhaps the wine? No. The two glasses she had had with dinner hadn't been enough to really affect her judgment. It wasn't the spirits she had found intoxicating. It had been Jordon's touch, his kisses, but surely her response to him could be attributed to nothing more than sheer lust. He was an exciting sensual man and she had never forgotten what a passionate and wonderfully generous lover he was. So perhaps she had allowed tonight to happen because of a very natural need to experience physical gratification. Or perhaps there was more to it. Inherently honest with herself, she couldn't dismiss the possibility that there was a deeper reason for tonight's response. Once she had felt so close to him; maybe, emotionally, she had needed to reexperience that closeness. She should have known better. Closeness had been a mere illusion before and would be again, no matter how physically fulfilling making love with him could be. And physical fulfillment simply wasn't enough.

It was a good thing she was a strong-willed woman. She could resist Jordon, despite all his charm. It might take a more intense effort than she had imagined, but she could resist him. She was certain. Yet as she ran water over the cups in the sink and added liquid detergent, as she stared out the window at the black, moonless night, a shadow of concern settled over her features.

CHAPTER THREE

Two nights later, on Wednesday, Amy worked late in her office. Jordon had also stayed late next door in his, but she was determined not to let that bother her. For the past two days she had been able to ignore him almost completely and the simple fact that they were alone together here was inconsequential. Besides, she was far too busy to think about him. Before her on the desk lay all the personnel folders in her files, which had to be updated on a monthly basis. Although it was six days until the thirty-first, she liked to keep ahead of things, knowing only too well how often emergencies cropped up at the last minute and kept her from routine duties. Sometimes Trudy jokingly accused her of being overly conscientious, but Amy regarded her habits as less a matter of being scrupulously careful and more a matter of pride. She had duties to perform; it only made sense to perform them as efficiently as possible and to the best of her ability. And to avoid that terrible curse of feeling driven, she was able to find relaxation in reading, swimming, and her dearest friends. She was satisfied with her life, or at least she had been until Jordon had reentered it.

Staring blindly at the folder open before her, she impatiently shook her head, as if to reassemble her thoughts. She had no time to waste thinking about Jordon Kent. She really was too busy, and with all the effort she could muster, she concentrated exclusively on the file on Jonah Fletcher, gardener for the Morrisons, the Lancasters, and the Meades. He had missed six days in the past four weeks but with good reason, a touch of the flu the residents of St. Tropez Run certainly hadn't wanted to catch from him. Besides, he had Deirdre Morrison's mums blooming in glorious profusion, a feat his predecessor hadn't been able to accomplish. And quoting Deirdre, who was "absolutely awed by the miracle he had performed," Amy was able to give him a glowing evaluation. Jotting down several highly complimentary comments, she smiled. It always pleased her immensely to give the employees at St. Tropez Run a good report, especially Jonah. She had hired him herself less than six months ago. Middle aged with a family to support, out of work and practically penniless, he had admitted he was nearly desperate for work but had so impressed her with his quiet strength and dignity that she had been pleased to put him on the payroll. And he hadn't disappointed her once.

Still smiling, she closed Jonah's file and laid it aside, but as she was reaching for the next on the stack, there were two sharp raps on her door and Jordon opened it and stuck his head in.

"Come with me, Amy," he commanded, his sun-bronzed face almost grimly serious. "I've just had a call from Renn Bushnell; he says someone was trying to break into his house until he scared them away, and since I've never met him I think you should go along to introduce us. He'll feel more comfortable with me that way."

Reacting quickly, Amy was already on her feet and moving across the office toward the door. "Someone was trying to break into his house?" she softly exclaimed. "Did he see anyone? What—"

"I didn't ask for details over the phone. I just said I'd be there immediately," Jordon replied, taking her elbow to rush her through the reception area and out into the night's refreshing ocean breeze.

Increasing her pace to keep up with his long strides, Amy hurried with him toward the white Ford. She slipped quickly into the passenger seat when he yanked open the door for her, and then he strode around the car to get in beneath the wheel. As they swung out of the clubhouse parking area and were waved through the gate by the guard on duty, Amy remained silent, realizing at once that she didn't need to direct Jordon to the Bushnell house. After only two days at St. Tropez Run he had obviously already familiarized himself with the layout of the community. He took the first street to the right, then a left, following the shortest route to St. Mark's Circle, where the Bushnells lived.

Jordon stopped the car in the driveway of a large brick Tudor house, ablaze with lights. Even the lushly landscaped lawn was brightly illuminated and a man rushed across the grass toward them while they got out of the Ford sedan. In his early to mid-forties, Renn Bushnell was an exceedingly thin man of average height with a pleasant face and a shock of unruly light-brown hair. In a highly agitated state he approached Amy and Jordon, expressive gestures accompanying his babble of words.

"I saw them! Through the study window! They were running into the woods behind the house," he breathlessly exclaimed, his hands in constant motion. "It wouldn't have done any good for me to try to chase them. They were moving too fast."

"It might have been dangerous to go after them anyway," Jordon said. "About how long ago did this happen, Mr. Bushnell?"

"Oh, four or five minutes, I guess. I called you right after they disappeared into the woods."

"You keep saying 'they.' How many of them did you see?"

"Oh, there were two of them at least, maybe more."

"Can you give me a description?"

"Oh, well, no, they were too far away for me to get a good look at them."

"Just tell me anything you can remember. Could you tell if they were children or adults?" Jordon questioned calmly. "Male or female?"

"No, no, I'm sure they weren't children. But they could have been in their late teens," Renn Bushnell answered, nervously running his fingers through his hair. "And I'd say they were both males. One was fairly tall, the other average height, both of them slightly built."

"Fine, that's a beginning." Jordon gave Amy a nod. "Why don't you and Mr. Bushnell wait in the house while I call Ted on the car radio? The woods extend over to St. David's Way and he can drive over to check out the area. I'll join you both inside in a minute."

Taking the older man's arm, Amy promptly escorted him into his home, where he suggested they wait for Jordon in the study. While he poised himself tensely on the edge of the oatmeal-colored leather sofa, she walked across the room to look out the window. Due to her nearsightedness the woods out back weren't distinctly defined. Although she could see the individual trunks of the pines, the lacy boughs of the trees merged into a deep-green blur even in the light of the back-lawn floodlamps. Squinting, she detected no signs of movement anywhere. Beneath the black canopy of the star-studded sky and the sliver of the quarter moon, the woods appeared quite peaceful but she shivered slightly, knowing that could well be an illusion. Danger could be lurking out there in the shadows and she was relieved to be safe inside.

Her heart seemed to turn completely over in her breast, then begin to drum too hard and too fast, however, when Jordon appeared from around the corner of the house, approaching the stand of trees. *If someone was hiding out there . . .* Shaking her head, she took several deep breaths, attempting to still her fear. Jordon was a professional; he knew what he was doing and how to be careful. Despite those self-assurances, however, Amy stood tensed at the window, watching as he moved along the edge of the woods, training the sweeping beam of the flashlight he carried onto the ground beneath the trees. For the next minute or two she couldn't take her eyes off him and finally breathed a sigh of relief when he started back toward the house.

Amy turned away from the window and found Renn Bushnell fidgeting on the sofa. Suddenly he jumped up and flitted from expensive mahogany desk to ceiling-high bookcases to antique floor lamp, as if he couldn't bring himself to be still.

"It's lucky I was home," he began, shaking his head disbelievingly. "And of course they didn't know that. All the lights were out because—"

"Why don't you wait to tell what happened until Jordon . . . Mr. Kent joins us? Then you won't have to repeat everything," Amy suggested gently. Growing concerned over the man's accelerated and somewhat shallow breathing, she motioned him toward the sofa. "It might be better if you sit down and maybe I could get you a brandy, if you think that might help settle your nerves."

"I think I could use one," he agreed. "Thank you, Miss Sinclair."

"Call me Amy, please."

"If you'll call me Renn."

She gave him a reassuring smile. While she walked toward the liquor cabinet across the study, Jordon entered the room, flashlight still in hand. She stopped, her eyes darting over to meet his, but she couldn't tell by his closed expression whether or not he had found any sort of clue during his exploration at the edge of the woods. Asking no questions, she properly introduced the two men, satisfying the amenity they hadn't taken time to observe outside. As Jordon settled his long form into the chair opposite the sofa, she poured a small amount of brandy from a cut-glass decanter into a snifter, then carried it to Renn.

With a murmur of thanks he accepted it and Jordon allowed

him time to take a couple of slow sips before he leaned forward, his elbows on his muscular thighs, his hands lightly clasped between his knees.

"I didn't find anything outside. The ground under the trees is covered with pine needles, so it's unlikely we'll find any footprints. Of course, we'll have another look tomorrow as soon as it's light enough to see. We might find something then." He stood, tall and rangy, towering over Amy and Renn, who were both now sitting on the sofa. He retrieved the flashlight from the chair-side table where he had placed it. "You told me on the phone that you heard noises, as if someone was trying to get a window open. In which room? I want to have a look."

Swallowing a sip of brandy, Renn inclined his head toward the same window Amy had previously looked out of. "They tried to get in the one over there."

Jordon went over to examine the window and after several moments came back to sit down. "The screen's been cut. Would you tell me exactly what happened before you saw the men running into the woods?"

"I guess I'd better explain why I was home in the first place. You see, Bootsie—that's my wife—and I were invited to the Osborn party tonight. The Osborns live on St. James's Court. Well, we'd both planned to go but I had a headache this evening and decided to lie down for a while to try to lose it. So Bootsie went on to the party alone and I planned to join her later. But as I was lying here on this sofa with the lights out, I began hearing noises at the window, so I switched on the lamp, then rushed over. That's when I saw the men running away." Renn tossed back another swallow of brandy, his frown deepening. "I suppose they were the burglars who broke into those other houses?"

"It's a possibility" was Jordon's noncommittal answer. He was taking nothing for granted and reserving judgment until he had more facts. He glanced around the expensively appointed

53

study. "I assume you and your wife keep some valuables in your home?"

"Enough to attract a burglar, I imagine. There's Bootsie's jewelry, my coin collection, and of course paintings and art objects, among other things."

Thoughtfully Jordon nodded. "Isn't there anything else you can tell me about the men you saw? Anything at all you can remember? You mentioned that they could be teen-agers. Is there something specific you noticed about them that gave you that impression?"

"All I could really tell was that they were both very slight of build. I guess that's what makes me think they might have been young men."

"Do you know any of the older boys who live in the boys' home nearby?" Jordon asked, raising a silencing hand when Amy started to protest. "In other words, have you had any contact with any of them?"

"You couldn't be more off track," Amy spoke up, refusing to keep her opinion to herself and giving Jordon a withering look. "I spend Saturday afternoons at the home tutoring some of those boys, and I've met many of the others. And I don't believe any of them could be involved in these burglaries."

"I agree with her, Mr. Kent," Renn said. "Although many of my neighbors suspect the boys at the home of being involved, I don't."

"You're probably both right," Jordon conceded. "But I'll still go over to the home tomorrow and talk to the director. It's important to check out every possibility."

Pressing her lips firmly together, Amy bit back a disgruntled sigh. Jordon would probably check out his own grandmother if he felt it was his duty. And though she understood the logic of conducting a completely thorough investigation, she still resented his uncompromising attitude. There were some people he should *know* he could trust—former lovers for instance, like her.

He had been close enough to her at one time to realize that she wasn't the criminal type.

For the next ten minutes or so Amy listened silently to the questions and answers Jordon and Renn Bushnell exchanged. In the end it seemed to her that they knew little more about the attempted break-in than they had known before they came to the house. Bushnell said he had been dozing when he heard the noise at the window and recollections of what had happened next were rather vague. Although Jordon did try gently to probe his memory, he was unable to provide many further details.

At last Jordon stood. "We'll check out the woods first thing in the morning and contact you if we find anything," he told the older man, before adding, "One final question, Mr. Bushnell. What sort of business are you in?"

"I'm semiretired—health reasons. But I'm still on the board of two computer firms in Houston and have to fly back there frequently on business. But why do you ask?"

"No special reason. I just never know what little bits of information might prove useful," Jordon answered casually, glancing in Amy's direction. "But, for now, I don't have any further questions, so we'll be going, Mr. Bushnell. I doubt if anything else will happen tonight, but if something does, call the guard at the gate at once."

"Oh, I certainly will," Renn murmured, escorting Amy and Jordon out of the study to the front door. Pausing with his hand on the ornate handle, he clicked his tongue against the back of his teeth and shook his head. "Unnerving experience, very unnerving. I think I'll drive over to the Osborns' party and try to forget what's happened for a while unless . . . unless you think the burglars might come back to finish what they started."

"I doubt whoever was here will risk returning tonight," Jordon reassured him. "But I'll tell Ted to drive by here several times an hour through the night, just in case."

"I'd appreciate that very much, Mr. Kent," Renn said, seizing Jordon's right hand and pumping it enthusiastically. "And I want to tell you that I feel better just knowing that you're with Security Unlimited. A fine agency, excellent reputation."

After voicing his thanks for the compliment and saying good night, Jordon indicated with a gesture that Amy should precede him from the house. Saying nothing to each other, they walked across the lawn, and as they reached the asphalt driveway, a Security Unlimited patrol car stopped by the curb in front of the house.

"I'll wait in the car while you go see if Ted found anything," Amy declared, leaving Jordon to get in the Ford sedan. She didn't have to wait long before he reappeared, got in with her, and turned the key in the ignition.

"Well?" she questioned hopefully while he continued around the circle drive and turned out onto the tree-lined street. "What did Ted say? Did he find anything on the other side of the woods?"

"Nothing, but I didn't expect him to. Bushnell's intruders had plenty of time to get beyond the woods and St. David's Way before Ted could get there."

Jordon's brisk, businesslike tone caused Amy to turn her head to look at him while worrying her lower lip with the edge of her teeth. His strongly carved, unyielding profile, limned in the soft light of the dash, reminded her of just how ruthless he could be. She knew that from personal experience, and contemplating what he planned to do tomorrow, she felt compelled to offer a few more words of protest.

"About the guys at the boys' home," she began softly, deciding she might be much more effective by reasoning with him rather than showing signs of hostility, "I think you know it's useless to go talk to Terry King, the home's director. You don't really believe any of those boys are involved in the robberies here."

"I'm going to check out the situation, Amy—I have a responsibility" was Jordon's blunt reply before he relented to some extent and, shaking his head, reached for her hand, bringing it

56

over to rest on his cleanly muscled thigh. "But, to set your mind at rest, I still doubt the boys at the home have anything to do with the burglaries. I still think they're being pulled off by somebody on the inside. And, to be honest, I doubt that Bushnell's intruders were responsible for the other break-ins, which all occurred very late at night. Right now it's only eight forty-five, far too early to fit the pattern."

Surprise widened Amy's eyes and for an instant she forgot that his thumb was playing idly over the tips of her fingers. "If they weren't the burglars, then who do you suppose they were? And what were they trying to do?"

"I'm not sure. I just have my doubts."

"Well, I have to admit that I wondered if Renn hadn't been mistaken about what he saw. I thought it could have been just a deer bounding away through the trees; we see them so often in the woods around here," she told him, but shook her head. "But Renn says he *saw* two men running away."

"Maybe he did, but if they were teen-agers, which he seems to think, they could very well have been been boys who live here and were up to some prank."

"I'd hardly call cutting someone's window screen a prank."

"Bored teen-agers will sometimes do some foolish things to entertain themselves," Jordon reminded her, a wry smile slowly appearing on his lips. "I should know; when I was that age, I pulled some foolish pranks myself—none quite this outrageous but silly nonetheless. I can imagine a couple of St. Tropez boys sitting around, bored to death tonight. One of them starts talking about the break-ins and finally they decide it would be fun to create some excitement by making it seem as though the burglar tried to strike again. To do that they at least had to make it look as though someone meant to break into a house."

"But for that to work, they would have had to know that Renn Bushnell was at home to stop them before they could get in," Amy debated. "And he shouldn't have been there. He would have been at the Osborn party if he hadn't had a headache."

"And practically everybody in the development . . . er, community, might have known he wasn't feeling well," Jordon countered. "From what I've heard about Bootsie Bushnell, she keeps few secrets from her neighbors."

Amy looked at him with grudging respect. He had certainly done his homework in the past two days. Bootsie Bushnell *was* a chatterbox, at least where her fellow residents were concerned. It was only the employees of St. Tropez Run, Amy included, to whom she wouldn't bother to give the time of day.

"I see what you mean," she mused aloud. "Now your theory's beginning to make more sense to me."

"But it's still only a theory," he readily admitted, then smiled too knowingly when she extracted her hand from beneath his as he braked to a stop at the gatehouse.

After Jordon had briefed Sam Wilson, the guard, on what had happened at the Bushnell residence, telling him to call him in his quarters if anything else happened during the night, he drove into the parking area before the offices of the vast clubhouse. Without waiting for him to come around and open her door, Amy got out of the car, fingertips still tingling from his casual, meaningless caress of her sensitive skin. She hurried into the reception area several paces ahead of him, feeling the oddest, most compulsive need to put a great deal of distance between him and herself. She thought she had succeeded after she'd gone into her office and he into his, but he appeared in her doorway as she was neatly stacking the remainder of personnel files on her desk, intending to get back to them first thing in the morning. She looked up at him, then hastily back down.

"It's been a long day and a hectic evening. I'm tired," she murmured, picking up her blue linen suit jacket before removing her purse from a drawer. "I'm going home now."

"In the morning I'll bring you my list of residents here," Jordon spoke up, intercepting her when she started across the office and blocking her route to the door. "I want you to check it over to be sure no names have been left off."

All too aware of how his height and the breadth of his shoulders seemed to dwarf the small room, she pressed the shoulder purse closer to her side while giving him a questioning look. "All right, I'll check it over. But why do you want me to?"

"I need a complete list of names for the investigations."

"Investigations? You don't mean . . ." She shook her head disbelievingly. "For heaven's sake, Jordon, you're not going to investigate the people who *live* in St. Tropez Run, are you? Why bother? Just to be able to move into this community, they all had to be checked out—so why do it again?"

"Because I can't assume the earlier investigations were thorough," he explained. "I know mine will be."

"Oh, I don't doubt that for a minute. And can you imagine how these people are going to react when they learn they're being checked out? They're really going to resent being considered suspects."

"Could be. But if they want to put a stop to the burglaries, they're going to have to put up with some inconvenience. Besides, the ones with nothing to hide shouldn't mind being investigated. The others will just have to accept the fact that I'm going to delve into their past. Of course, the reports will be confidential and I'm not interested in learning that someone was once convicted for cheating on his taxes. I'll only be looking for some possible link to the burglaries."

"Which you're not likely to find. Take a look at these people, Jordon. They're not exactly penniless; it costs a small fortune to buy one of the houses here, and since they have plenty of money, why should they steal? They're just not the burglar type."

"Stranger things have happened," he said, a glint of amusement lighting his eyes as he looked down at her. "Do you realize you've eliminated every suspect I've mentioned? According to you, none of the employees could be the burglar, none of the boys from the home, and now none of the residents. Who broke into those houses, then? Maybe you think some supernatural being is responsible, perhaps the very ghost that supposedly roams through the clubhouse?"

Amy had to smile. "My idea isn't quite that farfetched. I simply think someone from outside the community must be the burglar, even though you doubt an outsider could get past security so many times. You have to admit it's possible someone did."

"Yes, it's a slim possibility, and one I haven't ruled out yet. And, Amy, you shouldn't rule out any possibilities, either," he advised, both his voice and his expression gentling while he reached out to stroke lightly her shining hair. "If you keep on thinking that nobody you know personally could be the burglar, you might end up getting hurt if it turns out you're wrong."

His touch disturbed her immensely and she sought escape from it. "I'll keep that in mind," she murmured. "Well, I'd better be getting home now."

When she started to step away, Jordon lowered his hand onto her shoulder to keep her near him. "We've both already had dinner, but we could have a drink together before you leave. How about it?"

"Thank you but no, Jordon" was her polite answer. "Not tonight."

"When, then?"

"I'm not sure," she said, refusing to be trapped. "Just some other time."

"Amy," he said, his tone gently chiding, his gaze roaming over her face, detecting the firm resolve overlying her delicate features. She wasn't going to make this easy for him, but he had no intention of accepting defeat. Although her fascinating sapphire eyes no longer issued an invitation as they once had and issued a challenge instead, it was a challenge he would willingly meet. For too long a while he hadn't had much time for memories of the poignant, wildly passionate nights they had once shared. Yet seeing her again, touching her, made him remember often now, and he wanted them to share many more nights like that together. Patience was the key word; he knew it. He had hurt her in the past and regaining her trust would take time and a great deal of tenderness, tenderness he would gladly provide. Brushing a fingertip over her neck just at the top of her collar, he shook his head and faintly smiled. "You can't go on trying to avoid me forever."

"I'm leaving now," she muttered when he'd begun kneading her shoulder. "Good night."

"I can't let you go until—"

"No," she commanded as he lifted her chin and bent down— but it was too late. In an instant his lips were on hers, firm yet softly coaxing. His kiss was electric, and ill prepared for the tingling shock that scampered over her every nerve ending, she was powerless to struggle against him. Feeling held sway and his kiss was so expertly arousing that for a time she couldn't resist the pleasure it gave.

"Amy, you're so beautiful," he whispered, raising his head to look down at her, his amber eyes narrowed and glinting. Cupping her face in one hand, he drew the edge of his thumb over the gentle arches of her eyebrows, feathered his fingertip along the tip of her lashes, and slowly probed the curve of her high cheekbones before outlining the tender bow-shape of her mouth and creating such riotous sensations that she nearly trembled. This unhurried tactile exploration of her face was having an erotic effect on her senses, and although she realized how deliberately seductive he was being, he was reawakening the sensual woman inside that she had too long kept imprisoned. Her heart beat crazily. Her breathing quickened. A wave of relaxing warmth was sweeping through her and she didn't seem able to stem the tide.

Closing her eyes, she swayed toward him, allowing her lips to part beneath his questing touch. Whispering her name, he took her in his arms, holding her fast against him, and she offered no resistance. Yet the moment his warm minty-fresh mouth possessed hers once again, the remnants of sanity screamed a warning that was comparable to ice water thrown in her face.

Dragging forth all the willpower she could muster, she forced her head to overrule her heart and traitorous body. With a muffled cry of contempt for both herself and him, she struggled in his tightening embrace and turned her head aside to escape the sweet plundering power of his lips.

"Let me go," she demanded steadily. "Your gun's digging right into my side and it's very uncomfortable."

Allowing her to take a backward step, Jordon met her cooling gaze. "I'll take it off, then."

"Don't bother; I'm going anyway," she said, her tone chilling. And, after breaking free of his hands, she marched toward the doorway, stopping only to cast an icy glance back at him while busily tucking the hem of her blouse farther down beneath the waistband of her skirt. "And, Jordon, I don't want this sort of thing ever to happen again. Understand?"

"Oh, I understand, but I can't make promises, Amy," he answered with a teasing smile. "I don't think I'd be able to keep them, and I wouldn't want to deceive you."

Incensed by the obvious amusement in his deep voice, she called him a few nasty names and continued out the door with a pithy reminder that he would have to lock up when he left the offices.

She drove toward home a few moments later with a heavier foot on the accelerator, and it was all Jordon's fault. Glancing at the speedometer, she immediately slowed down, certain she would scream with sheer frustration if stopped by a patrolman and given a ticket which would simply add insult to tonight's injury. Anger seethed up in her, at herself and at Jordon. Tonight she had behaved like a weakling, and he had been himself—an impossible man.

"You son of a . . ." she uttered, but didn't finish the virulent epithet only because she was unwilling to malign his mother that way. She was a wonderful woman. How had she managed to have such a selfish, unfeeling son? Three years ago he had dumped Amy without a qualm, without a twinge of conscience;

but now he apparently believed he could waltz back into her life and talk her back into his bed as if nothing had ever happened.

"Fat chance, buster," she muttered, staring out at ribbon of highway stretching out before her. Yet, by the time she got home, her self-confidence was ebbing while her uncertainty was rising. And she was glad when Skeeter met her at the front door with a demanding meow. The cat gave her something to think about besides Jordon.

It was Friday, only two days later, when Amy received the second call for help from Renn Bushnell. Because Jordon wasn't in his office, Trudy transferred the call to Amy's and Amy listened attentively, her shoulder and neck muscles tensing while he explained why he had called.

"Just try to calm down, Renn. I'll have Mr. Kent or one of the guards at your house in a couple of minutes," she reassured him, quickly agreeing when he insisted that she come, too. After hanging up the phone, she rushed out of her office through the reception area without stopping to give the curious Trudy an explanation, and the moment she stepped outside into the bright afternoon sunlight, she spied Jordon talking to the guard at the gate. Despite her nearsightedness she recognized that tall, lean frame and casual, loose-limbed bearing, even though she couldn't clearly distinguish his face at such a distance. Half running, she crossed the parking area and entrance road to St. Tropez Run, and when she saw Jordon look up and notice her approaching, the abrupt solemnity that shadowed his chiseled features told her that he realized something serious had happened. With two long strides he moved forward to meet her.

"Amy, what—"

"Renn Bushnell called," she briefly and rather breathlessly explained, the top of her head seared by the sun's hot rays, which were tempered only by a too-gentle ocean breeze. Her cheeks flushed with rosy color, she waved a hand in the general direction of the Bushnell house. "He says he needs both of us over there as soon as possible."

Without asking questions, Jordon cupped her left elbow in one hand and hurried her back across the road and the asphalt parking lot to his sedan. It was only after they had sped past the gatehouse that he gave her a quick glance and asked, "What exactly has happened, Amy?"

"I don't know," she admitted, clutching at the armrest when the car suddenly veered into the first street to the right. "Renn sounded very upset. All he really said was that he might have caught a thief."

Jordon frowned but made no comment, driving on to the Bushnells' and stopping with an abbreviated squeal of rubber on the drive. When Amy opened the door and jumped out of the car at the same time he did, he waited for her to join him on the other side, then strode quickly with her beside him along the walk to the front door where he rang the bell.

Renn Bushnell opened the door and jerkily motioned them inside. Amy kept pace with Jordon as they were silently directed into the living room to the right of the entrance foyer. What she saw inside the room made her softly gasp: Bootsie Bushnell was looming over her blue-uniformed maid, Martha Trask, who sat wide eyed on a white velvet sectional sofa.

"*Martha!*" Amy exclaimed, taking several quick steps forward. "What's this all—"

"Oh, Amy, thank God you're here," Martha cried, jumping up to lope across the spacious, luxuriously furnished living room. Wringing her thin, red, work-roughened hands, she stopped in front of Amy, vehemently shaking her head. "What she's saying just ain't true and I can explain everything if—"

"She's lying," Bootsie Bushnell curtly interrupted, her thinly arched dark brown brows at variance with the platinum blond of her immaculately coiffed hair. Looking at her maid, she curled up her lips and sighed disdainfully. "She's a thief. I caught her trying to sneak out of the house with—"

"That ain't so, Miz Bushnell," Martha protested tearfully. "I didn't even remember I had—"

"Come now, dear," Bootsie haughtily interrupted with a falsetto giggle. "Don't try to insult us by lying."

"But I ain't lying. I—"

"Hold it," Jordon interceded, his deep, low-timbred voice demanding attention and obedience. He looked at the overwrought maid, then at Amy. "Take Martha into the study, please. And, Martha, you tell Amy exactly what's happened here this afternoon while I talk to the Bushnells."

Nodding, the maid rushed by Amy across the living room, through the vast entrance foyer, and into the study. She stood by the window and stared out blindly, wringing her hands once again.

As she watched her, Amy's heart ached. Martha was a simple countrywoman but one who had always possessed the utmost self-respect and dignity, and now she seemed lost, despite all her basic strength, in a tempest beyond her control. Stepping farther into the room, Amy closed the door quietly behind her and approached Martha. "Please tell me what's going on here."

"Oh, it's just such a mess. It truly is," Martha muttered, shaking her head incredulously. "I really can't believe it's happening, Amy. It just doesn't make a bit of sense."

"Come and sit down with me," Amy suggested, smiling encouragement as the older woman joined her on the leather sofa. "Now, just tell me what's happened."

"It's the biggest mix-up. You see, I was cleaning the master bathroom a couple of hours ago when I found one of Miz Bushnell's rings laying on the vanity top right near the lavatory. Well, I didn't want to take a chance on it getting lost down the drain or getting the cleanser I was using on it, so I just dropped it in my pocket. I do that all the time because Miz Bushnell leaves her jewelry laying round everywhere and I pick it up and put it on her dressing table. Well, I just plain forgot to today because I had my mind on my daughter's wedding next week. And anyway, the ring was still in my pocket when I started out the kitchen door to go home. I was saying good-bye to Miz Bushnell when I took my handkerchief out of my pocket and the ring came with it and fell on the floor. And all of a sudden, before I could say a thing, she was on me like a duck on a June bug, wagging her finger in my face and calling me a thief and lots worse things that I sure don't appreciate. I might be just the maid but she didn't have to talk to me that way."

"Of course she didn't," Amy agreed, angered by Bootsie's ridiculous behavior. "What happened when you explained how the ring got into your pocket?"

"She didn't believe a word I was saying and kept calling me a liar," Martha related, pushing a strand of graying hair back from her flushed face. "Then she started screaming for her husband to call up the sheriff and have me thrown in jail. But he said he'd call Mr. Kent and that's when I told him I wanted you to come here, too, because I knew you'd believe me when I told you what happened. And you do, don't you?"

"Martha, you don't even have to ask that. Naturally I believe you. I know you'd never steal anything."

"No, ma'am, I would not," Martha proclaimed, her words steel-edged. "Now, I ain't never had many things in my life, but I'm used to that, and besides, I got a healthy husband and healthy young'uns, and I'm pretty healthy myself. That's what's important and I'm happy. There ain't one thing in this fancy house that I want enough to take. It's Miz Bushnell who worships *things*, not me, I can tell you that."

Silently agreeing with that assessment, Amy nodded and stood up. "Well, let's go see if we can straighten out this silliness."

And silly was the word that aptly described Bootsie Bushnell. The moment Amy and Martha reentered the living room, she stuck her nose up in the air, her face a picture of unreasonable disdain. In her forties, fashionably gaunt, she tried to act and look as though she were fifteen years younger. Posed on a white velvet chair, she tapped a toe against the plush carpet, apparently

66

trying to draw attention to her tiny feet, of which she was unduly proud. In Amy's opinion, the woman's IQ and shoe size were a perfect match, both being four and a half. If she had a brain, she kept it well hidden, and this she soon demonstrated.

After Amy had quickly repeated Martha's story to Jordon and he seemed inclined to accept it as true, Bootsie snapped her head up high and glared at him indignantly.

"You don't believe that farfetched yarn, do you?" she sharply exclaimed.

Jordon folded his arms over the shirtfront of his crisp khaki uniform. "I think it's reasonable to assume Martha simply forgot she had the ring. Since she often picks up your jewelry to return it to your dressing table—"

"Oh, that's just another one of her lies," Bootsie interrupted, dismissing his words with a limp-wristed toss of one hand. "I *never* leave my jewelry laying around."

"Now, dear," her husband interceded, chuckling. "That's not exactly true. You know you're not very good at putting your things where they belong. And since you might be mistaken about Martha, I think we should forget the whole matter and give her another chance."

"Hah! I don't want that woman in my house. She's a thief."

"Mrs. Bushnell, I can vouch for Martha," Amy spoke up stiffly, disgusted with the woman's antics. "I hired her myself and she has excellent references."

"I thank you for saying so, Amy, but it doesn't matter. I don't want to work here any more anyhow," Martha said proudly. "I don't have to put up with being called a thief and I'm not going to."

"Now, Martha . . . Bootsie . . ." Renn Bushnell began. "Surely there's some way to work this out."

When no one offered any suggestions to accomplish that feat, Amy smiled reassuringly at Martha. "Call me tomorrow. I can probably help you find work somewhere else."

"Well, it won't be in St. Tropez Run, you can be very sure of that," Bootsie proclaimed. "I'll have her blacklisted here."

"Fortunately, Mrs. Bushnell, St. Tropez Run is not the center of the universe," Amy replied, her calm even tone belying the anger she felt. "There are other places, and I'm sure some family will be happy to hire someone as hardworking as Martha is."

"You'd better warn them to lock up their valuables when she's around," the older woman snapped cattily. "And I know all of you are going to feel very foolish about letting her get away with this, especially if it turns out she's the one who's been breaking into homes around here."

That idea was so blatantly ludicrous that when Amy's eyes met Jordon's and she saw the slight twitching of his lips, she had quickly to avert her gaze and press her fingers against her mouth to avoid laughing aloud. And after such an idiotic remark there was absolutely nothing left to be said. When Martha gathered up her worn purse and walked out of the house, her unrushed stately gait effective despite the slight stiffness of her arthritic knees, Amy and Jordon soon followed, escorted to the door by Renn, who apologized for his wife.

In the car a minute later Amy seethed, her anger coloring her cheeks a bright red. "What a shallow, petty woman," she muttered as Jordon drove out onto the street. "And what a snob. I doubt she's ever spoken to Martha except to order her around; she considers herself too 'good' to talk to the help. Oh, I wish this hadn't happened in her house. If Martha had worked for anyone else in St. Tropez Run, she wouldn't have been accused of being a thief."

"An unfortunate incident," Jordon agreed, passing the gate and turning into the parking area before the clubhouse. "I'm sure Martha's very upset."

"She's humiliated. And she doesn't deserve this. She's so honest that I doubt she ever stole anything when she was a child—and most children do, at least once. I did. I snatched a book of matches from our next-door neighbor, Mrs. Hundley, an elderly

68

woman who dipped snuff. Then I confessed to my mother and she made me take the matches back and apologize. That was so embarrassing I never stole anything ever again." Amy looked at Jordon. "But maybe you don't believe that? Maybe you think I defended Martha because we're both members of the same gang of thieves?"

Laughing softly, he looked over at her, shaking his head while pulling to a stop and cutting the engine. "Amy, you're trying to pick a fight; you should be ashamed of yourself. No, I don't suspect Martha of being a burglar. Besides having a touch of arthritis, she's a little too broad in the beam for climbing into windows. And I certainly wouldn't be swayed by any accusations Bootsie Bushnell made. She's one of the silliest, most immature women I've ever met."

"She's a bitch," Amy corrected, then gave him a sideways, half-hesitant glance. "And maybe I was trying to pick a fight. I apologize. But I feel terrible about Martha and, besides, even if you don't suspect her of being a burglar, you've told me in no uncertain terms that you're going to investigate me."

"And I've also told you the investigation's strictly routine."

Maybe to him it was, but she didn't feel that way about it. He should know he could trust her, and she was still rather hurt that he didn't. But there was no point in rehashing that difference of opinion. She simply had to accept the fact that he put his business before people. He always had.

Getting out of the car, she led the way into the reception area, frowning faintly when she discovered Trudy was nowhere in sight. Then she remembered. "Oh, that's right. Trudy had a dental appointment and had to leave early." She glanced at her wristwatch. "And since it's four forty and I've worked late three nights this week, I'm going to quit now too and go swimming. Maybe that'll take my mind off going back to punch Bootsie Bushnell in the mouth."

Jordon's dark brown brows lifted. "Swimming? Where?"

"On the beach. Even though I don't live here, I can use the

facilities and I always take a swim on Friday evening. By the way, you can use the facilities, too—golf course, tennis or handball courts, whichever you like."

"I'd rather swim. Mind if I join you in a little while?"

"I . . . no, of course not," she answered, only because the beach hugged the curving shoreline for nearly a mile and he might never discover her favorite secluded spot. Opening the door to her office, she stepped inside, planning to change to her swimsuit. "Be my guest."

"Where will you be?" he called after her.

She breathed an inward sigh. He was too practical a man, never leaving anything to chance, and now she was trapped. "There's a little cove I like," she reluctantly told him. "Outside your quarters there's a short path that leads to the beach. At the end of it turn right and go about thirty feet. The cove's right there beyond the rock pilings. You can't miss it."

Forty-five minutes later Amy stepped from beneath the outdoor shower installed on the beach. She walked back around the rocks to the cove and plopped down cross-legged on a large towel. Tilting her head to one side, she squeezed the excess water from her hair, then ran her fingers through it, allowing it to fall loosely around her shoulders so it would dry. Immediately afterward she opened a bottle of sunscreen and quickly applied some to the bridge of her nose, which had a tendency to pop out in fat freckles. Softly humming, she started rubbing lotion over her lightly tanned arms, but her humming abruptly ceased and she snapped her head around to look behind her when a small stone tumbled with a clatter off the low piling of gray rocks that enclosed three sides of the cove.

It was Jordon who had dislodged it, and her heart skipped a beat or two when he stepped into the sand and walked toward her. Clad only in black swimtrunks slung low on lean hips, he was the epitome of raw masculinity. His long, hair-roughened legs were darkly bronzed and subtly muscled, as were his tapering waist, broad chest, and shoulders. It had been a long time

70

since she had seen him with so few clothes on and the mere sight of him stirred up many old memories. She turned away from him to stare out at the shimmering waters cascading toward her. For a fleeting second she considered a hasty retreat. After all, she had been out here for a while and could reasonably say she had had enough of surf and sun, then simply leave. Yet she hadn't really planned to go this soon and after that brief moment of uncertainty passed, she decided she wouldn't. Her chin lifted a fraction of an inch. There was no need for her to run away from Jordon. If nothing else, he was a very interesting conversationalist and she enjoyed talking to intelligent people. Furthermore, she and Jordon had to work together now; for her own sake she needed to try to make the situation as tension-free as possible. But that didn't promise to be an easy accomplishment. When she glanced up a second later and found herself the object of Jordon's lazy roaming gaze as he took in the sleek line of her swimsuit. She almost felt she was being undressed by his eyes, but maybe part of that feeling came from the aura of sexual magnetism that clung to him like a second skin, which she didn't fail to recognize.

CHAPTER FOUR

Jordon sat down on the towel next to Amy, stretching his powerful legs out before him and leaning back on his hands. Industriously pretending to be intent on smoothing sunscreen over her forearms, she granted him only a quick, casual smile.

"How's the swimming?" he asked, watching her intently even

as she turned her attention back to what she was doing. "Did you enjoy it?"

"Umm, very nice. The water's wonderful—warm and silky soft," she replied without looking back at him. "You should go in. You'll love it."

"I will, but later," he said, dropping down onto his elbows. "And did the exercise help you get rid of those murderous thoughts you were having about Bootsie Bushnell?"

"I wouldn't go so far as to say that," Amy answered truthfully. "I still dislike her immensely and hate the way she treated Martha."

"You're not alone, then," he said. "I'm with you."

Some unidentifiable nuance in his tone seemed to add hidden meaning to his words and Amy felt the need to find a change of subject fast. "What did you find when you visited the boys' home yesterday?" she questioned, seizing the first topic that popped into her head. "Were all the boys in leather jackets and standing around with switchblades and chains?"

"Hardly, but then I didn't expect to find them that way," he said, apparently unabashed by her mildly sarcastic tone. "Actually, the young men Terry King introduced me to, those who fit Bushnell's description, impressed me as being earnest, dependable boys. Besides, they all had an alibi for Wednesday night. They threw a surprise birthday party for somebody, and according to King, who was there, all of them attended and were there from seven thirty until lights out at eleven."

"I see. As long as they had an alibi, you can't suspect them. So I guess your trip to the home was a waste of time."

"Depends on how you look at it. While I was there, King recognized me from my days of playing college basketball at Virginia and asked me if I would participate in basketball practice every Saturday afternoon."

Amy's head shot up. She stared incredulously at him. "And you agreed to do it?"

"King's a very persistent man," Jordon said, quietly, his darkening gaze capturing hers. "How could I refuse? Does it surprise you so much that I said I would?"

"Yes," she admitted candidly. "It really does. At one time you wouldn't have spared a second for all the orphans in the world."

"True, but a man can change, as I've tried to tell you."

Had he truly changed? Maybe he had. Or maybe he simply wanted to make her believe that? Conflicting emotions pulled at her; she wanted to believe him, yet didn't dare. Bewildered and greatly confused, she forced herself to concentrate on smoothing sunscreen onto her shoulders. Feeling his eyes upon her, she waved a hand toward the surf breaking in swirling foam against the sand. "You should go in now to cool off."

"Later. Here, let me do that," he commanded softly while brushing her small hand away from her shoulder and replacing it with one of his own. He took the bottle of sunscreen from her, squeezing a tiny amount into his palm. "Lie down."

"I . . . but I can do that myself," she protested, her legs going suddenly weak. "You don't have to do—"

"You can't reach all the places I can. Now, lie down," he insisted, turning her and lowering her face down onto the towel, brooking no denial. Slipping his fingers beneath the narrow straps of her navy maillot swimsuit, he slowly pulled them aside and off her shoulders, allowing them to drop down and drape her upper arms.

Laying her head on folded arms, she watched out of the corner of her eye as he knelt beside her. *Too close. And what was happening was too dangerous.* She felt she should put a stop to this madness right away, yet slowly began to relax beneath the ministering hands moving over her shoulders, smoothing lotion into her creamy soft skin. His touch was impersonal, almost professional, as if he were a masseur and she nothing more than another body for him to tend. He not only applied sunscreen, he kneaded and stroked taut muscles and the impromptu massage became so enjoyable that she lowered her arms to her sides without hesitation when he asked her to. She closed her eyes

73

while he worked tension out of her upper back, her shoulders, and the tendons rising to her nape. Yet they opened again only seconds later when he started rubbing lotion on the backs of her legs, his fingers lingering along her shapely calves before drifting upward to the slender lines of her upper thigh. Now his touch was far from impersonal, less a massage and more a caress. A shiver trickled down her spine while sweet sensation danced over the surface of her skin. She drew in a swift, shaky breath, as she imagined the muscles of his bronzed torso rippling as he bent over her, inducing erotic fantasies that she tried without success to block from her consciousness.

A moment later Jordon gently rolled Amy over on the towel. When her darkening eyes met his, she was nearly hypnotized by the emberglow illuminating the tawny depths. Suddenly it was as if everything in the world ceased to exist except the two of them and this magic secluded cove. The golden sun gilded the surface of the ocean and the creamy surf washed away the sand. Sea grasses whispered in a caressing breeze scented with brine. Amy felt herself floating into a wonderland of heightened senses and lacked the will to resist the dreamlike allure of the journey.

Lowering himself down, Jordon leaned over her, supporting himself on one elbow. His other hand cupped her face, moving gently against the smooth line of her jaw. He lowered his head, smiling faintly when he heard her swift intake of breath. He kissed her cheeks, her eyelids, then the hollows beneath her ears and her hair, stirring the soft gold strands. Pulsating thrills rushed over and through her, followed by an uncontrollable shiver. When Jordon dropped down onto his side and turned her over to face him, she went willingly. Perhaps it was because he did seem to have changed in some ways as he told her he had, and perhaps it was his having volunteered to spend time with the boys at the home that was weakening her resistance. Whatever the reason, resistance was ebbing, too quickly, promising soon to disappear altogether.

Amy trembled as his hand stole around her waist to seek the

74

enticing arch of the small of her back, his fingers seeming to scorch her skin through the thin fabric of her swimsuit. Looking deeply into his eyes, she found it impossible to avert her gaze. When he had first arrived at St. Tropez Run, it had been difficult to believe they had ever shared ultimate intimacies, that she had once reveled with him in long lazy nights of hot passions and needs gloriously fulfilled. But now, while his fingertips lightly probed the delicate flesh and bone structure of her back, setting off keen fluttering sensations deep within her, it was not difficult to believe at all. Once, she had adored all the pleasurable things they did together, adored the way he made her feel, and now, even after all the time that had come between them, she discovered she still did.

Caught up in a dreamlike state, beckoned by the promise of delight that shone in his eyes, she slipped nearer him on the towel, reaching out to skim her hands across his broad bare shoulders, pulses leaping when she felt the superb flexing of his muscles beneath her fingertips.

"Amy," he whispered huskily, pressing the edge of his thumb tenderly into the curve of her chin, rotating it in tiny circles until at last it feathered her lips, parting them. "You have such a lovely, inviting mouth. I never could resist it."

Anticipation erupted in her, intensified, and became feverish as he paused, simply looking at her, making her await his kiss. Never had a few seconds passed with such unbearable slowness, and a flaming pillar of fire seemed to be blazing upward inside her, warming every square inch of her skin, torching every nerve ending. At last, when Jordon's warm lips met hers briefly over and over again, her own parted wider, issuing an invitation which he accepted with a scarcely repressible insistence. Sensing the tight rein with which he controlled himself, knowing the fiery ferocity of the passion simmering just beneath the surface in him, Amy felt dizzy with the realization that his self-imposed control could snap at any moment and overwhelm both of them. In the blooming reawakening of her senses, she could hardly think.

Swept away in a tidal wave of primitive feeling, she could only experience emotions and longings that were a legacy from the past. The desire to be touched and to touch were as strong and unconquerable as the mighty pull of the ocean. Her hands floated down over his hard chest while his lips played on hers, exploring the full tender curves, sampling their sweetness, and exerting a strengthening pressure that graduated slowly from breeze-light enticement to dizzying fierce demand.

His even teeth nibbled at the lush full curve of her bottom lip, opening her mouth. Acquiescently she moved within the tightening circle of his arms, quivering at the compelling strength of his muscular chest against her now throbbing breasts. Her softly curved body yielded to the firmer line of his and still his kisses remained demanding yet gentle, taking yet giving, and she was soon lost in them.

Far beyond rational thought, she gave herself over to the tide of passion rising between them. Their kisses became less urgent but no less intoxicating as their lips touched and parted, touched and parted, again and again. Amy's fingers tangled compulsively in Jordon's hair, running through the crispy clean strands. With a low moan rumbling up from deep in his throat, his marauding mouth possessed hers. His large, warm hands wandered down her back, over the gentle swell of her buttocks to the sleek smoothness of her upper thighs, massaging her firm womanly flesh. His fingers played over her caressingly as he suddenly released her lips to arch her back slightly against his supporting palm. His free hand roved slowly back upward to cup her slender neck. Then, with deftness despite the slight shaking of his hand, he removed the detachable straps of her swimsuit and tossed them aside.

"Amy," he muttered roughly, pushing the fabric down.

Through drowsy half-closed eyes Amy watched as he gazed down at the exposed V of pearlescent skin which pointed into the shadowed hollow between her breasts. He lowered his head and she could have stopped him then, but never considered it. If he

76

had intended to go all out to seduce her, he was succeeding, because in that moment she wanted to feel his lips upon her body more than she had ever wanted anything. Her legs ached with weakness and she released her breath in a sibilant sigh when Jordon began to scatter evocative nipping kisses over her naked shoulders. The tip of his tongue flicked playfully over the beginning swells of her breasts, tormenting her warm cushioned flesh, her tickling satiny skin. She softly moaned.

"Amy," he said hoarsely, lifting his head to gaze hotly into her opening eyes. "You must know what I want now."

She took a shuddering breath. "Tell me."

"What I want simply can't be accomplished out here," he said, getting to his knees, picking her up in his arms, and standing easily, as if she weighed nothing at all. "I want privacy and long hours with you . . . in my bed."

Amy would never know what thoughts ran through her head or, indeed, if any had while Jordon carried her back along the path toward his quarters. Lost in time, as if caught up in rapidly changing sequences of a hazy dream, she lay pliantly in his cradling arms and nuzzled her head into the hollow of his shoulder, as the moment swirled about her as if it were a drugging mist. She was vaguely aware of being borne into his quarters, then his bedroom, yet it was only when he put her down gently on his bed and sat down on the edge beside her that she grasped the magnitude of what she was allowing to happen. She felt a flash of fear.

"Jordon," she uttered breathlessly. "I . . ."

"Hush. I won't rush you," he softly promised, his smile indulgent. "I'd never do that. We have all night and I want it to last."

That brief instant of fear evaporated when the heel of his hand glanced over her collarbone while his pleasantly rough fingers sought the wildly fluttering pulsebeat in her throat. His hand drifted lower.

"Amy, your heart's beating so fast. But then, so is mine."

She said nothing, was unable to. Looking up at him, she saw

77

the sudden tightening of his chiseled features, heard his tortured whispering of her name. Her eyes fluttered shut when his lips descended on hers, taking their full softness with rousing insistence. Wild emotion surged up searing hot and rapier sharp in her breast. She arched upward against him as he lowered his lithe body over hers. Her arms wound upward around the strong column of his neck. Her mouth opened like a budding flower to the sweet onslaught of his and she met the invading tip of his tongue with her own, drawing it farther into her mouth.

Groaning, Jordon molded her slight body to the long line of his and kissed her many times, his lips hungry and demanding complete surrender. Amy kissed him back, mesmerized by the rapid beat of his heart against her. She played her fingers through the thick hair that brushed his nape and kneaded the muscles of his wide shoulders.

His hands ranged over her back and along her sides in tender exploration, following the gentle swell of her hips up to her waist and upward farther still to cup the straining sides of her breasts. At his touch, her heated flesh swelled against his palms and when his fingers pressed gently into the resilient mounds, she trembled at the sheer power of the pleasure she felt. Her parted lips clung to his, sweet, eager, invitingly caressing.

The pink-orange glow of the evening sun shone on the window, filling the room with amber light and darkening the bronze tone of Jordon's skin. Amy's hands drifted up almost of their own volition to feather over his bare chest and she didn't pull them away even when she heard his quickly intaken breath and felt his muscles contract to steel hardness at her soft touch. Instinctively gauging the depth of desire he seemed to be trying to control, she half expected to be enfolded in his arms and fiercely kissed but with a determined hardening of his jaw, he merely caught both her hands in his, raised them to his lips, and slowly, seductively nibbled each fingertip in turn, then the curve of her palms, and the mounds of flesh at the base of her thumbs.

True to his word, Jordon didn't rush her. As if on a voyage

of rediscovery which also invited her to rediscover him, he plied her with the lightest of caresses, the briefest of kisses, and a visual exploration of her that left her feeling erotically vulnerable and nearly trembling. Her own hands cupped his sides while he swept her hair up and back until it fanned out in gloriously golden disarray on the pillow. His fingers glided through it, testing the silken texture, tickling her scalp, and smiling lazily as a small shiver ran over her. Amy's answering smile was somewhat hesitant yet decidedly sensuous, and even the mildly triumphant spark that flared in his eyes couldn't diminish the rising desire that held her captive.

Time seemed to stand still. Jordon lay beside her on one elbow, content to explore her face, his fingertips following the high rise of her cheekbones, the line of her small, straight nose, the bow shape of her lips, and the porcelain smoothness of her forehead to her hairline. And as much as she wanted him to continue touching her, she wanted to touch him. She turned onto her side toward him. Her hands sought his sun-browned chest while his spanned her narrow waist. Her palms played over his flat nipples, her nails gently catching in fine dark hair. There was some hint of triumph in her own smile when he made a low pleasured sound, his hold on her tightening. When he drew her to him, she eagerly awaited his kiss but his lips only hovered tantalizingly above her own for a few instants before seeking the hollow at the base of her throat, the length of her neck, then her ear, his warm breath drifting inside to tickle and torment until he caught the fleshy lobe between his teeth, nipping it.

Stiletto sharp, flame-tipped daggers of delight plunged through her. Her heart raced and the blood rushed through her veins, overheating her flesh. Her skin tingled, sensitized to his every touch; and captivated by her newly blooming sensuality, she allowed her hand to dance down over his flat, hard midriff, then around across his lower back to rake very lightly the edges of her nails up his spine. He shuddered, and although she expected him to really kiss her at last, he didn't.

"*Amy*," he moaned, winding her hair around one hand to tilt her head back on the pillow. He pressed her back into the mattress to rain kisses over her shoulders, his lips loitering here and there while the tip of his tongue etched tantalizing designs on her skin. Thrill after thrill pulsated deep within her and her hands feverishly caressed his broad back. He gripped one shoulder, holding her flat upon the bed, holding her prisoner while continuing to tempt and torment her with arousing forays of his tongue, until her breath was coming in soft, rapid gasps. She felt she might die if he didn't take possession of her mouth.

Yet, even when she cupped his face in her hands and her parted lips sought and found his, he kissed her lightly, fleetingly, teasing each corner of her mouth in turn, over and over, repeatedly. Playing with her, his big hands as clinging on her slender body as the swimsuit she wore, he seemed intent on evoking a volcanic eruption of passion in her. He was close to succeeding. Amy felt she was being drawn into a vortex of desire from which there would be no escape. He was driving her crazy, deliberately, with kisses light as a butterfly's fluttering wings, making her want more. Aching for a rougher, more impassioned kiss, she linked her arms over his back, pulling him down toward her while arching slightly toward him. Keen disappointment knifed through her when his grip on her waist tightened and he pushed her back down, denying her the warm contact of body against body that she sought.

"*Jordon*," she breathed with some urgency.

He turned her toward him then, his strong arms going completely around her though they still didn't press her tight against him. His lips continued to toy with hers, his teeth catching then releasing, catching and releasing the full lower curve before at last gently tugging downward to open her mouth beneath his. The fire inside her that threatened to consume her blazed hotter and hotter, expertly stoked by his purposely slow assault on her senses. He was seducing her, and very effectively, too. She knew it, but she also knew a few seductive tricks of her own. She had

80

learned them all with him. Spreading her fingers over the small of his back, she grazed her parted lips over the skin that hardened over his collarbone and upward along the side of his neck past the curve of his strong jaw. With the tip of her tongue she flickingly probed the curving ridges of his outer ear, smiling a secret smile at his swiftly drawn breath. She moved closer. Slipping her shapely leg between his, she sinuously brushed her smooth thigh against him and was pleased and fascinated by the responsiveness of his aroused masculinity, which surged throbbingly against her.

Jordon's low groan was muffled in the thick silkiness of her hair as he hauled her hard and fast against him, his lips hardening on hers, devouring their softness, exerting a slight twisting pressure on them, parting them wider to accept the gentle invasion of his tongue. It moved slowly inside her mouth, savoring her sweet taste until her own playfully parried, teasing and inviting. When the tip of his began rubbing tiny circles over the sensitized surface of hers, her nails pressed lightly into his back and she arched against him.

Their kisses deepened, lengthened, became intimacies in themselves, and Amy's senses were aswirl with long-lost delight. It was good to be with Jordon again, to be molded to his long, lean body, and to feel the heat of his firm male flesh permeating her skin to warm her to the marrow of her bones and the very core of her being. She had been cold for so long, but she didn't feel cold now, only alive with exquisite sensations that were rapidly intensifying to a power beyond any possible attempts at resistance.

Reveling in her ability to arouse him as much as he was arousing her, she wound her arms around his neck. Her supple body sought all his vital strength. She melted against him, sleek and shapely and feverishly warm. Her lips moved provocatively against his as she kissed him back with a near wanton abandon that would have astounded her if she had been thinking clearly.

As it was, she wasn't thinking at all. She could only feel, and when Jordon eased her down flat upon the mattress once more, she allowed her eyes to flicker open and gazed up dreamily at him. Her breath was released in a shuddery sigh as he drew a fingertip along the top of her swimsuit. The tenor of his breathing increased in time with Amy's. When the tip of her tongue came out to moisten her lips, he swiftly lowered his head and took them with marauding insistence, drawing her tongue in over his, pressing it against the roof of his mouth, exerting a delicious pulling pressure that sent shattering tremors over her and made her cling to him, her small hands sweeping over his broad back and lean, manly flanks.

"Amy," he uttered hoarsely, lifting his head only to seek access to the beginning swell of breasts just visible above the top of her swimsuit. His fingers caressed lightly her tanned skin, but that wasn't nearly enough for him. His narrowed tiger eyes captured and held hers, the amber glinting light impaling the drowsy blue depths. "I have to see you, touch you, taste you," he confessed. "And I can't wait any longer."

When he lowered the swimsuit to her waist, Amy felt her heart might explode with its frantic beating. Exposed to the gaze he swept slowly over her, she experienced a heady rush of pleasure, feeling daring and desirable, aroused by his intent appraisal. She liked having him look at her; she always had. He made her feel beautiful and delightfully vulnerable and sexually appealing. His mere visual possession of her bared upper body raised the fever raging inside her several degrees. Perhaps there was something of the exhibitionist in her, though she doubted that. She cringed at the thought of any man other than Jordon seeing her like this. Perhaps, then, she was merely a normal woman with normal needs, needs only one given man could assuage.

That very thought might have served as warning to her, but it was immediately lost when Jordon feathered his hands over her breasts, then cupped their weight in his palms. Arousing as it was, simply being looked at was nothing compared to being touched. Amy's fingers tangled convulsively in Jordon's thick

82

hair when his own played over her firm flesh, tracing concentric circles upward, ever upward to her delectable rouged summits. He took the rose-tinted peaks between his thumb and forefinger, rubbing, tenderly squeezing and pulling, arousing them to throbbing firm nubbles of flesh that seemed to beckon the tasting touch of his mouth.

"God, woman," he whispered raspingly. "You're such a sexy wench."

It was the worst possible thing he could have said. Her heart seemed to plummet to her stomach. *You're such a sexy wench.* He had said that to her before more than once in the past and she had allowed such words plus her love for him to lead her into intimacy followed by pain, disillusionment, and a general distrust of all men. The deeply ingrained need not to allow that to happen to her again burned away all desire, and when his mouth started to seek the pinnacle of one breast, she caught his face in her hands and stiffened.

"No. Enough is enough," she said sternly despite the flowering ache that was blossoming in her chest. "Let me go, Jordon."

For several heartstopping moments it seemed he didn't intend to release her so easily, but at last his hold on her relaxed. His glinting tiger eyes seared hers. "My God, Amy," he muttered, "you've certainly learned to play rough, haven't you?"

"I'm not playing. I just lost my head for a few minutes, that's all. I'm only a woman with . . . normal sexual needs," she said. "That doesn't mean anything. I still can't get involved with you."

"But you're not so sure you don't want to," he challenged as she slipped off the bed, tugging the top of her swimsuit back over her. "Are you, Amy?"

"I'm sure," she muttered. And gathering up what was left of dignity and self-assurance, she walked out of his bedroom without a backward glance.

In the bath adjoining her office a few minutes later Amy stripped her swimsuit off and stuffed it with more force than

83

necessary into a vinyl-lined beach bag to carry it home for a thorough rinse. Catching sight of herself in the half-length mirror above the lavatory, she made a low, half-tortured sound. Her full breasts were still faintly rosy from the touch of Jordon's hands and the nipples still passionately erect. Horrified, she spun around, escaping her reflection, and quickly dressed. *What was wrong with her?* How had she allowed the events in Jordon's room to progress as far as they had? Was she an idiot? Or was she beginning to hope he actually had changed during the past three years? What if he hadn't? What if he was simply pretending he had, thinking he would have a better chance of getting her into bed if he could convince her he was a changed man? And, more important, why should she even care whether or not he was actually different? Gnawing her lower lip, she shook her head. She didn't know why. All she knew was that she *did* care, but she didn't dare analyze the reasons why too closely.

CHAPTER FIVE

Jordon discovered he couldn't stay away from Amy. Patient as he was trying to be, he had to see her. Sunday afternoon over a week later he purchased a couple of chef's-cut rib-eye steaks, a definite plan in mind. Armed also with a bottle of Cabernet Sauvignon from the clubhouse, he arrived at Amy's apartment at about four thirty. And when she came to the door, disarmingly appealing in cutoff jeans and a faded denim halter, he was sorely tempted to deposit the gifts he carried on the floor and take her into his arms and then to bed. He resisted the temptation, however. He couldn't afford to be impatient, despite the fact that she was fast becoming an obsession with him. During the past few nights she had caused him to spend several sleepless hours, thinking exclusively about her. He wanted her badly, and not just physically. It was becoming increasingly important to him to win her trust again; her unfavorable opinion of his character bothered him far more than he would ever have imagined it could. And he *was* making some progress, he believed. In the past week he had detected a slight softening in her attitude toward him which had encouraged him enough to bring him here this afternoon, and as she stood in the doorway eyeing him speculatively, he gave her a slow, lazy smile.

"I thought of phoning first, then decided I'd rather surprise you. I come bearing gifts," he announced, producing a bouquet of white carnations from behind his back and handing them to her with a slight bow.

"What? No candy, too?" Amy quipped, concealing the fact that she was more touched by the unexpected gesture than she felt she should be. Burying her nose in the soft white petals, she inhaled appreciatively. "Umm, they're lovely, Jordon, but—"

"Wait, there's more. Something better than candy." He forged ahead, presenting her the bottle of wine. "To go with the rib-eye steaks I brought for our dinner."

"*Our* dinner?"

"I knew if I asked you to go out with me, you'd probably refuse. So I decided to appear on your doorstep with a bottle of Cabernet Sauvigon as a bribe. I hope you're impressed."

"Oh, I'm impressed, all right. How could I not be? Flowers *and* expensive wine."

"Does that mean you're not going to turn me away?" he asked with a somewhat boyish grin. "I'd hate to see these steaks go to waste, and I even volunteer to be chef."

On occasion he could be charming as the devil, and this was one of those occasions. Without really stopping to think about it, Amy opened the door wider and beckoned him inside. "To tell the truth I wasn't really looking forward to dinner very much anyway. Sunday evening is always potluck, which usually means soup and a salad," she said, wrinkling her nose. "Steak sounds much more appetizing, especially since you've offered to prepare it."

"You'll never regret it. I'm a master when it comes to steak." Jordon stepped confidently into the living room, closing the door quietly behind him. "But I do expect help with the dishes afterward. Deal?"

"Deal," she agreed lightly. But as his gaze lingered for half an instant on her bare midriff, she became more aware of her scanty attire, while swiftly taking in his. Damnably attractive in casual tan slacks and a navy cotton knit polo shirt, he was a pleasure simply to look at, although observing him wasn't a luxury she allowed herself for more than a split second. Turning away, she led him into her kitchen. "We'd better get these flowers in water."

"And the steaks in the refrigerator . . . unless you want me to start them now? It's early. . . ."

"Yes, it is, but I have an idea," she said, glancing back over her shoulder at him. "How would you like to have them charcoaled? I have a hibachi out on my tiny balcony which the apartment manager grandly calls a terrace. How about it?" When Jordon easily agreed, she directed him to the briquets in a lower cabinet, then toward the sliding glass doors that opened onto the balcony. "Why don't you start the coals while I find a vase for the carnations?"

Several minutes later, when Amy started out onto the small balcony, she found Jordon standing a couple of feet from the flames leaping up from the hibachi, which rested atop a round wrought-iron table. With a poker he was rearranging the coals to make them heat more evenly, and she paused in the doorway, watching him. Intent on his task, he looked almost . . . domesticated—maybe that was the word for it, although it was a word that certainly surprised her when connected with him. After his father's death he wouldn't have spared a moment for such a chore, but, judging by his wide, casual stance and the hand resting in the back pocket of his trousers, he actually appeared content, as if he might be enjoying what he was doing. A trace of a frown nicked her brow as she stepped out of the kitchen; then she sighed silently at the sight of her downstairs neighbor, Erica, sitting by the pool, staring up at Jordon, her very posture indicating intense curiosity, although Amy couldn't clearly see her facial expression from such a distance. She waved at the bride of eight months, knowing Erica would pay her a visit in the next day or two and undoubtedly ask innumerable questions about Jordon. At the thought Amy nearly chuckled aloud. How astounded Erica would be if she confessed Jordon was her former lover. Naturally she wouldn't describe him as such. She would simply say he was the new security chief at St. Tropez Run and fortunately, due to his cooperation during the past week, Amy had been better able to pretend to herself that that was all he was.

After what had happened between them Friday evening in his quarters, she had dreaded seeing him again; but when she had, he had made the encounter fairly easy by making no reference to what had occurred. In the following days he had been friendly and sometimes even gently teasing, though never in a very personal way. And, more important, he had kept his distance physically. He had never once attempted to touch her, which had been an immense relief. His touch disturbed her far too much, a fact she could scarcely cope with, but since he hadn't tried to lay a hand on her in over a week, she was beginning to feel more relaxed around him. And she wanted to be able to relax. After all, she was an adult and surely sophisticated enough to deal with him on a daily basis without feeling she was walking a tightrope. To some degree she was succeeding. Oh, he still made her tense, but the tension had somehow become vague and indefinable rather than being a product of her anger at him. That was fading, perhaps because she was beginning to sense something in him.

. . . Whatever it was intrigued her and had caused her to watch him with near fascination for quite a long time when she had seen him on the playground at the boys' home yesterday. . . . And it was that inexplicable something that was causing her to watch him again now.

Something akin to bewilderment flitted over her face, but she masked it with a polite smile when Jordon turned around and saw her stepping out onto the balcony. She gave the fire in the brazier a cursory glance.

"The coals should be hot enough in a half hour or so," Jordon said, laying down the poker to advance toward her. "In the meantime you sit out here and just relax while I take care of everything else in the kitchen."

"Oh, but you might be able to persuade me to do the salad."

"That wasn't part of our deal. I volunteered to be chef. Remember?" he insisted, reaching out to grip her upper arms lightly and gently impel her down onto the edge of the chaise longue beside her. "Now, just sit back and relax."

Amy sat but was unable truly to relax. Long after Jordon had left her to go into the kitchen, she felt as if he had left a tingling imprint of his fingers on her bare skin.

Later, when dinner was over and the kitchen had been tidied, the cat returned home from a jaunt outside. After dining on the few scraps of steak Amy had saved her, she meticulously washed her paws and face, then trotted on Jordon's heels out of the kitchen and into the living room. Jordon and Amy sat down at opposite ends of the sofa; immediately Skeeter pounced up and landed in Amy's lap, then decided to amble across the cushions to Jordon's. As he stroked her, she lazily arched her back up against his hand.

"That's a hint. No, it's actually a demand. She wants her back scratched," Amy explained, smiling indulgently as she transferred her knitting bag to the floor.

"Owning a cat and knitting isn't going to convince anyone

you're the spinster type, Amy," he drawled. "You just don't look or act like any spinster I've ever known."

"I'm glad to hear it, since I'm certainly not trying to project that image," she blandly replied. "And there's nothing old-maidish about liking to knit and owning a cat. The cat's a companion and knitting's creative. I've knitted some very beautiful and useful items. And another thing, spinster is an out-of-date word. No one is called a spinster anymore."

"I stand corrected," he murmured, one dark eyebrow lifting and a smile lightly playing across his mouth. "But I was only kidding anyhow, as you must know."

"I certainly hope so. I wouldn't want to think you'd stereotype people the way they were stereotyped twenty years ago. Surely you're more progressive than that."

"I like to think so" was his wry reply, but as he regarded her intently, his expression slowly sobered. "And speaking of being progressive, have the powers that be at Coastal Realty stopped giving you the impression you might be a suitable scapegoat if there are any more burglaries?"

Shrugging, Amy tucked her bare feet up beside her on the sofa cushion and wrinkled her nose, only a barely discernible shadow of darkness in her blue eyes revealing some concern. "I wouldn't say they've stopped giving me that impression. Last week was quiet—not even an attempted break-in reported—so Evan Price only called me a couple of times, insisting that something had to be done to make the residents and, more important, prospective buyers, feel that St. Tropez Run is the ultimate in safe, protected communities. After all, what we're selling is security, prestige, and luxury in that order. Evan's pat little speech," she said, shaking her head ruefully. "I've heard it countless times since the first burglary, as if he half expects me personally to stop the break-ins. I have been tempted on occasion to ask him if he'd like me to start carrying a loaded shotgun."

"I wouldn't risk it if I were you," Jordon warned. "He might think it's a good idea."

Amy laughed. "I wouldn't be surprised. That's why I've never said it. Ah, well, maybe there won't be any more trouble anyway. Security Unlimited does have a great reputation and maybe that will scare the burglars off."

"Maybe. Maybe not. Too soon to tell. We'll just have to wait and see while we go on checking out everyone who could be involved."

"Oh, yes, the infamous investigations. How are those going? Found any deep dark secrets about the employees or the residents? Or me?"

"We have a few possible leads, but they're very weak. We'll just have to dig a little deeper. But you'll be pleased to know that most of the preliminary investigations turned up nothing. Yours included."

"Oh, thank goodness," she countered with an exaggerated sigh of relief. "And I was so afraid you'd find out I did ten years in prison under another name."

Jordon chuckled. "You must have started your criminal career very early, then, no later than eleven or twelve."

"I'm just older than I look."

"I know, but not that much older," he countered. "You haven't changed much in three years, Amy, at least in appearance. You still look about twenty-two."

"Oh, you do know exactly what a woman wants to hear," she quipped, though she felt a sudden driving need to change the subject. And she did. "Why did you really come here, Jordon? You must be bored. In Alexandria you're involved with everything. That must be more exciting than a few burglaries one of your best men could have investigated."

"But this is a different kind of challenge. Most of our clients are corporations, and corporate crime can make for some very dull investigations. And running the agency isn't always exciting; some of the duties are very tedious. Fortunately I have a capable staff to leave in charge when I'm away."

"Then, you came here looking for a little excitement?"

"In a way. I told you before that I came because I wanted to see you, which is always exciting."

"I saw you Saturday," she said hastily, pretending she hadn't noticed his provocative tone. She clasped her hands together around one knee. "At the boys' home, on the playground."

"Oh? Why didn't I see you?"

"I don't know. Maybe because I was standing under that huge old oak tree and wasn't very noticeable. Or maybe you just didn't look my way. You were giving the boys all your attention and you really seemed to enjoy being with them."

"I did. Does that surprise you?"

"Yes," she answered candidly but without rancor. "It surprises me very much. Three years ago—"

"Was three years ago. And, Amy, it's time for you to let go of the past," Jordon said, his tone gentle yet adamant. "Even if I did seem to be an uncaring bastard then."

Steadily returning his gaze, she didn't disagree with that assessment but didn't continue the conversation about the past, either. She was realizing that whenever they discussed it, he had an advantage over her. Although he always explained his actions of three years ago quietly and calmly, she never felt calm. Her emotions were involved, but he could afford to be unemotional. He hadn't been hurt. She had, and was now suddenly unwilling to engage in yet another battle of words which he would win simply because her feelings got in the way and his didn't. So it was for her own reasons, not his, that she didn't pursue the issue.

"Well, since you enjoyed being with the boys, they obviously made a good impression," she said instead. "I told you they were a great bunch of kids, and they are, aren't they?"

Nodding agreement, Jordon smiled wryly. "But somebody should have warned me about their boundless energy. I could have gotten in better shape to take them on."

"It seemed to me you were keeping up with them without much difficulty. And although I only watched for a minute or two, I could see that you're very good with them, Jordon. You were patient with the younger ones who didn't follow your instructions and you were encouraging and friendly. They need supportive men in their lives . . . someone to look up to. I think you'll be very good for them."

The glint of surprise that flashed in Jordon's eyes altered to teasing amusement. "That sounded suspiciously like a compliment, Amy."

"You deserved it." She casually gave a toss of one hand, then averted her gaze from him to watch the cat leap from his lap to the arm of the sofa and on to the second shelf of the adjacent bookcase, where she curled up precariously close to the edge, settling down for a nap. "I'm fair minded enough to give credit where credit is due. And I'm not the only one who thinks you'll be good for the boys. Terry King is already singing your praises."

"He sings yours, too," Jordon remarked dryly. "Almost unceasingly."

"That's nice to hear," Amy said, obvious pleasure and satisfaction written on her face. "Terry's a fine man."

"What brought you to the playground Saturday?" Jordon quickly questioned. "Were you trying to find King?"

"Terry? No, he was in his office then, I think." Amy smiled fondly. "Actually, it was Joey's idea for us to walk over to the playground. He's nine and he's having trouble with fractions, so I'm tutoring him in math. He talked me into quitting early Saturday so he could come meet you. He's never known a former college basketball player before, and like all the other boys, he's terribly impressed."

"Why else do you think college men want to be jocks?" Jordon drolly replied. "It's a claim to fame, more or less. At least, it's enough to impress young boys while we're growing older. Makes us feel less insecure."

Amy's smile grew introspective as she thoroughly surveyed his tanned, strongly carved face. She was puzzled. Although he had always possessed a good sense of humor and had been able to laugh at himself, he had never done so as often in the past as he did now. Now he did seem more relaxed with himself and with everything else, almost as if some of his goals in life had undergone a subtle alteration. Oh, he was still iron-willed and obviously ambitious, yet . . . She tilted her head inquiringly.

"You know," she mused softly, "you do act like you've changed . . . a little."

"I've been trying to tell you that, Amy," he responded, his darkening gaze locking hers. "And now that you're beginning to believe me, maybe you don't hate me anymore."

"I never hated you," she murmured, unwilling to tell him that, because hate is sometimes the other side of love and might seem too revealing an emotion. Besides, it wasn't true; she had never hated him. Although she had tried desperately to, she had never succeeded. Initially his rejection of her had caused excruciating pain, followed by boiling anger and resentment, then bittersweet acceptance of what had been a severe error of judgment on her part. With his sudden reappearance in her life, anger and resentment had been rearoused yet hadn't ever evolved into true hate. Maybe she had every right to loathe him, but she had never reached that point. With a slight uncertain shrug she shook her head, eyes still held captive by his. "And I don't hate you now."

"Thank God," he muttered. "Amy . . ."

When he reached out and tenderly clasped both her hands in his, she allowed him to draw her toward him for a long instant in which she searched his familiar and once beloved face and sensed a different man behind it, a man who had mellowed and become more tender, a man who drew her as a moth is drawn to flame. Her body felt weak and warmly yielding, but her will proved stronger in the end. It was as if she were being pulled into a maelstrom of swirling emotion and the sudden surge of vulnerability she experienced was frightening enough to allow common sense to take tenuous control once again. She tensed, withdrew her hands from his.

"Jordon, no," she protested, concealing her breathlessness by some miracle. "I think you'd better go now."

He said nothing. He simply sat immobile for a long moment, then gently brushed the hair-roughened back of his hand over her left cheek before rising lithely to his feet.

Then he was gone. Amy heard him quietly close her door behind him on his way out. She was trembling. She pressed shaking fingers against her lips, then buried her hot face in her hands.

Early Tuesday evening Amy walked around the corner of the sterile brick building that dominated the grounds of the boys' home and smiled happily when she saw the familiar figure exiting a side door.

"Hi, Martha," she called out enthusiastically. "How's the new job?"

"Amy, bless your heart," the Bushnells' former maid called back, rushing toward the younger woman despite the obvious arthritic stiffness in her knees. She lumbered to a halt and kissed Amy's cheek. "I'm s'happy here, I can't begin to tell you. Miz Bushnell was no fun to work for, and I dreaded every day I had to spend in her house. But I love coming to work here. Oh, boys will be boys and and they leave messes for me to clean up sometimes, but I have three of my own at home, so I know how to handle these. All it takes is a lot of caring and a little teaching. Most of them try so hard to please. And I just can't tell you how much I thank you for getting me this job here."

"When Terry told me he had an opening on the housekeeping staff, I knew you'd be the perfect one to fill it. You're the motherly type and the boys here need someone like that," Amy said sincerely. "And speaking of boys, where are they? I stopped by to see how Joey did on his math test today—he was very worried about it—but I can't find him or anybody else. The whole building seems deserted. Do you know where everybody is?"

"Oh, they're all down on the playground. You wouldn't believe how exciting it's been here today," Martha answered. "Two tractor trailers pulled in this afternoon, loaded with swings and

94

slides and you wouldn't believe what else. That playground's going to be brand new when they finish setting up everything. The boys just couldn't wait to go see it all."

"And neither can I," Amy confessed, her smile beaming. "Excuse me, Martha, I have to go take a look, too. Terry told me that new playground equipment was out of the question in this year's budget but he obviously found the funds somewhere else."

"Looks more like he found a gold mine," Martha sang out after her as she hurried along the path to the recreational field.

Oceanside Boys' Home was actually situated about half a mile from the Atlantic, but the salt breeze drifted in over the complex, so the name wasn't fraudulent. Church operated, Oceanside had been constructed fifty years before and was a small facility, home to fifty to sixty parentless boys aged six to eighteen. The main building, housing the dormitories, was drafty, while the surrounding grounds were maintained as best they could be, considering an operating budget that provided for necessary expenses but very little else. Hearing the excited babble of voices coming from beyond the stand of pines straight ahead, Amy smiled. At least Terry had found a way to replace the old playground equipment, which the boys only half-jokingly claimed had originally come over the Atlantic on the *Mayflower*. They had no reason to complain anymore, however, as Amy discovered when she stepped out from beneath the trees to the recreational field. Her smile widened. Before her were sturdy shining new swings, a long gleaming slide, and climbing gyms, a dream come true for the younger boys. And there was obviously more to be seen, as evidenced by the crowd that had gathered on the concrete court to her right. She hurried over to the chattering mob and found Terry King in the center of the huddle, enthusiastically displaying new football, basketball, and baseball equipment. A rather short, stockily built man in his mid-thirties, he was gesturing excitedly and talking a mile a minute.

"I think Martha was right," Amy spoke up, taking in all the

bats, balls, gloves, and various other items. "You really must have found a gold mine."

"Isn't it fantastic?" Terry exclaimed, delight dancing in his warm brown eyes. He took her hand in a near bone-crunching grip and pulled her over for a closer look. His free arm waved about, pointing out the new basketball posts that towered over the concrete. "How about that? Brand-new posts, fiberglass backboards, new rims. *Rims with nets!* Can you believe it? It's wonderful, isn't it?"

"It really is," Amy agreed happily. "And it's all such a surprise. How did you—"

"Did you see the new swings and the slide?" Terry cut in, as much as or more excited than the grinning boys surrounding them. "I'm having a time keeping the fellows off the swings, but the cement they're anchored in hasn't set yet, so they have to wait until tomorrow to try them out." When a chorus of groans followed his statement, he laughed and shook his head. "No use moaning every time I say that. You're just going to have to be patient."

"It'll be worth the wait, won't it?" Amy asked the boys rhetorically. "Think about that old equipment, then take a look at all of this."

"But this isn't all of it," Terry proudly announced. "Come see what's over here."

Laughing, Amy followed as he cut a path through the boys and led her off the far end of the concrete onto the grass, where he stopped and extended a hand with a grand flourish. She stared out in front of her, squinting in the near-blinding glare of the early evening sun, and it took several moments for her eyes to adjust sufficiently to the brightness for her to see the series of white lines on the ground. Then her mouth nearly dropped open with surprise. "My Lord, a football field, too?"

Terry rocked back on his heels. "Lined out this afternoon."

"But what's this?" she joked. "No goalposts?"

"Those will be installed tomorrow."

Amy shook her head disbelievingly. "This is really incredible. Where on earth did you find the money for all this? How did you do it?"

Terry chuckled merrily. "That's just it. I didn't have to do a thing, except supply a list of what we needed. I didn't have to raise any money at all. Everything you see is an outright gift to Oceanside Boys' Home, no strings attached. We won't even have to call the football field Kent Field, although I'd like to and so would the boys, if Jordon wouldn't object. I'll talk to him about it."

Amy's heart lurched against her breast. Stiffly she raised a hand to place her fingertips against her lips. "Jordon," she echoed blankly, her brain on hold for an instant. Her gaze swept over the newly refurbished playground. "You mean Jordon, *Jordon Kent,* is responsible for all this?"

Perry stepped closer to her, lowering his voice so as not to be overheard by the boys several feet behind them. "Well, Jordon asked me not to broadcast the fact, but since the two of you know each other, I'm sure he won't mind my telling you. And I think the boys should know what he's done, too. I'm going to have to convince him of that."

"But . . . what . . . how . . ." Amy stammered, then regained control of her tongue and began again. "How did this all come about?"

"It's the damnedest thing," Terry said, shaking his head as if he too was still greatly astonished by this turn of good fortune. "I guess it all started Saturday before last, the first time Jordon came to work with the boys. He mentioned to me that our equipment was completely inadequate and most of it beyond repair. Of course I agreed, but thought nothing more about his remark. Then he called last week to ask for a list of everything we needed. He said he had friends who might want to contribute money to buy some of the items. Sounded great to me. I gave him a complete list, but I know how long it can take to raise funds for something like this and didn't expect to hear any more about it for a while. Then, lo and behold, two trucks show up here this morning and the drivers and their helpers unloaded and set up every piece of equipment I had included on the list. This afternoon two more men arrived to line off the football field and told me they'd be back next spring to lay out a baseball diamond and an outfield. You could have knocked me over with a feather. I never expected Jordon to accomplish this much so soon. Been trying all day to call and thank him but never got hold of him. I hoped he might come by this evening to see the new equipment, but he hasn't yet. Do you know where he might be?"

"H-he was still in his office when I left," Amy answered automatically. She was suddenly filled with a driving need to see Jordon, to talk to him about what he had done. He had never been a miserly, mean-minded person; she had never thought that about him. Yet what he had done for these boys far surpassed what she might have reasonably expected of him, which was no more than fulfilling an obligation to contribute to worthwhile causes and charities. No, this had been no obligatory gesture. It had been an act of caring, caring for a few boys who badly needed someone to care about them but, because they were so few, were easily forgotten by many people. Jordon hadn't forgotten or ignored them. He had generously fulfilled their need, not so much for new playground equipment—that was simply the symbol. In the giving he had bestowed something far more precious on these boys, the feeling that someone believed they were important, worthy enough to receive something better than they had previously had. A burning ache gathered behind Amy's eyes. She bit down on her lower lip.

"I have to run now, Terry," she murmured huskily, turning jerkily to walk with him back across the concrete. Pausing, she looked around once more at the transformed playground, but most of her attention was focused on the boys' excited, happy faces. "This is all just tremendous. I can hardly believe . . ." She shook her head, faintly smiled. "What does Beth think of all this?"

"She doesn't know about it yet. She took a day off to go see her mom, but I didn't call her there and tell her," Terry said, grinning mischievously. "I wanted to let her see this for herself. Won't she be surprised?"

"Bowled over is more like it."

"She should be back any minute. Can't you stay—"

"There's something I really have to do," Amy quietly said. "But tell her I'll give her a call tonight."

After exchanging good-byes with Terry, Amy started across the field, stopping only when she spotted Joey to ask how he had done on the dreaded math test. He had missed only two problems and was visibly proud of how well he had done. Amy praised him sincerely and playfully rumpled his thick flaxen hair. (She would have given him a kiss but knew that nine-year-old boys can't be kissed in front of their peers. Too embarrassing. It was only encouraging kisses given in private that were all right.) And after Joey ran off to gaze wistfully at the slide he couldn't swoop down on until tomorrow when the cement had set, Amy hurried to her car.

Ten minutes later she stepped up to the door of Jordon's quarters. She took a deep breath, then confidently rapped on the wooden panel. The door opened almost immediately, much sooner than she had expected, and when Jordon stepped forward, obvious surprise on his lean face, some of her confidence ebbed. In white tennis shorts and white shirt, his long strong bronzed legs and finely muscled arms were exposed to her darting gaze. When her eyes met his, she gestured uncertainly.

"Oh, I've caught you at a bad time, I guess," she softly said. "You're on your way out for a game of tennis."

"No, I thought about walking over to the court to find someone who wanted to play but changed my mind and decided on a walk along the beach instead," he told her. "I just got back. Come in, Amy."

She slipped past him, entering the sitting room, which had changed since she had left him there his first night at St. Tropez

99

Run. There were personal touches now, a book here, a family photograph there, a stereo with a stack of record albums next to it. When he motioned her toward the damask sofa, she quickly sat down on the edge, smoothing her ivory skirt over her slender thighs to cover her knees. She managed a convincingly natural smile as Jordon took a seat next to her.

"What is it, Amy?" he asked, tiger eyes searching her face. "Is something wrong?"

"Wrong? No, I . . ."

"You seem a little . . . nervous."

"Oh, not nervous. I'm just excited. I have some terrific news and that's why I dropped by—to tell you about it," she claimed, closely watching him.

While she told him what he already knew, about the new playground equipment, he responded like a well-rehearsed talented actor, conveying by his expression only suitable surprise, delight, and satisfaction at the news. When she'd finished, he nodded and sat back on the sofa, his long legs outstretched before him.

"They certainly needed new equipment—I'm glad they finally got it" was all he said.

Amy's blue eyes, riveted on his face, darkened to indigo. "I know, Jordon," she said after a long moment. "I know you did it."

"Did what?"

"Don't try to pretend you didn't. I *know* you bought all that equipment."

A frown creased his brow. "What gave you that idea?"

"Terry King. He told me that you said you were going to try to raise money for some of the equipment he needed. When it was delivered today, he knew you had to be the one who sent it."

Jordon tossed up his hands. "All right, I did have a hand in it. I ordered everything and had it delivered. But several other people contributed the money."

"Really?" she drawled dubiously. "How many?"

"Quite a few."

"I don't believe that. It would be nearly impossible to raise that much money in less than a week, and I think you paid for most of that equipment yourself."

"If I did, why shouldn't I just say so?" he countered easily, exhibiting considerable acting talent. "After all, I've been trying to tell you I've changed and you haven't believed me. This would be the perfect opportunity to make you change your mind. If what you're thinking were true, why wouldn't I just admit it?"

"I don't know why. But then, I've never understood you," she murmured, her voice lowering a bit in register when for a moment she lost herself in those magnetic amber eyes. She breathed in deeply, recalled her train of thought. "All I know is that you paid for most or all of that equipment and I think it's important for the boys to know you did. They like and respect you. Think how good they'll feel knowing you care enough about them to do that."

Jordon simply looked at her silently, then rose to his feet when she rose to hers.

"I just wanted to stop by and say thank you. You did something very wonderful and kind," she said, almost in a whisper. Stretching up on tiptoe, she pressed her lips against his right cheek, trembling when his strong corded arms went swiftly around her.

"You shouldn't have done that, Amy," Jordon muttered, desire flaring in the depths of his eyes. "I'm not sure I can let you go now."

And she wasn't at all sure she wanted him to as he drew her closer to his hard warm body and she tilted her head back to gaze up at him. She was only sure that he was right: she shouldn't have kissed him. But it was already far too late for regrets.

CHAPTER SIX

Amy continued to look up at Jordon, unable to speak. Time lost all meaning. It could have been seconds or it could have been minutes that she stood in the circle of his arms, awed by the sheer power of the sensual electricity that surged between them. As if enslaved by some invisible force that seemed to meld them together, she felt the strength draining from her. The moment and the feelings swirling within her were so intense she could hardly breathe. Her heart was thudding wildly and she was lightheaded as, with mounting anticipation, she waited and waited for him to wrap his arms tightly around her and gather her with rough urgency to him.

But he didn't do that. His large hands spanned her waist; yet when she swayed toward him, he still refrained from pulling her nearer. His piercing eyes impaled the soft blue depths of her. In his tightening jaw a muscle ticked.

"Amy, kiss me," he commanded softly at last. "Kiss me now."

Incredibly, she obeyed him. Stretching up on tiptoe once again, she brushed her lips over his, stroking lightly, teasing and tempting him, then lingering with feather lightness on the corners of his mouth. She heard his quick intake of breath, heard how ragged it was when he released it just as quickly; and when he didn't kiss her back and instead lifted her chin with one finger, her opening eyes darkened with disappointment and confusion.

"I've been waiting for you to do that," he whispered, his hot relentless gaze searching her upturned face. "Do you know how long it's been since you've come to me? Too damned long, Amy, but now that you finally have . . ."

At that moment further words were unnecessary. The promise of passion to come conveyed by his very touch said everything as he dropped back down on the sofa and drew her between his thighs and onto his lap. Mesmerized by the gentling of his carved features, Amy slipped an arm around his shoulders while her other hand floated up to rest against his chest, her small fingers spreading apart and beginning to move in slow, caressing circles.

"*Honey,*" he murmured, smiling tenderly. He tucked her hair back behind her left ear and cupped her face in one hand. Tilting her head to one side, he touched his lips to the side of her neck. With spellbinding slowness he blazed a trail of kisses along her jawline, over her left cheek to the quickening pulsebeat in her temple, then retraced the same path back downward again. Tilting her head to the other side, he bestowed caressing kisses on her right cheek and temple, too, but also kissed her eyelids when they fluttered shut, then the end of her nose, and at long last her mouth. Her soft lips were already parted and eagerly met the touch of his. As Amy moaned sweetly, her fingers clutched his shirtfront and his own lips hardened, taking the tender shape of hers with a gentle twisting pressure that made her moan softly again and wind her arms around his neck.

With a low, impassioned groan, Jordon crushed Amy to him and a rapier-sharp thrill shot through her. Her senses swimming, and feeling exquisitely alive, she tangled her fingers in the thickness of his hair and feathered the tip of her tongue into his mouth, succumbing gladly to a rush of delight when a shudder ran over his hard, rangy body. Her curved form yielded to the firm lineation of his and beneath her breasts she could feel his heart pounding as frantically as her own. Tucking her thighs close against his side, she returned his kisses with an ardor that equaled his; her warm, bow-shaped lips parted and closed, parted and closed, again and again, and toyed with his in reckless abandon. Catching the fuller sensuous curve of his lower lip

103

between her teeth, she gently nipped his firm, irresistible flesh, causing his arms to wrap more tightly around her and his slightly shaky hands to course over her frame in an arousing exploration. When Jordon drew her tongue deeper into his mouth, it parried his, flicking lightly over the tip and along the sides, rapidly intensifying the need rising between them. He tasted of mint and she couldn't get enough of his kisses. It had been so long since she had surrendered this completely to her desire and the fiery passion he conveyed with every caress was tempered by a tenderness she couldn't possibly resist. Warm, femininely pliant in his arms, she molded herself to him, fingers running feverishly through his hair.

"God, woman," he muttered huskily, abandoning her mouth to seek the hollow beneath her ear. "You drive me crazy."

". . . drive me crazy, too," she breathlessly whispered back, turning her face toward his and making a low pleasured sound as he nibbled the lobe of her ear. The need to touch him was a fever in her. And the moment her hands slid under his shirt to graze with provocative lightness over his heated flesh, his own hand curved over her hipbone and he pressed her down on his lap, then reached for the top button of her blouse. It was as if they were perfectly attuned to each other's desire. Both of them needed to touch and to be touched, and as Amy's nails caught gently in the fine hair of his chest, found and rubbed over the taut nub of his nipple, Jordon groaned her name while his unsteady fingers undid the second blouse button. Her drowsy blue eyes opened halfway to be caught and imprisoned by his fierce, glinting gaze. A sensuous smile curved her lips and she skittered her hands over his flanks, feeling the response of flexed muscle beneath her fingertips.

When the third button had been unfastened, Jordon's supporting arm arched her and he bent down to outline the opening V of her blouse with a strand of tiny kisses. His warm breath seared her skin, setting it afire, while hers began to come in quicker shallower intakes. Her fingers played over his midriff, then glided upward to stroke the tendons of his neck. He undid the fourth small cloth-covered button, exposing her rounded flesh to his probing lips and the tip of his tongue, which flicked into the shadowed valley between her breasts.

"Jordon," she breathed, delighting in the passionate caress. Aswirl in a whirlpool of heightening pleasure, she tried to turn in his arms and press against him, but he held her still to undo the fifth button, then the sixth. Freeing the tail of her blouse from beneath the waistband of her skirt, he raised her in his arms just enough to remove the garment completely and allow it to drift to the floor with a silken whisper. When he laid her back down on his lap, his narrowed gaze wandered over her, lingering on the rapid rise and fall of her breasts. He ran his palms lightly over them, kindling wildfires on her flesh through the inadequate covering of her brief bra.

"I have to see you. Touch you. Feel you against me," he said, his deep voice rough-edged. "Take off my shirt."

And she did. Wanting nothing to hinder her wondrous exploration of his torso, she tugged the shirt off over his head and tossed it aside, tousling his hair in the process, causing a tumbling swath to fall forward across his forehead. At once he looked more approachable, perhaps even a bit vulnerable, and certainly even more irresistible to her. An unbidden resurging tenderness for him enveloped her and she lifted a hand to brush back that crispy clean lock of hair, then dance a fingertip down along the bridge of his imperfect nose.

"Amy, honey, you're so sweet," he said hoarsely, weighing the heaviness of first one breast then the other in his hand, his fingers pressing gently into her warm mounds. Then the edge of his thumb scaled the uprising slopes to their rose-tinted summits, visible through the fine lace.

His touch was electric and a violent tremor shook her slight body. Her breath caught somewhere deep in her throat when he lifted her in his arms and bent down to kiss the swelling peaks, his firmly formed lips lightly brushing them and conveying something akin to worship. Her mouth slightly open with sensual ecstasy, she looked up at his smooth sun-browned face when he lifted his head and gave a lazy promising smile. Holding her bemused gaze, he eased a long finger beneath the front closure of her bra.

"They should have made them like this years ago," he teased, brushing a knuckle against her. "The hook in front makes much more sense, doesn't it?"

Amy could only nod agreement and gasp softly as he deftly unfastened the clasp.

"Ah, yes, a man must have designed this," Jordon murmured with a deep-throated chuckle of triumph and satisfaction. "Or else a very intelligent, very sexy woman."

As Amy gazed up at him, recognizing the tender amusement that mingled with and endearingly tempered the passion that glittered like topaz in his tiger eyes, an undeniable truth claimed her, body and soul, and brought with it both indescribable joy and bitter anguish. Her trembling hands cradled his face as she realized beyond any doubt that she loved him again. Or perhaps she had never stopped loving him, though she had truly believed she had. But the love she felt for him now was deeper, surer, and more invasive than it had ever been simply because he *had* changed. He had become the man she had believed him to be three years ago before he had cruelly proved her wrong. Now he was tender, caring, considerate, and it was impossible for her to resist him. Long ago she had wanted the man he was now with all her heart. She still did. And when he slowly peeled the sheer cups of her bra away and pulled it off her, exposing her breasts to his intent gaze, she knew she was hopelessly lost. She wanted him to look at her and longed for his touch and as he slowly drew the pleasantly rough hard edge of one hand down between her twin mounds of flesh, she entangled her fingers in the thick hair brushing his nape and urged him to her.

"*Kiss* me, Jordon," she commanded throatily. "Kiss me, kiss me. Never stop."

"I never intend to," he promised, his lips descending on hers to possess their soft sweetness with hungry demand.

Rising effortlessly with her in his arms, he carried her she knew not where and didn't care. The love she felt for him and had denied for such a long time overflowed in her now and swept her along in a mighty, relentless tide. Her parted lips clung to his. She entwined her shapely arms around his neck, releasing him only with reluctance when he laid her down. She opened her eyes, saw she was in his bed, and saw him towering above her, and reached up invitingly to him. The faint clang of warning that sounded in her mind was immediately silenced by emotions far stronger than fear—love and the aching need to give it. When Jordon came down on the bed beside her, she turned toward him eagerly, releasing her breath in a sigh of delight as his long, powerful leg pinned both of hers, holding her captive for an instant.

"Amy, *love*," he uttered unevenly, impelling her down into the softness of the mattress once again to lean on one elbow above her. "I want you so much. And you want me. Don't you?"

"Y-yes."

"How much?"

"Jordon, I . . ."

"Tell me, Amy," he persisted, catching her small chin between his thumb and forefinger. "Say it."

"I . . . want you."

"How much? As much as I want you?"

"M-more," she confessed, her soft azure eyes longingly exploring his beloved face. "I want you more."

"You couldn't possibly because I want—" His words broke off as he suddenly leaned down to kiss her hungrily, his demanding lips ravishing the sweet shape of hers while she kissed him back with all the love and passion in her.

Playing her hands over his broad back, she pressed him down closer, needing to feel his naked flesh against her own. The hair on his chest tickled her skin, and when his hand on her shoulder

107

started to roam downward, she eagerly guided it to her breasts, gasping softly with pleasure as he gently squeezed them in turn.

Inflamed by her responsiveness, Jordon turned onto his side and pulled her hard against him, holding her fast in his arms as they kissed again and again, each kiss deepening as warm lips met and parted, teased and tasted, and gave delight while also taking.

"I could devour you," he whispered as she tantalized the corners of his mouth with the end of her tongue. He felt her lips curve in a smile and took them once more, parting them easily with his own. He crushed her to him with a low groan while she drew her nails slowly down his back, causing his muscles to ripple beneath her touch. "Temptress," he called her, and in one swift, fluid motion flipped her onto her stomach to scatter nipping kisses across her shoulders and down her spine, sending shivers of delight over her.

"Jordon," she sighed, moving helplessly beneath his lips. "That drives me crazy and you know it."

"Yes," he admitted, pushing her hair aside to blow a prolonged breath gently over her overheated nape. "And I've only just begun to make you crazy, Amy. It's only fair, considering what you're doing to me."

With that provocative promise he turned her back over and knelt beside her, his eyes glinting with spellbinding intent tempered by tenderness. Amy's heart fluttered but, looking up at him, searching the strongly hewn features of his face, she loved him more in that minute than she ever had. She loved him too much and knew it yet couldn't help herself. And she trembled with anticipation when he reached down to unzip her skirt, pull it off, and toss it aside. His hands glided over her half-slip, easing it up to drape around her thighs. He leaned down to bestow a lingering kiss on her satiny skin.

She went weak with the emptiness that bloomed nearly full-flower deep inside her. She caught her breath and hastily cupped Jordon's face in her hands to urge his mouth up to hers again.

Her lips parted to the featherbrushing strokes of his. Then he raised his head and she opened her eyes, seeing him smile faintly in a way that seemed to convey understanding of her uncertainty.

"I'm not going to rush you, Amy. I don't want to," he said quietly, drawing the ball of one thumb over the delicate natural arches of her eyebrows. "I want this to last all night."

"But, Jordon, I—" She was silenced by his long finger pressed gently against her lips and she lay very still, enthralled by the thought of spending all of the night in his bed with him, but also regretful she had ever allowed this to begin. She hadn't even had time to cope with loving him again, and until she did that, she couldn't be sure what she wanted. Oh, she wanted *him,* wanted to give everything of herself to him once more. Yet conflicting emotions pulled at her until Jordon kissed her, catching her lower lip between his teeth to coax open her mouth to the slowly sweeping, tasting forays of his tongue. Then desire rushed through her like a whirlwind, driving out doubt on its way, at least temporarily. She felt as if licking flames of white-hot fire were spreading instantaneously all over her, consuming her, body and soul. Jordon was the one man she simply couldn't resist. He knew too well how to touch her, how to kiss her, and how, with words and caresses, to arouse passion in her to a feverish pitch. More importantly, she loved him and needed him and wanted to give him all of herself.

And Amy did give, as abiding love and physical need combined to banish all rational thought. Adrift in a sensual realm where nothing existed except him and her and the bed beneath them, she sinuously tangled her legs with his and ran her hands lightly down his sides, slipping her fingertips beneath the waistband of his tennis shorts. She explored the angular contours and planes of his face with her lips, sought and found the pulse beating with strong rapidity in the warm column of his neck, and when he turned to take her fully into his arms, she lowered her head and her golden hair fell down around her face in a silken curtain as she took the hard nub of his nipple between her teeth, lazily nibbling and flicking her tongue over and around it.

"Amy, *honey*," he groaned, winding her hair round one hand to tilt her head back. His hard mouth came down on hers, taking and giving and demanding total surrender while his hands ranged all over her body, touching everywhere. The light in the room faded as twilight gathered outside the window, and soon Jordon reached over to the lamp atop the bedside table and switched it on.

"I have to see you," he murmured, raising himself up on one elbow to look down at her, his gaze roaming with intensive slowness from the tips of her toes to the top of her head resting on his pillow. "Amy, you're so beautiful. Do you know how lovely you are?"

"I only know you make me feel lovely and . . . sexy and . . ."

"Wanted?" he questioned, a smile tipping up the corners of his mouth. "If you feel wanted, that's because you are. And I love to look at you."

"I love for you to," she confessed, very faint pink color rising enchantingly in her cheeks. "When you look at me, I feel . . . delightfully wanton."

Jordon's answering chuckle was deep throated and teasingly wicked. "Wanton? Hmmm, that's exactly the way I want you to feel. But I think you liked to be touched, too, don't you?"

She could only nod, adoring his playfully naughty smile, adoring those dangerous tiger eyes, adoring him with a love so powerful she wondered now how she had denied its existence for so long. She certainly could deny it no longer. It pulsated outward from the centermost core of her being, awakening all her senses to keenest receptivity while bewitching her with a drugging magic spell. She couldn't think straight, didn't really want to. At that moment she could only feel, and what she felt was a rising obsession to know all the strength of his hard male body and to know that her ability to arouse him could make him tremble in

110

her arms. Looking up at him, she lifted a hand to caress the line of his jaw.

"Don't you, Amy?" he persisted, breaking the silence she had commenced. "You do want me to touch you, too, don't you?"

A shy yet provocatively inviting smile trembled on her lips. "You know I do."

"Where?" He spanned the peaks of her breasts with his thumb and forefinger. "Here. And here?"

Her breathing quickened. "That's a . . . beginning."

Passion-fire blazed up in his eyes. He cupped her breasts in his hands. His fingers pressed gently down into her warm, resilient flesh while his thumbs drifted over her rounded slopes in slow circles to reach the summits. He gently squeezed and tugged at the erect tips, and when she gasped softly he leaned down to murmur against her lips, "I have to kiss, too. Here and here." He toyed with her lushly soft and cushioned flesh, rediscovering every rounded inch with questing fingertips before his hands drifted downward, ever downward, over her flat abdomen. "I have to kiss you everywhere."

"Oh, Jordon, I—" Her weakly attempted protest abruptly ended and the flash of uncertainty she had felt was vanquished when Jordon's warm mouth sought her left breast, closing on the nipple and drawing it inside. Shattering sensations radiated through the rounded flesh to rage wildly all over her. The central emptiness inside her opened to an aching chasm only he could fill and she touched his face, his hair, and his wide shoulders, outlining his corded muscles with her fingertips as his lips, teeth, and tongue took possession of both her breasts, left and right alternately, increasing the pulling pressure around each roseate peak until she was dizzy with loving desire.

"*Yes.* Oh, Jordon, yes," she uttered breathlessly, winding her arms around him, pressing her thigh deeper between the muscular strength of his, and encountering a potent hardness that surged demandingly against her tender skin. Feeling almost faint with longing, she trembled.

111

"Amy, we'll do the most delightful things together," he promised, raising up to kiss her again and again and again. "I only want to share all the pleasures with you."

That was what she wanted, too . . . although edging her consciousness was the realization that she was now doing what she had never thought she would do. She had sworn she would never get involved with Jordon again, but now she was involved. She loved him and was on the verge of giving herself totally, even though she knew only too well that if she did, she risked reexperiencing all the pain she had endured years ago. Jordon *had* changed since then, but that in no way meant that he loved her or ever would. He merely wanted her; his own words were proof, and she would be a fool to . . . Still, she loved him too much to deny him or herself the ecstasy she knew they would find together. But as he parted her legs and drew his hand slowly up her thighs, his fingertips describing erotic patterns against her secret feminine warmth, she cursed fate for making her so vulnerable to him that she would risk her own emotional well-being.

"Damn, *damn,*" she muttered, scarcely aware she had spoken the words aloud.

But Jordon heard them and suddenly tensed. "Amy, don't do this to me," he implored raspingly. "You can't say no because I'm not sure I can let you go now."

Loving him as she did, she could never have denied him what they both so badly needed but her voice quavered revealingly when she started to speak. "J-Jordon, I . . ."

"God, you're not ready for this," he uttered, his tone growing harsh as he released her with stunning abruptness and sat up on the edge of the bed. "If you're cursing me already, God only knows how you'd react if we woke up in bed together in the morning."

A certain relief surged up within her, killing all desire. He was giving her an out and she had to take it, although she felt horribly contrite. Sitting up also, she touched light fingertips against his back, but her hand dropped away when he impatiently shrugged it off. She gnawed at her lower lip. "Jordon, I didn't mean to—"

"Get up, get dressed, and leave," he commanded curtly, then caught her roughly by one arm when she slipped off the bed to retrieve her skirt from the floor. "Just remember this, Amy. I'm trying to be patient, but I'm only a man, not a saint. Another episode like this and we might have to make love whether you think you're ready or not. Do you understand?"

She did. *Completely.* And when he let her go, she hurried out the door into the sitting room, where she gathered up the remainder of her clothing. After dressing quickly, she rushed out into the night, but even the light breeze that caressed her couldn't cool the heat that was being generated internally. Less than two minutes later she sat in her car, resting her forehead against the steering wheel, her knuckles white as she gripped it tightly. She might have cried if she had been the weeping type, but she wasn't anymore. She had shed enough tears to last a lifetime three years ago and had resolved never to cry over any man ever again. Still, her nerves had been strained close to the breaking point tonight. Somehow she had done it again. History was repeating itself. She was still in love with Jordon, which meant she might let him use her once more. Judging by what had just occurred in his bed, her defenses against him were pitifully ineffective and weak. How much longer could she resist involvement in an intimate relationship that she yearned for yet also feared because she could end up being hurt badly again?

Not much longer. Amy moaned softly as intrinsic honesty forced her to face the facts. She loved Jordon, so it was the most natural thing in the world to need to be as close as possible to him. And that driving need was going to overcome all her fears very soon and allow her to become totally involved with him again. She knew it. Once again he was going to win and she was going to lose.

"Not necessarily," she suddenly muttered aloud, slamming her palm against the steering wheel. She sat up straight, shoulders squared. She simply wasn't willing to lose another time the way she had before. Maybe it was true that Jordon didn't love her simply because he had changed, but it seemed he had become a man whose love would be very precious to have. And since she would never be satisfied with a series of one-nighters with him, she needed to win his love in order to have much more than that. But how? A fantastic sexual relationship with him wouldn't make him love her. It wouldn't hinder, of course, but that alone was not the complete answer. She needed to become such an important part of his life that he wouldn't be able to end what they had together as carelessly as he had done before. *But how did she go about winning his love?* Amy thoughtfully nibbled a fingernail. She hadn't figured that out yet. All she knew was that she must try. Jordon could only be playing a game, but he had drawn her into it and now she had no choice except to play it out and do her best to win, because she remembered too vividly how much losing had hurt. Somehow, then, since the game seemed inevitable, she had to be certain of one thing: this time she and Jordon would play it by a new set of rules—her own.

CHAPTER SEVEN

Amy arrived at work earlier than usual Tuesday morning. Before she could walk across the reception area, Jordon stepped from his office, beckoning to her.

"Amy, come in here, please," he requested, both his expression and tone grim. "I just tried to call you at your apartment but you'd already left."

"Yes, I had a little work to catch up on and decided to come in early to take care of it." A tiny frown formed on her brow as she moved toward him. "But why did you try to call? What's happened? Not *another* burglary?"

He nodded. "Sometime during the night. We can't be sure exactly when, since no one we've questioned heard or saw anything."

"Dammit. I'd hoped we wouldn't have any more trouble. Whose house this time?"

"The Cabots'," Jordon said, placing his hand lightly against the small of her back to direct her into his office. "Mr. Cabot discovered his safe had been broken into when he got up this morning."

Stepping through the doorway, Amy discovered Foster Cabot sitting erect in a chair before Jordon's desk. The instant he saw her he began sadly to shake his head and she went straight to his side.

"I'm terribly sorry this happened," she said simply. "I want you to know that Coastal Realty, through Mr. Kent and his agency, will be doing everything possible to recover your belongings."

"Yes, I'm sure of that, but . . . well, the deputy sheriff who was at the house earlier this morning mentioned that stolen property has a way of just vanishing. He didn't seem very hopeful about anything being recovered," Mr. Cabot told her, glancing at Jordon. "At least that was the impression I got. How about you, Mr. Kent?"

"Deputy Craig wasn't very optimistic," Jordon agreed, then sat down behind his desk after Amy took the chair next to Cabot's. "But you have to remember the sheriff's department can't drop everything else to work full time on trying to solve these burglaries. But since Security Unlimited is involved, there's a better chance of recovering the stolen property. And, after all, these robberies haven't been typical home break-ins where televisions and typewriters have been ripped off—that sort of merchandise is very difficult to trace. But here, almost everything that's been taken is extremely valuable and usually easily identifiable. I have people in all our agency offices checking out pawnshops and known fences. Something should turn up."

"I hope you're right," Foster Cabot murmured, again shaking his head. "I just don't understand how anyone got into the house last night. After the other burglaries I had a security system installed that was supposedly fail safe. It failed."

"Unfortunately, no security system is infallible," Jordon said. "There is always someone who can get around it, usually by finding a way to shut it off."

"And obviously that's what happened last night." Raking his fingers through his thinning salt-and-pepper hair, Foster Cabot rose to his feet, then extended a hand to Jordon, who also stood. "I won't take up any more of your time. I hope that photograph of the ruby necklace I brought you will be of some help. Sorry I didn't remember we had it until after you and the deputy left, but I suppose I just wasn't thinking straight with Pamela so upset. I better get back to her now."

"Mr. Cabot," Amy spoke up hopefully before he started toward the door. "They didn't take Mrs. Cabot's collection of Fabergé enamels, did they?"

"My dear, they took *everything*. Even the collection which wasn't in the safe. Pamela kept it locked away in that teakwood display case that some burglars might not have noticed. But this one did and took it. Pamela's in tears. The collection was passed down to her from her grandmother."

"I know," Abby murmured commiserately. "I'm terribly sorry."

Nodding, Mr. Cabot made his way to the door, pausing to look back at Jordon. "If you find out anything . . ."

"I'll let you know right away," Jordon promised. "And I'd like to talk to you and your wife again sometime today when she's a little less upset. I have a few more questions I'd like to ask. I'll call before I drop by."

116

After the older man had left, Amy turned her attention to Jordon. Watching as he sat back down, she leaned forward in her chair. "Well, what do you think? Any clues this time?"

"Tell me something, Amy," he said, his chin resting on his long, steepled fingers, apparently so lost in thought he hadn't even heard her questions. "How did you know about the Cabots' Fabergé collection?"

For a moment she could only stare at him, then disbelievingly shake her head. "Gosh, I guess I let the cat out of the bag, didn't I?" she replied as blithely as possible at last. "Does this mean I'm now your prime suspect?"

"Just answer the question," Jordon reiterated, his tone flat. "How did you know about the collection?"

"Mrs. Cabot showed it to me several months ago. She invited me to lunch just so I could see it. She is . . . was very proud of it."

"Which probably means she shows it to nearly everyone who visits her house. That's what I wanted to know, Amy. That's why I asked how you knew about it."

"Oh. I see." Amy leaned back, regarding him soberly. "Then I'm still just a minor suspect?"

A flicker of impatience momentarily hardened his dark features. "Amy, I think you know better than that."

She simply gave a light shrug. Did she know better than that? She wasn't sure. Of course where he was concerned, she was rarely sure of anything—except that she loved him and still had no concrete plan on how to encourage him to return the feeling. *But this was hardly the time to worry about their personal relationship.* Thrusting such thoughts to the back of her mind while knowing they would resurface soon enough anyway, she concentrated on the matter at hand. "What about last night's burglary? Any leads at all on it?"

"None unless you count the deliberate clue the thief left. Cabot found a calling card in his empty safe—a playing card, to be exact."

"A playing card?"

"The king of diamonds. Obviously because our burglar steals mostly expensive jewelry. And I think maybe the card was left as a challenge. He seems to be saying: 'Catch me if you can.' "

"*He?*"

"I think we can assume the thief's a man since it was the *king* of diamonds that we found in the safe."

"Maybe the thief is a woman and she put the king in there to throw you off the track," Amy suggested, a trace of a smile dancing over her lips and belying her innocent tone. "After all, if I were a jewel thief and wanted to leave a calling card behind as a challenge, I'd want it to provide a false clue for whoever was trying to catch me. But, oh, dear, I guess I shouldn't have said that. Maybe I've just made myself a prime suspect again."

"Don't be flip, Amy," Jordon said, his eyes boring hard into hers. "In case you haven't noticed, we now have another unsolved burglary on our hands."

"Oh, I noticed all right. I can practically feel the heat from Coastal Realty's Virginia Beach office closing in on me right now," she admitted, her faint smile fading immediately. "I guess I was just trying to laugh off trouble instead of crying about it. I really don't like to think I might lose my job because of this situation."

"We will catch the burglar, Amy," Jordon promised, his expression gentling, his gaze losing much of its chill because of her admission. Suddenly she looked very vulnerable and somewhat lost to him and he wanted to take her in his arms and whisper reassurances; but he didn't. He suspected she would rebuff him if he tried and he simply looked steadily at her instead. "It may take some time, but we will catch him. Since he was cocky enough to leave a calling card last night as a challenge to us, he's obviously planning other break-ins and he'll slip up badly soon. The fact he's so sure he can't be caught will make him careless, and then we'll have him."

"I wish we had him now. But we really don't have any idea who *he* could be, do we?"

"I'm working on it, and expect to find some kind of lead soon. And in the meantime, if you get a lot of flak from Coastal, tell them to talk to me. I'm in charge of security here, not you. You can't be blamed for any of this."

"As the on-site administrator of St. Tropez Run, I guess I *could* be blamed for any problem. We'll just have to wait and see," she murmured, producing a smile that conveyed more confidence than she felt. "And speaking of Coastal, have you called there to tell them about the Cabot burglary?"

Jordon shook his head. "I thought you'd want to do that yourself."

"I don't *want* to," she confessed, but with a grin. "But it's my responsibility, so I'd better go give Evan Price a call right now."

When Jordon merely gave a silent nod of his head, Amy stood and walked to the door, glancing back to find him propping his feet upon his desk. Leaning back in his swivel chair, he crossed his arms behind his head, and because this was the position he most often assumed when he was deep in thought, she felt rather reassured. Those feelings of reassurance were threatened, however, before she could reach her own office. When the door to the reception area flew open and Renn Bushnell rushed inside, looking as agitated as he had the evening he'd chased intruders from his property, the bottom of her stomach seemed to drop out. She started toward him.

"Mr. Bushnell, what's wrong? What's happened?"

"That's what I came to ask you," he said, somewhat out of breath. "Bootsie heard the Cabots were robbed last night and insisted I come find out exactly what happened."

Relief washed over Amy, relaxing her tensed muscles. *At least there hadn't been two burglaries committed in one night.* Considering Renn Bushnell's dramatic entrance, she had expected him to say his house had been robbed, too. But he hadn't, and she regained enough composure to take a deep, steadying breath.

"No one knows exactly what happened, Mr. Bushnell, but—"

"Renn, please."

"Yes, Renn. Well, no one knows exactly what happened except that the Cabot home was burglarized. The sheriff's department and, of course, Mr. Kent are investigating right now."

"And those young men I saw running away from my house the other night? Did anyone see them around the Cabot house?"

"No one saw anybody, as far as I know. Mr. Cabot didn't realize he had been robbed until he got up this morning and found his safe open and empty."

"Dreadful, positively dreadful," Bushnell said, shaking his head. "It won't be easy telling Bootsie the burglar got away again. You can't imagine how hysterical she already is about all this."

On the contrary, Amy could well imagine Bootsie Bushnell's highly exaggerated hysteria, but naturally made no comment about the woman's great talent for melodrama. Instead she simply nodded. "I'm sure everyone in St. Tropez Run is upset because there's been another break-in."

"I certainly didn't expect it to happen here once, much less several times," Renn Bushnell muttered as if to himself. "And Bootsie's furious about it. She's insisting we discuss the situation with Evan Price. He sold our house to us, promising complete security, and now after all that's happened . . ."

"I'm sure Mr. Price would be glad to talk to your wife and you," Amy said politely when he left his statement unfinished. "As a matter of fact I was just about to call him. Would you like for me to tell him that you and Mrs. Bushnell want to see him as soon as possible?"

"Maybe you should," Renn said, though rather indecisively as he turned to leave. "Bootsie might decide she wants to sell the house here if we can't convince her it's safe to stay, so I'd appreciate anything you can do, Amy."

After Amy promised to do her best, and Renn departed, she turned around with a long sigh. Her shoulders fell slightly, but she straightened them at once when Jordon stepped from his doorway with a questioning frown.

"I thought I heard Renn Bushnell's voice," he announced. "Anything wrong, Amy?"

"Oh, it's just Bootsie on the warpath again," she answered with as much aplomb as she could muster. "Nothing I can't handle." But was that true, she wondered.

Jordon grinned and disappeared into his office once more and she went into hers to dial the number of Coastal Realty in Virginia Beach.

Tuesday afternoon began as inauspiciously as the morning had. By two o'clock Amy had listened to Evan Price repeat himself for nearly forty minutes but couldn't see that they had made any progress toward solving their problem. He said over and over that something had to be done to end the burglaries in St. Tropez Run and she agreed while trying to tell him that Jordon was the most qualified man he could have retained to find the solution they needed. Evan, unfortunately, acted as if he expected an instant miracle and she wondered if he expected her to produce it. Yet, as she watched him pace back and forth across her office, she felt some empathy toward him. He was only a lowly junior vice-president with Coastal Realty—it was possible he was as concerned as she was about being made a scapegoat for the burglaries occurring in St. Tropez Run. Still, much as she could empathize, she was having a difficult enough time reassuring herself enough to be able to reassure him.

Stalking back and forth before her desk like a caged bear, Evan stopped suddenly, looking at her and fidgeting with the knot of his tie. "Exactly what do the Bushnells want to talk to me about? Did Renn say?"

With an inward sigh Amy nodded. Though she hated to break any more bad news, considering the state he was in, it was her responsibility to tell him the truth. "Actually, I think it's Bootsie Bushnell who's insisting on seeing you," she said as matter-of-factly as she could. "Renn mentioned she had said something about selling their house."

"Oh, hell, the Bushnells, too! A few other people have been talking about selling out already. We can't afford to add the Bushnells to the list, especially when we're still looking for buyers for the new houses we built here this summer. These burglaries could ruin this entire project!" Evan exclaimed nervously, his square face flushed. "We have to do something, *anything*, to make the residents here feel like Coastal Realty is taking good care of them. Do you have any ideas at all, Amy?"

Amy didn't . . . at least for several long moments. Then the most wonderful thought struck her. Her blue eyes brightened to glimmering sapphire, and although the idea that had popped into her head served her purposes as much personally as professionally, she didn't hesitate to present it, especially since it was the only idea she could come up with.

"I do have one thought, Evan, but it's not very dramatic," she told him honestly. "I was thinking maybe I should move out of my apartment and into the quarters here for a while. At least then the residents will have someone representing Coastal Realty on the premises all the time. That might be a little reassuring, don't you think?"

Ready and willing to grasp at straws, Evan hesitated only an instant before nodding. "It's certainly worth a try, Amy, certainly worth a try. A symbolic gesture, to be sure, but sometimes those are most effective. So when can you move in here?"

"Probably by the day after tomorrow."

"Fine, fine," Evan murmured, continuing to nod. "I'll tell Mr. Braddock as soon as I return to the office this afternoon. He'll be pleased we came up with some sort of strategy. Now, I have to have a talk with Jordon Kent before I leave."

"He's just next door," Amy advised, and after Evan left her office, closing the door behind him, she fell back in her chair with a sigh. For better or worse, she had made a commitment to move into the quarters here and she wondered how it would turn out

122

in the end. It might save her job; it might not; it might make no difference either way. But, no matter what, she would certainly be much closer to Jordon with him living just across the hall and she needed to be near him as often as possible and hope that theirs could become a lasting relationship. At least today, she had taken a first step in that direction.

Amy moved into the quarters in the clubhouse Thursday afternoon. That evening Jordon came over to see her as she had hoped he would. Despite the tiny fluttering of nervous excitement in her stomach, she appeared perfectly serene as she opened the door on the fourth knock. In a white caftan that flowed prettily down to her bare feet and accentuated her lightly tanned skin, she was trying to look very casually appealing. Earlier she had applied her makeup meticulously but lightly, wanting to look her best but so subtly that he would never suspect she was trying to look especially nice. Even her hair, freshly washed and shining like spun gold, cascaded in loose waves down around her shoulders as if she had given it a quick brushing and allowed it to arrange itself naturally, when in truth she had done just the opposite. She had combed and brushed for nearly twenty minutes to achieve this "natural" look and now could only hope she hadn't wasted her time. And as she opened the door wider, giving Jordon a slight questioning smile, she was pleased to note that her efforts hadn't been in vain, judging by the appreciative light that appeared in his eyes as they drifted over her in slow appraisal.

"Just thought I'd drop over and welcome you to the neighborhood," he said, an answering smile touching his hard mouth. "Settled in yet?"

"Almost, but I really didn't have a lot to unpack," she replied, motioning him into the sitting room and toward the sofa. "I didn't bring all that much with me from the apartment since I don't know how long I'll be staying here. I guess it's possible the burglar could be caught tonight and I could be back home by tomorrow evening."

"Don't count on that, Amy. You'll probably have to be away from home for more than one night," he said candidly, dropping down next to her on the sofa, draping an arm over the back. "Do you mind very much having to move in here for a while?"

"Actually, I suggested doing it. Evan seemed so desperate for any sort of suggestions this afternoon that I offered the first one that came to mind," she said, altering the truth a bit. "I was surprised when he jumped at the idea the way he did, because it really isn't going to do any good for me to be here if another house is burglarized. I doubt my presence will placate the residents, but here I am nonetheless."

"But you didn't answer my question," Jordon persisted. "Do you mind very much having to move in here?"

"It isn't home," she murmured evasively, certainly wanting to give him no indication that being closer to him was the only reason she didn't mind. "I'm used to apartment living and this place is *so* quiet. It's almost eerie sometimes."

He gave her a smile that was somehow half-serious and half-teasing. "Just remember I'm right across the hall. In case you get lonely, I'll be happy to keep you company, anytime day or night."

The intimation wasn't lost on her and, although secretly pleased by it, she allowed it to pass by as if unnoticed and with a small sigh tucked her feet up beside her on the cushion. "Oh, well, I'll adjust to being here—have to put up with some inconvenience in any job, I suppose—but I'm not so sure about Skeeter. She's been miserable since I brought her here this afternoon, wandering from room to room, meowing mournfully, as if she's the most abused creature on the face of the earth. Everything's strange to her and she isn't happy about it."

Jordon glanced around the room. "Where is she now?"

"Taking a nap in the laundry basket, the only familiar territory she could find."

"I'm sure she'll get used to everything soon enough."

"Try convincing her of that," Amy wryly retorted, watching as his grin created those endearing semidimples in his cheeks, then allowing her gaze to lower momentarily. Although he had removed both his gun and tie, he was still in uniform, which apparently indicated he hadn't spent much time in his own quarters before coming to visit—and she could imagine why. "You worked late tonight, didn't you?"

He nodded. "A few reports came in from the Alexandria office and I wanted to go over them as soon as possible. I didn't think it would take as long as it did."

"Did the reports tell you anything that might help solve the burglaries?" Amy asked, her eyes brightening hopefully before he shook his head. She sighed. "Nothing at all?"

"Nothing earth shattering. A few minor discrepancies in three or four of the employees' histories which we'll follow up on, but that's about it."

"But I thought you'd already gotten the reports on the employees and found nothing suspicious in any of them. Why—"

"Those were only preliminary reports I mentioned to you before," he answered before she had to voice the question. "The ones I went over today were far more extensive."

"And you didn't find anything in them, either. I could have told you that."

"And you have, several times" was Jordon's dry reply. "But there were some discrepancies that we have to follow through on, Amy, whether you want to believe that or not."

"But you'll be wasting your time if you do follow through. I've told you before and I'm telling you again that none of the employees is involved in these break-ins."

"And I've told you before and I'm telling you again that, until that proves to be the case, I still have to investigate everyone who could possibly be involved," he declared, his voice deceptively soft. "When I'm personally satisfied that no further investigation is warranted, that'll be the end of it. That's just the way it is."

Heaving an inward sigh, she shook her head as she looked at him. In some ways he had changed while in others he was no different. She could read steadfastness in his eyes and the very alignment of his features, and although she personally thought that sometimes his strong resolve bordered on sheer stubbornness, she had to respect him for his professional integrity.

"You're an impossible man, Jordon, but as you've reminded me, I am from the hospitable South, so I'll offer you a drink anyhow," she said after a moment, deliberately exaggerating a drawl as she swung her bare feet to the floor. "What would you like? I have some Scotch, if you still like that. And cheese and crackers—I haven't been shopping yet so the cupboard's a little bare—if you haven't just finished dinner."

"As a matter of fact, I haven't had dinner yet," he admitted, shrugging. "I got wrapped up in those reports and—"

"For heaven's sake, why didn't you tell me you were hungry?" she demanded, getting up. "I'll make you something to eat. I ordered my dinner from the dining room, but I have some cold cuts in the fridge. I'll make you a sandwich."

"Amy, you don't have to," he murmured, catching her by the hand as she started past him. "I'm not really that hungry right now. I can order something from the dining room later or make an omelet. You don't have to bother."

"You have to eat, Jordon," she said, maintaining a steady voice despite the disruptive effect of his thumb brushing slowly back and forth across the pulse in her wrist. "You don't want to get sick."

"You almost sound worried about me, Amy," he gently accused, his eyes probing the depths of hers. "I'd like to think that means you've stopped disliking me enough at least to care a little . . . about my health, if nothing else."

"I care a great deal. After all, if you get sick, who's going to catch our burglar and save my job for me?" she countered flatly, extracting her hand from his. "So I'll go make that sandwich now and you'll eat it."

"Opportunist," he called after her, his chuckle following her into the kitchen.

Fifteen minutes later Amy watched Jordon wolf down the last bite of the sandwich, then fold his napkin and toss it onto the empty plate. She moved forward on the sofa cushion as if to stand. "If you'd like something else . . ." she began, breaking off when he shook his head. "More coffee, then?"

"Nothing, thank you, Amy. That was just what I needed."

Nodding, she sat back again, cradling her own coffee cup in her hands, curling her fingers tightly around it to still their sudden shakiness. A strange and dangerous intimacy seemed to radiate between the two of them and she wasn't sure if it was merely a product of an overactive imagination or a reasonable response to the indefinable nuance she had detected in his deep voice. Curling up in her corner of the sofa, smoothing the caftan over her legs, she sought to dispel the intimate atmosphere, real or imagined, that might prompt her to want to give too much too soon and thereby allow him to realize that she loved him again. That was the last thing she wanted to do. He had told her himself that she had scared him away three years ago by not hiding the fact that she regarded their relationship as very serious and hoped for a commitment from him; that was a mistake she didn't intend to make again. This time she would have to pretend *she* didn't want to make any commitments, either, no easy accomplishment, one that promised to tax to the limit her acting ability. As vague and risky as that strategy was, it was the only plan she had and she had no choice except to implement it. Perhaps her intention to deceive him concerning her true feelings should have made her feel like a cold, calculating woman, but that was not the case. She was simply a woman who knew what she wanted. She wanted him—enough to take a gamble and risk losing badly again. She couldn't *make* him love her but she could do everything in her power to win his love while hoping for the best. And she did have an advantage: she was no longer the naive little Amy she had been. She was three years older now and wiser and much more adept at handling her emotions and Jordon. Such thoughts boosted her self-confidence, and after idly picking a loose thread off her caftan, she looked up at Jordon, producing a casual smile while asking, "Had a chance to go see your new playground equipment yet?"

"Yesterday afternoon. It's certainly an improvement," he said, displaying obvious satisfaction but then firmly adding, "But it's not *my* equipment, Amy. It's the boys'."

"I know that, but you paid for it."

"I had help."

"Very little, I bet. I still think you paid for most of it yourself. But you don't have to admit that's true if you don't want to," she said, seeing by his rather closed expression that he probably never would anyhow. "I just want you to know, if you don't already, that the boys are so excited and so happy. Terry told me they would stay out on the playground day and night if he'd let them."

Jordon shifted restlessly. "When did you see Terry?"

"Just after lunch today. I dropped by over there before going home to start moving my things."

"Do you ever see him away from the boys' home?"

"Oh, sure. We—"

"How often?"

"Umm, pretty often, I suppose you could say," Amy murmured, strumming her fingers against her lips to suppress a rising smile. She liked the direction his questions were taking and was pleased by his brusque tone. It was encouraging to know he was interested enough in her relationships with other men to question her about them, but she feigned innocence and mildly added, "But why do you ask?"

"Are you interested in him?"

"*Interested?*"

"You know what I mean, Amy. Are you romantically interested in Terry King?"

"Well, he is a wonderful man and I certainly could be interested in him except for one thing: he's married to one of my closest friends and they have a three-year-old daughter" was Amy's offhanded reply. "But why didn't you know that already? Surely you've investigated Terry, too?"

"Not his personal life. We only ran a professional check," Jordon stated without apology. "And I'll answer before you even ask—we found no reason to investigate him further."

"Lucky for Terry he's not an employee at St. Tropez Run. *We* all have to be checked out thoroughly, don't we? So, what have you found out about me thus far, Jordon? I'm really curious to know."

"We've learned a great deal about you, as a matter of fact. For example, we know the names of all your teachers in grammar and high school and the grades you made. We have your college transcript and the names of friends you had then. We also have a copy of your personnel file from the Rosemont Hotel in Alexandria and a list of the friends you had then. Of course I knew a great deal about that time already, and it's the past three years that interest me most. We have a copy of your file from Coastal Realty, too, and know which resorts you've worked at, who your business associates were and still are. Friends, too. Terry King was on that list as well as a Beth King, but they weren't listed together and it didn't occur to me she was his wife—an oversight on my part. And we even have the names of the men you've gone out with." Jordon paused, his gaze narrowing as he regarded her more intently. And although his tone had been methodical, his deep voice suddenly lowered. "About all I don't know is whether or not you've been seriously involved with any of these men."

Amy's eyebrows shot up in surprise. "*Really?* Ah, well, check a little closer and I'm sure you'll find out that, too."

"Why don't you save me the trouble and just tell me whether you have been?"

She dismissed the request with a careless flick of the wrist. "Ladies never tell, Jordon."

A muscle began to work in his tautening jaw and the line of his mouth hardened. "You're enjoying this, aren't you, Amy?"

"Yes," she answered honestly, a mischievous glimmer lighting her eyes. "I guess I really am."

His own eyes never left her face as he nodded. "Is this your way of trying to get revenge? If it is, you'd better remember that seeking vengeance can be dangerous, Amy. You could provoke reactions you never expected."

"Oh, but I'm not seeking vengeance," she declared. And that was true. Revenge wasn't at all what she had in mind. She was merely trying to appear as alluring and mysterious as possible because she knew he had never been able to resist a mystery. *So let him wonder about her a little. It would do him good.* Meeting his darkening gaze directly, she allowed her shoulders to rise and fall in a shrug. "I just think it's sort of amusing that you're so suddenly interested in the details of my relationships with other men."

"I guess it's because I was your first lover," he countered, his voice taking on a caressing quality while he lowered his hand from the back of the sofa to touch her hair gently. "Maybe that makes me feel some kind of a responsibility for you."

"Well, don't. You don't have to. Nobody's responsible for me except me. I can take care of myself."

"Yes, now you can; you've proven that. But what about three years ago? Were you this independent then?" His hand on her hair stilled as he moved a few inches closer to her on the sofa, his lithe rangy body unusually tensed. "Amy, I'm going to ask you a question and I want a truthful answer. I wondered about it three years ago when I learned you'd left Alexandria so suddenly, but then I decided there was nothing to worry about because you didn't come to me. You would have told me, wouldn't you, if you had been pregnant?"

She was taken aback by his obvious concern and by the question itself. Yet even the mild astonishment she felt didn't prevent her from being perfectly candid. "You really think I would have

130

come to you for help?" she asked, then shook her head in strong denial. "Oh, you couldn't be more wrong about that, Jordon. That's the last thing in the world I would ever have done."

His hand dropped to her shoulder, lightly gripping it. "Are you saying . . ."

"I'm not saying anything except that I would never have come to you. I had some pride even then, believe it or not."

"Oh, I can believe it, knowing how independent you are now," he muttered, his fingers tightening over her shoulder, pressing hard into her flesh. "So maybe you just better tell me whether or not you had my baby."

"I didn't have your baby, Jordon."

"Which doesn't really tell me the whole truth, does it? You could have had an abortion."

"But I didn't. I was never pregnant," she said, unwilling to taunt him and make him wonder any longer. She loved him too much to do that. Her soft blue eyes sought his. "That's the absolute truth." He visibly relaxed and raked his finger through his hair, and she noticed the fine lines of strain around his mouth. He looked tired . . . even vulnerable . . . and suddenly she found herself touching his face. "Jordon, you—" she began, but the swift catching of her breath imprisoned the remainder of the words she had meant to say—he was moving much nearer.

"Amy, you're driving me crazy and I think you know you are," he murmured roughly, cupping in his free hand the small, slender foot that peeked from beneath the hem of her caftan. Smoldering fires glowed in the amber eyes that captured and held hers before he bent down to brush a kiss into the enticing arch of her foot, trailing his fingers, too, along her sensitized sole. And when she trembled, he raised his head and drew her inexorably to him, burying his face in her hair. "How am I supposed to be able to keep my hands off you when you look and smell the way you do, like you've just stepped out of a bath? God, I can't. You smell too good, feel too good, and underneath that pristine white robe of yours, I know . . ."

131

"Jordon, *don't*," she protested breathlessly as both his touch and his words became almost too evocative to resist. But the protest seemed to come too late, and when his lips sought the tender curve of hers, she eagerly kissed him back for several spellbinding seconds until common sense screamed at her to stop because it was too soon, too soon. She wasn't ready yet. She hadn't meant to seduce or be seduced tonight. She had meant it to be a time of rediscovery. That was important; she felt it. And, much as she wanted to let him go on touching her and to go on touching him, she knew she couldn't begin something she would not be able to allow to come to a fulfilling conclusion for both of them. She wouldn't lead him on. Best to call a halt now. And she did, garnering enough strength of spirit to push his arms down from around her while pulling away from him.

"You're tired, Jordon, and so am I. I was up half of last night packing," she muttered. "You'd better go now."

"My God, Amy," he whispered huskily even as he released her and rose to his feet to tower over her. "You've become a very tough lady in only three years' time."

You're the one who made me tough, she could have responded, but didn't, feeling that admission would be far too revealing. Instead she simply looked up at him, shaking her head. "I don't think I'm all that tough. I just know how to say no now, for practical reasons. We both need our rest. We have to think of our careers."

"Somehow I doubt that's what I'll be thinking about the rest of the night," he said shortly.

And as he turned and walked away from her, Amy watched him go with a welling up of regret even while she berated herself for being tempted to call him back and damn the consequences of such an insane act.

In his own quarters a few moments later Jordon slowly unbuttoned his shirt while walking through the bedroom to the adjoining bath. If there ever had been a time for a cold shower, this was it. Stripping off his shirt and pants, he shook his head thoughtfully. Amy had changed. She was tougher than she had been, but there was still a fire burning deep inside her that he could nearly feeling surging through her into him when he held her in his arms. And he needed to experience that inner warmth completely again. Somehow he had to regain her trust by convincing her he was more trustworthy now. But he wasn't sure how to accomplish that feat . . . yet. He was only sure that he wanted her more than he had probably ever wanted anything else in his life, and that was a disturbing certainty he just might have to learn to live with for a while—until he could make her change her mind about him.

CHAPTER EIGHT

A storm was brewing late Saturday night and Skeeter had been gone for over four hours. Still unaccustomed to the new surroundings, she usually stayed outside for only short periods of time and never strayed far from the door. This evening was different; she had wandered off somewhere. Amy had put her out around seven o'clock and then gone back to let her in a half hour later, but the cat had been nowhere in sight, which really hadn't been a cause for concern at that time. But as the evening had progressed and Amy had occasionally stepped outside to call "Kitty, kitty," with no luck, she had begun to feel a little worried. Now she once again checked the clock in the sitting room. Ten past eleven. She thoughtfully nibbled a fingernail. As skittish as Skeeter had been in this unfamiliar place, it wasn't likely she had suddenly decided to go off on a long journey of exploration.

133

"Asleep under a bush somewhere, probably," Amy murmured, wrapping her ankle-length clover-colored terry cloth robe more snugly around her and deciding to give it one more try. She padded barefoot out into the foyer to open the outside door. She looked down. Still no cat. She tried calling again, a bit louder this time in case Skeeter was snoozing somewhere nearby. No results. Amy sighed. The stiff, sometimes gusting breeze that lifted her hair off her shoulders brought to her the piney-sweet fragrance of rosemary from the gardens, and she took a deep breath of fresh perfumed air while peering at the far horizon. The dark band of clouds lacing the sky above the ocean was growing wider, and Amy didn't relish the idea of tramping out in the dark chasing down a cat on this kind of night; but didn't see she had much choice in the matter. With luck she'd find the wanderer before the storm got much closer.

A resigned look on her face, she started to go back into her quarters to dress but abruptly hesitated outside Jordon's door. She had heard him come in about thirty minutes ago and assumed he had been working late in his office again. Maybe when he had come in, Skeeter had followed him. Amy shook her head, doubting that had happened. Still, it was a possibility she shouldn't overlook. Pulling the lapels of her robe more tightly closed across her breasts, she stepped up to the door, knocked, then smiled somewhat uncomfortably when Jordon answered at once. Lean and rangy and overwhelmingly masculine with the top two buttons of his khaki shirt undone and his cuffs rolled up, he moved into the doorway, sweeping a speculative gaze over her.

"Amy, I'm glad you know you don't have to dress up to come see me," he said, a teasing note in his deep voice. "In fact I'd rather you didn't dress at all. But we can't have everything we want all at once, I guess. Come in, though."

"I . . . uh . . . no. I just wanted to ask if that cat of mine happens to be paying you a visit right now," she said softly, her face falling a little when he shook his head. "She isn't?"

"Should she be?"

"I hoped she was, since I can't find her. I put her out about seven and she never came back. It wouldn't be unusual for her to stay gone that long if we were at the apartment, but she hasn't gotten used to living here yet and she always stays very close to the door when she goes outside. I doubt she's built up enough courage to go wandering off, exploring."

"Maybe she wandered off for some other reason," Jordon suggested matter-of-factly. "Could be she felt the need to find some male companionship."

Amy shook her head. "No, she's been fixed. I had to talk hard and fast even to keep her in my apartment. The manager would never have put up with litters of kittens. So she isn't out looking for a boyfriend."

"Then she probably just got bored with sticking so close to home. Cats are natural adventurers."

"I know, but maybe she's lost."

"You're being a little overprotective, aren't you?" he asked, but with a slow indulgent smile. "She isn't a newborn kitten. She's nearly full grown and I imagine she could find her way back here even if she strayed away pretty far."

"You're probably right," Amy murmured, nodding as she half turned away. "But I still think I'll go have a look in the gardens just in case."

"Wait a minute." Jordon caught her arm and stepped out into the foyer in front of her. "Amy, are you really that worried about her?"

"Well, not worried exactly. I'm just a little uneasy," she replied, downplaying her feelings, which was becoming a habit with her where he was concerned. "You know how it is. Pets are nice, but they can be a lot of trouble sometimes."

"And you'd be lost without this particular one," he said perceptively, releasing her arm only to graze the hair-roughened back of his hand against her cheek. "I think you'd be heartbroken if something happened to her."

"She's such a nice cat. I guess I probably would be terribly upset," Amy conceded, a hint of a sheepish smile flickering over her lips. "Sort of crazy, isn't it?"

"I don't think it is at all. It just proves you're warm and tenderhearted," he answered, looking deep and long into her eyes before one corner of his mouth turned up in a resigned smile. "So, just to ease your mind, I'll go look for her."

"Oh, but you don't have to do that." Laying her hand upon his arm, she shook her head. "I didn't come asking about her, hoping you'd volunteer to go out and track her down for me."

"And I never imagined you did."

"I don't expect you to go chasing after a cat in the dark when I can do that myself."

"Don't be so damned independent," he chided. "I'm offering to help so let me. It makes sense for me to go. I'm dressed and you're not, and I'm going, Amy. No more arguments."

"But I'll go with you, then." She only partially retreated, despite the no-nonsense expression that lay over his chiseled features. "She's my cat and I'm the ninny who's worried about her, so I should share some of the inconvenience she's causing. Just wait right here. I can get ready in a jiffy. Be right back."

"I'll get a flashlight," he told her as she dashed across the foyer into her sitting room. Reentering his own quarters, he shook his head, but had to smile.

Five minutes later, after Amy had thrown on jeans, a cotton plaid shirt, and tennis shoes, she and Jordon followed a winding path through the gardens. She called the cat. He automatically took her left hand in his while in the other he carried the flashlight and played its far-reaching beam over shrubs and flowers and between ornamental trees. No big round reflective eyes glittered back at them. After a while they stopped still, listening, but the only sounds in the night were the muted swoosh of the surf breaking on the sandy beach and the whisper of the breeze through the leaves. Amy looked around, saw the brightly lit multipaned windows of the clubhouse towering above them, and quietly laughed.

"They're having a dinner-dance in the Peacock Room tonight and it just occurred to me that if anyone steps out on the balcony and sees us stalking around down here, we might be mistaken for the burglars," she explained when Jordon glanced down at her curiously. "If someone investigates and we say we're out here looking for a cat, they're going to think we're crazy."

"Do you really mind if they do?"

Although she could scarcely make out his features in the pale illumination cast from the wide tall windows in a silvery shimmer over the gardens, she looked up at him and shook her head. "No, I guess I really don't. Some of those people are as foolish about their pets as I am."

"You're not foolish, Amy."

"I'm not so sure of that," she said wryly. "It's nearly midnight and I've dragged you out here to help me look for an animal who's usually quite capable of taking care of herself. If that isn't foolish, what else can you call it?" And when he declined to answer that question, she called him a true diplomat.

A few minutes later they walked out of the gardens at the east end, near the ocean. If Skeeter was anywhere they had been, she had kept herself totally concealed and hadn't made a sound. Amy breathed a long sigh. Jordon looked up. In the purple sky the blackish arc was growing wider and a vanguard of wispy gray clouds, driven by increasingly stronger winds, swirled ominously before a pale half-moon. A roll of thunder rumbled in the distance.

"She obviously wandered farther than we thought," he commented, then looked back up again at the scuttling clouds. "And the storm's getting closer, Amy."

"I know, but . . ." She hesitated, hating to ask but felt compelled to anyhow. "Could we go a little ways along the beach? Not very far."

"I don't mind getting rained on if you don't" was Jordon's flat answer.

They had gone nearly a quarter mile when thunder rumbled again, louder this time. Flash lightning flared briefly in the far sky and Amy's fingers involuntarily tightened around Jordon's strong hand. Her shoes were filling with sand—his were too, she imagined—and she was getting irritable.

"Damn that cat, where can she be?" she muttered aloud. "If we go back and find her lounging on the doorstep, I just might disown—"

Jordon halted her words by pressing light fingertips against her lips as he stared into the copse of pines that edged the beach about twenty yards beyond the sand. "Listen," he commanded softly. "I think I hear a dog barking."

Amy strained her ears. "*Yes*. It—"

"Come on, I think we've just found your cat," he said, rushing her into the shadows beneath the trees, following the sound.

It was less than two minutes later when the flashlight beam settled on a huge black dog sitting at the base of a tall pine tree, head lifted, barking howlingly upward into the overhanging branches.

"Why, that's Sebastian, the Montgomerys' Newfoundland," Amy exclaimed with great surprise. "He's always been such a nice gentle dog. Why—"

"No dog's nice and gentle when a new cat comes around," Jordon said crisply. Giving the flashlight to her, he clapped his hands together and issued a sharp reprimand to the mastiff, who sprang up and scurried guiltily away into the darkness.

Amy hurried beneath the pine tree to shine the light up into the thick branches, feeling a surge of relief and happiness when two wide eyes glowed back at her. "Hello, Skeeter," she called gently, then grinned at Jordon as the cat protested the ill-treatment she had received with a loud, prolonged meow.

Amy called up to her to come down but it was Sebastian who answered the call, noisily crashing back toward the tree and his trapped prey. Jordon chased him off again. Amy tried calling Skeeter down again but the result was the same. The dog wouldn't give up and the cat wouldn't relinquish her safe haven in the tall tree.

Amy cursed. "Well, what do we do now?" she asked Jordon wearily. "She won't come down until that damned dog leaves and he won't leave."

"I've noticed, so I guess I'll climb up and bring her down," he answered, his voice heavy with exaggerated patience, as if he had almost run out of it. "Shine the light up at that lowest branch."

She did, then shook her head. "It's too high. You can't reach it, but I have an idea. Give me a foot up and I'll go up and get her and we'll finally get this over with."

"I don't think so, Amy. It's too high." His words were clipped, adamant. "I don't want you falling out of a tree, breaking your neck, even for a cat you love."

"I won't fall. I climbed trees all the time when I was a little girl. I was a real tomboy," she assured him. "Give me a boost up."

Finally he relented and, cupping his hands together to hold one small foot, hoisted her upward. Amy landed over the thick limb on her abdomen with an oomph and immediately realized it had been too many years since she had last climbed a tree and she was now too old to enjoy reexperiencing the feat. But since they had gone this far . . . As Jordon shone the light up, she moved from the first branch into the crook of the tree. She stretched out on the adjoining limb, groping for a hold on the cowering cat, whose claws were digging deep into the bark. Murmuring soothing words, she stroked Skeeter's thick, silken fur until the claws retracted and she scooped the cat up. Lowering herself to the first branch, she stretched out upon it and handed Skeeter down.

"Hold on to her. She might run away if you don't," she

advised Jordon, wrapping her arms around the limb and allowing her feet to dangle above the ground. "I can just drop."

"No. I can handle you both," he sternly insisted, tucking the flashlight into the back pocket of his trousers. He held the wriggling cat in one hand while clasping his free arm around Amy's waist and letting her slide down the length of his hard body until she could stand. Even then he didn't release her; in the circle of his arm, he held her near.

Amy looked up. Lightning briefly illuminated the woods and she saw his face clearly for an instant, long enough to want to kiss him and be kissed. But this was hardly the time or place to succumb to such feelings. She stepped back and took Skeeter. "I think we better get out from under these trees before that lightning starts striking closer."

"A wise idea," he agreed, shining the light back along the way they had come. He took her hand as they walked to the beach.

The lightning was getting brighter and the thunder louder by the time they reached the entrance to the gardens, and before they could get through them, fat plopping drops of rain began pelting them. They ran, Amy trying to hang on to the frantically squirming cat, Jordon slowing his long strides so she could keep pace with him. As they dashed toward the clubhouse, the entire situation struck her as funny and oddly exhilarating and she was laughing breathlessly when they at last reached the door. With a grin Jordon whisked her into the foyer, following as she went into her quarters.

"Maybe you'd better find somewhere to hide and lick yourself dry," Amy warned the cat when it hastily leaped from her arms to the floor then streaked away behind a chair. "And the next time a dog chases you, run up a tree near here and not one nineteen miles away or I might decide to let you rescue yourself."

"That I doubt," Jordon murmured, but smiled indulgently when she shot a quick glance at him.

Her gaze lingered, taking in the way his damp khaki shirt clung to his wide, finely muscled shoulders and the clean healthy sheen of his rain-darkened hair. She touched her own, found it more than slightly damp. "I'll get a couple of towels," she told him, waving him toward the sofa. "Please, sit down." She left him, returning a moment later from the bathroom with the towels. When he reached out to take the one she held out to him, she suddenly frowned, noticing the series of tiny raised welts on the backs of his hands. She caught his fingers in hers and bent down for a closer look. "That cat. The ingrate actually scratched you. I'll get something to put on those. Be right back."

"Amy, it isn't—" he began, but she was already halfway out of the room again. When she came back, carrying a basin of warm water and a bottle of antiseptic, he shook his head. "There's no need to go to all this trouble for a couple of little scratches. I wasn't mauled by a lion, you know."

Paying no attention to his wry comment, she attended to his hands, sluicing water over them to completely cleanse the reddened skin. After he had dried them, she applied clear antiseptic to the scratches, wincing for him as she did it.

"Do you think I'll live, nurse?" he asked theatrically as she finished. He laughed softly when she replied by poking the tip of her tongue out at him before leaving with the basin.

Reentering the sitting room, Amy found Jordon relaxed on the sofa, perfectly at ease, his legs outstretched and crossed at the ankle. Draping one long arm over the back of the sofa, he watched her approach with unabashed interest, an interest she no longer wanted to shun.

She inclined her head toward the kitchen. "After that little misadventure, we need some refreshment. I'll make hot chocolate, unless you'd prefer a drink."

He smiled. "Hot chocolate's fine."

Several minutes later Amy returned to serve him one of the steaming mugs she carried on a small enameled tray. His pleasantly rough fingertips grazed hers as he took it, and she didn't even try to suppress the pleasurable sensations instantly evoked by his touch. She sat down next to him toward the opposite end of the sofa, though not right against the armrest. Relaxing, she took a slow sip of the chocolate and sighed with satisfaction.

"Thank goodness I had marshmallows. Hot chocolate's nothing without them," she said, turning sideways on the cushion toward him, tucking her now shoeless feet up beside her. She glanced at the cat, who was next to the opposite chair busily licking her paws. Then her gaze wandered back to Jordon. "Thanks for going with me to look for her. I couldn't have gotten her out of that tree without your help."

"I told you not to be so independent," he teased, those fascinating semidimples making another appearance. "You see, you do need me for some things."

"Hmm, I guess I have to admit it," she murmured, her eyes alighting with mischief. "You are a cat-rescuer extraordinaire."

They talked quietly about everything and about nothing while the storm moved in around them, adorning the inky sky with fireworks of lightning and shattering the quiet with sharp thunderclaps. The wind rushed through the trees, driving rain against the windows in sheets, but in less than a half hour the more violent clouds had traveled on. The storm passed, leaving behind only a steady but gentle rainfall. In the sitting room Amy felt that aura of intimacy gathering around Jordon and her again but this time did not attempt to dispel it. The time seemed right, perfect in fact, and when he put his empty cup aside and then reached for hers, she allowed him to take it from her with no hint of protest and could only hope that the deep love she felt wasn't shining too obviously in her eyes as they met his.

He moved toward her. His hand on the back of the sofa came down to rest on her shoulder, his fingers drawing slow circles on her blouse. "Amy," he said softly, "you probably should get out of those damp clothes."

"So should you," she answered just as softly, trailing her own hands over his shirtfront, feeling his compelling body heat radiating through the damp fabric. She smiled mysteriously.

"Then again, it's a warm night and we're not all that wet, so it probably won't hurt us to keep these clothes on."

He smiled back, too knowingly. "If it's such a warm night, why are you trembling?"

"Oh, I don't know. Maybe it's just a delayed reaction from our misadventure with the cat."

"Little liar," he murmured, notes of both triumph and amusement in his deep voice. "You're not trembling because of the cat. You're trembling because of me."

"Could be," she confessed and, cupping his face in her hands, kissed him, her lips playfully tugging the lower curve of his. "Ummm, you taste like chocolate."

"And you taste like the marshmallow on top, soft and sweet and delectable." Pulling her into his arms, he turned her so that she lay cradled against him, smiling warmly as he blew a flaxen wisp of hair back from her left temple. "And I don't think you really know how delectable you are."

"Why don't you tell me, then?"

"Why don't I show you instead," he whispered, lifting her hand to his mouth to press a kiss into her palm, the tip of his tongue tenderly lashing her skin. He nibbled the ends of her fingers, each in its turn before the edge of his teeth sank gently into the mound of flesh at the base of her thumb. When she drew in a quick breath, his smile became sensuous as his darkening eyes held hers. He traced the outline of her parting lips with the edge of his finger, exploring their texture with a deliberation that was meant to arouse and was succeeding. Amy lifted an arm to touch his lips, too, then his hair, then his nape beneath his collar. Tilting her chin up slightly, he bent down, his mouth seeking and finding the quickening pulse in her throat, causing it to race even faster. After several dizzying moments he lifted his head to look down at her. "I can't get enough of touching you, tasting you—that's how delectable you are."

She gazed up at him. His beloved face filled her vision and she felt enslaved by his magnetic amber eyes. And as she stroked the

143

strong line of his jaw with the heel of her hand, she knew exactly what she was inviting. She didn't care. She had held her emotions in check too long; they had built up to an explosive intensity and she didn't know if she could control them much longer. She loved Jordon and even though he didn't love her and perhaps never would, she needed to give totally of herself to him. The point had been reached where she could maintain only one self-imposed restriction. He couldn't know why she was giving; she would have to keep words of love to herself, spoken in her heart but never aloud.

With an inward sigh of surrender, she feathered her fingertip down to the end of his slightly crooked nose, her smile secretive. "You're pretty delectable yourself but I doubt you know how delectable, either."

"Why don't you tell me, then?"

"Why don't I show you instead?" she countered, returning his own words to him. Sliding her arms around his shoulders, she rose up to scatter warm kisses along the column of his spice-scented neck to the hollow beneath his left ear. She nibbled his lobe, feeling the shudder that ran over him, and her breath caressed him as she whispered, "I can't get enough of tasting you, either. That's how delectable *you* are."

"Amy, you are a temptress," he half groaned, cradling the back of her head in one large hand, tilting it back so that she had to look at him. Passion flared hotly in the magic depths of his eyes as they held hers captive. "A merciless enchantress."

"And you're a seducer of helpless young women," she huskily replied. "You've always been."

"I don't know anyone less helpless than you are."

"Whenever you kiss me, I feel very helpless."

"Then I think I'd better kiss you again," he muttered, his low voice gruff. "And again and again and again."

And he did. His firm yet gentle mouth repeatedly took possession of hers, plying her with deepening heart-stopping kisses, and she kissed him back, feeling almost faint with a desire that rose rapidly to match his. Her lips toyed with his, inviting all their masterful persuasion and strength. Not that she needed persuasion now—she was already hopelessly lost in a madly swirling world of sensual delight where nothing had meaning except her love for him and the promise of ecstasy that surged between them. The very feel of his long, spare body inflamed her senses and made every nerve ending erotically receptive to the touch of his hands as they roamed over her slender, generously curved form, lingering on the swell of her firm buttocks, her trim waist, and the rounded sides of her straining breasts. And her hands conducted their own exploration, following the taut lineation of his superbly masculine body. She had almost forgotten how hard his muscles were and how close to the surface of his skin, but touching him once more without reservations, without fear, engulfed her in a deluge of memories of the many exquisite hours they had shared together in the past. Her body went weak when his tongue opened her mouth and found hers. They met, entangled, tantalized each other, tasting, parrying, playing. Her lips clung to his, eliciting their gentle, twisting pressure.

And somehow she was lying on the sofa, Jordon leaning over her. Her legs intertwined with his, one slender thigh brushing sinuously upward, and as she felt his response, the searing, aching shaft of emptiness deep within her clamored for the fulfillment only he could provide. Amy moaned softly, her own small hands demanding as they closed over the muscular hardness of the backs of his thighs. Moments later she had unbuttoned his shirt and her fingers were eagerly probing the firm planes of his chest and midriff. Her blouse had been unbuttoned by him and his lips were blazing trails of delight over the beginning swells of her breasts, then seeking the peaks outlined against the lacy sheerness of her bra. His tongue flicked over and around them, bringing the nubbles of flesh to aroused erectness against the moist fabric.

"God, Amy, if you say no now, I won't be able to let you go," he warned hoarsely, his mouth seeking the shadowed valley between her breasts. "And you aren't going to say no this time, are you?"

"I-I'm not sure," she answered breathlessly, enjoying the role of teasing vixen for an instant. "I haven't made up my mind."

"Does this help you make it up?" His mouth closed over the pinnacle of one breast after the other then grazed down over her satiny skin to the waistband of her jeans and the shallow bowl of her navel. He unsnapped them. "And this? And this? Will you say no now?"

"I won't say no," she softly gasped while he slowly lowered her zipper along the metal tracks. "I don't think I can now."

"Then take my shirt off," he commanded softly. *"Amy."*

Her shaky fingers fumbled with the buttons of his cuffs. "I-I've never undressed a chief of security before."

"Damned good thing," he uttered possessively, his lips descending on hers once again, his warm breath filling her throat as he murmured, "If you'd said no . . ."

"I couldn't . . . I c-can't," she confessed, wrapping her arms around him. "I guess rescuing cats during thunderstorms just makes me feel very amorous."

"Then God bless that cat," Jordon whispered as the weight of his body pressed her down into the soft sofa cushions.

And after that there was no turning back. There was only the promise of ecstasy that they would share.

CHAPTER NINE

Joyously Amy wrapped her arms around Jordon. Clasping the back of his head in her hands, she held him close. Searing deep tingling sensations streaked like electrical charges through her as he kissed her, his firmly carved lips devouring the softer curve of her own with innumerable tempestuous kisses until at last she had to turn her face aside to catch her breath and hopefully decelerate the beat of her heart. Gazing up at him, her eyes luminous and half closed, she smiled a bewitchingly sensuous smile while her hands skimmed over his broad chest, then pressed upward to raise him slightly before pushing his shirt off his shoulders.

"Let me help you with that," she said throatily, sweeping his sleeves down his arms, then tugging the shirttail from beneath the waistband of his pants. Taking her time to enjoy every prolonged moment, hypnotized by the fiery glint of passion in his amber eyes growing hotter and hotter, she stripped him of his shirt with a purposeful slowness that became a delicious torment of anticipation for both him and herself. Finally, when the garment had dropped to the floor beside the sofa, she touched his chest again, her lightly tanned skin a pale contrast against the coppery tone of his. With the ends of her nails she outlined his taut pectoral muscles, causing them to flex to iron hardness.

"*Amy*, this is a game two can play, and now it's my turn," he cautioned unevenly, sitting up beside her. He removed her blouse swiftly enough, but her lacy bra took considerably more time.

147

His fingers slipped beneath the straps, following them slowly front to back before easing them aside and finally lowering them from her shoulders to drop around her upper arms. Unhurried, he traced every small flower of lace, scorching her skin through the wispy fabric. Her rounded flesh surged tight beneath his expert touch. His thumbs played over and around the darker peaks clearly visible beneath the sheer filigree cloth. As she caught her breath and compulsively ran her hands along his neck and the slope of his shoulders, he automatically sought the front closure of her bra, and when he found none, a lazy smile moved his lips.

"Ah, you didn't make it as easy for me this time, did you?"

"I . . . guess I didn't." She smiled back. "How was I to know this would happen?"

"You should have known it could. It must be obvious to you by now that I can't leave you alone."

"Well, then?"

"Well, then, what?" he teased even as he lifted her enough to reach beneath her to undo the bra's hooks. Still unrushed, he didn't take it off, but instead leaned down to kiss her again.

Amy responded with an ardent urgency that was rapidly veering out of control. Her parted lips clung to his; her mouth opened wider to the sweeping tasting caress of his tongue until she felt her clothes were shrinking on her, suffocating her in the heat radiating from deep within, and she longed to be rid of them all. And when Jordon's kisses deepened in intensity, she drew his hands up to her breasts, pressing his palms down firmly against them.

Releasing her mouth, he raised himself up slightly. "Amy, are you sure this is what you want?"

"Jordon, I . . ." She paused, detecting the nearly concealed glimmer of triumph in his eyes and decided to prove to him that this was indeed a game two could play. "Maybe I'm . . . *not* sure," she countered with feigned uncertainty. "Maybe you're going to have to do more to convince me."

"I'd be delighted," he murmured, his fierce gaze holding hers while he deftly stripped the bra off her then caught her off guard with the swift, sure movements of his hands as he pushed her jeans down below her hips. Kneeling beside the sofa, he removed them completely and dropped them on the floor. Her panties immediately joined them there and she gasped softly at finding herself so abruptly totally naked and vulnerably exposed. And as his narrowing eyes wandered over her, she did feel vulnerable, yet the feeling had a wondrously primitive appeal. Wildfires raged through her, weakening her in their wake. His impassioned appraisal of her was more than arousing; it was spellbinding.

As Jordon looked down at her, desire surged in him to a nearly intolerable level. She was beautiful. Her fair hair brushing her bared shoulders, the somewhat shy yet sensuous expression that lay over her delicate features, her full firm breasts rising to roseate peaks that invited the touch of his hands and mouth, and the shapely contours of her long elegant legs—everything about her was so maddeningly and delightfully feminine that he almost wanted to take her at once, right then and there. Yet the need to be tender and to prolong the pleasure for her and himself was stronger than the need for instant gratification. He waited to touch her, allowing only his gaze to roam hungrily over her.

"You are exquisite," he said huskily, smiling indulgently as the mere words quickened her breathing and caused her naked breasts to rise and fall more rapidly. He had to touch them, but his fingers grazed across the nipples only briefly before he turned aside, lowering his head to kiss the end of each of her toes, the arches of her feet, and the curving of her calves. His lips traveled upward, ever upward, to linger at the tops of her thighs to caress and nibble her firm flesh. His loitering tongue inscribed sensuous designs on her skin, leisurely flicking and tasting and driving her wild.

Amy moaned softly. A piercing, pulsating force exploded in showers of fire deep within her. Piercing arrow-sharp thrills of delight shafted through her. And as Jordon's breath drifted against her, she cupped his face in her hands to urge his mouth up to hers once more.

"Kiss me," she breathed, her parted lips teasing the firm line of his until his mouth was possessing hers with all the demanding passion she had wanted from him. Winding her arms around his neck, she arched closer to him when he moved above her and opened her legs slightly.

"Amy, you're so sweet," he whispered, burying his face in her hair, catching the lobe of one ear between his teeth to nip at the tender morsel. "And such a sexy wench."

"And you always take advantage of my weakness."

"I try my best . . . too often without success. But now . . ."

"Now, I can't seem to help myself."

"Because you know I only want to do the most pleasurable things to you and you to me. We always did the most wonderful things together. Remember?"

She had never forgotten a second of ecstasy they had shared. And those memories, plus the fountainhead of loving desire that had sprung up uncontrollable in the very core of her being, combined to render her powerless against him. In that moment she would have done anything he asked her to do, given anything he asked of her and found rapture in the giving.

Unwilling to rush their lovemaking, however, Jordon whispered her name endearingly and lay down on his side next to her, turning her toward him. Tenderly he brushed the golden crescent of hair that curved across her right cheek back behind her ear, then ran his fingers through the silken strands. He kissed the end of her nose, then her temple. Taking her chin between his thumb and forefinger, he turned her face this way and that, seeking access for his warm lips that slowly explored her every feature. He kissed the corners of her mouth again and again until she trembled, expecting to feel the full force of his lips on hers at any instant. But she didn't. He pulled back instead, his warming eyes delving the soft depths of hers when they flickered open. The smile that curved his mouth was like a secret he meant to share with her, and she smiled back as secretively, unable to break the dizzying visual contact for many long moments.

Stroking his side and flat midriff, she was fascinated by the fine, smooth texture of his skin underlaid with taut bands of muscle that conveyed a superb male strength she yearned to experience totally. It was heavenly just to touch him, and when her fingertips drew circles over his chest and she felt his heart beating more and more rapidly, it was as heavenly to know he was far from immune from her caresses. She smiled again, this time a secret smile, but he saw and interpreted it correctly.

"Tormentor," he muttered roughly and took both her smile and her lips with the aggressive yet tender mastery of his. Her mouth opened slightly and his tongue entered to partake of the sweet moistness within, then tangled sinuously with hers. His fiery hands coursed over her, faithfully lining her every contour, sweeping over her slender thighs, gently squeezing her rounded buttocks, cupping the weight of her breasts.

Sliding her fingers beneath the waistband of his pants at the small of his back, Amy pressed tightly against him, unable to get close enough, and entwined her legs with his. She nuzzled her face against his chest, tracing the nub of his nipple with her tongue until a low groan rose from deep in his throat and, with awesome swiftness and little effort, he turned and brought her beneath him in one fluid motion. His left hand covered her right shoulder, pressing and holding her down in the softness of the cushions as he leaned over her, his mouth claiming the rosy pinnacle of one breast then the other, each in its turn, repeatedly, until the firm peaks were aroused to the ultimate and he tasted them with his lips and his tongue and his teeth.

Amy moved ecstatically beneath him, alive with rushing sensations that possessed her body and soul. Wildly licking flames consumed her, and her hands, roving eagerly over his back, kneaded and massaged and caressed. Arrows of delight shot

151

through each breast as he laid claim to their warmth and fullness with the right of possession he had always had. Pressing her nails against the tightly constricted muscles of his shoulders, she rubbed her thigh compulsively back and forth between his. His response was immediate, but when he started to turn over and pull her atop him, he was suddenly still. Despite his labored breathing, he softly laughed.

"Amy, much as I hate letting you go even for a second, I have to. I think I'd better take you to bed before one of us falls off this damned couch."

Her answering smile was tremulous. "Then, take me to bed."

"Now?"

"Right now. Hurry."

"Oh, no, I don't intend to hurry. We have all night and I plan to spend every minute of it touching you."

The kiss that followed his words was so indescribably tender that Amy's love for him knew no boundaries and she covered the hands that spanned her waist with her own as he sat up and drew her up beside him. Then he stood, gathered her into his arms, and strode with her into the bedroom.

After he had tossed back the bedcovers and put her down, she watched as he followed the shaft of light coming through the door from the sitting room to the window which he opened wide to allow in a rain-freshened breeze that billowed the curtains. From the shadowed bed she saw him turn toward her, pause a moment, then reach out to switch on the small lamp atop the bureau beside him, casting a soft glow over the entire room. His gaze captured hers.

"I have to see you as well as touch you. Do you mind?"

"I . . . no," she murmured, grateful for the smooth percale sheet beneath her which cooled her flesh at least temporarily. But when he came back to stand beside the bed, warmth suffused her again, as if liquid fire ran in her veins. Looking up at him as he quickly removed his shoes, she was glad he had turned on the lamp. She, too, wanted to see as well as touch, and as he started to unbuckle his belt, she sat up, her hands going out to move his aside.

"Let me do that," she said softly. "You undressed me, so it's only fair." Jordon didn't argue, and she proceeded, her fingers fumbling somewhat with the buckle but nonetheless accomplishing their task. Soon her gaze was wandering over his magnificent body and she took his hands in her own to pull him toward her with a sensuous smile. "Do you know you have very good-looking legs?"

"No, but I know you do," he answered, his grin rakish as he lightly gripped her shoulders to push her down upon the mattress again. He came down next to her and leaned on one elbow over her, cradling her face in his hand, his gaze possessive and conveying hot desire.

"You *do* have eyes like a tiger," she said, trickling her fingers through his hair. "You really look very dangerous sometimes."

"How about right now? Do I look dangerous to you?"

"A little."

"Scared, Amy?"

"Ummm, terrified," she said but her words were contradicted by the caresses she bestowed upon his broad, strong shoulders. And when she lifted her head a few inches off the pillow and, clasping her hands over the back of his neck, pulled him nearer, she proved that fear was not at all what she was feeling.

"Amy, I want you so badly," he uttered against her mouth. "I could go on touching you forever."

"Start now," she beckoned, her parted lips rubbing his. "And never stop. I'll never want you to."

The silence that filled the room was broken only by soft, dreamy sighs and muffled endearments. It was a time of rediscovery, a new beginning, and, for Amy, reminiscent of the first time she had given herself completely to him. Again she was giving, but despite the natural vulnerability she felt, she was an eagerly active participant in lovemaking's prelude. Their first time together long ago she had been inexperienced, far more

153

inhibited, but tonight her caresses were more confident, her kisses more beguiling, and as if it had only been yesterday, she recalled everything that pleased Jordon just as he seemed to recall everything that pleased her.

She trailed her fingers across his abdomen around to the small of his back and down over his hips and the backs of his thighs, knowing as she did that the caress had never failed to heighten his desire.

He swept her hair upward to lie in golden disarray on the pillow and grazed his lips slowly over her nape, knowing as he did that such kisses sent shivery chills dancing over every inch of her skin.

Remembering what the feel of her long legs did to him, she sinuously entangled them with his, joy surging through her when he responded with a husky groan.

Remembering how incredibly sensitive her waist was to any touch, he scattered hot arousing kisses around it, his teeth nipping gently at her skin, his tongue etching concentric circles over it until her breath was coming in soft, nearly inaudible little moans and gasps.

Her mouth sought his right ear, her wispy breaths entering to tantalize. A shudder ran over him.

His tongue flitted around and over and into the shallow hollow of her navel. She trembled violently.

Her hands closed over masculinely lean buttocks, pressing him nearer.

"God, woman, you always could drive me crazy," he growled. "And you haven't forgotten how."

"You seem to be pretty good at remembering yourself," she whispered. "You know exactly how to seduce me."

"There isn't anything I've forgotten about you. I remember everything, Amy."

Set adrift in the world of passionate pleasure they were creating together, she realized she neither believed nor disbelieved what he said. That would have required the sort of conscious thought which was beyond her capabilities at that moment. She could only feel, could only experience delight, could only float helplessly into a swirling whirlpool of heightening sensual pleasure. And she wouldn't have had it any other way. She loved Jordon and, deep in her heart, had awaited this night without consciously knowing she was waiting. Now she knew. She had never really gotten over him and had never stopped loving him completely, although she had desperately wanted to. All along she had suppressed the aching need to belong to him again. And now she no longer had to suppress that need. Now she could give and take and feel she belonged. Now she had to. It was too late to fear the possible consequences.

In the soft glow of lamplight they continued to explore each other. As he had promised, he didn't hurry to take her. Although his need for her was unmistakable, he seemed intent on heightening her desire to a level that matched his. And he was succeeding. Amy reveled in all the ways he went about gaining success. She had forgotten exactly how wonderful it was to be touched again and again, kissed repeatedly, and simply held. If his goal was to control her completely, it was useless to try to fight him. He was already winning.

Yet, controlling her wasn't Jordon's prime objective because, in actuality, he was as enslaved by her as she was by him. Oh, he *was* intent on making her physical needs as intense as his own, but that wasn't the only reason for his patience. He just couldn't get enough of looking at her, kissing her, touching her. She was exquisite, her body so shapely, her skin so smooth, so soft, so warm. He wanted never to let her go, wanted this time of their reunion never to end.

In the circle of his arms, her own wound around his neck, Amy danced light teasing kisses across his shoulders, over the skin that hardened over his collarbone, and up along the tendons of his neck to his chin. With the tip of her tongue, she toyed with the corners of his mouth until he crushed her against him and she felt his provoked masculinity against the sensitive skin of her abdomen. Her senses swirled. She thought he must take her then, but instead he caught both her wrists in one large hand to lift them up above her head, holding them fast there when she instinctively tried to pull them free. He leaned over her, his broad shoulders and bronzed torso blocking the light, casting a shadow over his angular features—accentuating his expression, which was somewhat amused yet more relentless.

"Amy, love," he rasped, "never say you didn't ask for this."

Keen thrills rushed through her with the warning but she moved her head from side to side on the pillow, laughing softly as she whispered, "You don't scare me, Jordon. Talk's cheap."

"Hmm, you're right. Actions do speak louder than words," he agreed an instant before he swooped down to cover her lips with his, parting them with an impassioned insistence that made her arch against him. His marauding mouth held her captive as much as the length of his body pinning her to the bed and she was swept along in a tide of pure emotion and sweet abandon that quite literally took her breath away.

When he lowered his head to lace kisses from the hollow at the base of her throat to the racing pulsebeat above, she inhaled in quick little gasps that did nothing to restore her equilibrium and couldn't while his firm lips remained on her neck. Involuntarily she nuzzled her face against his and shakily whispered, "All right, I . . . believe you. Your talk's not cheap. You can stop proving it isn't."

"Never," he promised gruffly and turned her over onto her stomach. He knelt astride her before releasing her hands at last and then it was too late to do her much good. In her position she was as helpless as she had been before and she certainly felt helpless indeed when he gently blew his breath slowly up and down her spine. She quivered and he explored with brushstroking fingers the delicate structure of her back. He leaned down to murmur, "Oh, I remember everything, Amy. Especially how much you liked for me to do this."

He demonstrated, and the second his tongue touched her skin, a breathless moan of pleasure broke from her lips. Long ago he had discovered and taught her that her back was incredibly sensitive, and that was a lesson he began reteaching her now. Amy clutched the pillowcase in both hands as he inscribed provocative messages over her shoulder blades, her smooth, firm flanks, and the inviting arch at the small of her back, messages she answered in the affirmative with ardent responses. Words weren't necessary. Jordon knew exactly what he was doing to her and that the flaming, finely honed sensations he induced were as uncontrollable as the awesome pulling power of the sea. When his lips and his tongue ceaselessly continued to score her skin until her entire back was ablaze and tingling with stimulative receptivity, the need to touch him, too, provided her with the strength to roll over and come up into his arms, her mouth seeking his.

"What a fascinating erogenous zone—your whole back," he teased as she drew him down against her, unmindful of his partial weight that pressed her down. "I guess that's why you're such a sexy wench."

"And you're a devil and a satyr," she murmured back. Her roundly curved body yielded pliantly beneath the hard, muscular planes of his, and she adored the feel of his rough skin against her own, adored the way the fine hair upon his chest tickled her breasts. She caressed his back, his shoulders, the length of his neck, then smiled sensuously up at him. "Now, hush and kiss me."

He complied, his lips tasting and taking the moist sweetness of hers while at the same time giving back as much delight as they took. When the tip of his tongue daringly invaded her mouth and she drew it farther into the honeyed darkness, he lifted himself up away from her but only to raise her knees, part her legs, and move between them. He branded her inner thighs with fiery kisses until she gasped softly, slipped lower beneath him, and guided his lips to her breasts. He buried his face in the scented valley between her resilient feminine flesh, feeling her

157

small fingers entangle in his hair, their tips lightly caressing his scalp. A tremor of excitement dashed over him. Clasping her shoulders in his hands, he scaled the rounded slope of one breast in concentric circles with his lips, leaving no area of skin unkissed. He reached the summit, gently closed his teeth around the rosy cushioned hard-tipped flesh, then drew it in between his tongue and the roof of his mouth, drawing hungrily upon it before doing the same to its twin.

"Jordon," Amy softly exclaimed, desire raging rampant within her. "I—" Her words were cut off along with her breath as his hand trailed downward across her abdomen, causing her muscles to quiver at his touch. His fingers moved lower, then lower still over her centermost warmth to rest possessively there but only for an instant. He touched her inner thigh. Almost of their own volition, her legs parted wider. And when his long fingers stroked over her again then gently explored every rise and hidden valley of feminine flesh, her own hands floated down to conduct their own exploration of him. She, too, stroked and caressed while he sought her innermost heat and his lips fluttered as lightly as a butterfly's wings over her midriff down across her abdomen, faithfully following the trail his hand had blazed.

Within moments Amy felt she might faint. Jordon was doing the most wonderfully sensual things to her and eliciting primitive emotions she hadn't experienced in a long time. Her caresses boldly became as sensual as his, but he held a tight rein on his passion and it was she who capitulated first. The searing sensations he created in her became too exquisite. She tried to shrink away from the piercing pleasure but was compelled to go on seeking it again and again, arching to meet his masterful touch. Physical rapture was roiling up in her, rising rapidly toward a peak—but that wasn't enough. This wasn't how she wanted it to be.

"Jordon, not this way! I need *you*," she softly cried, gripping his shoulders to pull her to him.

Lowering himself between her legs, he leaned above her, his

glinting tiger eyes impaling the azure softness of hers. "Say that again, Amy."

She caught her lower lip between her teeth. "Jordon, I . . ."

"That almost looks like a blush," he whispered indulgently, lightly touching her cheeks. "Amy, *love,* how can you possibly be shy with me? We've shared all the pleasures together so . . ."

"That was . . . a long time ago."

"Too long," he muttered hoarsely. "But we're going to share them all again tonight and I have to hear you say what you need. Tell me again, Amy, please."

"*You,*" she confessed, unable to deny him anything. "It's you I need. Take me now, Jordon."

"Amy, I want you so much," he crooned, slipping a hand beneath her hips to lift them.

Amy felt the pressure of him against her and her breath caught. Unable to avert her bemused gaze from his, she waited with mounting anticipation. When with a deep yet incredibly gentle thrust he entered her, her parted lips met his, her sweet sigh mingling with his murmur of delight as sleek feminine warmth flowered open to receive his hard body and he filled hers with potent strength. Then he was still above her and her mouth opened wider to the persuasive onslaught of his before he rained kisses across her cheek into the hollow beneath her right ear.

He raised his head to look down at her, whispering, "Better now?"

"Ummm yes," she answered honestly with a tremulous sigh. "Much, much better."

The light of triumph that flared in his eyes was tempered by his tender, sensuous smile. Supporting himself on his elbows, he swept back her gloriously tousled hair, then cupped her face in his hands, rubbing the edge of one thumb lazily back and forth over her lips until she began lightly biting at his skin. He arched her tighter against him, settling deeper within her and capturing

159

her breathless sigh of pleasure as his mouth descended upon hers once again.

Amy's lips met the caressing touch of his, her tongue boldly darting in to tantalize and tempt him. He made a low, tortured sound and plundered her mouth with rousing finesse. Their kisses lengthened, deepened, and Amy's adoring hands meandered over his powerful back. The emptiness she had felt no longer existed, and although the need for absolute fulfillment was still keen, she was content for the moment simply to hold him and be held by him. Tears of sheer joy pricked behind her eyes. Loving him with all her being, she was adrift in the stirring and filling enchantment of his virile possession. She threaded her fingers through his hair while he bestowed hot, nibbling kisses over her shoulders and gently curved neck.

"Your skin's like warm silk," he said, his voice even lower timbred than usual, his tone almost reverent. "So smooth and soft. And delicious. I could devour you."

"I won't mind if you do," she admitted, her faint smile beckoning as she gazed up into his tawny eyes, becoming irrevocably lost in the smoldering emberglow warming their depths. "But kiss me again first. I want you to kiss me."

Jordon's head came down. His mouth hovered just above her own, but it was Amy herself who initiated the kiss, her lips toying with his, playing over and around them until they hardened to exert a thrilling pressure on hers as he again began moving inside her.

"Oh, Jordon, yes, *yes*," she breathed. Winding her arms and legs around his body, she moved rhythmically beneath him, meeting each gently driving thrust with heightening ardor.

"God, Amy," he groaned urgently. "You feel so good."

"Oh, you do, too. So very good," she softly gasped, arching closer to him, unable to get near enough, happiness enveloping her when he whispered sweet endearments against her mouth.

Jordon was a patient, indescribably tender lover, yet demanding. His own subtle brand of aggression gained him everything he wanted from her, eliciting a white-hot response that bordered on wild, wanton abandon. An eager participant in their lovemaking, she gave him all her love in every way except spoken words, kissing him, caressing him, wanting him to find in her more intense pleasure than he had ever before known. Enslaved by his large exploring hands, his warm masterful mouth, and his superbly taut body, she sought to enslave him, too, and did. With each long stroke which she joyously met, his breathing became more ragged, and when she whispered messages she had never imagined she could utter in his ears, passion surged up in him nearly to the limit of endurance. She could feel his tension as he braced himself above her and she did everything to increase it, her own heart pounding as the throbbing flutters he created within her plunged ever deeper and with sharpening intensity into her very center, where shuddering waves of ecstasy originated and radiated throughout her.

They swirled upward from level to level of quickening sensation, each one binding them closer together as they shared ascending bliss. Amy pressed her nails hard against Jordon's shoulders as those deep-plunging flutters he was creating increased in frequency, coming faster and faster—so swiftly that, oh, she was soaring upward, ever upward toward paradise.

"Yes, Jordon, *yes*," she gasped as the exquisitely piercing flutters merged into a continuous crashing wave of pleasure. She felt the onrushing inevitability in him as well as in herself and clung to him.

"Amy, love," he roughly whispered, lost in her.

The wave crested. Together they were suspended on the sheerest pinnacle of ultimate ecstasy, and for Amy the world splintered in a blinding burst of fire and light. She had to bite down hard on one finger to keep from crying out her love as shattering swells of emotion and physical rapture broke over her. Then they were over the keenest edge and tumbling, lightly as a feather drifting, down into the warm contentment of completion and sweet fulfillment. The splintered pieces of the world fell back together again around Amy as they held tightly to each other, arms and legs entangled. Jordon turned onto his side, taking her with him, not letting her go, one arm draped around her narrow waist, his other hand resting between her breasts, his hard knuckles pressing lightly into her soft flesh. Her own hands lay against his chest, and as her heartbeat slowed to a normal pace, she felt his doing the same. The light fragrance of her perfume mingled with the faint spice scent of his aftershave on their glistening bodies, and when she snuggled closer to graze her lips against his shoulder, he gently stroked her hair back from cheeks, still rose-tinted.

Amy raised her eyes, met the warm amber of his, and drowsily smiled. "Umm, that was nice."

He cocked an eyebrow, a glimmer of amusement lighting his gaze. "Nice?"

"Wonderful, then," she admitted, realizing she could hardly pretend now that it hadn't been, not that she wanted to anyhow. She lazily stretched her lissome body. "It was just wonderful and you know it."

"Oh, yes, I certainly do," he murmured wickedly. "And if you don't mind my saying so, you were always great in bed, but now you're fantastic."

"Not getting older, getting better," she replied drily, smiling as he softly laughed. She trailed a fingertip down the bridge of his nose, then over his chest, in small circles, toying with the fine hair.

With his thumb he outlined the contours of her high cheekbones, his darkening gaze holding hers as he said, "I'm staying all night, Amy."

Nodding, she smiled secretively to herself. That was exactly what she wanted him to do. Stay all night every night. Forever.

For a long time they lay close together, looking at each other, speaking infrequently between light kisses and caresses, simply basking in lovemaking's precious aftermath. Amy ran a cupped hand slowly up and down the muscular arm around her waist, her bemused gaze flitting over his beloved carved features, and she felt no regrets. Oh, she realized all too clearly that by accepting Jordon as a lover again she was taking quite a gamble. Yet she had to take the chance, didn't she? She loved him, needed him, longed for a future with him. And in this instance the old maxim certainly rang true: "Nothing ventured—nothing gained." She had made her decision and, tonight, her total commitment. It was too late to back out now. Not that she could worry about that anyway as she lay in the circle of his arm. The warm contentment that filled her overcame all doubts, at least for the time being.

When Jordon touched his lips to hers, she sleepily murmured his name and nestled her cheek against the arm supporting her head. Her eyelids started to flicker shut but only for a few short moments before she realized his hands wandering over her were beginning to convey a certain rearoused desire. She opened her eyes, watching as he traced the lines that denoted where her swimsuit began. He followed the mark above her breasts and then the ones around the tops of her thighs, where lightly tanned flesh met skin never touched by rays of the sun that was alabaster smooth and pearlescent in the soft light of the lamp.

He seemed so enthralled by his exploration. She discovered she was quite susceptible to it. Quickening sensations pulsated within her and she closed her fingers around his. "Jordon, you . . . I was right to call you a satyr. You're insatiable."

He simply gave one of his most sensuous smiles. "It's been too long since we've been together, Amy, and I'm not going to be able to let you go to sleep just yet. Do you mind?"

Her answering smile was just as sensuous as she shook her head. "I don't mind at all," she softly said. Yet when he started to pull her into his arms, she stopped him by placing her hands against his chest. There was something she had to say, although it was a blatant falsehood. She looked steadily into his eyes. "This time, Jordon, there can't be any strings attached. We're obviously very sexually compatible and we'll just enjoy that. You

163

won't expect anything from me and I won't expect anything from you. Agreed?"

"Amy, honey," he began huskily, shaking his head. "You don't have to—"

"That's the way I want it, Jordon," she lied valiantly, managing somehow to sound convincing. "It really is."

He didn't answer, but a piercing glint appeared in his eyes. She clasped her hands together around the back of his neck and drew him close, her lips brushing his, teasing, rubbing, inflaming his senses. With a muffled exclamation he pressed her down on the bed and his mouth closed around the tip of her left breast with warm pulling pressure. And Amy felt his smile upon her skin when she drew in a sharp, sibilant breath.

Much later when they merged together as one again, Jordon was no less tender a lover than he had been before, yet he took her with a commanding urgency that heightened her own desire to a frenzy. He transported her so swiftly to the highest spire of delight, and fulfillment was so incredibly razor edged, that afterward she lay trembling and spent, although wondrously replete, in his arms, almost immediately drifting toward sleep.

"You're mine again, Amy. No one else can have you," he suddenly whispered in her ear. "You belong to me."

Drowsily she burrowed her cheek into the hollow of his shoulder, a faint smile touching her lips. He hadn't needed to tell her that. She already knew it.

When Amy awakened a little after nine the next morning, Jordon still lay asleep beside her. She was surprised. He was habitually an early riser—at least he had been three years ago—while she was more inclined to snuggle cozily beneath the covers whenever she had an opportunity. Today, however, they had reversed roles, and as she sat up to look at him, she smiled reminiscently. Last night *had* been rather physically demanding, so she supposed he could use some extra sleep. Able to observe him freely, she swept her gaze over him. In sleep his clean-cut features relaxed, giving him a more youthful, even a more vulnerable, appearance. Fierce and abiding love for him overflowed in her, and with a hopeful sigh she kissed the slope of his shoulder exposed above the top of the sheet covering him, and slipped silently out of bed. Quiet as a mouse, she walked across the room to the adjoining bath to take a shower.

Nearly fifteen minutes later Amy eased the bathroom door open again, then realized she had no reason to try to be very quiet. She saw Jordon sitting up on the edge of the bed, watching her with a faint smile. She stepped into the bedroom, clad in the clover-colored terry robe, bare toes peeking out from beneath the hem.

"My, you're lazy today," she said, pausing by the dresser. "For once I managed to get out of bed before you did."

"Not exactly," he responded, grinning. "Much as I hate to burst your bubble, I have to tell you I was up two hours ago and went over to my quarters to shave. When I came back over here, you still weren't awake so I decided to go back to bed myself and fell asleep again."

Amy wrinkled her nose at him. "Oh. I thought . . . Well, why didn't you wake me up?"

His grin became a wickedly suggestive smile. "Considering last night, I thought you could use all the rest you could get."

She had to smile back. "Really? That's exactly why I thought you were sleeping late."

"I have more stamina than that."

"So do I."

"Do you, Amy?"

In answer she strolled over to the bed to stop in front of him, her gaze taking in his sun-browned torso above the white sheet flung around his waist. Lifting a hand, she danced her fingertips along his jaw. "Umm, you did shave, didn't you?"

"Just for you. I didn't think you'd care to wake up beside a man with over a day's worth of stubble on his face."

"That was sweet of you, Jordon, and since you went to that

much trouble . . ." she began suggestively but didn't finish. Instead she slowly undid the tie belt of her robe, leaving the rest to him.

He didn't disappoint her. His hands came out to push the lapels aside, opening the robe. His eyes roamed lazily all the way down to the tips of her toes and back up again. He gave her an easy, teasing smile. "And you accused me of being a satyr. Who's the insatiable one now, hmmm, Amy?"

With a nonchalant shrug, she stepped back, closing the robe and securing the tie. "Ah, well, if you're not interested . . . How about breakfast, then?" She started to move away.

"Come here, woman," he playfully growled, catching her by the wrist.

Slipping free of his light grip, she darted back, shaking her head. "Oh, no, Jordon, you had your chance and now it's too late."

"That's what you think," he murmured, his tone a warning, his expression conveying passionate intent and no small amount of mischief. Tossing the sheet covering him aside, he sprang up and stalked after her when she dashed across the room to seek refuge behind the easy chair. Moving with the fluid animal grace of a big powerful cat, he advanced toward her, the glint brightening in his eyes making them appear more tigerlike by the second. Early-morning light cast a coppery hue over his naked body, and when he stopped in front of the chair, he reminded Amy of a pagan god sculpted in bronze, except perhaps he wasn't quite as classically handsome. Still, he was formidably masculine, which aroused a responsive chord of utter femininity in her and caught her up in the adventure of this age-old man/woman scene that they had begun to play out. Excitement grew in her while he surveyed her through narrowed eyes. Then, without warning, he lunged toward her, but she was light on her feet and quick. With a soft cry of surprise she jumped back just beyond the reach of his hands and then darted past him to the other side of the room (although she suspected she made it by only because he allowed her to).

Watching him stride slowly in her direction in purposeful pursuit, she warily backed up toward the bathroom door, a crazy exhilarating little flutter commencing in the pit of her stomach while her heart skipped a beat or two and then began to thud faster. Even when he was playing, he was an impressive man, and the latent power conveyed by that long, subtly muscled body made her realize he could easily take what he wanted if it wasn't willingly given. Not that she could deny him anything; last night had proven she couldn't do that. Yet . . . Excitement bubbled up in her, sent a shiver coursing down her spine. Backing up against the doorjamb, she extended one hand, palm out, intending to halt him in his tracks.

"Jordon," she uttered breathlessly. "Stop right there."

Eyeing her wickedly, he continued to advance and shook his head. "You're right about one thing. It *is* too late . . . for you. You've trapped yourself against the wall and now you're the prisoner of my lustful nature. And I don't intend to let you out of this room until I've had my way with you."

Fighting a smile, Amy threw the back of her hand up against her forehead and pretended to swoon. "Oh, sir, you don't mean . . ."

"I do mean," he whispered provocatively, stepping close enough to reach out, untie her belt, and toss open her robe with a cavalier grin. His gaze raked mercilessly over her naked body. "Ah ha, now you're mine to do with as I please."

His hands spanned her waist and when his fingers began to move, tickling her sensitive skin, Amy was surprised to find herself giggling. She hadn't giggled in quite a long time, but it was nice to do so again, and as the gentle rib-tickling went on and on, she began laughing helplessly.

"*Stop!* You know . . . th-that makes . . . me . . . crazy," she gasped, scarcely able to make herself coherent. "Don't, Jordon, I . . ."

"I could make you beg for mercy," he teased, pressing his fingertips along her sides at strategic points to make her squirm and laugh even harder. "But I won't do that. Instead I'll let you bargain. What will you give me to make me stop?"

"Y-you *devil* . . . anything!"

His answering smile was villainously victorious. "*Anything?*"

"You . . . know I will, if you'll just stop. *Jordon!*"

His fingers immediately stilled. His hands tightened around her waist and suddenly he hauled her to him, the expression on his hard-planed face convincingly hedonistic. "You've got a deal, Amy. But at what cost to you?"

"I don't know exactly," she countered, catching her breath while tilting her head back to look straight up at him. "Suppose you tell me."

"You innocent, can't you guess?" He swept the robe off her shoulders, removed it completely, then tossed it halfway across the room behind him while his gaze moved possessively over her. He trailed his hands up to the rounded sides of her breasts and back down into the curve of her waist again, then outward over the gentle swell of her hips. "I'll tell you, then: it's you I want, all of you, right now. Come here, wench."

Giggling again, Amy pretended to hang back and drag her feet while he pulled her toward the bed, and when he sat down on the edge and drew her between his thighs, the laughter that danced in her eyes lighted her face. Standing before him, looking down, she tried to arrange her features in somber, uncertain lines. "Oh, you're frightening me," she said in a small, contrived voice. "What is it you want to do with me, sir?"

"Everything. We'll do everything together."

"Oh, no! Oh, sir, I couldn't let—"

"You made a bargain," Jordon murmured dangerously despite his unmistakably amused gaze. "And now you have to honor it."

Amy suddenly relaxed in his hands. She shrugged. "I guess

you're right," she admitted lightly. "A lady should keep her word at all times."

Jordon softly chuckled. "You won't regret your decision, I promise."

"I think you're probably right," she confessed as he drew her down to cradle her in his arms. He smoothed the sun-gilded hair back from her face, and looking up into his, she shook her head. "We're crazy, Jordon. Do you know that? We're acting like a couple of teen-agers who've just discovered sex."

"I wouldn't say that. Oh, we may be just as obsessed, but I'm sure we know more than teen-agers do about making the pleasure last," he whispered into her ear. "And since it's Sunday, I may keep you in this bed all day to prove that."

"And we may die of sheer exhaustion in the process," she retorted, but drew in a sharp breath when he sought the curve of her breast with his lips. Yet, after he'd tumbled her onto the bed and rolled over above her, she realized this was her chance to get even. She fluttered her fingertips across the flat, taut surface of his abdomen, probing here, caressing there, giving him back a little of his own medicine, and when he laughed aloud, trying to escape her touch, she smiled impishly. "You seem to have some ticklish spots yourself, Mr. Kent. Maybe you started something you shouldn't have."

"Minx," he uttered, his voice gravelly. "I think you need to be taught a lesson or two."

Amy laughed merrily when he flipped onto his back on the mattress, pulling her over him, but her laughter ceased and so did his as his hands spanned her rib cage and he lifted her to close his mouth around the rose-tipped crest of one firm, full breast. Suddenly everything was different. Mutual teasing was replaced by mutual passion, passion that erupted with volcanic fury to burn into both of them with blazing ferocity.

"Jordon," she said, sighing tremulously. "Oh, Jordon, yes."

"Amy, *honey*," he whispered, rough urgency edging his voice. His lips and his teeth and his tongue ravished the aroused erect

169

nub of one nipple, then the other, before his hands dropped down to squeeze her buttocks. He positioned her above him, his legs slipping between hers to coax them apart. Then he claimed her, but with a fierce need so tempered by tenderness that his possession was nearly a form of worship.

Settling down upon him, Amy softly sighed, "Oh, Jordon," accepting the gentle invasion of his virile body in a relentless maelstrom of ecstasy. She hadn't realized she was so ready for this intimate union between them, but now she knew she had been, perhaps from the moment she had left the bath after her shower and found him sitting up in bed awaiting her return. Joy borne of love sang out in her. The shining curtain of her hair falling forward to veil her cheeks, she lay over him, feeling the guiding touch of his hands upon her hips as she slowly began to rotate them against him.

Wild sensation ran rampant over her, so soon, so exquisitely, that she felt she would surely melt in the swiftly spreading flames of loving desire. Hotter and hotter, delight doubled and redoubled, possessing her completely, hurling her into a raging physical and emotional tempest far beyond her control. The shallow tremors that radiated from her very center began to ripple outward in widening, deepening circles and she was flying upward, ever upward . . .

Until suddenly Jordon stopped moving, holding her still against him, wrapping his arms securely around her, soothing her by stroking her back. "Not yet, Amy," he murmured, brushing a kiss over her temple. "Very soon but not quite yet." Quivering, she relaxed upon him, her breathing ragged while the ripples within her abated in intensity to some extent, although her anticipation climbed. And when Jordon began moving again, she met his long, rousing strokes with ardent welcome.

They made love slowly, languidly, heightening mutual delight in gradual measure, prolonging sweet intimacy and experiencing its most poignant levels together until, at last, Amy's sinuous superheated motion dissolved the remnants of his self-control.

Groaning, he bore her up swiftly to the keen apex of ecstasy and joined her there, whispering her name again and again against her lips as they floated together back down to earth.

Considerably later Amy lay dozing in his embrace, a contented smile curving her lips as he weaved his fingers through her gloriously tangled hair, smoothing it back.

"I don't want this to be just a one-time thing, Amy, and I don't think you do, either," he abruptly murmured. "So I'll be staying with you tonight, too. In fact, when you think about it, we might as well share these quarters. Why don't I just move in over here?"

"W-ell, we'll see," she drawled, trying to sound anything but eager despite the burst of hope that bloomed in her heart. Obviously he wanted more from her than a few one-night stands. And while his desire to live with her wasn't exactly a firm commitment, it was, at the very least, a possible beginning.

CHAPTER TEN

Amy looked up from the tiny sweater she was knitting for a cousin's new baby. Next to her on the sofa, Jordon sat back perusing the contents of the file folder he held in one hand. A light frown marked his brow and he raked his fingers through his hair. He was frustrated with the burglary investigation, which was proceeding at a snail's pace. Although he constantly pored over reports, old and new, and followed up on even the slimmest of leads, he was making little progress, and that was a source of great aggravation to him. Amy knew that. Watching him, she smiled faintly. He really was a lovably intense man, especially lovable because he never directed his frustration toward her. Although it was obvious he was highly committed to his work, he could separate it from his relationship with her and was therefore attentive and tender and even affectionate. She could believe now he was genuinely fond of her. Of course, fondness wasn't abiding love, but it was a step in the right direction. And viewing it in that light, she had been happy the past twelve days. Living with Jordon allowed her to achieve a closeness to him that enabled her to know him better and better. And the knowledge she acquired merely served to deepen her love. Perhaps she was getting in over her head, but she had known that might be the case when she'd decided she must do her utmost to gain what she wanted. The entire situation frequently reminded her of an old proverb: *Nothing too easy is very worthwhile.* Well, winning Jordon's love promised to be no easy, simple task but if she succeeded, she suspected it would be even more worthwhile than she presently allowed herself to imagine. He had become such an incredibly wonderful person. Watching him interact with the boys at the home proved that to her beyond a shadow of doubt. Besides, he was so tender with her now that she thought if he could actually love her someday, she would become one of the luckiest, happiest women in the world. Of course the very strength of her need for him created an underlying tension that was always with her. Knowing how happy she could be if he ever did love her made the thought that he might not nearly unbearable, so she avoided thinking that way as much as she could. Besides, as long as she went on concealing the depths of her feelings from him, she wouldn't scare him away as she had three years ago. And the longer he stayed with her, considering how close they were in many ways, the more likely it was that eventually he would fall in love.

Chanting that comforting idea to herself, she turned her attention back to the sweater which she was knitting in a rather intricate design she wasn't too familiar with. She concentrated, not wanting to drop a stitch. And it wasn't until several minutes later that she looked up to find Jordon sailing the folder toward the coffee table, where it landed and slid a few inches across the polished top amid muffled but explicit oaths.

Amy regarded him sympathetically. "Nothing new, I presume?"

Thoughtfully he tapped his steepled fingers against his chin, shrugged, and grimaced. "That's the problem. There's nothing of great importance in that report at all, but something about it bothers me. And I can't figure out what it is, no matter how many times I read it."

"Maybe you should just put it aside for the time being and go back to it later," she suggested. "It might do some good to take your mind off the investigation for a while—so let's talk about anything else. How about some coffee?"

"Good idea, but I'll get it, since you're busy," he insisted, glancing at the half-finished sweater in her lap. Then he rose to his feet and strode into the kitchen, as at home in her quarters now as she was.

He returned several minutes later with two mugs, one of which he handed to her. As she laid the sweater aside, he grinned. "If you're making that for me, by any chance, you're a little off on the size. Shouldn't it be a little larger?"

"Not for a newborn baby, and besides, I just don't see pale pink as your color."

"Then it's *not* for me?" Pretending to be hurt, he settled down next to her on the sofa, closer this time. "I'm disappointed, Amy."

Giving him a sidelong glance, she smiled. "Is that a hint for me to knit you a sweater, Jordon?"

"I wouldn't mind."

"A pink one?"

"Well, maybe some other color would suit me better," he admitted wryly, stretching out his long legs. "Something in navy would be nice."

"I'll think about it," she replied noncommittally. Knitting him a sweater could be construed as a gesture made by a woman who wanted to be a wife, and that certainly was not the impression she wanted to give, since it touched too close to the truth. But then, he had made the request and she really would enjoy making something for him, so maybe she *would* do it. Besides, playing the part of Miss Super Cool was beginning to wear on her nerves sometimes. She loved him and wanted to be able to say so, but the memory of all the hurt she had suffered kept her silent. She could only wait and hope and pray that this time he could come to love her, too. That was the game of chance she had decided to play, and she had to stick by her self-imposed rules, even if there were many moments when she no longer wanted to. Now that she had come this far, it would be foolish not to go all the way, and as she gazed at him over the rim of the mug raised to her lips, she knew that the mere possibility that he might begin to love and need her as much as she loved and needed him was worth anything she had to do.

"You went over to see the boys today, didn't you?" Jordon asked, interrupting her reverie. "How's everything going with them?"

A fond but wry smile danced over her lips. "They're all fine, but Terry's going a little crazy. He says they're out on the playground from the minute they get back from school, and he has to practically round them up like cattle and drive them inside for dinner. And I can believe it. I went over this evening because Joey was very worried about a math test he has tomorrow. But when I got there, he wasn't acting the least bit worried. In fact, he was out on the court practicing those layups you taught them Saturday. I had to do some fast talking to get him back inside to study."

Observing her closely, Jordon reached over to touch her, rubbing the back of one hand slowly up and down over her cheek. "You really care about that kid, don't you, Amy?"

"Sure, I care about all the boys. But you're right, Joey is one of my favorites." Her voice softened, as did her features. "There's something . . . well, just special about him. He's so warm and loving and he tries so hard at everything he does and wants so very much to please. You just have to love him. It's a shame in a way that he only came into the home about six months ago. If he were younger, he'd be adopted so fast—but he's nine and people tend to shy away from older children. They don't know what they're missing."

Jordon moved closer to her on the cushion. "Have you ever thought you might have missed your true calling? You'd be terrific working with children."

"I guess I haven't really ever thought about it seriously because I enjoy what I do here," she answered honestly. "And besides, I think I'd probably get too emotionally involved if I worked with homeless children full time. I might do them more harm than good."

Shaking his head, Jordon cupped her jaw in one hand. "How could the love you would give ever harm them? Amy, you're so . . ." he began, then broke off with a rueful smile when Skeeter pounced up from the floor to land squarely in his lap, her motorboat purring already going strong as her big round eyes stared at him expectantly. For a brief time he lightly scratched her arching back; then he gently lowered her back onto the floor, despite her meowing protest. "Sorry, cat, I'll have to get back to you later. Right now I'm much more interested in stroking your mistress's back."

"I'm not sure I'll ever understand you," Amy confessed, laughing softly as his hands encompassed her waist and he started to pull her to him. "Now you have *this* on your mind, while only a few minutes ago you were all wrapped up in those new reports you got today, certain there was a clue in them you were missing."

Jordon tensed, drew back from her, and snapped his fingers. "Damn, I just thought of something. It might not mean anything, but . . ." He grimaced apologetically. "Would you mind

175

very much if I ran up to my office to check out something in my files? I have an idea that might—"

"Oh, go," she commanded good-naturedly, waving him toward the door with a flick of her wrist. "Never accuse me of standing in the way of an investigation."

"I'll be back as soon as possible," he promised.

Watching him leave, Amy shook her head, smiling wryly. In some ways he hadn't changed—he still couldn't resist a mystery and was as determined as ever to solve any that he came across. But in a much more important way he was different—tonight when he returned, he would put business completely out of his mind and concentrate exclusively on her. And that very realization gave her hope.

At eleven thirty, when Jordon still hadn't returned from his office, Amy went to bed without him. Worn out by a long, hard day, she fell asleep almost immediately and only partly awoke some time later when Jordon slipped in beneath the covers beside her. She turned toward him, murmuring contentedly as his strong muscular arms wrapped around her.

She was awakened by kisses that grazed her temples, then the center of her forehead, and finally her lips. Sighing softly, she wriggled down farther beneath the covers, never one to give up sleep easily.

Sitting on the edge of the bed, bending over her, Jordon avidly explored her appealing small face framed by sun-kissed hair. He kissed her again. "Amy, wake up, love," he whispered. "Amy."

With a drowsy smile she stirred, stretching lazily, then turned onto her left side to squint at the alarm clock on the bedside table. Moaning, she burrowed her face into the pillow. "It's only six thirty," she murmured sleepily. "I don't have to get up until seven."

"I know. But, Amy, I've just had a call from Alexandria. There's a crisis in the main office and I have to get there as soon as I can," Jordon quietly explained. "Ted Preston will act as security chief while I'm gone and I'll be back as soon as possible."

"A-Alexandria?" she breathed, coming fully awake, a sudden aching constriction painfully grabbing her chest. Her heart began to thud heavily as she opened her eyes to meet his. "You're . . . leaving?"

"Only for a few days," he muttered, his lips touching hers in a good-bye kiss. "And I'll call you tonight. You'll be here?"

"Y-yes," she managed to say despite the strangling tightness that squeezed her throat. And after watching him walk out of the bedroom and out of sight, she burrowed her face into the pillow with a muffled cry. *He said he would be back in a few days.* Yet she couldn't help remembering three years ago. His dedication to his agency had made him forget her then. It could again. And it was only sheer strength of will that prevented the hot stinging tears that gathered behind her eyes from flowing.

Wednesday evening, seven days later, Amy opened the outside door and entered the foyer, smiling when T. J. Preston, Ted's fourteen-month-old son, toddled out of the quarters his parents were occupying since Jordon was away. Despite his halting steps, he was quick and was soon several feet away from the doorway he had exited, an exhilarated, rather damp smile lighting his chubby little face. Stepping sideways, Amy headed him off, then swooped him up in her arms just as his somewhat harried mother, Kathleen, bounded out of the quarters after him.

"Oh, thanks, Amy," she said, coming to collect her runaway with a resigned shaking of her head. "I swear, that baby keeps me running from morning till night. I think he may grow up to be the fastest thing on two feet someday."

"A future Olympic track champion," Amy said, relinquishing T. J. into Kathleen's arms, where he wriggled, squirmed, and made impatient grunting noises, wanting to be put back down. "He is a handful, isn't he? A real bundle of energy."

"I think that might be something of an understatement,"

177

Kathleen replied, struggling to hold on to her small son while walking back toward her quarters. She inclined her head toward the doorway. "Come in and have a glass of the iced tea I just made."

Amy gladly accepted the invitation. "Sounds great."

"Just the thing to beat the heat, and it sure has been a hot one today, hasn't it?"

"Umm, hot and horribly muggy."

"And you look tired," Kathleen commented, shutting the door behind them after they had entered her sitting room. Releasing T. J., she watched with a sigh of relief as he scooted toward a stack of plastic building blocks instead of heading for the bookcase where three or four volumes he had preciously removed still lay on the floor. She turned back to Amy, her gaze sympathetic as she obviously noticed the faintly darker circles beneath her eyes. "A hard day in the office?"

"About the same as usual—too much to do and not enough time to do all of it. I think the heat's just beginning to get to me a little," Amy answered, not adding that she hadn't slept well since Jordon had gone away. "But the weather's affecting everyone like that."

"Everyone except T. J. Nothing slows him down," his mother said wryly, motioning Amy toward a chair. "Sit and I'll get the tea."

Five minutes later the two young women were engaged in conversation while sipping the refreshing freshly brewed tea from ice-filled glasses. Glancing around the sitting room, Amy noticed a few of the Prestons' possessions scattered about, none of which seemed to have found its proper place, no doubt because of the impermanence of the situation. She returned her gaze to Kathleen. "I guess you and Ted are looking forward to getting back to your own house again?"

"Well, there really is no place like home," the other woman conceded, tugging at a strand of her short auburn hair. "But I'm certainly glad I decided to come stay with Ted here. I would've missed him so much if I hadn't and besides, staying here is sort of like a vacation for T. J. and me. We go for walks in the gardens, and every day I take him down to the beach. Surprisingly enough I don't have to spend all my time chasing him across the sand. He's fascinated with the surf and will actually sit still in it for a pretty long time, giggling when the water rushes in over his legs. And of course, he's just in love with your cat, although I'm not sure she's all that fond of him."

Amy softly laughed. "Oh, I'm sure Skeeter likes him, too; she just likes to play hard to get." Her expression sobered. "Maybe it's a good thing you and Ted aren't minding your stay here too much, because when Jordon called today, he said he might be in Alexandria a couple more days. Of course, he's been saying 'only a couple more days' since the weekend, so who knows how long it will be?"

"As long as he needs us here, we'll be glad to stay. There isn't much Ted and I wouldn't do for Jordon Kent," Kathleen said in all sincerity. "He's such a fine man. He gave Ted a chance when no one else would. Ted's a Vietnam vet, you see, and he couldn't get a job anywhere until Jordon opened the agency in Norfolk and did the hiring of the staff himself. He said he was proud to hire Ted, and now he's allowing Ted to act as security chief here. We'll never be able to thank him for all the help he's given us."

"I know he realizes what a hardworking, conscientious employee Ted is," Amy assured her. "He speaks very highly of him. And I imagine Jordon makes it a policy to employ veterans mainly because they deserve special consideration after serving their country, and not just because he was in Vietnam himself."

Kathleen's brown eyes opened wider and round with astonishment. "Jordon was in Vietnam?" she softly exclaimed, shaking her head as Amy nodded hers. "But . . . he's never once mentioned that."

"It's not something he talks about much at all. He just mentioned it to me in passing, but he didn't offer any details about

179

the year he spent there. All I know is that he wasn't sure what he wanted to do with himself when he left high school and decided to postpone college a year, which turned into a two-year Army stint instead because he was drafted."

"We had no idea," Kathleen mused. "But then, he is a very quiet man, at least where his personal life is concerned, don't you think? I mean, he's very friendly and outgoing, but there seem to be things he keeps to himself. He's had dinner with us a couple of times and I had the oddest feeling that he's sort of a lonely man."

"Lonely?" Pensively Amy poked the topmost piece of ice in her glass with the tip of her little finger and watched it bob up and down. Her shoulders rose and fell in an uncertain shrug. "I'm not sure Jordon has time to be lonely. He's so . . . involved in his agency."

"Oh, I know that, but business isn't everything."

"To some men it's enough. Jordon may be one of them," Amy murmured, then decided it was too painful to discuss her doubts about him any longer, even with Kathleen, who had no idea how much he meant to her. After taking a few more long sips of her tea, she placed the glass on the coaster atop the table by her chair and rose to her feet, smoothing the skirt of her tan suit while giving her hostess an appreciative smile. "Thanks for the tea; it was delicious. But I'd better be going now. I think I may try to cool off some more by going for a swim."

"And I'd better check on dinner. Ted should be coming in any minute," Kathleen announced, automatically glancing over to check on her adventurous son, who, incredibly, was still haphazardly playing with his blocks. With a smile she accompanied Amy to the door. "After your swim, why don't you come have dinner with us? We'd love to have you."

"Thank you for asking, but could I have a rain check?" Amy asked, feeling the need for solitude at the moment. "I have the makings for shrimp salad remoulade waiting in my refrigerator, and I'm afraid the shrimp won't keep until tomorrow. And considering the price I paid for it, I can't afford to let it go to waste."

"Wow, isn't that the truth," Kathleen concurred wholeheartedly, promising Amy the rain check for dinner as she walked out the door.

Giving herself little time to think, Amy rushed into her quarters, stripped off her clothes and, after getting into her swimsuit, hurried out along the short path that led to the beach. The water was unusually calm and she stayed in, swimming energetically, until her arms and legs began aching from overexertion. Yet, despite that attempt to wear herself out physically, she felt no less tense nearly an hour later when she returned to her quarters for a shower and shampoo. Afterwards she prepared dinner while listening to Skeeter plaintively beg for tidbits of shrimp. She served the cat a tiny portion, then sat down at the table. Luckily her long swim had piqued her appetite enough to allow her to do justice to the meal. She even hummed to herself while clearing the table, but some minutes later, as she was washing the last of the dishes, she was no longer able to escape the intensifying loneliness she had been feeling since Jordon had left for Alexandria. Now she was beginning to wonder if he would ever return to St. Tropez Run. After all, there had been no burglaries committed in the two weeks prior to his departure and none since he'd been away; perhaps he felt his presence was no longer necessary here and was bored with the entire investigation. Perhaps he had once again become caught up in the excitement of directing all the varied investigations Security Unlimited handled, and maybe he would never return.

Discarding her apron, Amy wandered into the sitting room, berating herself for even considering such a possibility. She should be more confident, but self-confidence wasn't that easy to achieve. She couldn't help recalling that Jordon had chosen the agency over her before—that the same thing could happen all over again. Self-confidence is relative to past experiences, and assured as she might be in all other aspects of her life, she felt quite insecure where Jordon was concerned. The hurt she had experienced in the past could not be erased entirely from her memory, and she was afraid she had set herself up for inevitable pain once again.

Yet she had known what she was doing, had known the risks. Telling herself that, she sank down in the easy chair opposite the sofa, tucked her legs up, and wrapped her arms around them. Sighing tremulously, she gnawed at a fingernail and stared blindly across the room. The fact that she had walked with her eyes open into Jordon's arms once more provided little solace right now. She was afraid. Even a gamble entered into willingly can become very frightening when the possibility of losing looms larger with every passing day, every passing minute, every passing second. Jordon had called her three times in the past week, but each time he had been rushed and only able to speak to her briefly. And every time he postponed his return to St. Tropez Run, her heart had grown a little heavier. She loved him too much, needed him with her too badly, and what if his agency was luring him away from her again? What if he never came back to her? *What if . . . What if . . . What if . . .* Such tormenting questions chased one another incessantly in her head, and she could find no answer for any of them. She still didn't regret taking the chance she had taken, yet she hadn't really prepared herself for the possibility of losing Jordon again. This time she had meant to win but now had to face her growing doubts that it would turn out the way she had planned. The longer Jordon stayed in Alexandria, the more her hopes dimmed, and it was becoming increasingly difficult for her to square her shoulders, stiffen her spine, and remind herself that the game hadn't ended irrevocably yet.

But, curled up in the chair, she tried valiantly to do so just that one more time and nearly succeeded—until Skeeter pounced up onto her lap, seeking a scratching, but continued to meow loud and long even as Amy's fingers moved over her back.

"Oh, I guess I don't scratch you as hard as Jordon does, do

I? You miss him, too, don't you?" Amy muttered and, with the words, for some crazy reason, the tears she had suppressed far too long began to flow. She turned her face into the back of the chair as they cascaded in hot rivulets down her cheeks and silent sobs shook her shoulders.

And the cat, never having seen her mistress cry before, didn't seem to know what to make of the situation. Tilting her head to one side, she observed Amy with curious round green eyes. Then, apparently, sheer animal instinct prompted her to nuzzle her bewhiskered face against Amy's arm and hopefully meow.

CHAPTER ELEVEN

Amy was dressing to go to the office Friday morning when someone knocked loudly, rapidly, urgently, on her door. Buttoning her gray skirt over a white blouse and raising the zipper, she hurried from her bedroom across the parlor to the door. She jerked it open, and her blue eyes widened with surprise.

"Kathleen, what—"

"Ted just got a call and rushed right out, Amy," the other woman began, pulling her chenille robe more securely around her tall, slim body. "But he knew you'd want to know, so . . ."

"Know what?" Amy questioned rather sleepily, never at her best until after a second cup of coffee. "What's going on? I don't under—"

"Another burglary," Kathleen told her excitedly. "Last night sometime. At the Warner house."

"Warner?" Amy repeated vaguely, knowing no family with that name resided in St. Tropez Run. Then realization struck. "You mean the Warrens?"

Kathleen nodded vigorously. "Yes, that's the right name. I knew it was something like that."

"Oh, hell," Amy muttered, plowing her fingers through her hair. "And I was beginning to hope our 'King of Diamonds' had given up on breaking in houses here since Security Unlimited took over patrolling the place. Did he leave his calling card behind this time, too?"

"I don't really know. Ted answered the phone, jumped into his uniform, and ran out without telling me anything except to come over here and let you know what had happened because he thought you'd want to know."

"He was right. Thanks for coming over, Kath," Amy said. "And since all hell is breaking loose again, I'd better get up to my office as fast as I can."

Less than five minutes later Amy was presented with even worse news. While unlocking her office door, Ted Preston bounded into the reception area, his face tightly drawn, his lips pressed grimly together. Amy spun around to face him.

"Have you heard?" he asked.

"About the Warrens? Yes, Kathleen—"

"No, that's not what I mean. That's only the half of it," Ted replied, a deep frown furrowing his brow. "There were two burglaries last night, Amy."

"*Two?*" she gasped. "But . . ."

"After Fletcher Warren got up and realized his house had been broken into, he called Sam Wilson at the gate, who called me. *Then* Warren called one of his neighbors, and soon all the telephone wires around here were buzzing. When Malcolm Winters woke up to the news, he got up to look around his own house and discovered it had been burglarized, too." Ted slapped a hand against one thigh. "Damn, two in one night."

"Any clues?"

"None I could find. The sheriff's department is sending a deputy over right now but I doubt he'll find anything, either, except those two damned King of diamond playing cards. And while I'm waiting for him to get here, I thought I'd better give Jordon a call in Alexandria. He has to know what's happening."

"Yes. You have to call him," Amy said, turning to walk into her office, relieved to leave the task to him. Much as she wanted Jordon to return to St. Tropez Run, she hadn't wanted him to have to come back for something like this.

Early that same afternoon Amy was carefully checking the maintenance bills for the preceding month when Trudy knocked once on her door, then peeked inside, a disturbed expression on her face.

"There are some people here to see you," she rather worriedly announced. "Some of the residents who want to talk about the burglaries. I told them you were very busy, so . . ."

"It's okay," Amy said, sighing inwardly. She had half expected this visit and decided it was useless to postpone something she would eventually have to face anyway. Pushing the stack of bills aside, she nodded at the receptionist. "Please show them in, Trudy."

And in they came, Trevor Meade leading the way, followed by Candace Lancaster, William Marshall, and Clement Aldrich, with Renn Bushnell at the rear. Amy walked around the desk to greet them. Trudy returned with extra chairs, and after everyone was settled, Amy, too, sat back down and leaned forward. "I understand you're here to discuss the burglaries."

"Yes. We're representing all the residents of St. Tropez Run and we came here to tell you that something must be done about this situation, Miss Sinclair," Trevor Meade announced politely but very firmly. "Coastal Realty does have an obligation to this community. We were promised security, but that, obviously, is sadly lacking. One burglary was shocking enough, but seven of them, two in one night . . ." Clicking his tongue against the back of his teeth, he shook his head. "Intolerable, Miss Sinclair, intolerable. Everyone is upset and tense, wondering whose house might be hit next. All of us expected to have peace of mind when we moved here, but we certainly don't have that now. And it's Coastal Realty's responsibility to provide the tranquility we were promised. You represent Coastal, and we came to lodge a formal complaint on behalf of the entire community."

"I understand how upset and frustrated you must be," Amy replied in all sincerity. "And I wish I had a quick, easy solution for our problem. Unfortunately I don't have, but I want to assure you that Coastal Realty is aware of its obligation to this community and is doing everything possible to put a stop to these break-ins and to catch the person or persons responsible for them."

" 'Everything possible' doesn't seem to be nearly enough," William Marshall offered grimly, his arms clasped across his chest as he glowered at Amy. "This burglar is having so much luck in St. Tropez Run, there's no reason for him to quit and move on until he's hit every house here. He certainly doesn't seem to have to worry about being caught, and I wouldn't be surprised if he was somewhere laughing right now at the inept security forces that supposedly protect this community."

"Mr. Marshall, Security Unlimited has the reputation of being one of the best, perhaps *the* best, security agencies on the East Coast," Amy informed him calmly, clasping her hands together, her arms resting atop her desk. "And I'm sure the owner of the agency and the people who work for him didn't gain that good reputation by being inept. It just seems we're dealing with a very wily criminal in this situation, and wily ones are simply not that easy to catch."

"Well, he's wily, all right, and brazen, too, for that matter. Two break-ins in one night," Clement Aldrich remarked, rubbing the side of his nose. "Next he'll try burglarizing one of us in broad daylight."

"I doubt he'd want to take that chance. Jordon Kent, chief of security—I think you've all met him—believes we're dealing

186

with a professional burglar, a very self-confident one, but not one foolhardy enough to take chances," Amy told the delegation. "If he's as experienced as it seems, he probably believes he knows all the tricks to avoid being caught."

"How is anyone going to catch him, then?" Candace Lancaster softly exclaimed, nervously worrying the heavy intricately engraved gold bangle bracelet on her arm as if expecting it to be snatched from her at any moment. "If the burglar is invincible . . ."

"Not invincible, Mrs. Lancaster," Amy hastened to explain. "And it could very well be that his excessive self-confidence will prove to be his downfall. Mr. Kent says all criminals make mistakes eventually, especially if they feel they're infallible. This one—or maybe it's more than one person—will slip up sooner or later."

"This one hasn't made a mistake yet," Renn Bushnell spoke up, contributing to the discussion for the first time while sadly shaking his head. "Maybe he *is* invincible. Or maybe they are, if more than one person is involved."

"If that's true, everyone in the community will be robbed before he stops!"

"No one could be invincible if we had adequate security!"

"I don't understand how this is happening in the first place!"

"But if he's invincible, then we're helpless!"

All these comments were made at once, and as the babble of excited voices threatened to go on, Amy lifted a calming hand. "I know this is very difficult for everybody, but we all may just have to be patient a while longer. I know that Mr. Kent has been investigating this case thoroughly and will surely come up with an answer very soon."

"Well, very soon isn't good enough, Miss Sinclair," Marshall spat out brusquely, stiffening in his chair. "We want this problem solved now. We've run out of patience. None of us sank small fortunes into these homes to be harassed continually by the criminal element. We were courted and wined and dined by

187

Coastal Realty and promised total security and, by God, that's a promise we want kept."

"He's right, dear," Mrs. Lancaster agreed, nodding vigorously, though her expression warmed a bit as she looked at Amy. "Bennett and I did buy here mainly because we found the idea of tight security reassuring, but now we're becoming very disillusioned. And I'm afraid Coastal isn't going to placate us with rumors that you're going to be replaced. How silly. None of us holds you responsible for what's happening, so what good could it possibly do to replace you? No, we want this burglar caught or at the very least the break-ins stopped."

Although Amy had suspected more than once that she might be made a scapegoat in this situation, hearing that possibility spoken aloud by someone else stunned her. Yet she masked her reaction with a rueful smile and a casual toss of one hand. "I have to confess I haven't heard that particular rumor until now."

Candace Lancaster blushed slightly. "Oh, my dear, I didn't mean to—"

"The point, Miss Sinclair, is that you should tell your superiors at Coastal that we aren't going to be satisfied by any ridiculous purely symbolic gestures," Marshall interrupted, his face florid now. "We've had enough of this preposterous situation. Several people are considering selling their homes here and getting out before property values suffer tremendous losses, and I don't mind saying I'm one of those seriously thinking that way. And if we're forced to do that, it's highly probable that we'll take legal action against Coastal for misrepresentation. You tell them that."

"I'll relay your message," Amy calmly said. "Unless you'd like to relay it yourselves. Naturally, I called Evan Price as soon as I heard about last night's burglaries and he'll be arriving here later this afternoon. Perhaps you'd like to speak to him personally?"

"We most certainly would," Marshall answered sharply. "When he arrives, give me a call and he can come meet all of us at my house. And I advise you to warn him we're not willing to listen to meaningless platitudes. As I told you before and I'm telling you again, we want these break-ins to end immediately. In other words we want fast results instead of worthless promises. You do understand that?"

"Maybe you should be talking to me instead," a deep voice suddenly spoke out, surprising everyone, since the door had been opened noiselessly. Trim and tall in crisp khaki uniform, Jordon strode into the office, glancing at Amy before focusing his full attention on William Marshall, apparently self-appointed spokesman for the five-person delegation. He coolly inclined his head. "I see no reason for you to discuss security with Miss Leighton. That's not her responsibility. It's mine, and I'll be happy to answer your questions if you have any."

"Oh, indeed we do, Mr. Kent. We have quite a few," Marshall began.

But Amy tuned the rest of his words out while her gaze lingered on Jordon. She had never been so glad to see anyone in her life as she was to see him right then. Or was she? The moment after joy bloomed in her chest, conflicting emotions began pulling at her. Part of her was ecstatic because he was here, while another part (perhaps common sense) was plagued with dreadful doubts. If she could have believed he had returned to St. Tropez Run simply because he couldn't stand to be without her, she could have known a happiness more intense than any she had ever before experienced. But deep inside she knew better than that. He hadn't felt the need to return to her for over a week. It had taken two burglaries in one night to bring him back here, and for her, that realization made all the difference.

Early that evening Amy walked slowly across her sitting room to answer the knock on her door. It was Jordon waiting out in the foyer; she knew it because Ted and Kathleen Preston had already said good-bye to her before departing for home, since Jordon was reassuming his position of security chief at St.

Tropez Run. So it had to be Jordon who was knocking, and despite all her misgivings, she forced herself to open the door, assuming a casual expression as she did so.

In one long stride Jordon entered the sitting room. He took Amy into his arms and kissed her. "Amy," he whispered, his kiss deepening as she pressed closer to him.

Despite her confused state of mind she could resist neither his embrace nor his kisses. The need to touch him and be touched ran so deeply in her now that it almost frightened her to realize how much she was beginning to depend upon him once again. She was going to be hurt if she ultimately lost this gamble, but, then, she had known all along that that was the risk she was taking, and as long as she was able to conceal the depth of her feelings from him, she at least retained some control over the situation. Mentally reminding herself of that fact, she broke off the kiss that was swiftly becoming more impassioned, and instead lightly touched her lips to his cheek then stepped back out of his arms.

"Welcome back . . . I guess," she made herself quip, leading the way to the sofa and smiling blithely as they both sat down. "Unless I've become a suspect again because of the break-ins last night. After all, nothing happened for two weeks before you left here, and since I'm the only person besides your men who knows you don't just work for Unlimited—you own the agency—and since I know how determined you are solve this case, maybe I just waited to pull off another burglary while you were gone when I was less likely to be caught. Under those circumstances I suppose it's reasonable for you to be a little suspicious of me."

Grinning, Jordon shook his head. "I think it's safe enough to scratch your name off my list of possible suspects, Amy."

"You're sure?" she countered wryly. "I *could* be the head of a burglary ring. You know, sort of the Ma Barker of St. Tropez Run."

His answering chuckle was deeply resonant. "You're not mean enough to be the Ma Barker type."

"It's nice to know you're starting to have some real faith in my ethics," she replied, but her grin slowly faded. "I've only seen glimpses of you all afternoon, Jordon, when you were either hurrying in or out of your office with the deputy sheriff and Ted. So tell me, any clues from last night's burglaries that you can follow up on?"

"Nothing besides those two playing cards, *except* a personal message for me left at the Warren house."

"Personal message! What did it say?"

" 'Better luck next time, Mr. Kent.' "

" *'Better luck next time'*? That's all?"

"That's it."

"But the note itself should provide you with some clues, shouldn't it? I mean, even if it was typed, all typewriters are different and can be traced."

"Unfortunately our 'friend' is perfectly aware of that fact," Jordon told her, his lips thinning to a grim line. "He composed the note on standard stock note paper with the words cut from magazines, and I'm sure he was smart enough to get rid of the magazines he used immediately. And they found no fingerprints on the note at the sheriff's department. Just another dead end."

"But if he addressed it to you personally, do you think that might mean he knows you own Security Unlimited?"

"I think that's probably exactly what it means. And I assume you haven't told anyone the truth about me?"

"Nobody at all," Amy said. "Oh, I've almost let it slip out a couple of times but remembered in the nick of time to clam up about it."

"And my men are all certain they haven't said anything to anybody," Jordon murmured, thoughtfully stroking his jaw with one finger. "Which means the burglar recognized my name. It's not unusual for professional art and jewel thieves to learn all they possibly can about the security agencies that might be involved in trying to catch them, but, until now, I didn't realize we were dealing with someone that highly organized. Oh, I knew he was a professional, but now I think he's more than that; he's probably a man obsessed with flaunting authority and, to him, I'm a challenge he can't resist, which explains the personal note to me. But the fact that he knows I'm involved in this investigation makes me surer than ever that these burglaries are inside jobs committed by someone with easy access to St. Tropez Run, maybe someone we both see every day."

"But *who?* Who could it be? I can't imagine," Amy pondered, nibbling her lower lip. Looking at Jordon, her eyes suddenly brightened. "That night before you went back to Alexandria, you rushed up to your office to check something out. Was it—"

"Not much more than just an instinctive feeling I had and still do, as a matter of fact," he said, although with a qualifying shrug. "But suspicions aren't concrete facts, so I have someone following through on mine. Trouble is, finding the truth will take some time. We seem to be following a sharply twisting trail that might lead exactly nowhere in the end. We'll just have to wait and see, and in the meantime, hope there are no more break-ins, especially two in one night."

The even edge of Amy's teeth sank deeper into her lip as she observed him, blue eyes darkening. "I guess it was inconvenient for you to have to come back here because of what happened last night," she said softly. "I'm sorry you had to leave that crisis at your home office."

"No problem" was Jordon's easy answer as his broad shoulders rose and dropped in a shrug. "It was a crisis that should never have developed in the first place and was fairly easily solved. One of our client companies was being sued and Security Unlimited and I, personally, were named as codefendants. The man we caught embezzling from the company decided to sue the firm and us for invasion of privacy in investigating him. Since I had headed up the investigation, I had to meet with all the attorneys involved several times. By this morning there was every indication the suit was going to be dropped, so I only had a few loose ends to tie up. I decided my staff could take care of those, so it wasn't a problem to fly back here. I'd planned to come back tomorrow anyway."

"Oh," Amy murmured, wishing she could believe what he'd said yet not quite able to. The painful way their relationship had ended three years ago still made it impossible to trust him completely now. But that was something she didn't like to think about, and to push such thoughts far back in her mind, she veered the conversation off in an alternative direction. "Well, I guess it wasn't very pleasant for you to get here and run straight into that delegation of residents in my office. William Marshall was getting pretty abusive before they finally left."

"I try to ignore people who are abusive, just because they seem to enjoy being that way," Jordon said flatly, but his gaze narrowed as he intently surveyed Amy's face. "I just hope he didn't give you too hard a time before I got there."

"Oh, it takes someone more impressive than William Marshall to get me ruffled," she answered honestly. A small, resigned smile played over her lips. "But I did learn some interesting news during that meeting. Seems there's a rumor going around that I might be replaced as coordinator of St. Tropez Run. Of course, I shouldn't be surprised, should I? I always suspected Coastal might start looking for a scapegoat."

"Dammit," Jordon swore heatedly, taking one of her small hands between both of his. "I'm sorry, Amy. Maybe if I spoke to Evan Price . . ."

"I doubt that would help much. Evan came to my office this afternoon after his meeting with Marshall and the others, and frankly, he gives me the impression he's afraid his own neck is on the chopping block, too." With a rueful twist of her lips she threw up her free hand. "Just imagine, our mystery burglar may have created a two-scapegoat situation here. And if he's the egomaniac you think he is, I'm sure he'll be deliriously happy if both Evan and I get the ax."

"It's an absurd situation, Amy, and I wish I could do something about it right now."

"Oh, but I expect you to very soon," she responded glibly. "You'll catch our thief and save my job and Evan's in the process."

"I'm trying, believe me," he muttered earnestly, rubbing his thumb slowly across the back of her hand, then steering the conversation to a more pleasant topic. "Well, how have the boys been since I've been gone?"

"Fine. Still neglecting their schoolwork by spending all the daylight hours on their new playground. But they've really been missing you."

"Have they? And how about you?" Jordon asked, his voice lowering. "Have you been missing me, too?"

Recognizing the hot glint that appeared in his tawny eyes, she haltingly began, "Well, I . . ."

"God, I hope you have," he softly but roughly exclaimed, "because I've been missing you like hell."

Before Amy could react, she found herself wrapped in his powerful, possessive arms while his lips descended to part hers with raw sensual insistence. And for several long moments there was no suppressing all the love she felt. Her sweet mouth opened like a flower blooming in the warmth of the sun and her body yielded pliantly to his. The beat of her heart thundered in her ears, an involuntary response he was always able to evoke, and for a wondrously spellbinding fraction of a second, she was tempted to give all of herself once more and allow him to take what he wanted from her. But suddenly, from the deepest recesses of consciousness, something—perhaps it was pride plus the very human self-protective instinct—surfaced, and she remembered she could not know for certain Jordon would have ever returned to St. Tropez Run if last night's burglaries hadn't occurred. He said he had missed her, yet could she truly believe him? Maybe he simply thought that was the right thing to say— and if he did, he must consider her a most gullible fool. And she couldn't allow him to think she was that easy. Confusion seemed to scramble her brain. She loved him, wanted him, *but* . . . Maybe it would be wise to reconsider her game plan, and to do that she must have time to think. Bewildered by her own conflicting emotions, she stiffened and pulled away, laying her hands against Jordon's chest and holding him back when he tried to draw her into his arms again.

His eyes narrowed quizzically. "What's wrong, Amy?"

"There's nothing wrong, exactly," she said. She clasped her hands together in her lap, meeting his questioning gaze. "It's just that . . . well, I think maybe it would be a good idea for us to . . . cool it—for a while at least."

"Cool it?" he repeated tonelessly. "You mean our relationship?"

"Yes."

"Why?"

"People are talking about us," she answered with some degree of honesty. Trudy *had* hinted more than once that were some rumors going around about them. "I think quite a few of the employees and residents suspect our relationship isn't strictly professional."

His jaw tightened. "And that bothers you?"

"I think it has to, and it'll bother you, too, if you just consider for a moment what it might mean," she said softly. "I mean, we can hardly afford to be the objects of gossip. My career's hanging by a thread already, and you . . . well, people might assume you're not really concentrating very hard on catching the burglar if you're wasting time carrying on a torrid affair with me. And I know you value the reputation of your agency above anything else."

"You know that, do you?" His eyes flicked over her coolly. "No, Amy, I'm beginning to believe you don't know anything at all about me."

"Well, I've always admitted I've never understood you, but I *do* know how devoted you are to Security Unlimited, and it's crazy for us to jeopardize our reputations. And it's not as if this were a decision I made for personal reasons. It's purely professional," she lied, trying to sound cool and ultrasophisticated to avoid giving him even a tiny hint that she was, in actuality, using this quite reasonable excuse to play for time to sort out her feelings and to decide how to handle him from here on. "I just think we should back away from each other for a while until the rumors die down, at least."

"Meaning I should move back into my own quarters?"

"That would be best, don't you think?"

"It's up to you." Rising swiftly to his feet, Jordon towered over her. "If this is what you want to do, fine with me."

He was angry. Looking up at him, she recognized the icy impatience in his eyes and in the tension conveyed by his rigid stance. Had she simply wounded his ego or had she finally touched some deep feeling in him? Praying that she had and that she might prompt him into making some kind of declaration, she began, "It's not exactly something I *want* to do, Jordon. It's—"

"Purely professional. Yes, you said that." He shrugged. "And it's all right with me if you want to let your personal life be ruled by your loyalty to a company that's certainly not showing any signs of being loyal to you."

A sharp gasp caught in Amy's throat. Defensive anger erupted in her and defiance flashed in her eyes. "That was a rotten thing to say, Jordon, since you know I'm worried about losing my job anyhow," she said heatedly. "It's not very fair of you to taunt me with nasty remarks like that."

"Maybe not," he conceded with an unpleasant smile. "But I don't particularly feel like playing fair at the moment."

"That seems to be a habit with you," she retorted, feeling as if rapier-sharp ice shards were piercing her chest. "You were a master at unfair play three years ago, and obviously you're just as good at it now." And for an instant the pit of her stomach fluttered violently when he swiftly moved, as if he meant to reach out and grab hold of her. But intrinsic pride wouldn't allow her to back down, and she added in a laconic drawl, "But at least you're consistent."

His eyes hardened as he raked them over her, a stony expression masking his features. Apparently he hadn't been able to convince her he had changed, and frankly he was damned tired of trying. Without bothering to answer her charges, he pivoted on one foot and stalked toward the door that opened onto the foyer. Placing a hand on the knob, he coldly glanced back over his shoulder.

"I'll move my things out of here tomorrow," he announced, his tone chilling. "Unless you're in a real hurry for me to get them out right now."

"Tomorrow's fine. As long as it's early in the morning," she snapped back. But after he had closed the door quietly but very firmly behind him, her anger dissipated abruptly, leaving her as confused as she had been before their bitter confrontation.

"It's better this way," she muttered aloud, trying to convince herself that it would do him a great deal of good to know he couldn't take her for granted. He couldn't just waltz in and out of her life and expect to be welcome in her bed simply because she was there and convenient. So the action she had taken tonight had been correct. If he felt nothing more for her than lust, then she would be cutting her losses by ending their renewed relationship right now. And if he cared more than that, he would be back, trying to win her over again, perhaps even voicing some commitment to her. That was what she wanted, what she had to have, what she had been seeking all along since realizing she still loved him much more than she could probably ever love any other man. So, yes, she had been right to send him away tonight and force him to think about her a little. Yet the knowledge that she had made the right move was cold comfort as she glanced around the lonely sitting room, occupied only by herself and the curled-up cat snoozing peacefully in the opposite chair.

CHAPTER TWELVE

One stubborn person involved in a difference of opinion can complicate a situation, but two stubborn people at odds with each other can make a resolution practically impossible. Both Amy and Jordon were stubborn individuals, and the tension between them mounted daily in leaps and bounds. By the following Friday, a week after Jordon's return to St. Tropez Run, Amy's nerves were stretched taut, near the breaking point, and to her dismay she found herself reacting even to minor problems with uncharacteristic impatience. Once she actually spoke very sharply to Trudy, who simply gave her a rather morose but understanding smile, which made Amy feel terribly guilty. Valiantly she tried to thrust all thoughts of Jordon to the back of her mind but that was an impossible feat. She couldn't stop thinking about him and wondering if she had made a grave mistake in breaking off their intimate relationship, although she had meant the break only to be temporary. She had hoped with all her heart that he would come to her, seeking to mend the rift between them by showing her some deep affection, but he had not come and her hope was fading fast.

Although she still couldn't regret the chance she had taken, it hurt to think she might already have lost. She and Jordon avoided each other as much as possible, conversed only when necessary, and then their words came out stilted, while their shallow courteous manners were forced. Sometimes she felt he was a stranger and there was a constant ache in her breast because they had lost all the warm feeling of intimacy they had shared before he had left her to go to Alexandria. She hated the entire situation and was miserable. And if she hadn't felt she must pretend she wasn't the least bit unhappy, she might have been better off. The mere pretense was too taxing on her; day by day and long night by long night, she became increasingly tense until she felt she might have to cry out in frustration. And she was certainly in no mood for Friday afternoon's unexpected visit from Evan Price.

The man almost drove her berserk as he paced back and forth across her office. Although she longed to tell him to light somewhere and be still, he *was* her boss, so she remained silent, which merely heightened her tension to a nearly intolerable level. Pure strength of will prevented her from repeatedly pulling the rounded tip of a thumbnail between clenched teeth while resting her chin on her tightly clasped hands.

"Amy, how the devil are we going to put a stop to this madness?" he exclaimed, anxiously rumpling a tuft of his hair. "What can we do?"

"I don't think there is anything *we* can do," she responded candidly. "You're the executive director of St. Tropez Run and I'm the coordinator who supervises the clubhouse and sees to the maintenance of the streets and recreational facilities and screens the domestics before they are hired by the residents. Those are my responsibilities, and yours is to see that I do what I was hired to do. Neither of us should be expected to stop these break-ins or catch whoever's responsible. That's a job for security."

Halting in midpace, Evan stared at her. "Obviously you don't know that William Marshall has half the residents here threatening to sue Coastal Realty. And you must not be aware of how damaging this entire situation could be to both our futures."

"Oh, but I do know all about the threats of lawsuits and I've also suspected for some time that Coastal might try to use me as a scapegoat," Amy flatly replied. "And since I've heard the rumors that I might be replaced here, I've known exactly how damaging this situation could be to my career."

"Oh. Well, I . . . You can't . . ."

"The thing is, I don't think it will do much good to replace me with a new coordinator," she continued over his uneasy babbling. "The people of this community aren't stupid. They know I really have nothing to do with security, so Coastal will be wasting their time replacing me."

"Now, Amy, where did you get the idea you might have to bear the brunt of responsibility for these burglaries?" Evan asked smoothly, reverting to his most charismatic affectation. "I assure you that's not true."

"Oh, come on, Evan, face the facts," Amy bluntly said, tired of all the game-playing. "You know damned well I'll be the chosen scapegoat if the burglar's not stopped soon, and I think you know, too, that you'll be the second chosen if he's not stopped after I get the ax."

"Amy, you—"

"I suggest you talk to Jordon about security," she cut in tersely, all patience spent. "Because I see no point in our discussing this subject further. Potential scapegoat or not, I'm not about to accept the responsibility for stopping these burglaries."

"Well, hmmm, naturally I plan to talk to Jordon." He craned his neck as if his buttoned collar and knotted tie had become very uncomfortable suddenly. He cleared this throat, then gave Amy a rather sick, quite unconvincing smile. "As a matter of fact, I think I'll go speak to him right now."

With a nod she watched him leave the office, feeling some pity for him. Yet she was proud of herself for not having allowed him to infect her with his terror of losing his position with Coastal Realty. In fact she had ceased to be all that scared she might be fired, because Jordon's cutting remark last Friday night kept echoing in her head. Why *should* she be fanatically loyal to a company that showed her no loyalty whatsoever? She was beginning to wonder if she even wanted to continue working for such an organization.

Ill with a mild virus, Trudy didn't come in to the office Monday. Much of Amy's morning, therefore, was spent answering the phone calls the receptionist usually handled herself. A call she received around ten thirty struck her as wonderfully funny, but the resident making a complaint sounded so disgruntled that she bit down hard on her bottom lip to keep from laughing aloud. After reassuring the caller that the problem would be taken care of at once, she said good-bye and called Sam at the gate.

"I have an important and very glamorous assignment for the guards," she told him, amusement edging her voice. "It seems that Sebastian, that cat-chasing Newfoundland who belongs to the Montgomerys, has given in to his instinctive love of water and jumped the fence around our Olympic-size pool. At this very moment he's merrily swimming laps, according to one very irate resident. Guess you'd better send someone over to haul him out."

"Might be better to send for a crane," Sam retorted, chortling. "That dog's so big it's going to take more than one person to get him out of the pool, maybe even more than two. But we'll manage somehow and take care of it right away, Amy."

"Best of luck," she said, laughing as she hung up the phone. Merriment danced in her eyes while she glanced over all the paperwork on her desk. She shook her head. Too bad she had so much to do. If she weren't so busy, she would have succumbed to the temptation to go over to the pool to watch what promised to be quite a hilarious spectacle. She could just imagine what a time even more than two men were going to have trying to get the soaking-wet one-hundred-sixty-pound Sebastian out of water he didn't want to leave. Personally she thought they should take the easy way out and lure him from the pool with a thick, juicy steak. And she suspected that in the end that might be what they'd have to do.

For the following thirty minutes Amy was able to work without any phone calls coming in to interrupt her. But she knew the peace and quiet couldn't last and, sure enough, someone soon knocked on her door. "Come in," she softly called out, glancing up and tensing when Jordon stuck his head into the office.

"I just came in and found someone out here waiting to see you," he announced, his tone no more than polite, his eyes and face conveying no particular expression. Then he stepped back out of Amy's sight, allowed an elegantly dressed elderly lady to precede him into the office, then followed her inside. He inclined his head toward Amy. "Mrs. Grant, Amy Sinclair, the coordinator of St. Tropez Run. Amy, this is Mrs. Eloise Grant. She's moving into her new house on St. James's Court today."

"Oh, yes, Mrs. Grant, welcome to St. Tropez Run," Amy said, already on her feet to extend a hand to the rather slight woman with a kind delicately rouged and powdered face. Then she motioned her into the comfortable leather chair across from her desk. "Please sit down. We were expecting you today and I'm sorry no one was in the outer office to greet you, but our receptionist is ill today."

"Oh, it's perfectly all right. I had only just arrived when Mr. Kent came in," Mrs. Grant said, giving Jordon a warm, appreciative smile. "And he kindly offered to play receptionist for me."

Amy looked up at him. "Thank you, Jordon."

"Any time" was his offhanded reply. And the semblance of a smile that moved his hard mouth became much more genuine when he transferred it to Mrs. Grant, said good-bye, and excused himself.

After he had left, Amy relaxed in her chair. "Well, as I said, we're very happy to have you here, Mrs. Grant. I know that the movers were at your new house yesterday and that your interior decorator was there to supervise, so I'm sure you'll find everything in order when you get there."

"Oh, yes, I know that everything will be fine. I may have to rearrange a few things, though probably not very many. But of course, I will hang my art collection myself. I never allow anyone else to do that."

A tiny worried frown nicked Amy's brow. "Do you have an extensive collection, Mrs. Grant?"

"It's rather large and some of the paintings are very valuable. After I have it all arranged, I'd love for you to visit and let me show it to you, if you'd enjoy that."

"I would, very much, thank you," Amy murmured sincerely, masking the rising concern she was feeling. She looked at the three strands of moderate-sized richly lustrous pearls lying against the bodice of the woman's simply cut blue silk jaquard dress, the three-strand bracelet that matched, and the delicately elegant earstuds that completed the ensemble. Eloise Grant was the subtle picture of great wealth—a perfect potential victim for the burglar in their midst. Was Mrs. Grant at all aware of the present situation here? Unsure, Amy felt it her obligation to mention it.

After the explanation Eloise sat silent for several long moments, strumming her fingers against the arms of her chair. The sunlight pouring in the window behind Amy's desk caught in a large diamond solitaire, creating shimmering rainbow colors while illuminating the bluish-red, simply mounted ruby upon the other hand. "I had heard some stories about trouble here," she answered at last. "But I was given the impression that everyone expects this burglar to be caught very very soon."

"Every effort is being made to catch him, of course." Amy drew in a deep breath, wondering how much Evan had downplayed this problem simply to sell Mrs. Grant a house. Obviously enough to succeed in getting the sale. Feeling the need to issue a warning, she quietly added, "But until he is caught, I think you should take special care in locking all your doors and windows. You understand, just be as cautious as you can."

"Dear, you just don't know me yet," Eloise responded with a chipper smile. "My friends accuse me of having made my home a fortress, my former home that is. But since being widowed, I've been a firm believer in having several locks installed on every door and also locks for the windows."

"That should help," Amy said, somewhat relieved, although she couldn't help feeling a bit concerned. But she had done all she reasonably could. She could hardly warn Eloise Grant not to move into her new house; she would sound like an alarmist if she did, so she let the matter drop until she could take it up later with Jordon. She smiled at the older woman. "Now, is there anything I can do for you right now? I guess you'll be wanting domestic help, and I can arrange that for you. Just tell me what you need."

"A temporary maid will probably be enough, especially during the first month or so because I'll be spending most of that time in California, visiting my son and his family."

Nodding, Amy jotted a note to herself. "Would someone coming in on Tuesdays, Thursdays, and Saturdays be all right with you?"

"Oh, I think just Tuesdays and Thursdays will be sufficient, if it's possible for you to schedule that. Even before I leave for California, I doubt there'll be all that much for a maid to do." Eloise smiled wryly. "You see, I'm an exceptionally neat person."

Amy smiled back. She liked Mrs. Grant. Unlike Bootsie Bushnell and the few others like her in St. Tropez Run, Eloise didn't seem to have a pretentious bone in her body, thank heaven. The last thing in the world anybody needed was another Bootsie. "And since you're so neat and tidy, you'll probably never want a full-time maid, will you? Just someone to come in two times a week?"

"If you can possibly arrange it that way."

"No problem. Several of our residents have maids in on Mondays, Wednesdays, and Fridays, so by assigning one of them to you the other two days, she'll be able to have a full workweek."

"Wonderful, it works out just right for everyone this way,

then, doesn't it?" Standing, Eloise smoothed the skirt of her dress. "Well, I won't keep you any longer. I can see you're busy and you've already been a great help."

Rising to her feet, Amy removed a brochure from a desk drawer and carried it around to hand it to Mrs. Grant. "I'm sure you were given the grand tour of the recreational facilities before you bought your house, but if you can't remember exactly how to locate them, the map in here will help. You shouldn't have any trouble finding the tennis and handball courts, the golf course, and the pool."

"Ah, well, I'm a bit too stiff for handball and tennis. Now, I might play an occasional round of golf, but it's that pool I'm really interested in. I love to swim."

"Do you? So do I."

"But you can afford to. I'm sure you look very nice in a bathing suit, but I'm afraid that at my age, everything has started to sag," Eloise quipped. "But it doesn't matter. I still enjoy swimming."

"Then, that's all that counts," Amy told her, walking her to the door and opening it. "By the way, if you didn't know, the pool is heated. During the winter months the lifeguard is only on duty from noon to five, so you'll want to go during that time. And if a black bear of a dog ever leaps over the fence and joins you in the pool, don't be scared. It's only Sebastian, the Montgomerys' Newfoundland. He crashed in for a dip just today, as a matter of fact. He loves swimming too."

"Then I look forward to meeting him," Eloise said drily.

Amy escorted her across the reception area to the outside door, where they paused. "After you get settled in, I'd be happy to come over and introduce you to your neighbors, if they haven't already introduced themselves."

"That would be very kind of you."

"Of course there will a party in your honor here in the club-house very soon, anyhow, to welcome you to the community."

Something akin to a flicker of uncertainty crossed over Mrs.

Grant's face and she hesitated an instant before asking, "Would it be possible to postpone that party until after my California trip?"

"Whenever it's convenient for you. After all, it's your party," Amy assured her. "And if there's anything at all I can ever do for you, please call me and I'll do my best to help. That's why I'm here."

"Yes. And I have a feeling you're a very dependable young woman," Eloise said, stepping out the door when Amy opened it for her.

When they had said good-bye and the older woman had left, Amy felt she had just made a new friend, which strengthened her resolve to speak to Jordon about her concern for Eloise. She walked across to his office door, knocked, then entered when he called, "Come in."

She went over to stand before his desk, trying to ignore the faint lines of strain around his mouth and the jumble of papers and files atop his desk which looked as if he had been rifling through them futilely for some sort of clue that might help him put a stop to the burglaries. He sat far back in his swivel chair, his hands clasped together across his flat midriff, staring expectantly at her, and she simply stared back.

"I just wanted to talk to you about Eloise Grant," she tautly announced, clenching her own hands together behind her back, loving him while at the same time wondering why she did. "She's obviously an extremely wealthy woman. She told me she owns a fairly large and apparently quite valuable art collection which she intends to keep in her house. And, judging by the expensive pearls and rings she's wearing today, she probably has quite a bit of equally valuable jewelry. It seems to me that our burglar's going to notice her right away. That's why I wanted to mention this to you, so you could start watching her house more closely."

"Thanks for your concern, but I already know all about Eloise Grant," Jordon replied, his tone as bland as his expression. "In fact, we knew practically everything there is to know about her almost before she closed the deal on her house."

"I see. I guess I just forgot for a moment how very thorough you are. Well, since you already know everything I came to tell you, I'll go," Amy muttered, spinning round on one heel on her way toward the door.

Watching her leave, her shoulders squared, her head held up proud, Jordon cursed explicitly beneath his breath. Suddenly he'd had more than enough of this nonsense. Springing lithely to his feet, he stalked after her, catching her by one arm as she put a hand on the doorknob. "Just a damned minute, Amy," he commanded tersely. "Don't you think enough is enough?"

She looked up at him, her round blue eyes seeming to convey innocence. "Enough of what is enough?"

"For God's sake, do you have to be so hostile?"

"Me?" she inquired, feigning surprise by pressing her free hand against her upper chest, hoping to slow the feverishly quick beat of her heart. "If I seem hostile, I assure you I don't mean to. Why should I be hostile toward you?"

"I'm not a game player, Amy, so don't try any on me," he said harshly, his fingers tightening around her upper arm and then loosening again as he seemed to relent a little. "Look, since we're working together, don't you think we can at least talk to each other without speaking through clenched teeth?"

She shrugged. "I don't know. Can we?"

"I think we damn well better try. You were so worried about people gossiping about us being involved in an intimate relationship, and if you think you've squelched the rumors by ending what we had together, you're wrong. Considering how we've been avoiding each other and talking only when we have to, I'm sure most people believe we've had a lovers' quarrel and will be back together, hot and heavy, very soon."

"Oh, really?" Valiantly trying to numb herself to the hurt that stabbed with abrupt sharpness through her breast, she snatched her arm free of his grip and jerked open the door. "Just goes to

207

show how wrong people can be sometimes, doesn't it?" she drawled on her way out.

CHAPTER THIRTEEN

Nearly seven o'clock the following Tuesday evening Amy finished the work she had stayed late in the office to do. She started to push her chair back from her desk, then had second thoughts and picked up the phone to call Eloise Grant, just to say hello and ask how she was doing. After Eloise answered, sounding terribly pleased by Amy's call, the two women chatted as companiably as longtime friends. Over ten minutes later, when Amy hung up the phone, she smiled to herself. Eloise was such a warm, friendly person and fun to talk to, although she had told Amy one thing that concerned her, something Jordon needed to know.

Not particularly eager to seek him out, however, Amy walked slowly from her office next door to his. She knocked lightly; no answer from inside was forthcoming. She turned the knob to see if the door was locked. It was, which surprised her a little. Usually Jordon worked later in the evenings than she did.

"Wonder what's up tonight?" she mused aloud, speculatively tapping her chin with one fingertip as she went to get her purse. Then she shrugged, trying to dismiss the question. After all, she didn't have to see Jordon this evening; the information she had for him could wait until morning. And since she hadn't been looking forward to going to him anyhow, this allowed her to postpone doing it. A reprieve, so to speak. A rueful half-smile twisted Amy's lips but didn't reach her eyes as she switched out all the lights and left, locking the door to the outer office behind her.

When she stepped into the foyer several minutes later, she found Jordon in the doorway of his quarters, bending over to deposit Skeeter gently on the floor.

"Sorry, cat," he was saying. "But that's all the scratching you're going to get from me tonight."

Halting midstep on the threshold, Amy watched as he gave Skeeter's narrow, silky black back one last, slow stroke. Then Amy's softening blue eyes were captured and held by his when he suddenly straightened to look directly at her.

"I'm sorry if she's been making a pest of herself," she said, flicking a hand toward Skeeter, who lazily stretched and then padded silently toward her mistress. "I hope she didn't bother you too much."

"She didn't bother me at all" was his flat reply. "If she was a bother, I'd never let her come visit me in the first place."

Amy simply nodded as misery abruptly welled up in her, assaulting the back of her eyes with hot, stinging pricks. They spoke to each other as if they were practically strangers, no more than neighbors who were scarcely acquainted, and she was becoming less hopeful and more depressed with each day that passed. She longed for him to come to her and show her some sign that he missed her even half as much as she missed him, but he stayed away. And she wouldn't have known how to approach him even if she had been able to allow herself to take that step. It was a stalemate and she was terribly unhappy, knowing that he couldn't let things go on this way if he cared anything at all about her. So obviously he didn't.

Searching for something to say to break the lengthening silence between them, as he continued to lean in the doorway looking at her, she glanced down at the sleek, slim cat winding around her ankles. "Well, she can be a bit of a bother sometimes, you know." Amy smiled wanly. "She's a very demanding animal."

"She just knows what she wants and goes after it."

"And usually gets it, lucky girl," Amy murmured too quietly for him to hear. Wondering ruefully if Skeeter might share the secret of her success with her, she turned toward the door, at which the cat was now scratching. But when, out of the corner of her eye, she saw Jordon take a step back into his sitting room as if he considered this brief encounter ended, she hastily looked directly at him. "Could you wait a moment?" she softly requested. "There's something I want to talk to you about."

The dark-brown slashes of his brows lifted, lending a hint of mockery to his expression. "You actually *want* to talk to me, Amy?"

She nodded, ignoring the faint sarcasm that laced his voice. Opening the outer door, she watched Skeeter crouch down, warily look right and left in the deepening twilight, then, at long last, step with extreme caution across the threshold before streaking under a nearby shrub. "And don't come scratching to get back in for a while," Amy called after her. "You need the fresh air and I know you're not scared to be out there anymore."

"What is it you want to talk about?" Jordon asked after she'd closed the door and started toward him.

"It'll only take a second. I just needed to tell you that you might want to keep a closer eye on Eloise Grant's house starting next Monday. I talked to her a little while ago and she told me she'll be leaving then for a trip to California."

Jordon smiled faintly. "Yes, I know exactly when Eloise is going because I'm paying her air fare."

"*You're* paying her fare?" Amy softly exclaimed, following him into his sitting room. Utter confusion written over her face, she stared at him. "What are you talking about?"

"Sit down and I'll tell you all about it." He motioned her to the sofa, and after she had subsided stiffly onto the edge of a cushion, he made himself far more comfortable than that near the other end. He met her perplexed gaze. "Amy, Eloise is not a wealthy widow. She *is* a widow, but all those trappings of wealth are purely for show."

"But . . ."

"Eloise Grant is her real name, though. She was my father's secretary until she retired a couple of years before he died. I asked her to help me try to catch our burglar."

"But that house and expensive car and her jewelry and clothes! And that valuable art collection! Where did she get—"

"All willingly provided by Coastal Realty after I told Evan and his associates that we might not be able to save St. Tropez Run from ruin if we didn't find a quick way to lure the thief into a trap."

"You mean you're using Eloise as bait?" Amy cried, astonished and appalled. "Jordon, how in the world can you do that to such a sweet, helpless lady?"

A fond smile gentled his lean face. "Helpless? Eloise? She wouldn't like to hear you say that. As a matter of fact, she told me she's loving every minute of this little adventure."

"Maybe she is right now, but I don't see how you can live with yourself, taking this kind of chance. If the burglar breaks into that house . . ."

"Remember the nephew who's visiting with her until next Monday? Well, he isn't. Not Eloise's nephew, anyhow. He's one of the agents from our Baltimore office."

"Even though she isn't alone there, she could still get hurt if the burglar decides to strike before next Monday."

"He won't," Jordon proclaimed confidently. "And that's why I wanted Eloise to stay in the house this first week, so people would have a chance to meet her, then gossip about her jewelry and especially her art collection. Could be our burglar's already been in the house—and if he has, I'm sure he's managed to find the precise location of the wall safe. Amy, this man doesn't just break into houses when the mood hits him. He plans every job he does down to the smallest detail, which is why it's been impossible to catch him . . . until now. He won't hit Eloise's house this week, but he will eventually, and we'll have him."

Amy stared at him incredulously. "You almost sound like you know exactly who the burglar is."

"I have my suspicions."

"Then who—"

"I want to keep that to myself for a while. I don't have any concrete evidence yet, so I could be wrong. But I seriously doubt I am."

"Well, why didn't you tell me about Eloise, anyway?"

Both Jordon's jaw and lips tightened slightly as he closely surveyed her face. "We don't talk very often these days, Amy, so I guess there was never a real opportunity."

"There was so. The day Eloise arrived, last Friday, I came to tell you I was concerned about her being robbed. You could have told me the truth about her then but you didn't. Why not?"

"When she first got here, I thought it was best not to tell you," he answered calmly. "The fewer people who know a secret like that, the better."

Something in his nonchalant, unapologetic tone irritated her immensely. Anger rose up in her. She glowered at him, her hands tightening over the top of her navy leather clutch purse. Then she jumped up and started to flounce past him. "And I guess that means you had put me back on your ten most wanted list again, then?" she snapped. "Did you think I might be the burglar's partner and would naturally tell him that you were setting a trap to catch him if I was?"

"Oh, for God's sake, Amy, don't be a nitwit," Jordon snapped at her, grabbing her by the wrist before she could sweep by him. His fingers tightened, pressing down into her flesh as he stood to glare down at her, his eyes glinting like intensely hot, smoldering coals. "You're being silly. Ted didn't even know the truth about Eloise until earlier today."

"That just proves you don't have faith in anybody. You're jaded and I'm *not* being silly," she shot back. "I'm just tired of you changing your mind about me every two minutes. First you say you suspect me; then you say you don't. And the next time I turn around, you're saying you do again. And I'm damned tired of your insinuating I'm not trustworthy."

"And *I'm* damned tired of you giving me the cold shoulder."

"You give it to me."

"Then we're both acting stupid, aren't we?" he countered, his tone altering to convey something more disturbing than mere anger. "We must be idiots, Amy, or you wouldn't be sleeping alone in your bed over there every night. Or I wouldn't be sleeping alone in mine over here."

"I believe you have a serious problem, Mr. Kent," she announced as haughtily as possible, drawing herself up to her full height despite the raw pain that arrowed through her chest, the combination of bewilderment, hurt (old and new), and a niggling uneasiness evoked by Jordon's relentless expression. Hiding her true feelings behind a frigid mask, she disparagingly shook her head. "Can't you ever think about anything besides sex?"

"Sometimes" was his quick answer as his eyes searched the depths of hers as if foraging for every single secret. "But I must admit that, right at this moment, that's mainly what I'm thinking about."

"Then you'd better get your mind on something else," she coldly advised him—then gasped when he took her purse forcibly from her to toss it onto the sofa. As his purposeful hands grabbed her waist, she clenched her teeth. "Let me go this instant."

He shook his head.

"I want you to take your hands off me right now."

"No chance," he whispered roughly, drawing her toward him with unnerving slowness. "This time I'm not going to let you go, Amy." And, enclosing her in his arms, he lowered his head.

"No!" she said breathlessly; but then his warm lips descended. And, as if by their own volition, her own parted to welcome their brushstroking touch, which swiftly became fiercer and more

213

potently demanding. Amy drew in a sharp, labored breath; exquisite sensations rioted wildly through her as his fingers tangled in her hair, tilting her head back to expose the length of her neck to the strand of burning kisses he lavished over her creamy-smooth skin. Yet, drawing from an intrinsic strength of will, she overcame her clamoring desire long enough to press her hands against his chest and push herself back in the binding circle of his powerful arms. "Jordon, no! I can't; I don't want—"

"Oh, yes, love, you do. You have to, because I won't let you go now," he muttered, deftly stripping her suit jacket off her, then seeking the top button of her blouse. With passionate intent he surrendered to his own raging need of her and with a quick jerk tore the blouse open. Tiny buttons made soft pinging noises striking the hardwood floor at their feet, and as he wrapped his arms tighter around her lissome body, he rained burning, pressing kisses over the swell of her breasts peeking out above the lace-edged top of her pristine white slip.

"Don't. Don't, *don't,*" she uttered weakly while still valiantly trying to resist the rousing touch of his hands, of his compelling lips. Mustering all her willpower from the deepest recesses of her being, she struggled to free herself from his merciless embrace— wanting to give everything he demanded of her, yet afraid to give. She twisted against the sheer male power of his imprisoning arms, arched backward, desperate to put some distance between them. She succeeded, but only for an instant. Her heart somersaulted violently when she was swiftly hauled back hard against his body. Something akin to panic plunged over her, and she turned her face aside as he sought to kiss her again. "No!" she gasped, despite the deep running thrills shooting through her. A low moaning sound escaped her parted lips. "Jordon, *don't. No.*"

"Hush," he softly commanded, holding her effortlessly in one arm while sweeping the straps of her slip off her shoulders. He dragged it down until it was draped around her waist. Arching her back slightly, he placed a light kiss between her breasts before his fingertips began climbing them in closing concentric circles.

"Jordon," she breathed, tormented by the expert caresses. Her legs went weak beneath her. *"Stop."*

"I don't want to ever stop. And you don't want me to, either," he whispered. He bent down, his lips retracing the circles his fingers had drawn. His warm breath scorched her skin through the sheer fabric. "You like what I'm doing to you, the way I'm making you feel, so relax."

"No, no," she murmured but each time the word sounded more reluctant and less convincing. Wicked warmth blazed over her as he masterfully rekindled fires of desire. Resistance was being consumed in flame and her traitorous body was too easily weakening. With the last of her fading resolve she tried to shrink away from his seductive lips moving upward, round and round one breast. *"No."*

"Be still," he coaxed, his large supportive hand against the center of her back pressing her close once more, not allowing her to escape the tantalizing warmth of his mouth. "Hush, love, hush."

And at last she did, unable to voice further protest. A soft moan of delight was the only sound she made as his slowly flicking tongue played with her nipple, arousing it to supreme erectness which strained against the lace dampened by his questing mouth. Electric currents of sensation careened deep inside her. She trembled and watched through half-closed eyes as he lifted his head and rubbed his fingers over the dark nubble of flesh, squeezing, pulling gently, caressing. Then somehow her own right hand was covering his, pressing it more firmly into her breast.

"Amy," he crooned, triumph edging his deep melodious voice, his seeking lips capturing hers.

When he dropped his hand away from her back, his fingers moving deftly to unfasten the side button of her skirt, she could have easily stepped back and ended the madness in an instant.

Yet she didn't. By then she could only wish it would never end and that she could forever bask in the heated pleasure he never failed to arouse in her. She was lost, hopelessly so, betrayed by her own physical needs and an abiding love for him. When he lowered her skirt zipper, allowing the garment to tumble to the floor around her feet, she stepped out of it, then also her slip after he pulled it down. She kicked both slip and skirt aside along with her shoes, when she had stepped out of them. And she looked down at him, tangling her fingers in his thick hair as he knelt to peel the summerweight pantyhose completely off her. Her breath caught repeatedly as he slowly rose again, forging a searing path of nipping kisses along her legs and thighs. Then his lips burned her skin through the sheerness of her panties before probing the shallow hollow of her navel. He straightened. Still in his shoes and with her barefoot, he seemed to tower above her. Lightly gripping her upper arms, he held her back from him, allowing his impassioned gaze to drift over her from the golden halo of silken hair framing her face all the way down to her bare toes.

Then his smoldering amber eyes lifted to meet the deepening cornflower blue of hers and a slow, sensuous smile gentled his strongly chiseled mouth. "God, you are beautiful," he said, his voice appealingly rough. "And I want you so much."

Drawn to him, almost as if hypnotized, Amy stepped without hesitation into the arms held out to her while her own wound around his neck. Looking up at his face, she released her breath in a slow, quavering sigh. "You defeat me every time, Jordon," she accused, her gaze holding his. "You always win."

"Not always, Amy."

"Almost always, then. Why do I let you?"

"Because, as I've told you many times, you're a sexy wench," he softly declared, cupping her jaw in his hand to outline the full bow shape of her lips with the tip of his thumb. "You enjoy what we always have together when we make love, as much as I do. Underneath that cool, calm professional exterior, there's a very passionate young woman, hot desire simmering very close to the surface."

"I guess so," she conceded, although she knew there was far more to it. The physical delight they shared always tempted her, but she could have resisted temptation more consistently if the love she felt didn't continually trample down all the defenses she tried to build up against him. But it did. He had touched her too deeply three years ago, and now she knew beyond all hope and doubt that his touch had been lasting, branding him indelibly in both her memory and her soul. No matter if he could never love her in return—she loved him, and in that moment as in so many others she had experienced with him both in the past and recently, she knew she could not prevent herself from expressing all she felt for him, in willingly giving, although not in words.

His fingers swept through her hair, tickling her scalp, and as he cradled the back of her head in one hand, tilting her face up, she signaled willing acquiescence with another sigh, and her tremulous smile was resigned.

"Amy, you . . ."

"I surrender, Jordon. You win again."

"We both win, love, because you want this as much as I do, don't you?"

"Yes, and you know it," she told him, but as his fingers started to slip beneath the straps of her bra and move them off her shoulders, she stilled his hands, shaking her head. "No fair. You're still dressed. Let me take off your shirt first." And she heard his swiftly intaken breath as her own fingers skittered down from his shoulders to find the first button beneath the one already undone on his khaki collar. With an unhurried deliberation that was meant to entice and inflame, she undid the first button, the second, the third, and the two or three below with tormenting, drawn-out slowness, reveling in her power over him when she felt the rippling of his hard muscle beneath the grazing touch of her knuckles. Then, finally, with Jordon's fingers running feverishly through her hair, she began to tug his shirttail from beneath the waistband of his pants. A secret sensual smile played over her lips while she skimmed her hands over his broad chest, playfully tugging at the fine dark brown hair, winging butterfly-light caresses over the bronzed skin that hardened over his rib cage. The iron-hard muscle of his flat midriff flexed and relaxed, flexed and relaxed, as she inscribed slow widening circles with the heel of her hand ever downward over it until she daringly, boldly eased her fingers beneath his waistband.

"Oh, God, Amy," he groaned. "I was such a fool to ever let you go."

Hope surged up, threatening to fill her heart with long-sought-after happiness, but she urgently tamped it back down, still afraid to trust in mere words. In the impassioned heat of a moment such as this, a man might say anything, and she couldn't bear the thought of allowing hope to soar to the heights only to be dashed cruelly to the ground once the moment had passed. Uncertainty enabled her to shake her head in denial even as her eyes rose to meet the hot flaring glint in the depths of his.

"I'm not so sure you were a fool at all," she told him, managing to maintain a credible tone of voice. "If you hadn't ended it with me, you might never have expanded the agency as you have, and I might never have gone this far in my career. So, sometimes things do work out for the best, don't you think?"

Jordon didn't answer and Amy suspected he hadn't even heard the lie she had uttered. Then she was sure he hadn't when his arms closed around her, lifting her up against him until only the tips of her toes grazed the floor and his lips claimed the softness of hers with hot possessive power tempered by incredible finesse. He kissed her many times, each kiss deepening, and she kissed him back, wrapping her arms around his neck as his tongue pushed intimately into her mouth, caressing the veined flesh of her inner cheek and lower lip and meeting the responsive parry of her own. With each sweep of his tongue's pleasantly rough tip, sensation danced over every inch of her skin in sweet shivers and plunged with sharp keenness to her very center. She forgot the untruth she had just told, forgot everything except Jordon, the love she felt for him, and the glorious promise of the ecstasy she knew they were about to share.

Practically lifted off her feet, held fast against him, she clasped her arms around his neck, her hands easing beneath his shirt to massage his hard-muscled shoulders and upper back. She lightly raked the edges of her nails over his skin, causing him to shudder. When he lowered her until her feet were flat upon the floor again and his hands ranged all over her, charting every graceful sweeping line and rounded curve, his touch conveyed an indisputable mastery and a promise of all the pleasure to come. Anticipation made her tremble. As his hands wandered down her back coming to rest over the firm rounded swell of her buttocks, she brushed against his taut thighs, thrilling to the virile physical power unleashed in his response and aching to experience fully all his potent power once more. His obvious desire heightened hers while hers heightened his, on and on in an endless progression that soon swept them far past the point of no return.

Emboldened, Amy cradled the back of his head in her hands and stretched up on tiptoe to entice him with playful yet erotic kisses, catching the fuller sensuous curve of his lower lip between her teeth to nibble and nip, then flicking the tip of her tongue over one corner of his mouth then the other, over and over, repeatedly, until at last he could stand it no longer.

With a rough moan he claimed her lips in a swiftly deepening kiss, his own hardening and gently twisting their softness, parting them with irresistible demand. Widening his stance, he molded her to him. He couldn't get enough of touching her warm, creamy skin nor enough of her intoxicating kisses. For a dangerous instant he wanted to tear off the rest of her clothes along with his, then push her backward onto the sofa and take her quickly. Yet he didn't. He needed to make her as crazy for him as he was for her. When the tip of her tongue conducted a daring little foray into his mouth, he captured it, pulled it deeper inside, and exerted a drawing pressure upon it until a violent tremor ran all over her. He continued to ravish her with kisses and gained him her most ardent response. A shiver raced down his spine when she nibbled the lobe of his right ear, then throatily breathed his name into it. Groaning softly, he abruptly put her away from him to shed his shirt. But as he gripped her narrow waist, intending to pull her close again, her hands floated down upon his larger ones, her slender fingers catching his and slowly lifting them up, directing them at last to the front closure of her bra. Genuine warmth gentled his features as his tawny eyes plumbed the pure blue depths of hers, a lazy smile crinkling the corners of his.

"Ah, that clever little device again," he murmured, rubbing a fingertip over the plastic clasp. "If I knew the inventor's name, I'd send him a personal note of thanks."

Amy's answering smile was sensuous, inviting.

"Shall I unfasten it, then?" he asked, curving a finger around the clasp and under it, his gaze never leaving her face as he rubbed his knuckle up and down over her skin. "Well, Amy, shall I?"

"Yes," she murmured.

"Now?"

"*Yes.*"

"Right now?"

"*Jordon.*" She softly protested his teasing, amusement dancing in her eyes. "Yes, now, right now. Undo it."

"If that's what you really want." His deft fingers quickly opened the clasp but moved much more slowly as he separated the lace cups, peeling them back over her alabaster-smooth breasts and never pausing to touch until after he lowered the straps from her shoulders, removed the bra completely, then allowed it to drop from his fingers to float silently down to the floor. Even then, he didn't touch her immediately. A brilliant, impassioned light shone in his eyes and his free-roaming gaze almost seemed to worship her.

"Tiger eyes," she whispered as she had often before. "You really do have them."

A small smile quirked at one corner of his mouth. "All the better to see you with, my dear."

"No, no, you're getting all mixed up. It's the big bad wolf who says that."

Unabashed, Jordon shrugged. "Same thing."

"You know, in this case, I think you may be right," she conceded, laughter bubbling up in her voice. But the laughter faded when at last, with near reverence, he touched her.

Rubbing a tendril of spun-gold hair between his fingers, he seemed fascinated by its very texture. Then he touched her cheeks, eyebrows, the tips of her lashes, even the end of her nose before beginning to draw the edge of one finger back and forth across her lips and applying light pressure between them. They parted and when she caught his finger between her small white even teeth to lazily nibble at his skin, fire leaped up to replace the smoldering glow in his eyes. His free hand dropped to her waist, sliding beneath the elastic of her panties and gliding completely around her before circling back to the place he had started. The palm of his hand rested against her navel while his fingers extended down over her flat abdomen, moving in slow, seductive strokes over her skin, provoking wild flutters of muscle beneath his caressing touch.

"Take them off, Amy," he quietly commanded, easing her panties down only an inch or so himself. "Take them off now."

And she did, unhurriedly pushing them down her long legs, making him wait. Then she straightened to stand naked and vulnerable before him; yet the sense of vulnerability she felt wasn't the least bit unpleasant. He was looking at her as if this were the first time he had ever seen her. But, then, every time seemed like their first together somehow. Their mutual excitement never seemed to abate and even expanded perhaps. Maybe it was because her love for him flourished day by day and maybe it was because he was a real, earthy man with driving sexual

221

needs which she always so eagerly fulfilled. Only able to hope he felt more for her than that, she accepted her fate—she loved him too much and couldn't help herself—and stood relaxed under his ranging, compelling gaze.

His eyes took in every lovely inch of her, the faint rosy glow mantling her cheeks, her slender, almost delicate frame shaped by lush, exotic contours. The rounded curve of her hips swept inward to her finely drawn waist, and he was bewitched by her shapely arms and long legs and slender hands and feet . . . *everything*. And her beauty was not merely physical. Strength of character was mirrored in her face along with intelligence and compassion. As his gaze locked with hers, he was mesmerized by a beauty that was much more than skin deep.

"Amy, honey," he uttered hoarsely, "I do love to look at you."

"But I like to look, too. So . . ." she answered suggestively, reaching out to unbuckle his belt before issuing the same demand he had earlier issued. "Take them off, Jordon."

After he quickly stripped, he took her into his arms, his insistent lips seeking and finding hers. Arching her back, he leaned down to encircle her swelling breasts with fevered kisses, ascending the slopes and tormenting the soft yet firm undersides with slow, sweeping circles drawn by his tongue before closing his mouth over one tumescent crest and then its mate, tasting each in its turn again and again and again until Amy was quivering in his embrace.

"*Jordon,*" she gasped. Dizzy with desire, she lifted his head, nuzzling her hot face against his chest, her own teeth and tongue and lips toying with the tight hard nub of his flat brown nipple. While his hands coursed over her, touching her most secret places, her own dropped down to thoroughly explore him.

"My God, woman," he moaned, his deep voice strained and his breathing ragged as her intimate stroking caresses continued, rousing hot passion in him close to the unbearable level. Winding a thick swath of her hair around one hand, he tilted her head back to seek with his lips the wildly throbbing pulse in her throat, muffling his words against her skin. "If I didn't know I taught you everything . . . Amy, tell me you've never done all this with any other man. Right now I can't stand the thought of you with anyone else."

The truth rose to her lips but she bit it back and didn't answer him, guided by an age-old instinct to exhibit some uniquely feminine mystique. Let him ponder his unanswered question. Every woman deserves to keep a few secrets. And now Amy chose to keep the fact that he was her one and only lover strictly to herself. Arms tightening around him, she probed his powerful back and whispered, "Don't talk. Just kiss me."

And when he did, her opening mouth met the forceful taking pressure of his while he picked her up to carry her out of the sitting room. Without waiting to throw back the quilted coverlet, he gently put her down and came down beside her, his body hot and hard against the tender curves of hers. His lips possessed hers, then the straining peaks of her breasts, then the supple smoothness of her abdomen, while he slipped his fingers between her thighs, opening her legs and innermost warmth to questing caresses.

His touch wandered everywhere, followed by his kisses, until his warm mouth had heightened her desire to a wild frenzy. She scampered her feverish hands down his back to grip his tapered waist and slipping them wider apart, urged him between her long elegant legs. She pulled him closer.

"Take me," she beseeched, her eyes issuing an invitation as evocative as her words as they met his. "Take me, now. *Now.*"

"Oh, yes, love, right now," he whispered back, his hands easing beneath her hips, squeezing their rounded form to arch her upward. "I can't wait any longer."

Braced by his arms, he lowered himself upon her, thrusting gently upward, and Amy's soft sighing of his name mingled with his murmuring of hers, both accompanying the swift penetrating union of flesh.

It had never been quite this same way between them, never so wildly abandoned. Perhaps because it had begun in anger and then had become something wondrously different, it was all the more enticing. Raging need enslaved them both, spinning them upward from plateau to plateau of keen sensation, each one more deliciously shattering than the one before. Unrestrained passion made him less gentle with her than he had ever been, yet he never once hurt or abused or humiliated her. As much as he took, he gave back to her, and she wound her arms and legs around him, lost in her love for him, lost in the ecstasy they found together.

When completion came for both of them, it came with a sunburst of piercing delight that singed every inch of her and warmed her clear through. Later, as they lay wrapped in each other's arms, their breathing slowing to normal, she basked in a joyous contentment beyond control, beyond even conscious thought.

"We missed dinner, lady," Jordon reminded her softly, his warm breath stirring wisps of her hair. "Hungry?"

She was and said so, although she regretted losing the feel of his body close to hers when he swung his feet onto the floor and got out of bed, grabbing the short beige terry robe draped over the back of the easy chair beside him and putting it on.

Sitting up in bed, the sheet tucked beneath her arms to cover her breasts, Amy smiled hopefully at him. "What about your navy robe? Think I could borrow it?"

"You could if it weren't in the laundry basket," he told her with a wry grin. "But if you'd like to have dinner just the way you are right now, I certainly won't mind. Or you could just stay in bed and let me bring it to you, if you'd prefer. I make a great omelet."

"I know. I remember," she said, unable to prevent herself from grinning back. "But I'd rather help you with dinner if you can find me something to wear. I'm just not used to working in the kitchen in the altogether."

Jordon's answering laughter was soft and deep. "Okay—if you want to be a spoilsport, how about one of my shirts?"

"Fine," she agreed, taking the khaki uniform tunic he brought out of the closet. She put it on and stood, then wrinkled her nose when she caught sight of her reflection in the mirror. The shirt hung off her shoulders and reached down to midthigh, not exactly high fashion but adequate covering nonetheless.

"Um-huh," Jordon murmured, nodding as he eyed her appraisingly. "You look terrific in uniform."

"But you have to admit it suits you better," she retorted wryly, rolling up the excessively long sleeves. When he strode out of the room a moment later, she padded into the adjoining bath and, after trying to smooth her tumbled hair, joined him in the kitchen.

The fresh green salad she made was perfect with the cheese-and-herb omelet he prepared. Amy enjoyed every morsel of it, and when she had taken one last sip of coffee she rose from the table to start clearing away the dishes. "This is the first time Skeeter's missed joining us for dinner," she commented, transferring plates to the counter. She walked back to the table. "She may never forgive us for leaving her out."

"Amy," Jordon said, taking her arm to draw her between his legs. Resting his hands on her hips, he looked up at her solemnly. "You don't seem very upset."

She tilted her head to one side questioningly. "Upset? What about?"

"What just happened. I guess it shouldn't have, but I won't apologize because I'm not sorry we made love, Amy. I am sorry for the way it all began," he explained, both a disturbed and disturbing darkness in his tawny eyes. "We were both angry and maybe I took advantage of that because I had to have you. And I'm not sure I would've let you go even if you had tried to refuse to go to bed with me—not a very honorable thing to admit."

"These things just happen, I guess," she murmured, steadily meeting his gaze, although she wasn't at all sure how to interpret his words. "And you don't have to apologize to me. I'm not about to try to pretend you took me by force. I was willing."

"But vulnerable."

Involuntarily she nibbled at her bottom lip. Where he was concerned she was always vulnerable, but she had been trying to hide that fact from him. Obviously she had failed. Had he guessed she was hopelessly in love with him? If he had, would that scare him away again? She hesitantly moved one hand, having no idea what to say. "Well . . . I . . ."

"I know how worried you are about your job and the damage rumors about us could do to your career . . . and my professional reputation," he continued, his fingers gently stroking her waist, warming her skin through the khaki fabric. "And that's made you more vulnerable to everything, everybody."

Amy heaved a silent sigh of relief. *He thought she was vulnerable because she was afraid of losing her job.* If he knew the truth—that it was him she was afraid of losing again—and if he knew what it was she truly wanted: him, all his love, and a strong commitment, he would . . . But he didn't know. Thank goodness. Perhaps there was still some hope of her winning this game eventually after all, especially if she could continue to hold her cards close to her chest and give him little or no indication of her true feelings. With that in mind, she maintained what she hoped was a suitably bland expression while finally inquiring, "And that 'everybody' I'm more vulnerable to includes you?"

"It seems that way, doesn't it? Less than two hours ago you were mad as hell at me and ready to stalk out of here. Then I lost my temper, too, and was determined to do everything in my power to seduce you. Maybe it seems to you that I took advantage of the situation by deliberately channeling already deep emotions from anger to desire. If you think that, it's not true. At least, I didn't take advantage consciously. I only needed to be with you, believe me."

Amy's eyes searched his face, looking for . . . What? She wasn't sure. She only knew there was a sudden expectant stillness in her heart. "Why . . ." she began, but a funny little catch in her voice forced her to start again. "Why are you telling me all this, Jordon?"

"Because I don't want you to feel like I manipulated you tonight. I want you to trust me, Amy."

"Okay, I trust you."

He shook his head, his hands tightening around her waist. "No, you don't, Amy."

No, she didn't. He was right. It would take more time for her to learn to trust him again, if she ever could. Oh, she wanted to, but she was still far too unsure of him and too many old memories continued to linger. This time he would have to prove beyond a shadow of doubt that he was worthy of her trust before she could ever let her guard down enough to reveal her true emotions. Now it was too soon, and looking down at him, she forced her shoulders up, then let them fall in a contrived nonchalant shrug.

"I don't think I understand why you care whether I trust you," she told him. "After all, we resumed this relationship with no strings attached. Remember? This time I expect nothing from you, so I don't have to trust you."

"But, Amy, you—"

"You're making too much of what happened tonight," she hastened to add, retreating behind that Miss Super Cool façade once more. "You really don't need to apologize to me. I'm not twenty-two anymore, so sexual interludes are no longer such traumatic experiences for me."

A muscle ticked with fascinating regularity in his tightening jaw, but even that didn't make his expression at all readable. It was as if his features were carved into an enigmatic mask as he said, "I hope no sexual interlude with me would be traumatic for you, but you *did* say you wanted us to 'cool it.' But tonight was anything but cool, and I thought you might be a little upset about that."

"Well, I don't think we can make evenings like this a habit.

227

Some of the rumors about us seem to be dying down, and we can't afford to stir them all back up again."

"I see," he murmured, his tone lowering as he slipped his hands beneath the shirt she wore to cup her firm, round bottom. "So I presume that means you'd say no if I asked you to spend the rest of the night here with me?"

The caressing touch of his fingers on her bare skin was nearly her undoing. Sensual longing, greatly enhanced by love, threatened to overwhelm her; yet she knew she didn't dare go so easily into his arms and back into his bed only moments after telling him they couldn't risk reviving the rumors again. To do so might reveal too clearly how susceptible she was to him. And she was afraid to do that. Steeling herself to the invasive deep plunging effect of his possessive touch, she drew in a long, calming breath and shook her head.

"It's not as if I wouldn't like to stay," she admitted, then followed the truth of that statement with a partial lie that served as excuse. "But it wouldn't be wise for me to. Sometimes one of the guards has to come here to see you about security matters, and it wouldn't do for someone to come tonight and find our clothes strewn all over the sitting room. That's probably how some of the gossip about us started, anyhow. When you were living with me and anyone came to see you, they always found you in my quarters instead of here. I know it wasn't hard to figure out what was going on between us. Even the best of security guards gossip about personal matters. It's human nature, and it would happen that way again. You know it would."

Jordon didn't answer, although his eyes became like topaz ice shards that impaled the depths of hers.

"So I'd better leave," she finally added, compelled to break the silence between them that seemed to her to last an eternity. When he abruptly released her, his large hands dropping away, she remained immobile for a moment except to reach out compulsively to brush back the curve of thick brown hair that had fallen forward and to the side across his forehead. His gaze imprisoned hers, conveying a message she couldn't understand, yet she longed to throw herself into his arms without regard for the possibly painful consequences of such an act. But in the end common sense and a certain amount of fear of being devastatingly hurt again prevailed. Taking a backward step, she forced a tight smile to her lips. "But before I go, I'll wash the dishes in exchange for a delicious dinner."

"Leave them," Jordon commanded, his voice deceptively soft. "I'll take care of them myself. Maybe you should go now because, as you said, you never know when one of the guards might come by."

"Yes. I guess you're right," she murmured. "So I'll say good night, then."

"Good night."

She left him but as she walked along the short hall to the sitting room, she hesitated for an instant in the grip of an awesome longing to return to the kitchen, then stay the night as he had asked her to do because with him was really where she wanted to be. But she didn't go back. Something intuitive told her not to. Even so, her emotions seemed to be pulling her in two as she went across the sitting room, and suddenly she wanted to gather up her clothes and dash naked across the foyer to the sanctuary of her own quarters, simply to escape Jordon and her own driving need to be close to him. But she didn't dare give into that impulse, either. She could just see herself standing in the buff trying to get her door unlocked when one of Jordon's men happened to enter the foyer on his way to see him. What a lovely scandal such a little scene would cause! She had enough on her mind now without creating new problems for herself, so rather than making a mad dash, clothes clutched in her arms, she dressed quickly instead, hearing the chink of dishes from the kitchen. After slipping on her shoes, she stared for several long moments in that direction but at last turned and went out, closing the door noiselessly behind her.

CHAPTER FOURTEEN

Much later the same night Amy was finally drifting to sleep. After hours of tossing and turning and thinking incessantly about Jordon, sheer exhaustion had claimed her at last. Her eyelids had become too heavy to open. She was floating somewhere in that half-aware state between total consciousness and deep restorative repose. When a naggingly persistent noise tried to intrude on that wonderful deepening drowsiness, she tried to ignore it, burying her face in the mattress and clamping her pillow over her head. That didn't help. The noise didn't go away, and in fact became more and more strident, dragging her back against her will from the edge of sleep she had been seeking far too long already.

"Dammit to hell," she swore, sitting up straight in bed to fling her pillow halfway across the room. Hot tears of weariness and sheer unmitigated frustration pricked her eyes until she realized the noise was actually hard quick knocking on her front door. Any unexpected late-night intrusion makes the heart pound. And Amy's was thudding wildly in her breast as she hopped out of bed and threw her robe around her. She hurried into the dark sitting room, ever mindful of trying not to tread upon Skeeter, who made getting underfoot her life's work. But she didn't encounter the cat and made it to the door without mishap. Switching on the overhead light, she blinked and squinted her eyes in the sudden glare before jerking open the door with some impatience and irritability. Then she felt as if her breath had been

230

knocked out when she found Jordon on the threshold, clad in nothing more than the terry robe he had been wearing when she had left him hours ago.

"Jordon, what the devil—?" she muttered sleepily, glancing back over her shoulder at the clock on the far wall then back again at him. "Do you know what time it is? Nearly three in the morning. What—"

"Amy, I need you."

Her blue eyes widened in stunned disbelief. "*You what*? You can't mean—"

"No, that's not how I need you . . . not at the moment anyhow," he cut in, even his short chuckle sounding rather grim. "I need you to get dressed and go with me to the Morrison house. Mr. Morrison is away on business and his wife's alone, and since you know her better than I do, I thought you might be able to calm her down."

Amy's face paled. "Oh, no! Not another break-in?"

Jordon nodded. "Mrs. Morrison heard a loud noise downstairs, went to investigate, and found someone in the study, but it was so dark she could only see a shape. When he ran away, she called her neighbor, Fitzpatrick. He alerted us. Sounds like she's hysterical, so maybe you can help me with her. How soon can you be ready to go?"

"F-five minutes."

"Try to make that three or less," he commanded, turning away from her to stride back toward his own open door. "Meet you here as soon as you can get ready."

Less than five minutes later they were in Jordon's patrol car, zipping past the gate, a deputy sheriff arriving to follow close behind them as they swung onto St. Michael's Way. Lights blazed in every house on the short street, which ended in a cul-de-sac.

"Good news sure travels fast," Jordon muttered, braking to a halt before the Morrison house located to the right in the circle. A moment later, as they were hurrying along the brick walkway,

231

a young deputy sheriff caught up with them. He inclined his head politely at Amy, then looked at Jordon.

"I'm Don Hodges, Mr. Kent," he introduced himself. "Think the burglar's hit again?"

"Looks that way" was Jordon's reply, his voice hard edged with unmistakable frustration and anger.

Lawrence Fitzpatrick met them at the door of the Morrison house, his hastily thrown on clothes slightly askew. With an expression as grim as Jordon's and the deputy's, he directed them into the study where his wife, Patrice, was attempting to calm Mrs. Morrison, unfortunately to no avail. The moment Deirdre Morrison saw Amy and the two men enter the room, fresh tears flowed down already streaked cheeks as she sat trembling uncontrollably, wringing and twisting a fine lace-edged handkerchief in her hands.

"Oh, dear. She's crying again," Patrice announced unnecessarily, her own hands aflutter. Her helpless glance darted from Amy to her husband, then to Jordon and the deputy, as if she were desperately seeking assistance. "I just don't know what to do. Nothing I say to her seems to help."

"I'll pour her a brandy," Amy offered, going to the small bar across the study from which she took two snifters, deciding Patrice as well as Deirdre could use something to soothe the nerves. After she took the drinks to the two shaken women and gently urged them to take a couple of slow sips right away, she watched as Jordon and the deputy visually examined the expensive marble-inlaid stand that lay on its side on the floor. The bronzed bust that had once sat atop it had landed a foot or so away and didn't appear to be damaged, but Amy could just imagine what a frightening noise it had made when it was knocked over.

"Better get your fingerprint expert over here," Jordon suggested, touching nothing. "Although I know he isn't going to find anything."

"Maybe this time he will," Hodges said, thoughtfully tugging

232

at one earlobe. "I wasn't in on any of the other burglary investigations, but I've heard some of the fellows in the department talking about them. During those break-ins nothing in the houses was ever disturbed, was it? I mean, knocked over like this? So maybe the man who pulled the other jobs didn't pull this one, and maybe whoever did was careless enough to leave prints."

As Jordon walked around the thick mahogany stand, the line of his strong jaw tightened grimly. "No, it was our man all right," he muttered, flicking a hand toward the corner of a playing card peeking out from beneath the wood. "He's left us his calling card again and probably another personal message for me under it."

"This is outrageous. When are you people going to put a stop to this crime wave?" Lawrence Fitzpatrick irately put in, standing ramrod straight by his wife's chair. "Or perhaps a better question is: Are you people capable of putting a stop to it?"

"I'll go call in," Deputy Hodges said quietly, ignoring the blatant insult. "They'll send someone from the lab right over."

Jordon simply nodded. Then he, too, ignored Fitzpatrick and instead looked expectantly at Amy before flashing his eyes over to Deirdre Morrison.

Amy interpreted the silent message and sat down beside the distraught woman on the sofa. "Are you feeling a little better now, Deirdre?" she asked kindly, noticing that Deirdre was no longer shaking quite so violently as she had been before. "If you're up to it, Mr. Kent needs to ask you some questions. Do you think you could answer some now?"

"I-I . . . yes . . . no. I don't think so . . . not yet," Mrs. Morrison squeaked, clutching the small snifter in both hands. Her lips trembled. "I . . . my mind just seems to have gone blank."

"There's no rush; finish your brandy," Jordon told her, his deep voice conveying genuine understanding and reassurance. "When Deputy Hodges gets back, we'll give you all the time you need to tell us what happened."

233

A wan, appreciative smile appeared on Deirdre's face, but faded fast. As they awaited Don Hodges's return, only the Fitzpatricks' muted whispering broke the silence. While Jordon moved around the study, his trained eye scanning everywhere, obviously searching for any clue, Amy looked up and found Lawrence and Patrice glaring reproachfully at her, and her heart sank a little. She felt as if the words "Coastal Realty" must be emblazoned across her forehead; as their representative in St. Tropez Run, she was quickly losing the respect of many of the residents because she worked for the company they felt had cheated them. They might not blame her for the burglaries, but she was the most convenient person to resent nonetheless. And although she realized it was only natural for them to feel that way, the realization didn't provide much solace, especially since she knew Coastal was considering making her the scapegoat in this situation anyhow. Yet she set aside her worries about her future and turned away from the Fitzpatricks toward Mrs. Morrison again.

"I'm so sorry this happened, Deirdre," she said, her tone truly compassionate. "I know it's been a dreadful night."

"Horrible, perfectly horrible. I've never been so terrified in my life," the woman said shakily, tears welling up in her eyes, threatening to overflow again until she abruptly sat up straighter, trying to take hold of herself. She shook her head. "I'm not sure I'll ever be able to stay at home alone again. If only Paul had been here. . . ."

Don Hodges returned to the study a few seconds later, and after Jordon had assured himself that Deirdre was ready for their questions, they began. At least he began. Don, who looked young enough to be a rookie and showed some lack of confidence, seemed more than willing to let Jordon do most of the questioning, which he began very gently.

"I understand you were awakened by a noise, Mrs. Morrison?"

Dabbing at her eyes with the handkerchief, she nodded. "I

234

never sleep soundly when Paul's away, and the crash I heard down here was so loud that I shot straight up in bed. Then I didn't hear anything for several minutes except the wind blowing. I told myself the French doors in here must have blown open and the wind had knocked something over, so I came down to check."

"But you did wait a few minutes after you heard the crash before coming downstairs. Do you know about how many minutes?"

"Three or four. Something like that. And when I opened this door and saw that . . . that man silhouetted in the French doors, I just froze. I mean it. I was petrified; I couldn't move. And instead of running away, he just stood there for the longest time and I could feel him looking at me." Deirdre shuddered. "I couldn't see his face; I couldn't see anything except his shape but I was so afraid he thought I *could* see him and was going to come over and . . . kill me. I tried to scream, but I couldn't even do that. Then, suddenly, he just turned around and ran out. I thought I was going to faint but I managed to phone Patrice and Lawrence."

Taking notes, Jordon turned to the Fitzpatricks. "Did either of you hear or see anything before Mrs. Morrison called?"

"How the devil could we hear or see anything?" Lawrence snapped imperiously. "Dammit, man, it was three o'clock in the morning so naturally Patrice and I were asleep until Deirdre rang us."

"We all know what time it was," Jordon said, undaunted by the man's rude, rather condescending manner. "But people do get up in the middle of the night occasionally. I had to know if either of you had." He turned his attention back to Deirdre, his expression gentling once more. "What was taken, Mrs. Morrison?"

Her face was anguished. "I . . . well, everything from the wall safe in our bedroom, I suppose. You see, I couldn't bear the thought of that man having been right in my room while I was sleeping, so I didn't go up and check. Lawrence did and he was just coming back down when you arrived, so he didn't have a chance to tell me what he found."

"The safe's empty," her neighbor blurted out. "Sorry, Deirdre."

A flash of impatience flickered in Jordon's eyes at the insensitive, tactlessly abrupt revelation.

"Oh, no. Oh, no," Deirdre responded to the news, her eyes glistening even more brightly. "Everything . . . everything gone . . ."

"What was in the safe?" Jordon asked.

"Oh, my jewelry—some lovely heirloom pieces. The beautiful emerald choker and matching bracelet that first belonged to Paul's paternal grandmother. And my pearls and . . ." Deirdre ticked off the list as if stunned, then added, "And a small amount of cash. Oh, but nothing matters really except those heirloom pieces." She looked at Jordon, hope overshadowed by despair on her face. "Is there any chance of getting those back?"

"I can't make you any promises except that we'll do our best to retrieve your property," Jordon honestly answered. "But if you have photographs of your jewelry made for insurance purposes, they would be a great help to us."

Deirdre's deeply tanned face brightened for the first time. "Yes, we do have pictures. I remember now. They're in the filing cabinet. I'll get them for you."

Before she could rise to her feet, Jordon placed a hand upon her arm, regarding her somberly. "Mrs. Morrison, would you say your jewelry was more valuable than anything else you keep here in the house?"

"Oh, yes, certainly. My weakness is jewelry, and luckily, Paul likes to give it to me. We do have a few ivory and jade statuettes in the parlor, but all of them together wouldn't be worth as much as Paul's grandmother's emerald choker."

Nodding, Jordon let his hand drop from her arm, the expression on his lean face almost broodingly musing as she got up to

236

rush across the study. When she returned a minute or so later to give him a manila envelope, he opened it, examined the color photos briefly, then replaced them to hand the envelope to Deputy Don Hodges.

"I need copies of these as soon as the department can get them to me," he said. "All right?"

"I'll have them for you tomorrow," Don readily agreed.

The front doorbell rang. The fingerprint expert had arrived. While he started dusting for prints in the study, and then up in the bedroom where the safe was located, Jordon and Don went outside with flashlights, looking for telltale footprints.

"Nothing," Don was grumbling nearly ten minutes later when they returned. "Too many pine needles."

"Amy, we can go now," Jordon told her, and when she came to him after saying a few reassuring words to Deirdre Morrison, he drew the young deputy aside. "If you turn up anything with these prints, have someone give me a call, will you?"

Don nodded. "And if there's a personal message for you underneath that king of diamonds, I guess you'll want to know what it is?"

"Anything that might give us some insight," Jordon answered flatly, then went to tell Deirdre Morrison he might send someone to question her further later in the day.

Cupping Amy's elbow in one hand, he escorted her out of the house into the fresh brine-scented air of very early morning. Looking at him, seeing the stony hardness of his clean-cut profile dimmed by the lights spilling from the windows, Amy tiredly sighed, sensing his frustration.

"Well, at least he *is* getting careless, as you said he would," she offered. "Making all that noise and letting Deirdre even get a glimpse of him."

"Amy, that bust and marble-inlaid stand weren't just knocked over," he told her, his hand on the front passenger door handle. He shook his head. "Our 'friend' knocked that over deliberately just to wake up Deirdre. Then he waited three or four minutes for her to come downstairs and see him."

"But I don't understand. Why would he want—"

"He really believes he's invincible, and maybe the game's become too boring for him—so he's decided to play with us, taunt us. But he's wrong, Amy. He's not invincible," Jordon said tersely, opening the door and handing her into the car before coming around to lower himself in beneath the steering wheel. He added determinedly, "And I'm going to prove he isn't. No matter how long it takes, I'm going to catch the bastard."

Aware of how lost in thought Jordon was, as he obviously was mapping out some sort of strategy, Amy said nothing as he drove them back to the clubhouse. They walked around along the dimly moonlit path to their quarters. Inside the foyer they stopped outside her door.

From his considerable height he looked down at her. "I have to leave tomorrow, Amy," he told her solemnly. "But I'll be back here in a few days."

She gazed up at him, her blue eyes wide and darkening. "Something to do with catching our thief?"

He nodded. "Yes, and it's something I've decided I want to handle myself. It might not pan out, but whether or not it does, I'll be back here this weekend."

"Okay," she murmured, believing him this time. He might not come back because of her, but he would return because he was determined to catch this burglar of theirs. Impulsively she stretched up on tiptoe to lightly kiss his cheek. "Good luck, Jordon. I hope you find what you're looking for. I want you to catch this horrid man. I'm so tired of the whole thing."

"Amy, wait," Jordon uttered huskily as she sank back down upon her heels and turned toward her door. He drew her back around to face him, his eyes searching the depths of hers. "About last night . . ."

"If you're going to apologize again, can't it wait until you get back?" she asked, concealing a yawn behind her hand. "Right now I'm just so tired I . . ."

"All right. Later, then. I'll be back soon, Amy," he promised and bent down to bestow an exquisitely tender kiss upon her lips. He opened her door, then, after she had stepped into her sitting room and turned on the light, closed it behind her. Touching her fingertips to the lips he had kissed, she wandered into her bedroom, stripped off her jeans and shirt, and fell into bed. Languidly she stretched out one arm to switch off the bedside lamp. Merciful darkness soothed her tired, burning eyes and they fluttered shut. Although the imprint of Jordon's firm lips seemed to linger upon her own, she couldn't rouse herself from the drowsiness creeping over her. Even if he only came back to St. Tropez Run to catch the burglar who was so blatantly challenging him, *he would return*, and at that moment knowing that was enough for her. And succumbing to total physical exhaustion, she drifted into a deep, dreamless sleep.

Jordon didn't get back until late Sunday afternoon. When he drove into the clubhouse parking lot and saw that Amy's car wasn't there, he smiled knowingly to himself, virtually certain of where she was. Without even going to his quarters first, he drove on to the boys' home, arriving there just as she was getting out of her Chevette. He pulled into the empty parking space next to hers, receiving a surprised smile when she saw him.

"I didn't expect you back today," she told him, overjoyed because he was but trying not to too blatantly show it. "How was your flight into Norfolk?"

"Not bad," he answered, loosening the knot of his tie and undoing his collar button, his eyes never leaving her face all the while. "A little bumpy."

"Hmmm. And what brings you over here?"

"You. When I didn't see your car at the clubhouse, I figured this was the place you'd probably be, and I was right. You are."

"Terry called and told me to rush right over if I wanted to hear some good news," Amy said, walking toward the front double doors of the plain brick building. As Jordon fell into step beside her, she looked hopefully up at him. "And maybe you have some good news, too? Did you find out something important about the man you suspect is our jewel thief?"

"I found out some things that are important to me, at least. Everything I learned just confirmed my suspicions."

"Oh, Jordon, that's wonderful!" Impulsively stopping to throw her arms around him, feeling as if a heavy weight had been lifted from her shoulders, she suddenly found herself held lightly but firmly against him.

"Now, this is the kind of welcome I hoped to get a minute ago. Instead, you asked me how my flight was," he gently chided, lifting her chin, lowering his head, and kissing her.

For a few warm cozy moments Amy responded, her lips parting slightly to the brushing touch of his until, finally, she remembered where they were and somehow managed to overcome her natural deep-rooted reluctance to surrender to the glorious embrace of the man she loved so much. Pulling away, she stepped back, shaking her head.

"This is hardly the place for such shenanigans, Jordon," she said, her tone as light as she could possibly make it. "What if one of the younger boys saw that? You're their hero and they might never forgive you for doing something so 'yucky' as kissing a *girl*. You know how some boys at certain ages are."

The smile tugging at the corners of Jordon's mouth became a teasing grin. "I do seem to recall being a girl-hating boy once upon a time, but I grew out of it. These guys will, too, so if any of them did see me kiss you, I'm sure I'll be forgiven eventually when they begin to understand now nice and exciting 'those awful silly *girls*' can be."

"You're impossible; you have an answer for everything. Let's just go inside," Amy said, smiling back despite herself as she led the way up the short flight of stairs to the doors that opened onto a sparsely furnished lobby. "Now, tell me exactly what you found out about your prime suspect while you were gone. And *who* is he? Has the sheriff arrested him yet?"

Halting midstride in the center of the small lobby, Jordon gripped her elbow to turn her around to face him. "Amy, it's not going to be that simple. I didn't mean to give you the impression that we've cracked this case and caught our man. I did gather up quite a bit of evidence to confirm my suspicions, but all that evidence is so circumstantial I doubt any judge would give the sheriff a search warrant on the strength of it."

She drew in a deep, long breath, looking up at him. "Oh, I thought—"

"But we will catch him and soon," Jordon assured her confidently. "He has that one self-destructive flaw—he thinks he'll never be stopped. That's why he enjoys challenging me. But I've accepted the challenge and set a trap. Eloise leaves for California tomorrow, and with that house empty, I don't think our man will be able to resist breaking in. The art collection alone is enough to lure him there."

"But who is 'our man'?" Amy exclaimed softly. "Can't you tell me exactly who he—"

At that moment Terry King inadvertently interrupted her question by stepping out of his office. "There you are, Amy. And you've brought Jordon along with you. Good." He hurried forward with greetings, his brown eyes warm and friendly as he kissed Amy on the cheek then nodded his head at Jordon. "Glad to see you back. The boys were mighty disappointed when you weren't able to make it for basketball practice yesterday afternoon."

"I hated to miss it but it couldn't be helped," Jordon said. "But I thought I'd give them a rain check by coming over tomorrow at about four, after they're all home from school, if that's all right with you."

"Terrific," Terry said, nodding exuberantly, then turning back to Amy with a mischievous wink. "Now, try to guess what the good news is."

Amy laughed. "There's a lot of kid still left in you. You aren't really going to make me guess, are you? I have no idea what your news could be."

"Try to guess anyhow."

Amy and Jordon exchanged amused glances. She tossed her hands up in the air. "Does the news have something to do with you and Beth? Where is she anyway? She's usually here with you Sundays."

"She's back at the cottage feeding Angie her dinner. And, no, the news isn't about us."

"Have you finally been given the money to renovate the kitchen, then?"

"That's not it, either."

"Hmm, then have you . . ."

"Oh, you're never going to guess it in a million years. I'll just tell you," Terry cut in, bursting with excitement, unable to keep his secret another second. "Joey's been adopted! How's that for great news?"

"Oh, I'm so happy for him!" Amy softly exclaimed, beaming at Terry, then at Jordon as well. "How won-derful." Her voice suddenly faltered, a certain shadow seeming to pass over her face. "You . . . mean he's gone already?"

"Oh, no, not yet. He won't be leaving until next weekend."

Amy released her breath in a sigh of relief. "Thank goodness. I don't want him to go before I can say good-bye to him."

"No chance of him letting that happen. In fact, he asked me to call you over here so I could tell you the news, and then he could talk to you," Terry said, inclining his head toward his office. "He's waiting for you in there. You go on in, too, Jordon. He'll want to see you."

When Amy and Jordon entered Terry's inner office, they found Joey peering into a small aquarium, seemingly fascinated by the flashy cavorting goldfish. Hearing them walk in, he quickly turned around, a smile growing on his face as he swiped back the somewhat tousled flaxen hair from his forehead.

Deep fondness welled up in Amy, but she resisted the desire to give him a great big hug. He might *die* from embarrassment if she did that in front of Jordon. Instead she sat down on the rather worn sofa across from Terry's none-too-tidy desk and beckoned Joey to her, giving him her warmest smile when he plopped down next to her.

"We've just heard the great news," she said softly. "And we're so happy for you. You must be so excited."

"Real excited," Joey admitted, his smile widening a bit while he wriggled into a more comfortable position. "Just sorta surprised it happened so fast."

"Fast?" Jordon inquired, taking a seat on the other side of Joey.

"Sorta fast. The Wilsons never saw me till about two weeks ago and now they want me."

"Just proves they know a terrific kid when they see one," Jordon answered, playfully messing the boy's hair. "Sounds to me like you're going to be part of a very smart family."

Nodding agreement, Amy added, "And I bet the Wilsons are very nice, too."

"Oh, sure, real nice. Both of them but especially Mrs. Wil—" Joey broke off with a grimace and some of the light seemed to go out of his face. "It's hard to remember to call her Mom. But she's real nice anyway." A hint of red colored his cheeks when he glanced at Amy. "She looks a little bit like you, but not as pretty."

Suddenly Amy was close to tears but held them back and produced a cheeky grin. "You men learn very early in life how to say just the right thing to a woman, don't you?" she teased, and when Joey snickered, she gave his arm a quick squeeze. "But I'll always remember you said that to me, Joey. Thank you."

"Where do the Wilsons live, Joe?" Jordon asked. "In town or in the country?"

"Sorta in the country, I guess. They got a real big house; it's nice and all, but . . . it's near Charlottesville, and that's a long

243

ways from here," Joey said, his voice lowering to a murmur. He ducked his head and stared at his scruffy sneakers, turning his toes toward each other. His smile faded and finally vanished completely. "I mean, I guess I'm going to miss . . . things here. You know, like that neat new stuff you gave us for the playground, Jordon. It's still hot weather and I like playing out there a lot. And . . . I'm going to miss everybody here, too, I guess."

Over the child's lowered head, Amy and Jordon looked at each other, but before either of them could say anything at all reassuring, Joey went on.

"And I'm just getting used to my teacher in school. Now I'll have a new one. And I still get all mixed up in fractions." He glanced sideways at Jordon, then looked at Amy with some desperation. "But I'm not going to have you to help me with 'em after I go."

Detecting in that quick glance the boy's need to speak to Amy alone, Jordon abruptly rose to his feet. "Excuse me, but I remembered I have to talk to Terry about something. I'd better go track him down." With a smile he reached out to mess Joey's hair once again, and this time his large hand lingered a bit longer—but not too long—before he strode to the door. "See you at basketball practice tomorrow, Joe."

When he was gone, silence filled the small office for several moments. Joey stared at his feet again, nibbling restlessly at a fingernail, and Amy had to blink back the tears that sprang to her eyes.

"You know, I bet you might be a little scared," she quietly said at last. "I know I would be if I was going to live somewhere new with people I didn't really know very well yet."

"Yeah," the boy muttered. "But you're a girl."

"That doesn't make any difference. You've been listening too much to some of the older boys' talk. Boys don't have to be ashamed of being scared any more than girls. In fact, Joey, anybody with any sense should feel scared sometimes, even men.

Even Jordon and Terry are afraid of some things; I know they are."

Joey jerked his head up to stare disbelievingly at her. "I bet there's nothing they're scared of."

"You lose your bet, then," she said with a reassuring smile. "I think I'll ask Jordon to tell you how he feels about high places. He hates them. He told me he doesn't even like to climb a stepladder. I'm surprised he doesn't get dizzy just from being so tall."

Joey had to giggle, but eyed her suspiciously nonetheless. "Is that really so?"

"It really is. And I'm going to have Jordon tell you that himself," she promised, taking one of his hands in both of hers. (It was safe—no one was there to see him let her do it.) "Joey, listen, I'm know you're a little afraid and I would be, too. Anybody would. But it'll be okay. You'll make new friends fast; I *know* you will because you're such a nice person, everyone wants to be your friend. And you'll get used to a new school and new teacher quicker than you think. If you have trouble with fractions, your mom or dad will help you. They really *want* you, so they're going to take good care of you and try very hard to make you happy. And you're not the only one who's a little scared, Joey. I'm sure they are, too. Maybe they're afraid you won't like living with them or that they'll do something wrong to make you not like them. After all, you're as new to them as they are to you. But I bet they already love you a lot. How could they not? Everybody loves you. I know I do."

"Oh, I'm gonna miss you," Joey muttered thickly, propelling himself against her, wrapping his arms around her shoulders, his young body shuddering with dry sobs until at last resolve failed him and he allowed the tears to fall. "I'm gonna miss you more than anybody."

"And I'm going to miss you, too. So much," she confessed, the tightness in her throat and chest causing her voice to quaver. She held him close for several minutes, stroking his hair as he clung

245

to her, his warmth and vulnerability arousing all her protective instincts. Finally she gently held him from her, swiping at her own eyes while he swiped at his. She gave him a tremulous smile. "What *am* I talking about? I'm not going to give us a chance to miss each other. I'm going to write you letters and you'd better answer them, even if you'd rather go out and play basketball. Got that?"

On his smooth, tear-streaked face a small smile dawned. "I got it."

"And I bet your mom and dad wouldn't mind if I came to visit you once in a while."

"You'd really come to see me?"

"You just try to stop me. Remember. I love you, Joey Wilson."

"I kinda like that name," he said, his expression brightening with renewed confidence. "It's not so bad, is it?"

"*Not so bad?* It's terrific. Joe Wilson—that's a perfect name for a future pro basketball star."

Engagingly he tilted his head to one side. "How'd you know I want to be a pro basketball star?"

"How could I not know? You've only told me about three hundred times since Jordon started coming over to practice with you guys," she teased, steadying her voice, although her self-control was quickly slipping as she touched his still rather babyishly round cheeks. "And speaking of practice, you should be out on that playground in the fresh air right now, young man. You're going to be seeing enough of me every day next week."

"Promise?"

"I promise," she murmured huskily, hugging him to her briefly then letting him go again. "Now, scoot. I'll see you tomorrow afternoon."

"Okay." Joey jumped up and sprinted to the door, opening it with youthful exuberance. "Bye, Amy."

"Bye," she called gaily after him. But when he was gone and she could no longer hear his footsteps in the corridor, her

246

straightened shoulders drooped slightly and she turned to press her face into the back of the sofa to muffle an irrepressible sob. This, however, was hardly the time nor the place to indulge in a crying binge. By swallowing repeatedly and taking several deep breaths, she managed to compose herself sufficiently to get up and go to the door. She opened it and cautiously looked out. Mercifully the hall was empty, and she shot out to sprint through the spartan lobby, out into the unseasonable heat and glaring sunlight to her car, her straw shoulder purse banging against her left hip. All she cared about was getting home—home, where she could privately give in to the tears that threatened to erupt in a veritable torrent.

Around thirty minutes later Jordon stood in the foyer outside Amy's door and rapped his knuckles sharply against the wooden panel. He listened, heard no movement inside her quarters, and knocked again, a deepening frown creasing his darkly tanned brow.

"Amy, I know you're in there. Now, let me in," he called out at last, just as the door opened and she appeared before him, her face unusually pale, her lips tightly compressed, Skeeter cradled securely in one arm. The cat's eyes widened at the sight of him and she meowed, apparently begging for a back scratch. He ignored her, his gaze riveted instead on Amy's drawn face and the faint red splotches surrounding her eyes. Tenderness and a heartfelt desire to provide comfort surged through him. He stepped forward. "Amy . . ."

"Jordon, I . . ."

"It's Joey, isn't it?" he asked, taking the cat and lowering her gently to the floor before he took Amy into his arms. "I didn't know where you had gone. You just disappeared. I found Joey out on the playground, and when he seemed much happier and less fearful than he had in Terry's office, I knew you'd somehow managed to reassure him by tearing yourself to pieces. You really love that kid, don't you?"

247

"Yes," she mumbled, the tears she had finally staunched cascading down her cheeks again in renewed freshets. Her own arms wound around his hard male, comfortingly warm body. "And I'm so ashamed of myself. I should be happy that Joey's been adopted, and I *am*. I really am. But I'm sad, too. I'm going to miss him so much. He's such a special little boy."

"Come here," Jordon commanded softly, guiding her to the sofa, where he pulled her down upon his lap, cradling her close against him, whispering words that stirred tendrils of her hair. "You shouldn't feel guilty, honey. You love Joey and he knows that; that's what's important. You made him feel like a valuable person."

"S-so did you."

"And we both can let him go now, can't we?"

"I . . . don't want to."

"But you can whether you want to or not. I know how strong you can be. You can let Joey go and be happier that he's found the family he needs than sad for yourself."

"I'm trying," she rasped tearfully, burrowing her damp face into the spice-scented column of his neck and pressing tight against him. "I'm really trying, Jordon."

"I know you are," he whispered, wrapping his arms around her slight, trembling frame, seeking only to give comfort. "It's all right, Amy. Try to relax now."

And within minutes she did, lulled by his soft reassurances and his gentle, caressing hands. Already emotionally overwrought, she succumbed too easily to the pleasure evoked by his stroking touch and endearing tenderness. And her love for him conquered what little ability she possessed to pretend she didn't really need him. She *did* need him. She needed to be as close to him as she could be and needed the warmth that emanated from him to soak into the very center of her being. And when his fingers kneadingly massaged her spine down to the small of her back, she lifted herself up in his arms and closed her parted lips over his.

"Amy," he whispered huskily, recalling her fear of the rumors about them that could damage her career. "Maybe I should leave now."

"Don't go," she whispered back, kissing him again and again and again. "Don't leave me. I need you."

"Amy, I—"

"Stay with me."

"You know I will."

"All night?"

"All night long."

"Hold me," she whispered. "Hold me close."

"I may never let you go," he whispered back gruffly, his arms tightening around her lissome body, his lips descending to possess the tenderness of hers.

CHAPTER FIFTEEN

Amy's room was bathed in the pale gray light of dawn. Jordon awakened to sweet, lingering kisses and light, sweeping caresses. Desire stirred strongly in him and he opened his eyes to look up at Amy leaning over him. Her thickly luxuriant flaxen hair had cascaded forward across her shoulders to veil her cheeks and tickle his chest as she danced bewitching kisses along the tendons of his neck, down over his collarbone, and into the hollow she found there at the base of his throat. Soft light shimmered on her bare skin as she moved to pull the sheet that covered him down. She sought his flat brown nipples, toying with each in its turn with brushstroking fingertips before the end of her tongue drew moist circles over the dry ones her fingers had drawn. A tremor rippled over him and he felt her lips curve into a small smile against him.

"Amy," he pleaded huskily, lifting his hands to cradle the back of her head.

"Let me touch you," she whispered, bracing herself on her elbows to look into his eyes, the blue of her own darkening with distinctly sensual allure. "I like to touch you. And you like me to."

"Very much," he said, and when her mouth drifted down to make too fleeting a contact with his, the responsive hardening of his lips was echoed throughout the length of his body. He started to wrap his arms around her, but, playfully, she slipped free and lowered her golden head to scatter nibbling kisses over his broad chest, and then the taut midriff. With a low groan, he cupped the weight of her full, firm breasts in his hands, his fingers tenderly yet compulsively pressing into the warm enticing flesh, which swelled to his touch; and the swift hardening of her nipples against his palms conveyed her passion and fueled his.

Turning onto her side, Amy moved her lips along his neck and took the lobe of his right ear into her mouth, tormenting the flesh with her teeth, tongue, and breath. She knew she was bringing a white-hot vital force to life within him, and delicious anticipation filled her. Feeling the quickening rate of his steady drumming heartbeat beneath her fingers, she guided a hand over him, following the line of his hair-roughened arms and legs, tracing contouring muscle, probing the texture of his bronzed skin. When his hand kneaded and squeezed and played over and around the rise of her right breast, a deep, thrumming thrill surged like high-voltage electricity through her. She grew bolder. Slipping her leg between his, she leaned on an elbow above him to draw a wispy tendril of hair across his lips. Her eyes held his; she saw the fires ignited in their tawny depths and gloried in the superheated response she evoked. Her mouth found his, her tongue darting inside to tangle languidly with his. When he suddenly turned toward her and curved a hand over her rounded bottom to arch her to him, she encountered his forceful, rigid virility and sinuously brushed her smooth abdomen against him.

Jordon's warm lips took hers, exerting a slowly graduating pressure that claimed their tenderness as exclusively his. His tongue darted into her mouth again and again, savoring the ambrosia within while flicking lazily over the sensitive flesh of her inner cheeks. Inhaling the faint fragrance of her perfume, fascinated by the satin smoothness of her skin, he eased his slowly rotating hand up over the swell of her hips to the small of her back, then brushed his fingertips along her spine, pausing to explore its finely boned, lithely muscled structure before grazing over to stroke lightly the side of one breast. The feel of her flesh was a delight, and her impassioned response to his caress an aphrodisiac. He needed her to absorb the very essence of his soul into her being and to allow herself to be absorbed by him, two hearts and two minds intermeshed and inseparable. He had never felt as close to anyone, even her, as he did in that moment, and her sweet warmth became all that existed for him, all that he could imagine could ever exist.

In the cool gray morning Amy was caught up in her role as seductress. The rippling of hard muscle beneath her hand intrigued her. And as the kisses they exchanged became more feverishly intense, veritable preludes to ultimate intimacy, she surrendered all inhibitions to the promise of shared pleasure. Adrift in sensual delight, she nuzzled her cheek against his hand, which cupped her slender neck, while her own traveled down his side to slip between them. Enthralled by his swift intake of breath, she explored him with ardent caresses, her senses swimming as he stirred potently against her palm.

With a deep-throated moan, Jordon pressed her back upon the bed, pinning her beneath him. "You like to be touched, too, my love, and I'm going to touch and kiss every inch of you," he whispered, his deep-timbred voice rough with urgency as the hot pressure inside him surged to nearly unbearable levels. His lips

251

ravished hers yet with a gentleness that defied description. Hard, manly, calloused hands roamed freely over her, defining the slender length of her thighs, her delicate waist, and the soft tenderness of her throbbing breasts; but his touch was exquisitely gentle, reverent. Her honey-colored skin beckoned his caresses. The sweetness of her kisses made him hunger for more. Raised on one elbow beside her, he looked down into her softly glowing eyes. The sensuous smile that graced her lips was hypnotic and he was obsessed by her loveliness, a loveliness that transcended the physical. She wasn't the most beautiful woman he had ever known, but she was the most desirable perhaps, because he knew what explosive warmth simmered just beneath the surface of her cool exterior. And tonight he wanted to ignite a raging inferno in her, towering shafts of fire that would hopefully burn all the barriers she had erected between them and reduce them to ashes so she couldn't rebuild them. Every time they made love, she gave all of herself physically, but emotionally she held back. Tonight he wanted her to let go. He didn't merely need to possess her body. He was consumed by the need to possess her very soul.

His burning gaze roamed over her, followed by his hand, which wandered over and under and all around the graceful sweep of her legs for several long minutes as if he were lost in their texture and form. His eyes, his touch, adored her, and although the intimate fluttering of her small fingers upon him caused a blazing fire to run through his veins, he held a tight rein on his own passion. He ran his hand lightly over the gentle curve of her slender neck, tipping up her chin with his thumb. He bent down, his eyes holding hers, her lovely, fine-boned features filling his vision until her lids flickered shut and he closed his also. He kissed her, then retreated only to kiss her once more, then retreated once more, over and over, repeatedly, until her breath was coming quicker and mingling with the ragged tenor of his own. As their lips met and parted, met and parted, he was certain he had never known anything softer than her mouth.

"Ummm, this is a nice way to wake up in the morning," he

whispered, the tip of his tongue flicking over the leaping pulsebeat in her throat. "Late as it was when we finally went to sleep, I thought I'd have to drag you out of bed today."

"Just proves what a bad influence you are on me," she whispered back, nibbling his earlobe. "Maybe I'm becoming a slave to passion."

"I hope you are," he murmured, raising himself up slightly to search her face and delve her mysterious blue eyes. "But I want us to share all the pleasures this time."

"We always do, Jordon."

"*All*, Amy. Not just the physical delight. I want to share all your feelings, too, and know you share mine; that's the most precious pleasure we can find together."

"*Together*," she softly repeated, subconsciously evasive because she was still too fearful to reveal to him her true emotions. Her gaze darkened, plumbed the tawny depths of his, but she remained uncertain, afraid she might be overestimating, even imagining, the strength of affection she thought she detected in his eyes. No, she couldn't share all her emotions with him nor voice her love—not yet, anyhow. But needing to give that love in the only other way she knew how, she caught his hand in hers with an enticing smile and drew it upward to rest in the deep valley between her breasts. "I want us to be together."

"But, Amy, I—"

"Touch me. I need for you to touch me now."

"Honey," he muttered, not immune to such a provocative request. His gaze lowered to her full breasts, their ivory satin sheen and erotically darker crests creating a wild searing desire to ravish them with his mouth. He roughly added, "You can't begin to know how much I want to touch you. Everywhere."

"Then, do," she invited. "Start now."

And touch he did, first bridging her breasts with his thumb and forefinger, which rubbed and teased and brought the roseate peaks to hot burgeoning erectness.

Amy moaned, the sound that rose in her throat low-pitched and tremulous.

"You need to be touched? Here, too?" he uttered with sweet savage intensity while the hard edge of his hand drifted down to part her thighs and then grazed upward too fleetingly against the most sensitive part of her.

"Oh, Jordon," she quietly cried, arching against a touch that too quickly ended as his lightly calloused hand drifted back to rest between her breasts again. Instinctively she drew her nails over his taut abdomen until her fingers traversed the hard length of him to the straining evidence of his need, which she gently squeezed and caressed.

"God, Amy," he groaned into her ear. "What a brassy woman you are."

"If I'm brassy . . . *you* have to take the blame for making me this way."

"Or the credit, which I'll happily take . . . as long as you promise you'll be like this only with me."

She didn't answer in words, but deep in her heart she knew she could never so eagerly share such intimacies with any man other than him. He was her one true love and, vaguely, she wondered why he didn't realize that as her intimate touches became more deliberately arousing until, with a muffled groan, he raised her arms above her head, pressing them into the softness of the pillow, his strong fingers pinning down her delicately boned wrists.

Longing to go on touching him, she resisted captivity, her heart thundering, her breath quickening as she arched upward, trying to escape his imprisoning grip. "Jordon!" she gasped. "Let me—"

"I can't, love. Don't make me take what I want until you want it as much as I do," he uttered, his low-timbred commanding voice at variance with a husky undertone of appeal. "Now, be still."

She couldn't be, as his hand cupped her right breast while his mouth closed compellingly around the tip of the left, drawing it deeper in over his rough-surfaced tongue while his fingers tenderly pulled and tugged at the hard nubble of the other. Held captive, transported by the compelling pressure of that tongue and those fingers, Amy gasped with pleasure as an endless series of erotic thrills began cascading through her. She trembled while his merciless lips plundered her breasts, kissing the soft undersides, nipping at her skin, forsaking one only to bestow equally arousing caresses upon its twin.

Jordon circled kisses back up to one rose-tinted peak. His slow, stroking tongue ringed its circumference before he once again took the succulent morsel deep into his mouth and exerted such a strong yet gentle drawing pressure upon her that she softly cried out. And the responsive throbbing of the hard nipple tore a low groan of delight from down deep in his throat as well. He felt he could never get enough of her creamy skin, her warm flesh, of her sweet basic essence which he longed to extract completely and take into himself. With tender lips and teeth and tongue, he pillaged the warm breast cupped in his right hand, and he wanted to never quit. He knew what he was doing to her; she moved ecstatically beneath him, her breath coming in fast, shaky gasps, but the rapid rise and fall of her breasts only served further to inflame his senses. He couldn't yet stop possessing her this way.

Amy was dizzy with hot desire. Her fingers itched to sweep through his thick hair; her arms ached to hold him, "Jordon," she implored. "Let me go. I want to touch you, too."

"Soon, love, very soon."

"But—"

"Hush," he coaxed, his rough voice muffled as his wandering lips climbed the rounded flesh of her other breast to its inviting crest. "I have to taste here, too, Amy."

Then his mouth was closing warmly around her again. Hot liquid lethargy spread throughout her as he continued to tantalize and seduce her for what could have been an instant or might have been an eternity—she couldn't tell. Time had become meaningless. She could only relate to the scorching passion winging to higher and higher levels within her. After one last loving lash of his tongue when he raised his head, leaving a sweet dampness upon her skin, she was certain he would release her, allowing her to caress him too once more. But he didn't and she tried to free her wrists from the light grip of his fingers, which were pinning them against the pillow above her head, but to no avail.

"Be still, love," he whispered, grazing her parted lips with his. He gazed down into her eyes and softly smiled. "Just be still."

Nearly transfixed by the fierce amberglow of his penetrating gaze, she could hear her own heartbeat pounding in her ears. Yearning to hold him close and return his kisses, she moved restlessly under the partial weight of his powerful upper body. "I like to touch you, too," she murmured breathlessly. "Let me go so I can."

"Be patient, honey. I'm not through making you want me as much as I want you."

"But I do . . . want you and you know that."

"Not enough yet."

"Too much, already."

"There's no such thing as too much, Amy, although I hope to make you want me more this time than you ever have."

The impassioned intent in his deep voice and tiger eyes made her breath sharply catch. *"Jordon . . ."*

"I will let you go very soon," he promised. "But first . . ."

Muscles fluttered in her abdomen as the heel of his hand drifted over it to gently pivot between her thighs. His fingers, roving lower, began to chart the secret contours of her soft warmth. A violent quiver shook her slender frame, and she saw the flash of triumph blaze up in his eyes, but didn't care. His touch felt so good and he was creating such intensely pleasurable sensations that she arched against his slowly moving hand. Yet even those intense delights were mere preludes to the ultimate completion she now more urgently needed. She pulled in a sharp breath when he too briefly sought the heated inner flesh, opening an aching emptiness deep inside her that clamored for satisfaction only he could give.

"Oh Jordon, you have to . . ."

"Not yet."

True to his word, he continued to hold her wrists fast, and as his thorough, masterful, expert exploration of her also continued, she trembled with each gloriously intimate caress. She moved her head from side to side on the pillow. He was making her wild, carrying her into that realm of utter abandon.

When at last he released her wrists, she wound her arms around him, her mouth seeking his.

"Oh, God, Amy, I love you so much," he said huskily an instant before his devouring lips descended to possess her mouth.

With his words, joy bloomed in her heart, but she tried valiantly to hold it in check. She wasn't so lost in him that she could trust him without reservations. Three years ago he had said those same words and probably believed he meant them. As it had turned out, he hadn't and this time she had to be sure he did before she could let herself say them back. As he buried his face in her scented hair, she murmured, "You don't have to say that to me, Jordon. Remember? No strings attached."

"But, Amy, I—"

She halted his attempted protest with a sweet giving kiss. Her hands coursed caressingly over his broad back, along his hard thighs, then between their bodies, to resume their own intimate journey. He shuddered, his hot marauding mouth claiming hers with near savage insistence. Then they were lost in each other, no longer aware of individual kisses and caresses as what they shared blended into a kaleidoscope of motion without beginning, without end. In the tangle of sheets his lips meandered over her, kissing her everywhere, as hers did him. Morning lengthened; brighter light filled the room, but neither of them noticed, enthralled and consumed as they were by this ritual of love and passion. Amy's slight, roundly curved body responded to every nuance of his ranging hands; the longer, firmer length of his was hers to command. All that broke the spellbinding silence were hushed endearments and soft sighs of rapture.

"You feel so good, Amy," he murmured into the shell of her ear some time later. "You smell so good, so sweet, and taste so delicious."

"Oh, so do you" was her fervent answer, teeth lightly nibbling the rise of his sun-browned shoulder. "And it's so good being close to you."

"Close, yes, but not close enough. Not yet."

"Soon, make it soon."

"I'll have to," he confessed hoarsely, her eager words causing desire to heat up to near the boiling point in him. With supreme strength of will he contained it, not convinced yet that her ardor matched his, and he wanted that, needed that, had to *know* that her need was as great as his. Winding the silken swath of hair that fanned across the pillow around one hand, he held her quiet while his tongue glanced through the shadowed hollow between her breasts, before his mouth surrounded one erect crest, then the other, once more exploring all the supple softness of her breasts.

Amy's low moan was followed by another and another. Desire was a fever raging through her. His fingers were still conducting their lazy expedition along every rim and hidden recess of her warmth. Deeper rippling sensations were soaring upward into her, sensations she was powerless to resist yet was afraid he might bring to a peak too soon. And as he sought her heated inner flesh, then withdrew again and again, she longed for a more invasive, more filling touch and breathlessly commanded, "Take me, Jordon, *now.*"

And he could wait no longer. Her slender fingers, gripping and stroking him, were tumbling him too swiftly toward the brink. With a muffled groan, he raised her knees, parted them wider,

258

then lowered himself between them, extended arms bracing him above her like an eagle poised to swoop down. Her eyes flickered open to meet his. He held her smoky gaze as, with a gentle thrust, he entered her.

Amy's sweet murmur of satisfaction mingled with his. She had awakened, consumed by the raging need to feel him inside her. Now he was there, his hard length filling her physically, his tender warmth fulfilling her emotionally. And it was exquisite. She wound herself around him as their lips met.

Jordon took the sweet, ardent kisses she offered. He was enclosed by her vital feminine warmth, intensifying the throbbing pressure as he whispered, "Amy, honey, it's so good to be inside you."

"Yes," she murmured, catching his lower lip between her teeth. "Yes, *yes.*"

They made love languidly, rhythmically, bodies merging into one, minds and souls joining in a rapturous union. Adrift together in a dream, slowly revolving in timeless wonder, they soared together through far-off galaxies of pleasure, restraint forgotten as he drove deeper, taking care not to hurt, into eagerly receptive warmth. Keen sensations, ever wilder and more untrammeled, fluttered through her. She was free-falling through space, then was swept along the sheerest, highest apex of poignant ecstasy. And as Jordon joined her there, the hot essence of him flowed into the innermost depths of her arching body.

Later they lay, physically spent but replete, lightly embracing each other. Abiding love for him warmed her completely as he swept her tumbled hair back from her face and his lips lingered against her left temple, and he murmured, "You've worn me out, lady, and it's going to be a long day. We're starting a twenty-four-hour surveillance of Eloise's house tonight, and I'm on for the eleven-to-three shift."

"Then, you think our burglar will try to break in?"

"Maybe not tonight, but within the next few days. I'm sure of it. And since I can't afford to doze off while I'm on duty, why don't you have Ted drive you over with some coffee for me around midnight, if you don't mind doing that?"

"I don't mind. I'll be there."

"And will you mind if I try to go back to sleep for a while right now?"

"I don't mind that, either. Rest," she whispered, lightly massaging his broad back until she heard his steady, even breathing. Her own drowsy eyes traversed the angular but now relaxed planes of his tanned face. How she adored him. And now that he had said he loved her again, the hope building in her was harder to contain, although she couldn't quite bring herself to trust him totally. But he *had* spoken those words tonight and that, in itself, seemed a step in the right direction.

Later that day, in the early afternoon, Amy sat behind her desk, barely aware of Evan Price, who paced the floor of her office, wringing his hands. Her thoughts were far away, focusing on Jordon. If he did truly love her this time, he might be willing to make a real commitment. He meant too much to her and she loved him too deeply to be happy with a casual, nonbinding, perhaps on-again, off-again relationship with him. What she wanted was the promise of a future they would share, and in her heart she knew her own sense of self-worth wouldn't allow her to settle for less. But was that a promise Jordon could make? If he did indeed love her, did he love her enough to make such a binding commitment? Could he ever? Pensively Amy stared at her fingers strumming the top of her desk. Those were questions she supposed only time could answer, and in the meantime she would simply have to cope with the niggling fear that was always in the back of her mind—after Jordon caught his burglar and left St. Tropez Run, he *could* just forget her. It had happened that way before; it could again.

Lost in her reverie, she heard only the continuous drone of Evan's voice until he suddenly stopped pacing and spoke her name rather sharply.

"What's the matter with you? I don't think you're listening to a word I'm saying."

She gave him an apologetic smile. "Sorry. I've just got a lot on my mind today."

"The only thing you should have on your mind is the terrible fix we're in," he intoned, fussing with his tie. "I hope you realize how serious this situation is."

"I know it's very serious."

"So serious we both might lose our jobs."

He might. She wouldn't, she suddenly decided, sitting back in her chair to observe him blandly. It was time now to take the step she had been considering for several days. "I'm leaving Coastal Realty, Evan," she calmly announced, watching surprise spread over his face. "I'll write a letter of resignation, of course, but I wanted to tell you in person. My contract calls for thirty days' notice, which I'm giving as of today."

"Now, now, Amy, don't be so rash," he spluttered, uncomfortably fidgeting with his cuffs. "I was exaggerating a little before; I admit it. I don't *really* think you might lose your job because of these burglaries. I know you imagine you could be made a scapegoat, but don't let that silly little fear cause you to give up a very good position."

"It's not only that," she stated as diplomatically as possible. "I think it's time for me to move on anyway. I have a friend who's with an employment agency in Washington, and while we were talking on the phone the other day, she told me about some administrative openings in the D.C. area and some of them sounded very interesting. One was even with a children's home, and I'd like to get into something more service oriented. I'm ready to get away from resorts and exclusive communities."

Evan's expression was pained. "You mean you've already started looking for a new position?"

"I've made some inquiries, yes."

"Oh, we really have to talk this out. I'm sure I can convince you not to leave us," he hopefully insisted. "I certainly don't want to lose an employee as valuable as you are."

Neither did he want to lose a potential scapegoat, Amy suspected. If she left Coastal, he might well be next in the sacrificial-lamb line, if Jordon wasn't able to put a halt to the break-ins very quickly. Declining to voice her suspicions, however, she simply shook her head. "There's really no use in talking this over, Evan. I've made my decision and it's final. I'm leaving Coastal."

"But you don't want to—"

"I'm sorry but my mind's made up."

"But . . ." His voice trailed off. Obviously convinced he could do nothing to alter her decision, he sadly shook his head. "I certainly wish you didn't feel this way."

"It's not just a matter of feelings," she truthfully assured him. "It's also a career move I think I should make, since I am interested in something more service oriented."

"I think what you do now is service oriented."

"Yes, it is. But the residents of St. Tropez Run don't need my help in the same way parentless children would," Amy explained. "And I've decided I'd feel more useful helping provide a social service, if not for disadvantaged children then maybe for the elderly in a convalescent home, something like that."

"I see. Well, then, I'd better get back to my office," Evan replied, drifting to her door. "I'll see you later."

"See you," she called after him as he started out—then compassionately added, "And try not to worry too much, Evan. Jordon's sure the burglar's going to fall into the trap he's set for him within the next few days, and when he's caught and arrested, that'll be the end of everyone's problem."

"I just hope Jordon's right," Evan hopefully said, stepping across the threshold.

When he had pulled the door shut behind him, leaving Amy alone, she turned her swivel chair around to look out the window at the line of pines in the distance, her nearsighted gaze only able hazily to define their forms. She sighed. So now it was done, and a great feeling of freedom washed over her. She was leaving a job that lately had kept her perched on the edge of tension and uncertainty to seek one which she would find more emotionally gratifying. She couldn't regret making that decision. Besides, if she could find a new position in D.C., she wouldn't be that far from Alexandria after Jordon wrapped things up here and returned to his home office. She didn't intend to chase him down, but it certainly wouldn't hurt to be closer to him than she would have been here at St. Tropez Run. It was only logical to believe he would be less likely to forget her again, the nearer she was. At least she hoped that would be the way it worked.

CHAPTER SIXTEEN

Amy sat next to Ted in his patrol car. He turned onto St. James's Court, driving slowly to the cul-de-sac at the end of the short road. Straining her eyes, Amy saw the dark Mercedes parked in the darkened far side of the circle, a classy car that could have belonged to a visitor to any one of the nearby homes. In it was Jordon, waiting and watching Eloise's house, hoping their infamous burglar would choose tonight to strike.

"I'm going to pull up right behind him, Amy," Ted explained. "I'll stop and get out to pretend I'm checking out the car. While I'm doing that, you slip out behind me and stay in the shadows to go around to the other side. And don't forget to tap on the window before you get in, in case Jordon forgot to switch off the overhead light so it won't come on when you open the door. We don't want to take a chance on scaring our man off."

263

"That's the last thing we want to do," she said, repeating his directions mentally. "I'll be very careful."

Ted nodded, pulling up behind the Mercedes and grinning as he glanced over at her. "This is service. How did Jordon con you into bringing him coffee?"

She grinned back. "He just asked. I guess because he knows what great coffee I make."

"Well, I'll just ask, too, since I have this shift tomorrow night. How about bringing me some?"

"Sure, I'm always ready to help a man in uniform," she quipped.

"Terrific. I'll be glad to have you to talk to for a while. Maintaining surveillance is the most boring job in the world."

"I can imagine. Maybe that's another reason Jordon asked me to bring coffee."

"Could be," Ted agreed with a chuckle as he switched off the engine. "Now, this overhead light won't come on, either, when I open the door, so there's no chance of our man seeing you, dark as it is under these trees. And I'll be back to pick you up in about a half hour."

"Right" was her short reply. And when Ted got out of the patrol car, she scooted across the seat beneath the steering wheel to follow. Unaccustomed as she was to such intrigue, her heartbeat quickened slightly as she made her way around the Mercedes to the passenger door, staying low while Ted convincingly acted as if he were thoroughly checking the vehicle. His footsteps receded along the asphalt and he got back into his car to drive away—waiting until he had passed the Mercedes to switch on his headlights. It was then that she tapped lightly upon the passenger window. The door opened. She closed it noiselessly after slipping inside, detecting the faint spicy scent of Jordon's aftershave. In the dark cavelike interior he was only a dark form, but a small smile curved her lips anyway, though he couldn't possibly see it.

"Here's the coffee I promised," she said very quietly, holding up a small Thermos. "But I'm not sure I can pour it without spilling it. It's so dark in here."

"You don't have to whisper, Amy," he told her. "We're a long way from the house."

Looking out through the windshield at the two-story home silhouetted in moonlight, she asked, "Who's watching the other side?"

"Kiley's in the Lincoln Continental up the street."

"And obviously nothing's happened yet."

"Nothing."

"Maybe nothing will. The moon's so big and bright tonight. Any burglar would be a fool to try to break into a house on a night like this."

"Either a fool or a man who believes he can't be caught. It's just a hunch, but I think he'd pick a night exactly like this to commit another robbery because he wants to prove to us that he's smarter than we are."

"Sounds like you think you know a lot about him," she murmured, cautiously pouring hot steaming coffee into the cup that had capped the Thermos bottle. When it was nearly filled, she handed it to Jordon. His shape was becaming more defined as her eyes adjusted to the darkness. "Care to tell me exactly who your suspect is?"

"I'd rather wait until I can find more conclusive evidence."

"But I need to know," she softly exclaimed. "You think it's someone on the inside here and I just can't imagine which employee it could be."

"It isn't an employee, Amy."

"But . . . what do you mean? Are you saying you suspect someone who *lives* here?"

"Yes. I do."

"But *who?*"

"Let me tell you that when I have more proof."

"But, Jordon . . ." she began then to realize he wasn't going to divulge the name until he was good and ready. She had no choice but to accept that, although she did so with yet another question. "But if you're so sure he's going to break into this house, why are you out here watching for him? Why aren't you inside, waiting?"

"Because I want to catch him leaving, loot in hand. That way no crafty defense attorney can try to convince a jury that no one can assume he's a burglar since there's no proof he ever stole anything."

"Surely no lawyer, even the best, could convince a jury of that if he was caught inside the house?"

"Probably not, but stranger things have happened. And I don't want to take any chances with this bastard. I want to catch him and see him convicted."

Amy murmured agreement, then shook her head. "What I really don't understand is why anyone who can afford to live in a place like St. Tropez Run commits burglaries."

"It's the perfect place for him to live. He's able to socialize with his victims and case out their houses. It's really too easy for him. Maybe that's why he doesn't just operate here. I've found out that wherever our man travels, there's usually an increase in burglaries in the more prestigious communities where the homes are rigged with security systems only a pro could get past. And he travels frequently. A regular one-man crime wave. Unfortunately, there's no hard evidence to connect him to those break-ins, either."

Curiosity highly piqued again, Amy touched Jordon's arm. "But *who* is—"

"I'm not going to tell you," Jordon quietly but firmly cut in. "He may not show tonight, and if you see him tomorrow . . . Amy, sometimes your eyes give away what you're thinking, and I don't want to make him the least bit suspicious."

She heaved a sigh. "Here we go again—you're saying you don't trust me."

"I trust *you*," he told her, some amusement edging the sincerity in his voice. "It's those beautiful big blue eyes of yours that might betray us."

Reassured by his truthful tone, she shrugged. "Okay, keep your secret to yourself. I promised Ted I'd bring him coffee tomorrow while he's watching the house, so maybe I can get him to tell me who you suspect."

"Don't waste your time," Jordon advised with a low chuckle. "Ted knows when to keep his mouth shut. He's a good man."

Mentally Amy conceded defeat. After all, he didn't realize that she had been compelled to learn how to conceal her emotions much better than she had ever been able to three years ago. Since he had walked back into her life again, she had hidden her deepest feelings from him, and it was a good thing he didn't know that . . . yet. Before she dared confess how she truly felt, she had to win abiding love and a lasting commitment from him. So, with another exaggerated sigh, she grumbled halfheartedly, "You're right. Ted probably won't tell me anything. You men always stick together."

"Not always. Our burglar is a man and we're going after him."

"He's different."

"He certainly is," Jordon grimly agreed, swallowing the last sip of coffee while staring at the house. Then as he put the empty cup up on the dashboard, he turned toward her. "But enough about him. There's something more important I want to talk to you about."

"Oh?"

"Amy, I . . ."

"*I think he's taking the bait, Jordon.*" It was Kiley Scott's excited voice, suddenly coming over the two-way radio. Jordon immediately tensed. The message continued, "He's moving up along that line of trees from the beach toward the rear of the house."

"Can you keep him in sight?" Jordon radioed back, momentarily forgetting Amy. "I want to know exactly how he gets into the house."

"Through the sun porch," Kiley came back a minute or so later. "Damn, it didn't take him long to disconnect the security alarm system."

"I didn't think it would; it was only installed to keep him from getting suspicious," Jordon responded. "All right, we'll take him when he comes out. I'll be covering the sun porch while you cover the front of the house in case he goes out some other way. First, alert Sam at the gate. And, Kiley, keep low approaching the house. I don't want him to know he's trapped. He may be armed."

Kiley quickly signed off, and Jordon reached for the door handle. Amy clamped her hands around his arm. She was getting scared. "Let Kiley go with you to the sun porch. You know he's going to come out that way, and it's too dangerous for you to be there alone when he does."

"I can't take a chance on his getting out some other way. Kiley has to watch the front of the house, just in case."

"I could watch and beep the horn if he comes."

"*No.* I don't want you involved in this. So just stay put," he brusquely commanded, though his hands were gentle as he eased hers from around his arm. His strong fingers squeezed hard for an instant. "It'll be okay and all over soon. We've got him now."

Then he was gone, sprinting off into the darkness, not bothering to shut the door behind him. Trembling, Amy stared after him, but he was quickly swallowed up in the shadows and she only saw glimpses of him whenever he moved through patches of dappled moonlight that filtered between the trees. She glanced at the house, which looked rather blurred to her from this distance.

"Damn. Blind as a bat," she muttered beneath her breath, wishing she had brought her glasses along. She tried to relax but that was an impossibility. There was a burglar in that house and Jordon was on his way to confront him. She was frightened. The man might be armed and what if . . . She shook her head. No, she wouldn't think such thoughts. Jordon knew how to take care of himself. He'd be just fine. She sat mentally chanting that reassurance for several long minutes, but it didn't help much.

Even the night was eerie, too still, too silent. No breeze stirred, and it was unseasonably hot for late September. The heavy, muggy air soon felt almost suffocating to Amy. She caught the side of her left forefinger between her teeth and began gnawing at it while a few minutes more ticked by with excruciating slowness. Staring at the house, she wondered what was happening. How long did it take to burglarize a home, anyhow? Surely the thief would come out soon now; Jordon would catch him and it would all be over, as he had said.

Amy shifted restlessly in the passenger seat, too uneasy to sit still. All the time that had passed was beginning to seem like an ill omen and fear was creeping steadily deeper within her. Finally she jumped out of the car. She couldn't just sit and wait any longer. She had to get closer, where she would be able to see what happened.

Cautiously, noiselessly, she made her way through the stand of trees close to where it bordered the lawn, then bent down low to move into the shadow of a neatly manicured hedge, following it for some distance. There were plenty of ornamental shrubs to provide cover for her as she approached the brick home. She reached the back corner, pausing there a moment to take a deep breath before peeking around. Everything looked so deceptively peaceful. All was perfectly quiet and she saw no sign of Jordon. The sun room was located at the other side of the house, but she knew the outside door opened onto the back lawn. When the burglar came out, she would have a perfect view of him.

Now that she had gotten out of the car and taken some action, she felt better about the situation. At least she didn't have to suffer the uncertainty of not knowing what was going on. She stood absolutely still except for the times she warily peered around the corner. Her ears were attuned to every sound, even the softest of natural night noises, and at last she heard, very faintly, the opening of a door. Her throat tightened and went dry, and when she looked around and saw the dark figure emerging from the sun room, her heart lurched.

"I expected to see you here tonight," Jordon's deep voice suddenly came out of the shadows of the rose arbor about ten feet away from the sun-room door. He stepped out onto the moonlit lawn, switched on a flashlight, and turned the beam on the shorter, slighter man who had stopped dead in his tracks and now stood frozen, his back to Amy. But as Jordon called out for Kiley, the burglar quickly recovered from the shock of the unexpected encounter, threw down a bag, and ran, heading across the lawn toward the beach. But he didn't get far, as Jordon loped after him.

Stepping away from the house, Amy watched tensely as Jordon grabbed the thief, who proved he was tough and wiry despite his small size. Desperate to escape, he put up a fight. Etched in moonlight, the two men struggled for several seemingly endless seconds. Then, suddenly, without warning, there was a burst of light and the sharp, horrifying crack of a gun going off. As if trapped in a hideous nightmare, Amy saw Jordon fall.

"No," she screamed, terror ripping into her as she flew across the lawn, barely aware of Renn Bushnell, who now turned the gun toward her—in consequence turning his back on Kiley also. From behind, Kiley tackled him. Both men went sprawling while the gun flew across the grass to land close to Amy. She automatically grabbed it while dropping to her knees by Jordon's side.

"*Jordon!*" she softly cried, running her hand across his chest, relief making her feel almost faint as he tried to sit up. He was alive and she had been so terrified that . . . Urging him not to move, she held him back. "Just lie still. W-where are you hit?"

"In the leg. It's not so bad, Amy. I'm all right." He removed her hand from his chest, sitting up despite her protest. "Give me the gun." When she reluctantly did so, he aimed it at Bushnell, who was struggling frantically with the young guard. "Give it up, Renn. Your luck's run out. I have the gun now."

The man went limp until Kiley pulled his arms back behind him to get a secure grip on him. Then he produced a cocky, unconvincing smile. "*You* sure got lucky, Kent, staking out this house tonight."

"Luck didn't have much to do with it. Eloise Grant isn't quite as wealthy as you think. Truth is, she was once my father's secretary" was Jordon's dry reply. "Now, why don't you tell us what your name is. I know the real Renn Bushnell lives in Hawaii."

The cocky smile remained firmly affixed. "Why don't you just call me George Washington, since I'd rather not say what my real name is."

"Suit yourself. I'm sure the sheriff will be able to identify you soon enough after getting a set of your prints."

"Sorry to disappoint you, old chap," the burglar shot back sarcastically. "My prints aren't on file anywhere. Never been arrested."

"Then, prison will be a brand-new experience for you, one I guarantee you won't like."

"I won't be there long."

Ignoring that bravado remark, Jordon glanced over at Amy, who had moved down to push up his right pants leg. As she softly gasped, he shook his head. "It's really not so bad, just a flesh wound."

"Not so bad?" she exclaimed, briefly focusing a glare on Bushnell. Fury, fueled by an intense protective instinct came to a quick boil in her. He had hurt Jordon, and for an instant she longed to tear him apart. Then the moment passed and she lightly touched Jordon's ankle while meeting his eyes. "But it's really bleeding."

"It looks worse than it is. Here," he said, handing her his handkerchief. "Press that against it."

Doing so, Amy looked at Kiley. "Do you have a handkerchief, too?"

"Yes, ma'am, I sure do."

271

"Bring it to me."

"Face down on the ground first, hands behind you, friend," Jordon commanded, punctuating his words with a downward flick of the gun aimed at the thief, who resentfully obeyed. When Kiley came over to give Amy a neatly folded white handkerchief, he added, "Kiley, go radio Sam. Tell him to ask the sheriff's department to have the deputy they send over here bring a warrant with him to search Bushnell's house."

"Yes, sir."

"You'll never connect me with those other burglaries," the Bushnell impersonator claimed.

"I'm sure going to give it one helluva try," Jordon drawled, nodding at Kiley. "Get going."

"And have Sam call for an ambulance, too," Amy sang out as the young guard sprinted away. "Tell him to do that first thing."

"I don't need an ambulance, Kiley," Jordon quickly added.

"Kiley, do as *I* say. Ambulance first," she reiterated firmly. "Got that?"

"Yes, ma'am," he called back.

"Amy, I don't need an ambulance," Jordon protested, holding the gun steadily on "Bushnell." "One of the men can drive me to the hospital. Or to a doctor. All I need is a tetanus shot and a bandage."

"Will you be quiet and stop acting like Macho Man? That's not your style," she told him emphatically. "Take my word for it—an ambulance is a good idea."

Maybe she was right, he decided by the time some neighbors who had heard the gunfire were beginning to gather around. He was feeling a little light-headed, and when one of the men offered to cover "Bushnell," he handed the revolver over to him gratefully and stretched out upon the lawn.

"Hurt much?" Amy gently asked, hovering over him.

"Well, since I'm not a masochist, I can't say it feels fantastic," he admitted, but smiled. "It's not unbearable, though."

"The ambulance should be here soon," she promised.

And her words proved prophetic. Within minutes a screaming siren split the quiet night, accompanied by a flashing red light. A moment later, when Jordon was gently moved onto a stretcher, Amy bit down hard on her lower lip. Tears pricked her eyes. She couldn't bear to see him in pain, but she followed the attendants as they carried him to the ambulance, and she rode along with him, clutching his hand, to the hospital in Virginia Beach.

Over two hours later Jordon insisted he be released from the hospital, and Ted Preston and Kiley Scott were there to drive both him and Amy back to St. Tropez Run. Limping, he rested an arm upon her shoulders as they entered the foyer of their quarters. He started toward his own door.

"It's not locked," he told her. "If you'd just help me to my bedroom, I—"

"No way. You're staying with me tonight. The doctor said you had a deep flesh wound that could start bleeding again, so you need someone to be with you."

"But I thought you were worried about gossip," he murmured. "If anybody finds out I stayed with you, people will talk."

"Let them. I don't care," she responded.

And Jordon didn't argue.

The next morning Amy stood beside her bed, gazing down at Jordon, who was still sleeping peacefully. The dark fringe of his lashes lay against his sun-browned skin and the love she felt burgeoned up irrepressible in her. What would she do if he could never love her the way she loved him? she wondered. *She would survive,* she answered her own mental question, despite the push and pull of her emotions. She *was* a survivor, and if he could never really love her and make a commitment, she would find contentment in life, if not total happiness. She knew she could; after all, she had managed to accomplish that same feat during the past three years. She could do the same again. Yet she ached for his love.

She gently raised the sheet to examine the bandage wrapped around the calf of his right leg and breathed a sigh of relief when she found the gauze pure white, untinged by red. Jordon stirred. Her eyes darted to his face, and as his fluttered open, she smiled.

"Morning," she softly greeted him. "Feeling better?"

"A little sore, but not too bad," he answered, smiling back sleepily. "What time is it?"

"Ten after ten."

"Damn, I can't remember ever sleeping this late in my life." She laughed. "I can't say the same about myself."

"But you're such a lazybones sometimes. Never on workdays, though, and this is Tuesday. Why aren't you upstairs in your office?"

"Because I'm here taking care of you. Trudy can cope with anything that comes up." She sat down beside him on the edge of the bed, pulling one side of her clover-colored terry robe more securely over the other, looking down at him with a small frown. "You're really not in a lot of pain?"

"No, I'm not. I'd certainly let you and some doctor know if the pain was unbearable."

"Good." Her frown disappeared. "Are you hungry, then? How about breakfast?"

"In a little while. First I want to know if 'Bushnell' was bluffing last night about never having been fingerprinted?"

Amy sighed. "It doesn't look like he was. I talked to Ted this morning and he said the sheriff can find no record of his prints anywhere. They've checked with the FBI and the military. No luck. But—"

"And I don't suppose they turned anything up when his house was searched?"

"I was just about to tell you that good news," she answered, her face brightening. "They found Pamela Cabot's collection of

274

Fabergé enamels hidden in Bushnell's attic. I guess it was one thing he wanted to keep for himself too much to sell it."

"Damn, he was even cockier and more self-confident than I thought," Jordon mused, tapping his finger against his jaw while shaking his head. "I asked for the search warrant without much hope of it turning anything up because I figured he was too crafty to hold on to any of the property he had stolen."

"I'm sure Bootsie wishes he hadn't kept anything. Ted said she was hysterical when the deputies found the collection. Until then she kept telling everyone they had arrested an innocent man and that their lawyer would make mincemeat of everybody involved. Apparently she really believed that because she and Renn, or whatever his real name is, have only been married a couple years, and obviously she didn't know all that much about him. Now she does. And she's already left St. Tropez Run." Amy wrinkled her nose. "I guess I should feel a little sorry for her, but she's such an obnoxious woman that I . . . just can't. I'm not that noble."

"You're noble, Amy," Jordon said, smiling softly at her. "It would take a saint to feel much pity for someone as pretentious and silly and insensitive as she is."

"And after the way she treated Martha Trask . . ." Amy's lips tightened for a second before she dismissed Bootsie with a toss of one hand. "Enough about her. Now, will you *please* tell me how you knew this man wasn't the real Renn Bushnell?"

Propping himself up on one elbow, Jordon ran his fingers through his slightly tousled hair. "One thing led to another. We were watching the activities of all the employees and residents, and when I checked with the airlines about that trip Bushnell took alone, supposedly to Houston, there was no record of him on any flight there. He flew to Boston instead, which made me suspicious enough to check the Houston references he'd used to get into St. Tropez Run. They checked out again, of course, but I still had a hunch he might be our man. Finally I flew to Houston myself and found out that a Renn Bushnell is a member of the boards of a few corporations but that he's become a fairly inactive member. When I showed people who knew him the photo we'd secretly taken of our Bushnell, I was told he wasn't the same man. But that didn't prove our Renn was a burglar, which meant we had to lure him into a trap."

"How devious. Just to assume the identity of somebody else. And he nearly got away with it. If you hadn't checked up on that Houston trip . . . But since you did do that, you must have been watching everyone *very* closely."

"We were."

"Including me?"

"Amy," he softly chided, brushing his knuckles lightly over her left cheek. A teasing smile touched his hard mouth. "I always watch you closely."

She lifted her eyes heavenward. "That's not what I mean. I—"

"I know what you mean. And I've told you I never considered you the Ma Barker type. Aren't you ever going to believe me?"

Although she knew she almost did already, she simply shrugged. "I'll have to think about it some more. But for now, how about that breakfast I promised?"

As she stood, Jordon sat up in bed, paying no heed to the sheet that fell down around his waist, exposing his tanned bare torso. His attention was riveted completely on Amy, on the way the morning sun glimmered in her hair, on the full soft shape of her mouth, on the velvet blueness of her eyes. Suddenly, with swift intensity, he caught her by the hand to draw her down onto the edge of the bed facing him.

"Tell me what I can do, Amy," he implored, his voice hushed and nearly raw-edged, touching her slender fingers to his lips. "Whatever it is, just tell me and I'll do it."

Her steady gaze met his and she ignored the mild tremor of excitement that scampered through her. "Do about what, Jordon?"

"About *you*. About convincing you to trust me again, about making up for what I did three years ago. Aren't you ever going to forgive me, Amy?"

276

Her heart felt as if it were performing a joyous somersault, but she didn't answer. She simply looked at him, willing her expression to reveal none of her true emotions.

"Amy, listen," he insisted, feeling as if he had come up against a stone wall. His hand tightened around hers. "There must be something I can do to make you give me another chance."

This time it was more difficult not to respond, but she managed to remain silent.

"Say something, anything," he muttered, the knot of tension in his chest squeezing tighter. "Dammit, Amy, I love you!"

Those words, spoken with what appeared to be great sincerity, were nearly her undoing, but he had left her with scars and hadn't yet said enough to make them fade completely. Holding in check the emotion swelling in her, she continued to look into his amber eyes.

He uttered a mild oath beneath his breath. "God, woman, you're driving me crazy."

She could answer that and did, as calmly as possible. "You won't have to be crazy much longer, though. Now that your job here is done, you can leave soon—today even, if you want to."

"I'll leave here, but I won't be leaving you," he declared, desperation clutching at him. His large hands shot out to span her waist and hold her still when she tried to rise to her feet. His eyes bored into hers as determination sharpened his carved features. "I'm not going to let you go, Amy. That's a promise. Somehow I'm going to make you love me enough to agree to marry me."

The hope that surged up to incredible heights made her tremble inwardly, but she still cautiously replied, "Marry you? But I thought the very idea of marriage scared you to death?"

"That was three years ago when I was young and a fool. I should have married you then and this time I'm going to, no matter what it takes to persuade you," he vowed, his thumbs moving against the undersides of her breasts as he added with

277

some anguish, "Amy, I love you like hell, and you have to tell me what I can do to get you to love me again, too."

As she recognized the depth of true emotion conveyed by his spellbinding gaze, unbridled happiness flooded her being and her chin wobbled slightly with the sheer force of it as she nearly hurled herself into his arms, her own winding around his. "You big lanky nincompoop, I already love you," she murmured thickly, burying her face in his neck. "Maybe I never really stopped. I thought I had, but . . . All I know is that I love you more now than I ever have."

With a deep-throated groan he crushed her against him, holding her fast as if he could never bear to let her go again, while shakily whispering, "Amy, are you sure?"

"I've never been so sure of anything in my life," she confessed, his long sigh of relief making her love him all the more. "I do love you, Jordon, so much. I tried to fight it—"

"And did a fine job of it, too," he complained, kissing her left ear, then the hollow beneath it. "What made you decide to give up the fight this morning?"

She softly laughed. "This morning? Oh, I lost the battle weeks ago."

"You sure had me fooled. I think you missed your true calling. You could have been an award-winning actress. I've been going out of my mind, trying to win you back. Why didn't you let me know I had?"

"How could I? I scared you away the last time by acting like I wanted and needed a commitment. I didn't want to do the same thing again."

"No chance of that this time," he whispered, cradling her in his arms and tilting up her small chin to gaze deeply into her warm, happy eyes. "I hadn't been here a week before I knew what a terrible mistake I'd made when I let you go before. And I'll never make the same mistake again."

"Don't. I'm not sure I could stand it if you did," she whispered back, touching his lean, angular face with her loving fingertips. "Oh, Jordon, I love you so much."

"And I'm so glad because I adore you. I'd do anything to keep you, Amy, even buy you a house in St. Tropez Run, if that's what you want."

Detecting a subtle lack of enthusiasm in his tone, she smiled tremulously and shook her head. "That won't be necessary. I'd rather live out there in the real world where most people do, than live here."

"My sentiments exactly. See how compatible we are? But I *will* move the agency's home office to Norfolk, and we can live anywhere you like so you can go on working here."

Amy caught her breath. "Y-you'd really be willing to do that for me?"

Jauntily Jordon snapped his fingers. "Just like that."

For the first time he was saying she meant as much as or more to him than Security Unlimited, and the realization made her eyes mist as she drew a fingertip along the bridge of his nose. "Oh, I *do* love you, and it's wonderful of you to offer to move your home office, but that won't be necessary, either, because I won't be working here much longer. I gave Evan Price thirty days' notice yesterday morning, because you were right. Why should I be loyal to an employer who's not loyal to me? And I want to get into something different anyhow. There's even a chance I might get a position on the administrative staff at a home for children in D.C. If not that, there are openings in some of the convalescent centers in that area, too. I'm sure I'll be able to find something I like."

"That would be perfect, wouldn't it? Washington's not far from Alexandria."

"Ummm, I know that," Amy admitted with a wry but provocative smile. "Why else do you think I called my friend Jocelyn there to see if the employment agency she works for had anything at all suitable for me?"

His gaze narrowed. "I hope that means you were willing to pursue me?"

"Not quite. I wouldn't have chased you down," she explained. "But I did want to be near enough to you to make it harder to forget me after you left here."

"As if I could have forgotten," he murmured, sweeping his fingers with some urgency through her hair. "I love you, Amy. Marry me. Tomorrow."

"Give a girl a chance," she protested halfheartedly. "At least give me until the end of the week so that we can invite your family and mine to the ceremony. And then I guess I'll be a deserted bride while you go back to Alexandria and I work out my notice here?"

"Fat chance," he retorted emphatically, his arms tightening around her. "I don't plan to spend one night away from you for the next fifty or so odd years, so while you're working out your notice, I'll just have to find something to keep me occupied in our Norfolk office."

"Promise?" she questioned, smiling blissfully at him. "Or are you just saying that because you know I was willing to move to D.C. just to be close to you?"

"You are a shameless hussy, no doubt about it. But that's only one of the reasons I love you so much."

Warmth born of a happiness more intense than any she had ever before known radiated through her as she draped an arm across his shoulders, her hand curved over his nape and exerting a light pressure to urge his mouth closer to hers. "I love you, too, Jordon, and I want you to know that . . . there hasn't been anyone since you."

"God, I'm glad. I'd still love you like crazy if there had been, but I'm so glad there's been no other man," he said roughly, stroking back a golden arc of hair from her temple. "I can't bear to think of anyone having you except me. You're mine, Amy."

"I've always been," she confessed, raising herself up in his arms to touch her lips to his.

For a long while they simply held each other, kissing and touching, until the familiar hot passion erupted between them, passion made even more intense by the professions of love they could now freely exchange. Soon they were stretched out in the bed on their sides facing each other while his hands upon her body became more possessively demanding and hers explored the taut, virile contours of his.

Jordon drew back slightly to look into her eyes. "I've missed hearing you say 'I love you.' I've missed you."

Smiling faintly, she touched the slight, endearing hump of his nose. "I've missed you, too, Jordon. It's been a lonely three years."

"For me, too, although I didn't realize how lonely I'd been until I saw you again."

"As long as you realize it now . . ."

"Oh, I do," he said, while at the same time untying the belt of her robe, opening the lapels, and exposing her slim form, clad only in a sheer cotton chemise that barely reached the tops of her thighs. His gaze ranged slowly over her, lingering upon her rounded curves outlined against the thin fabric. "Hmmm, this is convenient. You don't have much on."

"No, because it's already promising to be another hot day."

"And it's going to get a lot hotter," he told her. "Very soon now."

"But, Jordon—" Her words were cut off by a slow rousing kiss as he removed her robe swiftly, then released her, only to pull the chemise over her head. He tossed it away and finished undressing her completely before throwing back the sheet to strip naked himself. Afterward he kissed her hair, her temples, the end of her nose. "Amy, I need you so much."

"But . . . your leg?"

"What leg?"

"Jordon, be serious," she breathed even as her body involuntarily sought closer contact with his. "The doctor said you shouldn't move around much for the next couple of days."

"Then, I won't move all that much. I'll let you. I like it that way, too," he whispered into her ear, arching her nearer. "Now come here, woman."

Her hands came between them against his chest. Leaning back slightly, she looked into his narrowed tiger eyes. "Jordon, are you sure you're up to this?"

He hugged her tight, softly laughing. "What an unnecessary question to ask, love. Can't you tell I am?"

"Wicked man, finding innuendoes in the most innocent questions," she admonished, but had to laugh with him until his lips met hers and their laughter swiftly altered to muffled endearments.

In the still warmth of the morning they explored each other as if they had never done so before, luxuriating in their new beginning, the delight they always found together greatly enhanced by whispers of love. The adoring fingers that probed her back and the satinesque texture of every inch of her skin once again branded his mark of possession indelibly upon her, while her own hands moved over his body in sweeping caresses, performing an intriguing dance of adoration and claiming him as hers. The lips and mouth that tenderly tasted then lingered long upon the peaks of her breasts stoked the fires of desire that were always smoldering just beneath the surface in her until her breathing was ragged and she cupped his face in her hands to urge that warm seductive mouth up to hers. And when feverish passion enslaved them both, Jordon took her in his arms and swept her over him. Their bodies merged in a union more wondrous than they had ever known before, binding them together emotionally at last as well as physically.

"Amy," he roughly murmured, his gaze holding her as his hands drifted up from her hips to her breasts to her shoulders, then came to rest against the silken hair that framed her slightly flushed face. An indescribably tender smile gentled his features. "Honey, I love you."

"And I love you, too, more than anyone else in the world,"

she freely told him, smiling back as they began to move together in slow synchronization.

When completion came, sensation peaked with an exquisite keenness. Tidal waves of ecstasy crashed within her. Softly she cried out Jordon's name and felt the deep shudder that ran through him at the same moment. He wrapped her in his arms as they glided down together into warmest contentment. She felt very well loved.

Later Jordon leaned above her on one elbow, a hand curving into her waist. Now his smile was teasing. "Are you convinced now that I'm not in a lot of pain? I think I proved I was up to that, didn't I?"

An answering smile played over her lips. "You were superb."

"And you were a delight. You always are. You know, I never thought I'd have reason to feel grateful for a burglar, but I have one now since he brought us back together."

"I guess the king of diamonds will always have special meaning for us, won't it?"

He nodded. "And speaking of diamonds, what kind of engagement ring do you want?"

"I haven't really thought much about it. I've been spending all my time concentrating on how to get you to propose."

Laughing, he placed a kiss on the tip of her nose. "Brazen."

"No. I just knew what I wanted."

"Thank God you did. And now that you've got me, you're never going to be able to get rid of me."

"Promise?"

"I promise."

"That's what I've needed to know," she murmured, touching his face. "Now, are you hungry yet?"

"Starved."

"So am I. I'll make breakfast and serve it to you in bed. But only because of your leg. Don't get the idea that this will happen every day of our married life."

"I'd never think of it," he replied, amusement in his resonant voice. But as she slipped naked from the bed to reach for her robe, he took her by the hand, his expression growing more serious. "And, Amy, I thought that someday when we decide we want to have children, you might like to adopt an older child, too."

She squeezed his fingers, her blue eyes misty again. "You mean someone like Joey?"

"Yes, like Joey. And a girl, too. Why not both?"

"Oh, I *love* you," she whispered huskily, dropping down onto the bed to wind her arms around his neck and press close. Some moments later, as he held her cradled against him, she smiled adoringly up at him and a hint of mischief brightened her already sparkling eyes. "And just think, I'll get to tell all our children and grandchildren that you once suspected me of being a burglar and that was after you'd already broken my heart three years before!"

He pretended to be grievously wounded by the words and sadly shook his head. "You're not ever going to let me live down what I did, are you?"

"Never," she murmured, even as she raised herself up to brush her lips along the strong line of his jaw. "If I let you forget, you might not pay me as much attention."

"You have nothing to worry about there. I plan to spend the rest of my life making you realize how much I love you and how empty my life would be without you in it," he vowed.

And as her teasing lips were captured in a deepening kiss that conveyed a wealth of emotion, she knew his was a promise he truly intended to keep. At last he understood a truth she had known a long time ago. They were made for each other.

LOOK FOR NEXT MONTH'S
CANDLELIGHT ECSTASY SUPREMES

CANDLELIGHT Ecstasy Supreme

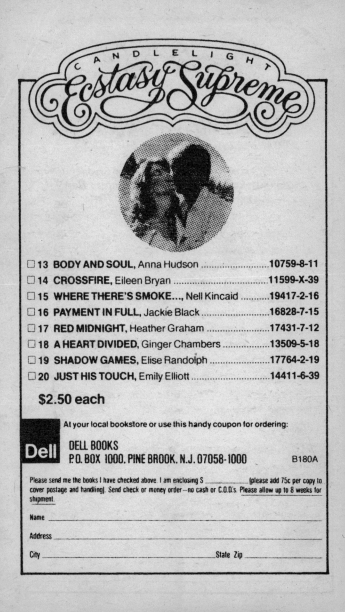

Candlelight Ecstasy Romances™

$1.95 each